Dr. Cartier had propositioned me several times, but I turned him down. He took his rejection good-naturedly and even told me that I would probably get quite a charge out of some of his nude male models. Especially one named Eric who had a spectacular physique which no one on campus had touched. He was an enigma, a real loner who stayed pretty much to himself, but who worked out daily with weights and in the gym.

This particular art professor was notorious for his blatant flirting with good-looking males. I was small for my age, five-foot-three, with curly golden-blond hair, large blue eyes, and a compactly built physique. Men had always been attracted to me, and that can make you bold and confident. And when I saw Eric that cold afternoon, I vowed to myself: "Sooner or later, I am going to have you."

ERIC'S BODY

JASON FURY

Originally published by Masquerade.

Copyright © 1993, 2000 by Jason Fury

978-1-5040-3001-4

Distributed in 2016 by Open Road Distribution
180 Maiden Lane
New York, NY 10038
www.openroadmedia.com

For Cochise—You Are Not Forgotten

ERIC'S BODY

Our Unregenerate Author	9
Barbed Wire	13
Animal	29
Janu	43
Strange Young Man	59
Forbidden Fruit	79
Kiss Me, Kill Me	95
Eric's Body	107
The Return of Bubba Lee	123
Mr. White Lightning	137
Poochie Woochie	155
The Leader of the Pack	171
A Merry Little Christmas	185
Cock of the Walk	199
Wild, Wild Young Men	217
White Gods	233
Dance with the Devil	251
The Bull of the Blue Ridge Mountains	271

The Bastard of the County   285

Him   301

They Won't Forget   315

Miracle on 55th Street   335

The Faggot and the Redneck   355

King of the City   367

The Last of the Seven Beauties   381

OUR UNREGENERATE AUTHOR

I was raised in the Deep South by a large family of eccentrics.

My father was so incredibly good-looking he could have been a movie star. Instead, he chose to end his days in a tiny cowdab of a town (the "Carson City" of my stories). My mother was obsessed with Thomas Wolfe (the writer) and was such a bitch that even today she makes Bette Davis seem like Vanna White. One of my brothers became a famous artist, one became a big-time financier, and another became a brilliant alcoholic. I was determined to be a writer.

During the fifties, aspiring writers were supposed to follow in the hallowed footsteps of Faulkner, Hemingway, and Fitzgerald. They all bored me stiff. I yawned through their pages of lovemaking. I wanted to read stories about men stripping off their clothes

9

and doing all those things churchgoing Dixie boys weren't supposed to even imagine.

I became obsessed with Nancy Drew, the girl detective. She was my idol, but I drooled over her father, Carson Drew, and her hunky boyfriend, Ned Nickerson. When a schoolteacher asked us fifth graders what we aspired to be one day, I screamed, "Nancy Drew!" My mother whipped me good. In secret, I wrote dozens of stories about Jason Drew, a boy detective who did things with his father and boyfriend, Ned Dickerson, that would have had him committed to Cherry Mental Hospital (where all known homosexuals in that area were sent).

At fourteen, I wrote a weekly column for the town newspaper about being a teenager, describing what was going on in our one-room schoolhouse and reporting what teen queen was dating Mr. Football favorite. But secretly I yearned to write about some of the dazzling young farmboys I knew. I wanted especially to write about gorgeous, sixteen-year-old Tommy Robb Hamilton III who lived in the swamp area of our community. We dated secretly on the weekends, and he treated me just like a girl. He brought me Cokes and candy and, now and then, such boyish gifts as perfume. (Yeah, it was cheap, but oh, boy, did it smell great to me!) He even gave me a pair of his white BVDs (which I kept until a year ago, when I had to throw them away because they had disintegrated!).

At Brevard Junior College and East Carolina University, both in North Carolina, I was quickly labeled "the campus queer." This was in the early sixties, when nobody had ever seen an out-of-the-closet gay boy before. I hid nothing and managed to bed down some of the most macho guys on campus. My track record became legendary. Gay men had noth-

10

ing to do with me: I was *too* obvious. That didn't bother me; my "straight" bed partners kept me too busy to worry about public opinion—something I've always ignored, anyway.

Still determined to write, I became a successful newspaper reporter and columnist for the Associated Press and several Southern dailies. I was deeply frustrated, though, because mainstream magazines continued rejecting the short stories I sent them. Like most homosexual writers, I was trying to disguise my plots and characters behind a facade of heterosexuality. It didn't work, and I felt like a hypocrite.

In August 1978, my professional life took a dramatic turn: Montgomery, Alabama's, first adult bookstore opened. Naturally, I was among its first customers. I was startled to see a magazine called *Blueboy* on the shelf. It was slick, filled with beautiful photographs of naked men, fiction for gay readers, articles. I couldn't believe it. *Blueboy* was the first upfront, over-the-counter publication made available to millions of emerging gay men. I studied it carefully that night and then worked like a demon on a story called "Garage" and sent it off to *Blueboy*.

In less than two weeks, I received a rave acceptance from editor Bruce Fitzgerald. He said I was writing something "new and fresh" and even compared me to the French author, Colette, one of my literary idols.

A few months later, my first book, *I Love My Daddy* (did I ever!) was published by Greenleaf Publishers. For reasons known only to him, the editor gave my book the ghastly title of *Daddy Stud* and gave me the even worse pseudonym of Jerry Tucker. Even so, the book still sells—more than ten years later.

Since then, I've sold nearly all of the 150 stories

11

I've written under my pseudonym of Jason Fury and several others which are fairly well known. I love using pen names because for each one, I have a complete literary persona. Jason Fury is probably the best known. He is basically a romanticist, and when he finds Mr. Right, he doesn't sleep around. He's a one-man man with a penchant for complex, rugged hunks.

Two of my most popular stories, "Wild Boy" and "Barbed Wire," appeared in *FirstHand,* and both have interesting histories. Editors at three other gay magazines rejected both manuscripts, describing them as "corny" and "absurd." One editor even said, "Gay readers don't want to read about people dying. They want happy stories about fucking and sucking."

Luckily for writers like me, there are other editors in the world who realize that homosexual men are like other human beings. A good cry never hurts anyone and if some people criticize me for being corny at times, well, I've been accused of worse things.

I still read Nancy Drew mystery books now and then, and I think the best kissers in the world are preachers, priests, and bodybuilders. The worst are cops, construction workers, and college boys. In bed, though, I would probably reverse this order.

BARBED WIRE

Forget the louse...forget the prick...forget that sono-fabitch...

My windshield wipers had been clicking out that message since I'd left New York City the night before.

During the ten hours I had spent on the road since then, my mind conjured up hundreds of variations on this theme whenever I thought of Paul: The Asshole of the Century. The man with whom I had lived and loved for five years. And who, a week ago, had casually announced he was moving on to "better things."

"Better things" meant a new apartment—minus me—and the addition of a new lover. His new lover was a male stripper, which made him more appetizing than a writer. I knew it would be years before this pain fully died away. You can't wipe out the memories of a handsome rogue who was the sole focus of your life for five years.

Like barbed wire, he was entangled in my psyche. And when I tried pulling him out, the memory just dug in deeper.

I had actually thought little of my destination. A fellow writer had raved about the Chantrell farm—how beautiful, inexpensive, and restful it was. A call to Mrs. Chantrell the day before had assured me that the price was indeed right—and there was a cottage by the sea available. Now I saw for myself the white-capped waves a short distance to the left. Smoke billowed up through the gray rain from the big farmhouse. *This is exactly what I need,* I thought.

And I was certain of it after being greeted warmly by Mrs. Chantrell—a spry, white-haired older woman. She showed me the cottage, and I loved It. A roaring fire welcomed me. In the kitchen, she had prepared a platter of sandwiches, a pot of coffee, and a spice cake. Proudly she showed me the handmade furniture, the patchwork quilt on the featherbed, and the large windows which provided me with a spectacular view of the sea below.

"I think you'll like it here," she said. Most people do. I'll send my son, David, up to help you move anything around and get a fire going in the oil circulator. The fireplace is okay, but it's going down past the freezing mark tonight."

"I think I'll spend five years here instead of a month."

We both laughed, and I was surprised to realize that the gloom which had hung over me for a week was lifting rapidly.

When I answered the door half an hour later, I was

half-expecting David Chantrell to be a straw-chewing bumpkin—or maybe even a horny young redneck. But instead I was stunned by the vision before me in a fur-lined leather jacket, chino pants, and desert boots. *Good God*, I thought, *What is this hunk doing out here in this isolated part of the world?* With a charming smile, he introduced himself. My hand vanished into his big one, and I acted like a half-wit.

"Oh, oh, hi, yeah, I'm Jason," I stammered. "Oh, won't you come on in, David?"

A cigarette hung from his full lips as he strolled to the oil heater and prepared it for fire. If this man had walked into any gay hangout in the world, he would have been considered prime rape bait. He was that extraordinary phenomenon: a man in his forties who looked more enticing and luscious than most men half his age. He had the aura of a man who had been around and done things. As he knelt down before the stove, the back of his chinos slid down to disclose white BVDs. They dazzled against his tanned, hard back.

Thick hair the color of coal was graying at his temples. He had taken off his jacket, and his amber cashmere sweater hugged a powerful torso which betrayed no signs of forties flab.

Soon a fire was burning steadily in the heater. Task accomplished, he stood up, lit another cigarette, and looked down at me. I'm short for my age—about five-foot-five—with gold curls and big blue eyes which often give me the look of a high-school kid, instead of a man on the wrong side of twenty.

I was overwhelmed by his eyes. A luminous blue, they were nonetheless nearly hidden by thick lashes. But there was so much pain in them! This man had suffered terribly somehow—he had the haunted look of a small lost boy. This made him instantly attrac-

15

tive; who could resist such a powerful combination of vulnerability, muscularity, and beauty?

My breathing quickened. Through some quirk of fate, I had chosen to come here, out of a thousand places I could have gone to—and here was the most beautiful man I had seen *anywhere!*

"You must be dead," he said, smiling, "Driving all the way here from New York in that little Volkswagen."

"Dead, but not too tired to cook you and your mama a big Italian supper tonight!"

"All right! Sounds great! I get a little tired of this Southern cooking after a while."

His eyes scanned my face briefly, as if suddenly seeing me for the first time; then he quickly looked down at the floor. We went into the kitchen, where he washed his big hands in the sink. He glanced from the wood stove to me.

"Know anything about lighting one of these suckers?"

"I'm a whiz!" I lied.

He laughed. "Something tells me you're gonna be calling me up here for some help."

"No way!" I boasted. Grinning, he told me about the woman artist who had had the cabin before me. She had been so frightened of the strange night sounds that he had had to sleep on a couch on the front porch during her last week there.

A lock of hair had fallen over his forehead, giving him an irresistibly boyish look. "You mean she didn't invite you into her bed?" I teased.

He blushed. "A sixty-four-year-old woman with gray hair and bad breath don't exactly give me a hard-on." He squeezed his well-packed crotch. My eyes followed his gesture. When I looked up he saw my expression and rolled his eyes comically.

16

"Whew!" he laughed. "Changing the subject, we'll just move right along."

Slowly, a bond of some kind was forming between us. His eyes were beginning to gleam when he looked at me. Somehow I sensed that nothing I did would ever repulse or irritate him. He was acting as if I were a kind of creature he'd never encountered before—but which he was much enjoying.

As he arranged the work area for my writing, he stripped off his sweater. It left his big chest covered by only a thin sleeveless T-shirt. It was obvious that he had acquired his magnificent physique from lifting weights. When I commented, he offered me his biceps to feel. It was smooth and hard like metal. Then he lifted his T-shirt so I could feel the ripples in his stomach. Our eyes met again; he blushed and looked away as he pulled his sweater back on. He promised to be over at seven with his mother.

I watched him from my window as he walked through the drizzle back to the farmhouse. His buttocks undulated beneath the thin, damp chinos.

He looks so beautiful, I thought, *but so lonely, too! I'm going to change that.*

Naturally, when it came time to prepare supper, I couldn't get a flicker of flame in that goddamn stove. And naturally David was only too happy to come and fix it. He managed to keep a straight face for only about two minutes before he burst out laughing. I had to join in his hilarity when he mimicked me: "I'm a whiz!"

The supper proved a great success. The only incident that marred it was when we discussed the recent Veterans Day parade in New York City. Thousands of bystanders gave the Vietnam veterans a rousing reception.

17

"It's about time!" I declared. "It's horrible the way they were treated when they returned home from the war."

At that moment, I noticed that Mrs. Chantrell seemed to be shaking her head slightly at me. David had turned pale. Sweat was trickling down his handsome face.

She swiftly handed her son some pills from a metal box she had in her pocket. He swallowed them, and within a few minutes, was back to his normal self. But it was a chilling reminder of how little I knew about this luscious male who had so captivated me.

"I hope I didn't say anything out of place," I murmured.

"Forget it," Mrs. Chantrell said with a smile. "David here was a Vietnam vet, and he wasn't treated too well when he returned. But let's get back to that book you were telling us about."

Shortly after this, she got up and said she was going to watch "Dynasty." "I wouldn't miss it for the world! But you two men stay up as long as you want, and don't worry about me." After she left, David asked me to accompany him for a walk along the beach. I threw on my trench coat, and together we went out into the freezing cold of that February night. The wind was icy, but his warm, hard body brushed against mine many times. He helped me over the dunes and logs. Each time it was like a bolt of electricity whenever I touched him.

And he talked. In Vietnam things had happened to him that still gave him unpredictable flashbacks. They were so horrible that he had buried them deep inside his mind, but they resurfaced now and then to haunt him. I reminded him of a close buddy of his—Gary, a small young guy whom he had looked after.

18

"Didn't do much good," my companion sighed later as we sipped hot buttered rum before my fireplace. "He was the first one killed in our platoon."

As the days passed, I forgot many times that I had ever known a bastard named Paul. His memory receded steadily. In its place, growing larger each day, loomed the image of a new man: one with black hair and a gorgeous smile who lived a quiet life away from the outside world.

We saw each other several times each day. He dropped by in the morning for coffee and at night for a nightcap. He was always concerned about my welfare. He checked my windows and doors carefully. Why I don't know—it was such an isolated part of the North Carolina coast. He made certain there were always plenty of logs for the hearth and oil for the heater.

It didn't bother him when he brushed up close to me while reaching over my head to fix a light bulb. He seemed totally unaware of the intimate contact which nearly made me faint.

I can always judge what kind of man I'm dealing with when I show him my published stories. They appear mostly in gay magazines. If a man glances through them and a contemptuous sneer crosses his face, I forget him fast. I showed David my newest story. He glanced through the publication with keen interest. While I scribbled on my writing pad, he read my story about a love affair with a Southern trooper. Finally he handed back the magazine. "Wow! That was great. You're a great writer, I've never read any of these magazines before."

I lit a cigarette and asked, "Does it bother you to read gay stories, David?"

He shook his head. "Naw. Gay people are like

19

everybody else. They just chose a different life-style, that's all."

How I loved him at that moment. "You're a beautiful man, David!" I said quietly. "I don't just mean physically. I mean the way you see things."

"I'm just a good ol' Southern boy," he grinned. "Nothing special."

"You're something special—and don't you forget it!" I replied.

Usually, I'm very cautious with a man—especially after living in New York with its great number of human animals. But with David, I felt unusually at ease. Before long, I found myself telling him about being ditched by Paul the Asshole.

"He sounds like a real jerk-off," my admirer muttered, "I'd like to get my hands on him. You deserve somebody better than that slime."

"Any suggestions?" I drawled.

David pretended to glare at me when he saw my look. "Okay, now. Let's don't get any ideas."

Both of us burst out laughing. His expression clearly revealed that he was not in the least bothered by such an idea.

David's mother went to Florida for a week, to visit her sister. Except for a dozen farmhands who left for their own homes each afternoon, David and I were alone. On the first night, I prepared us a big Southern feed. Hush puppies, chicken fried in bacon grease, candied yams—the works. He was stunning in a black turtleneck sweater and clinging wool pants of the same color. His dark hair fell over his forehead: his eyes seemed even bluer, his muscles even bigger.

It began sleeting heavily at around ten, He prepared to leave, although I begged him to stay. As he slipped on his leather jacket, he looked at me intently and asked, "You get scared out here, Jason?"

"You bet your balls I do! Don't be surprised if I come running up to your bedroom tonight."

He seemed to be studying something on the wood floor. "You—you want me to stay over tonight?"

His offer astonished and delighted me. "David, that would be wonderful! I'd feel so much better!"

I was leaning against the kitchen sink when he came closer. As he put his cup of coffee in the sink behind me, his body pressed lightly against mine, I looked up into his eyes.

"You've only got one bed," he said.

"I'll fix you a place on the sofa—"

"Wouldn't it be easier if we just slept together? I might snore, but I don't bite."

He bent down and kissed me; the touch of his mouth was electrifying. It was so warm, soft, and moist. Putting a powerful arm around me, he walked with me to the bedroom.

Now, from beneath the gold comforter, as a scented candle flickered in darkness, I watched him undress. Outside, sleet froze on the windows, and the sea sounded furious. But within this cottage on an isolated bank of the Atlantic, we were alone—two men who had been adrift, but had now miraculously come together.

He walked toward me now, naked, and winked reassuringly as if to say: "Don't be nervous. I'll take care of you." New York and its bleak bitterness were forgotten as David's big arms pulled me easily against him.

"Last time I balled was with a fifty-dollar whore in Wilmington, six months ago. Never did it with a guy before—but the minute I saw you, something weird happened. I wanted to see what it would be like."

His kiss was awkward at first—tense, uncertain—but then it gained power. I slid my mouth from his, down onto his right nipple, then moved it to the left one. Both swelled up. Then, with my tongue, I explored that beautifully chiseled stomach, which was rising and falling quickly now. Diving from there, I hungrily enveloped his uncut penis, which pulsed insistently against his navel. There was such a profusion of precum syrup oozing out, and the oval tip felt so solid, that I knew he was on the verge of exploding. I had hardly started to suck him when he did ejaculate. He cried out and writhed as he flooded my mouth, and spattered his thighs, with sperm.

"Nobody can complain of you being impotent, David! Can you do it again? Are you worn out?"

He laughed. "I'm just getting cranked up. You'd be doing me a big favor if you could relieve me—if you could suck out all I've got inside me."

I was struck by those words: "all I've got inside me." It felt as if he was presenting me with a special and rare gift. Now, as I concentrated again on the smooth hard rod of his manhood, I realized that I had his essence in my mouth. This was what made him tick; this was his center of existence.

I turned his beautiful body over, and found another treasure facing me. His ass was one of the most incredible I had ever encountered. David's rear was perfectly rounded, and glossy as marble. I pulled his genitals up between his thighs and sucked on them while resting my face on his firm rear end. It was wonderful to again taste semen surging out of that love muscle.

It wasn't just a night of passion. Holding me close, he finally began to describe the hell he had endured in Vietnam, seeing his buddies murdered, mutilated, driven insane. And when he returned home, he didn't receive a hero's welcome; he was spat upon and called "murderer" and "baby killer."

I hugged him. "But you're alive, David! Be thankful for that! At least you came home: thousands of other men didn't."

But he still had those horrifying flashbacks. Many Vietnam vets had them. A loud noise, or somebody discussing the war, or even some completely inexplicable thing could set him off. He couldn't remember anything he did while having a flashback.

"Lots of times I wake up screaming; I can't help it. I keep those pills with me at all times." The metal box of pills was right beside us on the nightstand. David muttered that he was afraid of sleeping with me because he might wake up screaming.

"Go to sleep, David," I urged him. "You'll never scare me. You won't repulse me because you could never do that." Around dawn, both of us finally slept.

But, sure enough, I was awakened by screams of terror. My companion was sitting up in bed with his eyes bulging. I grabbed the pills.

"Swallow, David!" I shouted at him. "Swallow the pills!" I held down his convulsing body as best I could, struggling to force the pills into his mouth. I don't know what medication they were, but within minutes I felt him calming down. When he awoke, an hour later, he remembered nothing—which made it even more frightening to me. Anything might have happened during that time.

"Did I—?" he started to ask. I nodded my head. He covered his face with his hands. "Oh, shit! I'm sorry; I'm really sorry. You must've been scared out of your mind." I hugged this troubled man, and he clung to me. But he managed a weak laugh when I threatened him: "If you don't sleep with me every night, I'm gonna whup that gorgeous butt of yours."

23

The following week, I was enjoying some freshly baked chocolate cake and coffee with Mrs. Chantrell. Through her big kitchen window, we watched her handsome son and three workmen unload a grain truck.

I was startled when she said finally: "I think you two like each other a lot. He's been like a different person since you came here, Jason. If it's love between you two—I couldn't be happier. After what he's gone through...come with me for a moment, Jason. I think I can trust you."

Opening a locked metal cabinet, she showed me rows of medicine bottles. They were all David's. "He has to have them every day. It's those horrible flash-backs of his—sometimes in public, while we're eating or in church. That's why he's been such a recluse these years. It's why I keep him here. The war nearly destroyed him. He won't see anybody."

Her face hardened when she locked the metal cabinet. Suddenly it flashed through my mind that maybe there was an even darker side to all this. Her next words confirmed my fears.

Mrs. Chantrell told me that she had to keep her rifle and sharp knives locked up. And the farmhands were warned to watch David carefully, especially around sharp machinery. He might try to kill himself.

I was horrified. Surely he wouldn't.

She held up two fingers and nodded grimly. "Twice he's tried it..."

I seldom thought of Paul and, when I did, David sensed it. He said he would make me forget him, and he almost did. He was a powerful lover, and the fact that he had been virtually celibate since coming home from the war made him a man of extraordinary stamina and passion. I never ceased to be amazed by

24

the abundance of his sperm and the number of his ejaculations. I adored his lustrous skin, the deep cleft of his smooth buttocks. Most of all, though, I loved him for his kindness and protectiveness, and for his sense of humor.

Since he knew that his Vietnam problems didn't repulse or frighten me, he let me accompany him one day to the nearby VA Hospital, where he went twice a week for therapy. As he waited to have his drug prescriptions filled, his psychiatrist, Dr. Erwin, invited me into his office for coffee.

"I'm mighty glad he's found someone like you, Jason," said the silver-haired man. "I've never seen him so optimistic and upbeat."

Every time the doctor saw someone bright and handsome but troubled—like David—it reminded him, he told me, of a hunting trip he had taken in Georgia. "We came across a magnificent deer which was almost dead. It had gotten caught up in this coil of barbed wire. Each time it moved, the barbs dug deeper into its flesh. Finally it just stopped moving. The pain was too horrible. Then it died."

That was how Dr. Erwin saw some of the vets, like David. The war was like barbed wire, even to those not maimed physically. Although they tried to escape it, the metal prongs sank deeper into their psyches. Eventually, some just gave up and died.

"He won't give up," I said fiercely. "And he's not gonna die!"

"We're all behind you, Jason, If you can help him out."

But I *had* to return to New York. My bank account was dwindling at an alarming rate. I had magazine assignments that I hadn't even touched; there were editors I needed to see. And my landlord called to say that Paul had been seen taking things out of my apartment. I needed to get back before he wiped me out.

When I told David, he appeared resigned to my leaving, and said he would fly up to stay with me in April. For my last night, he took me out on the town: we pigged out on pizza and beer and then went to see *Nightmare on Elm Street*, of all things. I was terrified, but David just laughed as I squeezed his big arm all through the harrowing movie.

We were in bed by midnight, and David immediately began loving me more fiercely than ever before. He fucked me steadily for several minutes before he had his first ejaculation. His semen hadn't stopped surging before I had his penis in my mouth.

David gasped as he slowly produced yet another orgasm. He had several more before dawn. I got up quietly and walked around the room. I wanted to memorize everything in it. David watched me from bed as I pressed my face against his fur-lined jacket, his chino pants, his white underwear, the quilt on the bed, the pillow we shared.

"What are you doing?" he asked, smiling. I told him I wanted to forget nothing about this snug, warm little room, which had brought me such peaceful serenity and so much love.

David got up and began to dress. "You'll forget all about me," he muttered as he sat on the edge of the bed. Chunks of ice bobbed in the gray ocean beyond the window. His face was grim when he added, "If you do think about me, it'll be as that fucked-up Vietnam vet who suffers flashbacks. I don't know why they didn't finish me off in the war."

I protested furiously and flung my arms around him. I reminded him that he was flying to New York within a month to spend some time with me. But when I tried kissing him, he pushed me away and walked back to the house with his head down.

His mother visited me before I left. David was taking my leaving pretty hard, she said, "but he'll get over it—I hope." Sure enough, after I returned to Manhattan, he wrote me a passionate letter about how much he missed me—and how he would definitely be flying up in April.

The first week in April, I received a package from Mrs. Chantrell. I should have been warned when I opened it to see David's black leather jacket. But I had to read that brief note and study the small newspaper clipping attached to it several times before I fully realized the truth.

He was dead. "David Chantrell...self-inflicted gunshot wound...a decorated veteran of the Vietnam War..."

For hours on that snowy afternoon, I sat with his jacket around my shoulders, watching the snow fall outside my apartment, fifteen floors above Broadway. Then, a little bit drunk on gin, I called Mrs. Chantrell. Although quiet, she sounded remarkably calm.

She was happy that he had found someone to love. His body was found in my cottage—in the bedroom. As she spoke, I vividly recalled that little room facing the ocean, the fireplace, the smells of the strawberry candle, and the beautiful man I had slept with for a month.

The note she found in his pocket had asked for the following words to be used as his epitaph: "I run to Death, and Death meets me as fast, and all my pleasures are like yesterday."

"Are you okay, Jason?"

"No, I'm not. I'm thinking about barbed wire—and that war. That goddamned war."

Animal

August 3, 19—

If I told my friends about the man who has become an obsession, they would howl with disbelief. I've heard some of the other faculty members and a few of the girl students refer to him as "a slob...an animal."

Because he's uninhibited. That's exactly why I've flipped out over him. You would never confuse him with a clean-cut preppie. With his husky build, he's more of the redneck wrestler type.

He's strictly hands-off. Even if he did serve a stint in the marines before enrolling here, he's still a student. And school policy fires any instructor who has sexual relations with a pupil.

So I'll have to be content with casting furtive glances at his near nudity as he sprawls at his desk in the back of the room. Those powerful legs springing from cut-off jeans, slit so high at the hip that you see generous glimpses of white BVDs. I've even seen his cotton-covered crotch as it bulges out from the leg opening. During the whole summer session, he's worn the same tank top, a washed-out red, chopped off at the midriff to reveal a stomach beginning to show the first signs of a beer gut. When he stretches his arms or puts his hands behind his head, his top zooms up to air big pink nipples.

His sandy hair looks greasy; it's combed back in ripples.

You can't see his eyes, since he wears shaded glasses, but I know he watches me. His eyes follow me around the classroom. When I walk close to him, I can hear his heavy nasal breathing and smell his scent. His white skin, completely without hair, glistens with moisture; and once, when I put my arm next to his while pointing out a passage in a book, my own arm came away wet. His clothes are grungy with food stains and God knows what else.

In the hallway, I see him with his buddies. He's always smoking, slurping a Coke while pulling at his crotch. When he laughs, his blunt features crinkle up like a bulldog's. When a pretty girl walks by, he squeezes himself and humps his hips so his friends can snicker.

From my office window in the Administration Building, I've studied him through binoculars as he plays tag football. They play on a green quadrangle nearly hidden by Lombardy poplars. Like a bull, a bear or a water buffalo, he runs sturdily around the field, nude except for his chopped jeans.

Last week something happened that confirmed my suspicions. He's got to be a nudist, an exhibitionist—something like that.

He'd caught the ball. The other players tackled

him and covered him with their bodies. When they got up, four of the guys held him down while two others stripped off Jack's shorts and BVDs.

Completely naked, he chased the culprit and retrieved his clothes. He took his time, laughing about it all; he even shook his genitals at the Administration Building. That's how I got to see a big white boy, stark naked, slipping on his shorts outdoors.

His butt was big, solid, mounted high. When he turned sideways, I finally glimpsed his penis. It was the dick of a mature man: heavy, dark, thick. One of the boys grabbed Jack's foreskin and yanked on it. He just growled good-naturedly and knocked the hand away, as if he were used to people grabbing at him.

The next time I saw Jack, he and his buddies were eating pizza and slurping beer at a fast-food place downtown. Jack had stuffed his mouth till it bulged. Fragments of cheese and anchovies spilled down his chin, onto his shirt. He was laughing and trying to talk while spitting out crumbs of food. His friends were staggering around, howling with laughter.

Maybe he is an animal, but there is something exhilarating about his indifference to the niceties of society. He doesn't have time to be well groomed or charming, yet he possesses a powerful charm.

He can be sexy, funny, incredibly macho, and sweet. Around me he is always casual, witty, and irreverent. But he keeps me at arm's length. It is as if he were studying me, assessing me before coming to a decision.

I've already been fired from one school for "conduct unbecoming a teacher" because I had developed a fatal passion for a devil named Danny.

The school board refused to believe it was Danny who had seduced me. He was eighteen, I was twenty-

31

three. Age ruled in his favor. He was a bold one. He'd squeeze his hard-ons at me whenever he came to my office. An oversexed little bull, he would grab my hand and push it down onto his crotch. I still remember how his dark eyes flickered hotly as he pushed my face down in his lap and forced his penis into my mouth. He always wanted to cum.

After a month, I came home one night and found him in my bed, sipping chilled vodka and smoking a joint. Ready for me. Right after he ejaculated, he kissed me for a long time and then whispered in my ear, "I need some money—bad." I gave him everything he wanted until I was ruined financially. When I told him, "No more money, he reported me to the school board, saying I had repeatedly forced him into sex in return for a passing grade.

Nowadays, I have only to evoke the specter of Danny to help me keep my dirty little hands to myself.

August 5, 19—

I've been reading the students' first chapters of the novels that all of them are supposed to be working on. I've Xeroxed Jack's twenty pages. He's writing about me!

He brought it to me in my office. I greeted him with undisguised delight.

He leaned back in his chair, chewing gum, and folded his hands behind his neck. His tank top zoomed up above his nipples. Both were pink and hard-looking. Even from where I sat, I could smell his warm skin, moist with sweat.

"I'm kinda embarrassed to be showing this to you." he said in a musical Southern drawl. "I mean, it's real dirty. Full of sex stuff. But remember, it ain't about me. A buddy told me all this. He's an over-sexed dude and—well, read it."

32

"Come off it," I teased. "That's what every writer says when he's written anything sexy. You look hot-blooded enough. I'll bet this book is all about you."

"Naw, it ain't. Huh-uh. It sure ain't."

"I just know I'm going to blush when I read it."

He laughed. "I hope it makes you more than blush."

"Angel of Light," he had written, "who visits me at night and makes me think of doing things I'd be killed for in my hometown...you've returned to tempt me. With your hair glowing in golden curls, those big eyes of blue and that little-boy torso swishing around me, making me all hard and wet...you're tempting me again. I take out my big, floppy thing and flap it around on my palm and on my thigh, hitting it enough to make it thicken into a rosy cucumber...you run your tongue over the pink opening, pushing apart the lips of my dick door, licking the insides of it until the syrup drips down like strands of clear honey...and when I shoot it all up into you, it's like death...a beautiful kind of death and rebirth because each surge makes you a part of me. My cells become your cells. I hold my thing out to you again, making it big and plump for you—you, who have taken control of me and turned me into the animal you see before you."

August 7, 19—

Outside in the hallway, he waited for me. Everyone had gone home, for it was Friday. He had stripped off his tank top and used it to mop the sweat dripping from his face and chest. He smiled when I came out of the office.

"You have time to read my stuff? I've been dying to get your reaction. Christ, it's hot. Let's get on outside." I followed.

33

Around the corner of the old building, thick trees grow close to the wall. Students go there to sneak a smoke, a swig of beer. Now it was deserted. I leaned back against the wall. Jack stood in front of me, leaning forward slightly with his hand propped up above me. I saw the sweat rolling down his chest, dripping from the pink nipples...heard his heavy breathing through his nostrils. I told him how excited I was by his writing. It was naked, vivid.

"Oh, Angel of Light," he whispered with a smile, "you mind if I take just a tiny little piss? I swear to God my bladder's gonna bust open if I don't piss out that six-pack of Molson Gold I jus' done drunk."

He didn't wait for a reply. With one hand still braced above me, he unzipped his britches, pushed his BVDs down and grabbed hold of the pink organ that was already bobbing about in semihardness. He ripped back the wattle of flesh so the bullet-shaped tip zipped out. Running a finger back and forth over the moist urethra, he let the golden water stream out.

It spattered against the wall, just an inch or two from my leg, but I didn't move. With his piss and his big, wet body, he'd worked a spell on this cloudy afternoon, on a deserted campus. His buttocks twitched, and he shuddered now and then as the urine gushed out. To the sweet smell of newly mown grass was added the darker aroma of fresh piss. It drenched part of his shorts, but Jack didn't move. He seemed to be in a trance, grunting softly in satisfaction, staring at the yellow stream as it trickled out onto the sidewalk.

When the last drops had fallen, he squeezed his foreskin, twisted it, flicked away the remaining liquid, and sighed. Looking at me through the shaded glasses, he smiled.

"That was a good piss. It felt wonderful coming out. Did you enjoy it?"

"It was beautiful."

"I thought you might enjoy it. I've felt a weird kind of bond going on between me and you. Could you let me borrow some of your Kerouac books?"

"They're at my house, Jack."

He waited for me to invite him over, but I forced myself to say nothing.

"Well, could you maybe bring 'em by the dorm if you're over that way tomorrow afternoon? I'm playing some football, but I'll be in my room around three."

He was testing me—wanting to see how strong a hold he had on me. "I'll be there at three, Jack."

August 9, 19—

When I'm nervous, my voice almost vanishes. It was like that today when I got off the elevator at the fourth floor of Jack's dormitory. I know the danger I was courting by being seen here. I know people gossiped about "the mysterious Dr. Fury," whom no one ever saw on a date with a woman. Nor did I seem to have any male friends. It had taken ten years to repair my professional reputation after the Danny fiasco. And now, here I was, throwing caution to the winds over a man who acted like a pig, a bull.

There were voices coming from Room 401. I stuck my head timidly in the door. Two boys in towels lounged on the beds. One boy was drying off. Jack stood buck naked at the sink as he shaved.

The boys looked shocked to see me—the popular Dr. Fury suddenly appearing in their midst. Jack looked over his shoulder: "Hey, come on in. Thanks for the books. Just put 'em down." Casually, he knotted a towel around his middle, but one of his beer-swigging companions quickly ripped it off. Another grabbed at his foreskin and stretched it out, as if it

35

were latex. Jack just growled and reached for another towel.

"We're using your room for a while, Barry. We can't talk in this zoo."

"Using it for what?" Barry hooted. The other boys snickered as we left.

Barry's room looked uninhabited. Dust was thick, and the heat was suffocating Jack took off his towel and began to wipe the sweat from his wet body. Sitting down on the edge of a desk, he beckoned me to come closer.

"Thanks for the books. You're such a little guy. You should be in movies. Some of the guys thought you looked like that TV kid—whatsis-name, with blond hair?"

"Did it hurt, Jack, when that guy yanked on your foreskin?"

I was staring down at his genitals, which were moist and dark. They hung over the edge of the desk. He ran a hand over his privates, weighing them. He dried them with his towel, carefully, proudly.

"Naw. They do it all the time. I never wear any clothes around here, and I'm always up for grabs. Sometimes we play a game with it, when we've all had a few beers. Look."

He took the loose covering of his penis and began to stretch it upward, pushing the tips of his finger into its rim to make it wider.

"Some of them try putting their fingers inside to see if they can touch my cocktip. None of them can do it. Go ahead. Push your second finger in there. Betcha can't do it."

I pushed my finger into the wet opening. It felt sticky and warm and spongy inside. I edged it in far-ther, but no matter how hard I tried, Jack simply stretched some more. Soon it was as if he held a col-

36

umn of pink flesh. Then his grip relaxed, and the funnel shrank. I felt the rubbery surface of his penis tip.

"Just keep pushing, and get it inside my dickhole," he urged "It don't hurt. Go on. I can take it."

Parting the lips of his urethra, the first joint of my finger sank into the tunnel of his cock. Carefully, I applied more force until I felt my fingertip encased in sticky snugness.

Jack's penis had been hardening. He let his foreskin curl around my finger as his fist began to slide up and down his shaft. I saw it begin to expand, to lengthen, felt it grow more firm and hot. Sweat trickled from his vast body, collecting around him in small pools on the desktop. His body trembled, and I heard him say softly, "Okay, take it out now. I'm gonna pop open."

I was startled to see how large his opening remained. And when his sperm squirted out, the spray was thicker than any I had ever seen. There were several more gushes, liberally spattering his chest and thighs. Jack barely grunted. He held his cock tight, watching me and smiling. He ran a thumb into his penis opening and brought out a glistening gob of semen.

"Did you like that?" He seemed genuinely curious.

"Can you come to my house next Friday—after class? I need some work done around the place. I'd pay you. We could have supper, watch some videos."

"And?"

"It'll be the end of class. We can unwind and let our hair down."

He stood up. He made no attempt to wipe the semen from his body or from the floor. As I left the room, I heard a whisper: "Oh, Angel of Light!" He laughed softly.

37

JASON FURY

August 15, 19—

We were both in a carefree mood when Jack and I left the Humanities Building. We headed for my house on the edge of campus. Through a little wood, it was only a thirty-minute walk.

The campus was dead. I had thrown a small party in the classroom and given all the budding Stephen Kings and Judith Krantzes passing grades. With the exception of Jack, I saw no future for any of them in the literary world.

My companion had stripped off his jersey and stuck it in the back pocket of his shorts. The string-up work boots made him look even more rugged. We'd said nothing about my visit to the dorm—yet I had thought of nothing else but the sight of his penis with its enormous urethra...the huge squirt of sperm...his splendid nudity.

There really were some jobs to be done around my house, jobs for someone tall and strong. Jack rehung a gutter, fixed my back door, and carried several heavy boxes into the cellar.

Around five, I stuffed several $20 bills into his pocket. "Go on up and shower. We'll have supper in an hour. I'll bring up some beer."

He whooped and laughed and, stripping off his shorts, he threw them at me. Naked and sweating, he bounded up the stairs.

When Jack came out of the shower, I dried him off. I ran the terry cloth down into his deep cleft. When I got to his genitals, I pushed back his foreskin and patted the penis tip. Even freshly cleaned, his crotch still exuded a powerful aroma of sperm and musk and skin.

Taking my hand, he led me to the bed, where he stretched out on his back and pressed my fingers against his nipple. He gulped down a cold Molson

38

Gold, and then another one. His glasses still hid his eyes, but I didn't ask him to remove them.

"What do you want to know about me?" he smiled. "Ask me anything you want to. Ask me something filthy."

"Has any guy ever blown you? Your cock looks like it's been used a lot. Sucked on or something."

"A guy at the dorm blew me last night—"

His words ended in a gasp as I began sucking his nipple. It was as warm and thick as I thought it would be. For several minutes, the room was silent, except for my loud slurping. Quickly, I found my way down to his lap. He had already yanked down his cocksock and was rubbing the slit of his penis, which dripped transparent lubricant. I began sucking on it wildly—for the first time in months, I was fellating a man I really wanted to.

My fists grasped the thickening stalk, the tip like a big lollipop of flesh. Suddenly its burden erupted. I swallowed his sperm and was startled by the number of squirts that emptied into my mouth.

Jack turned over on his stomach, pushed his big white butt up into the air, spread his cheeks. I sank my face into it. My tongue pushed its way into his rectum. Hanging down beneath were his moist genitals. I began tugging on them while still rimming him.

His penis grew hard. Pulling it up from between his legs, I began sucking him like that, and eventually Jack fed me yet another abundant ejaculation.

I licked and kissed his powerful legs, his testicles, nibbled at his big tits again, and once more lost myself on his penis. He fucked me expertly, then had me fuck him with my fist without using any lubricant.

Around midnight, we were watching the storm outside my window. I lay curled up in his arms, my lips once more wrapped around his swollen nipple.

39

He bent down and whispered, "I really need some money bad."

I really need some money bad. Slowly I sat up and looked at him. He got up and began moving around my room, fingering my clothes in the closet, peering into my dresser drawers.

"I *gave* you money, Jack."

Without turning around, he said, "That was for work. I need some for this kind of work. Sex work."

"Sex work? When I read your writings, Jack, you kept mentioning your Angel of Light. I thought it was—"

"Linda? Thought you might recognize her."

"Linda? Who's Linda?"

She was the bleached blonde who sat in the front row of my class. Jack said he fucked her nearly every night. "Oh, boy, could she give some good head."

"Do you charge her for sexual services, too?"

"Ha. Fun-neeee. You got some more bucks?" He had taken his glasses off. I could see why he might want to hide his eyes. They were a dead gray with no sparkle or expression. I thought of a water moccasin.

"What happens if I don't give you any more money?"

He shrugged and lit up a cigarette. "I hear the trustees don't think too highly of professors who seduce students."

I stared for a moment at his nudity, the thick neck, the square head. Then I went to the dresser and gave him two more twenties. He slipped them into his pocket and grabbed a new bottle of Seagram's gin from my bar.

"Might get a little thirsty tonight."

"Can you come back tomorrow Jack? I'll give you some more money. I really do need some more work done—I'd like to get fucked by you, too."

40

He smiled in delight. "I'll need a lot more money. Maybe some new clothes. I still might have to go to the board and tell them what happened."

"I'll pay you, Jack. With your body, you'll make a fortune. Why, you're—just like an animal. Some people love the caveman type."

"An animal, eh? That'll cost you extra." Suddenly he shouted, "Goddamn it, I'm not a goddamn animal! I got some class, some brains!"

I watched him swing down the path and into the woods. The triumphant hunter, he clutched his bottle like a trophy. No. Crashing about in the shadows, he was more like a clumsy beast than a hunter—a grotesque creature with his fleshy body and big head and cold eyes. In a few years, he'd be fat.

Later, in my bath, I sipped the champagne I had chilled for Jack and watched the sun come up through the window. And thought.

In my basement, there was a small room. Tomorrow Jack would paint it. The walls were thick. The door snapped shut in a flash. And on the door was a powerful lock....

I had never trapped an animal before. It was time I began.

Janu

1

Janu.

I whisper that name in dread, sometimes in hope, and shriek it many times in ecstasy.

Janu.

He commanded me to await him in this dark room on the outskirts of Nowhere, and I obeyed him, as I always do.

He visited me last night the first time in many days. When I awoke and felt him pressed close to me in that narrow cot, I nearly fainted from joy...and from terror. He creates in me always that inexplicable emotion that has gripped me whenever I know that he is near.

Janu is a jealous god, and he knows better than I that someone is seeping into my thoughts. His eyes, the color of amber, of sand beneath seawater, glowed in their almond-shaped sockets as they looked into mine. He mounted me, and while he sank his long tongue into my mouth and while his sword of flesh began its swift journey into the center of my universe, his thoughts become part of mine:

"Someone is trying to steal you away. There will be no more games. He must be destroyed. You will help me. You must go to the end of the line on the midnight train. There, you will find a hotel beyond the station. Your room will be ready for you. You must not leave it for a moment. Then, either I...or the one who tries...will come to you."

His power was filling me up, like an inner ocean. I could say nothing as the tip of him searched within for my heart. It was found, and that signaled his release, which was violent as an earthquake. It shot bolts into me, recharging my heart, and the bed shook so it nearly cracked in two. Janu's arms were on either side of me, his hands gripping the railing. His thighs pinioned my hips. I was his prisoner, and he smiled as I thought that.

"Yes...my prisoner, forever. For you will never escape me...."

I carried out his instructions.

I took the small train which was empty and left The City.

The train flew through the night like a silver column of energy, carrying no one but me. I passed through the small station, where only rats and snakes moved about, and I came shortly to this hotel. It was so tall that I could not see the top of it as it shot upward, stretching farther up than any skyscraper I have ever seen.

The lobby was empty, but on the counter was a large, square envelope that bore my name. Inside, on a piece of cardboard, I read: Room 10,001. I took the elevator up to this floor, passing rows of closed doors and wondered what lay behind them. I found my room. It was identical to my austere chamber at home. There is a narrow bed, covered in white muslin, in the corner; a table with a chair, and on the table a silver platter bearing hard bread, a metal pitcher filled with water, and a crystal goblet. On the bed is a small volume, bound in black with a single word printed in red: *Poem*. I will read that later. There is a window here, too, one with bars through which I can see the gigantic moon, filling up the entire sky, like the mirage of a desert one sometimes sees in the Sahara. The sky has turned into golden sand. I look through the bars...far below, almost hidden behind layers of mist are the forests and mountains I have crossed and the ravines, which resemble silver threads.

I sit down on the edge of the bed and pick up the thin book. Janu left it here...or, perhaps, it was the other one.... I can almost imagine the footsteps of Janu thundering in the past as they try to reach the present. I open the cover of *Poem* and begin reading:

"I fled Him, down the nights and down the days;
I fled Him, down the arches of the years;
I fled Him, down the labyrinthine ways
Of my own mind; and in the mist of tears
I hid from Him..."

Yes! Yes! All of that is so true. The poem could be a biography of my life with Janu. I read on:
"All things betray thee, who betrayest Me."

I have tried to flee from him constantly, but he has always found me, recaptured me, and made me cling to him more. I knew I could try to hide from him until eternity ends, and he will still find me...through

45

the years, into all my hiding places, even into my own mind...and those feet will always follow...follow after.

2

There is a period in my life when I was very young and there was no Janu. Strangely, I can recall hardly any of those days. In the small village where I lived, I spent most of my time in the house where only my father and the servants lived. I knew none of the other children and had no wish to. I was happy in my own self and spent my time studying religion and philosophy and walking in the thick forests surrounding our house. I was aware, even then, of a quality of waiting. It was not something one could define verbally. It was a hidden thought, but it convinced me that something fantastic would one day happen to me. I never doubted that for a moment.

There was one tract of land, near our estate, where Father forbade me to enter: the Star Woods. It was called that lovely name because Indians once believed that certain stars would descend from the skies at various times of the year and settle down for the night among those trees and magic rituals would ensue.

Often, while my nanny would walk with me on the outskirts of Star Woods, I would look at those black trees and the strange white flowers that grew in such abundance there and long to enter among them. A silent voice seemed constantly to urge me to enter.

I would beg of my old nanny to let me slip into that wood, even for a second, but the very thought made her face grow pale.

"The Dark One dwells there," she said once, "it is his home and one must never intrude upon his privacy. God forbid!" I could not get her to say anything more about The Dark One.

The years passed quickly, dreamily, and I took all my lessons at home from private tutors. Soon I was sixteen and ready to enter the university, a hundred miles away. The day before I was to leave for school, I did something I had dreamt of endlessly but never dared attempt: I entered Star Woods. I felt no fear as I slipped into that forbidden area, shunned and loathed by the village people. The pale flowers, almost translucent, covered the ground, but no sounds of wind or animals disturbed the sanctity of that eerie place. There was no path, but my feet seemed to move of their own accord and led me to the edge of a glimmering pool, filled with black water. No leaves or bracken floated on its still surface. Suddenly I noticed the bubbles and the widening ripples of something coming upward. It was a huge man, a naked man, who erupted out of the water and stepped lightly onto the bank of the pond. His eyes glowed large and yellow through the dim light. A smile grew on those thick, sensuous lips and he held out two arms towards me. He was very dark, indeed, the perfect image of the Dark One my nanny had whispered about. But his skin had a greenish pallor to it, and I thought immediately of underwater kingdoms and a race of people who live far below the surface of the earth. Two small antennae grew on his forehead above his eyebrows. His immense phallus twitched and lashed itself around his knees like a serpent. Although his lips did not move, I read his thoughts perfectly:

"So. You have come to me at last. The waiting has been long. But I am happy now. Here, don this." And he placed a wreath of soft leaves on my head like the one he wore. His phallus began darting around my feet and legs. It wrapped about my waist and pulled me to him. Although his skin was moist and hot, I could hear no heart beating beneath the skin of his chest. With a lunge, he toppled us over the side of the pond, and we began falling through the water for several long minutes, traveling at an incredible speed as the result of his powerful strokes. I was not frightened because I knew I was safe in the arms of this supernatural creature.

The darkness began to fade, and a pale light grew stronger below us. The man flew with me across green tiled floors bearing drawings of strange beings and animals; past crumbling columns, through a large square in the middle of the floor into a gigantic chamber, so huge I could not see where it ended nor how far up the ceiling went. Placed in the center of the room was a pyramid, and my master flew with me to the top. There was a raised dais there, and he laid me down upon it. Gently, he placed his massive bulk over me and he put the back of one of his hands behind my head. Smiling, he thought:

"I am Janu and have waited long for you. You are not your father's child, but one of royalty from the planet Xidan, brought here by an enemy of your original parent. You were found a short distance away by a shepherd and adopted by your father. It was foreordained that you should be mine. Millions of years ago it was predicted that you would come here, The One Who Is Yet to Come.

I felt his penis creeping up the inside of my leg. It began kissing my opening, and then it gained entrance and loved me deeper. I felt no pain and I realized that through some powers of his own, Janu had reduced his monstrous organ to accommodate me, who was then a virgin. Then Janu began to move his hips in a steady rhythm. His insistent gestures became more frenzied. Suddenly his thoughts were gasping, almost sobbing. And then I felt my internal self become drenched in a marvelous balm that soothed me, but made me want more of it. Janu complied with my newfound desire, and many more times did he issue forth that magical elixir that made me want to never leave him. Finally he raised himself away from me, and his organ resumed its natural dimensions; it wrapped around me and pulled me against his chest. Then Janu swam with me up to the surface and out of the pond.

"No matter where you go," he thought, slipping back into the water, "I will be there. No matter where you try to hide. I will be there. So farewell...for now."

Thus began my fervid courtship by Janu.

3

He came regularly—almost nightly—into my room off campus. He enjoyed surprising me so that I never knew what hour he would be there. I could be engrossed in my studies when suddenly something would wrap around my neck. It would be Janu's phallus, and he would laugh at my fright. And then he would carry me to bed, which was much too small for him, and he would straddle it and he would begin to enter me...again...and again until I would nearly faint from exhaustion and from the lunatic desire for more of his penis. But just when I would beg him to stay in and to not draw out, he would vanish...like the picture on a television screen after you have turned it off.

This went on for several months. I knew that it would have to end. My physical health was deteriorating, my studies were suffering and I found myself thinking of nothing but penises. They became my obsession. It came to the point that I sought sex by day, not able to wait for Janu. But, to my horror, I discovered that men I had sex with during daylight, would eventually end up dead. A biology student who spent several hours in my bedroom was found on the side of a highway the next morning: victim of a hit-and-run accident, the newspaper said. A football player ended up a heap of crumpled flesh and bone at the bottom of an elevator shaft. I began to avoid any contact with males of any type. I did not want a kiss from me to send them to their young graves.

I tried moving and hiding in a large mansion on the outskirts of The City. I should have known better. The first night in my new quarters, just when I was preparing to sleep, Janu boomed into my room, his phallus lashing around him furiously…it swept over to my bed and pulled me through the air. Janu caught me in his powerful arms and then he began to rape me, with his penis flashing in and out of me like an automotive piston. Faster and faster he penetrated me, and his movements did not slow as the night wore on. Suddenly he vanished and left me sobbing and frustrated on my narrow cot. He did not visit me for a month, and all I could think of was his return, so that he could take me, in a way no man would ever be able to do.

I managed to keep up with my studies. Soon my fever for him abated, only to return when he returned one night. I looked up from my desk and he was standing there, watching me tenderly. His organ stretched out and pulled me gently to my master as he carried me to bed. He was very quiet…and sweet, kissing me softly, something he had never done before. His huge eyes, so golden and glowing, were wet.

"What do you want from me, Janu?" I whispered.

"What are you trying to do to me? I cannot keep living like this."

He touched his mouth to my throat and then raised his head and looked at me. I felt his penis creeping up my leg, spreading fire that shot up into me.

"I want to move all thoughts out of your mind so that you will think only of Janu. You want to study and learn, and that will only create a barrier between us. I cannot allow that. I am going to rid you of that desire. There can be no one but Janu in your life."

And the room trembled with his powerful pelvic thrusts as he sought to rid me of my earthly desire: to learn.

4

My thirst for knowledge could not be quenched so easily by the power of lust, however, and although I quit my classes, I still haunted the library. I searched through all those volumes that year for any information I could find on Janu.

Through moldering, worm-eaten tomes to new-smelling volumes, my quest grew almost as feverish as my anticipation, mixed with fear, of seeing Janu again.

And finally I found what I sought. It was an English translation of the extraordinary *Zharbhxcizt,* believed to have been written by the Mayans and later translated by the enigmatic Comte de Jacombzch, a ghoul and prophet who lived in the Black Forest of Germany in the eighteenth century I turned the pages very carefully for several hours and learned this:

In the age before time began on Earth, there evolved a battle between Janu, king of darkness, and

51

Jozna, god of light, that was waged for millennia. The universe resounded and shuddered from this titanic battle fought under rolling crests of ocean waves and up above the red clouds. There was no winner in this struggle and the two had to finally part from each other in mutual defeat. Their magic was considerably dimmed as the gods of Greece replaced them in the pantheon of deities. The object of the furious war between Janu and Jozna was over who would possess the One Who Was Yet to Come.

I read further in that ominous book for more information on the briefly mentioned Jozna. At the back of *Zharbhxcizt*, the Comte de Jacombzch listed all of the ancient gods, including Janu. And for Jozna, he made this startling statement "...believed to have been the bastard brother of Janu. The power of Jozna was much less than that of his warlike kin, but he was more dearly beloved than any of the other immortals during that elusive age."

His brother! I had to read this small smattering of facts over several times, but was afraid to put it down in my notebook. Janu would find it. But then, if he were still dwelling upon Earth, then perhaps his brother was, too.

That afternoon. I went to the seashore, a mile away from the library. There was no one about, for the day was a gray one. I chose an isolated section of sand, spread my overcoat, and lay down upon it. Then I thought of what I had uncovered there in the library.

I must have slept for perhaps an hour when I opened my eyes and saw a strange man studying me: a magnificent, beautiful man, all gold and silver, with eyes so light blue they looked like spotlights trying to see my soul. He stood there naked above me, and I saw his penis writhing and curling around his wrist.

"You...," he whispered and sank down beside me. "I thought it would never happen. I have been here at this place for centuries waiting for you...."

"Are you—?"

"Yes, yes," he laughed happily. "I am Jozna and was once the god of light. But now, my power, like that of my brother, has failed, to a great degree. Other gods have long replaced us." Somehow I found my head against that massive chest and I was sobbing out my torment at the hands of his brother.

"Can you help me?" I cried. "I am possessed by him...yet I would do anything to escape." But my silent thought was: Would I? Would I really have the courage to give up such a monster lover as Janu, who tormented—yet fascinated me—with his brutality, and then with his unexpected quirks of gentleness.

His brother pulled me close to him and I felt his phallus stroking my cheeks and neck.

"There is nothing I can do...except to fight him for possession of you. We did this a long, long time ago. No one won because you had not come yet This time it will be very quick and very quiet. This time there must be a victor."

He began kissing me and quickly removed my clothes, laying me back on top my coat. Although he was as large as his dark brother, he was much more gentle, and his penis, instead of teasing and torment-ing me, went quietly and directly into me and he kept it there while turning it around hungrily, exploring every part of me internally. While his hips gyrated faster, he continued to kiss my eyes, my ears, and finally my mouth. His tongue sliding down my throat felt like a bolt of lightning, illuminating my inner visions of him and Janu to an incredible degree. I felt his tremendous organ swell larger, and then felt it pulsating as it shot forth love for several minutes. But he did not withdraw after that tumultuous orgasm, nor after the countless other times that afternoon on the beach.

"There is more," he would whisper each time, "Much more."

It was dark before he finished. Then he pulled out of me quickly.

"Darkness is the time Janu roams about...I must leave you," he said sadly.

"How can I see you again?"

"Here...come back tomorrow and I will be waiting...as I have through the centuries. Put this on...no one but you can take it off." He put a ring of pure silver around the second finger of my right hand. "It is a sacred ring of the Sun, and it means that you and I are friends. After Janu and I meet tomorrow, I hope that we will become much more than friends. Janu loves you, too; but if you become his companion, you will have to efface yourself totally."

"I will come back tomorrow...before you and Janu come together."

"You must," Jozna said as he waded back—and then disappeared—into the winterish green ocean.

When I returned to my house, I knew that Janu knew. Furniture was smashed against the walls, my books were ripped and torn apart, the windows were smashed, and snakes and rats slithered and crawled around the floor. He stood there in the middle of the floor, a dark giant with his fists on his hips, his eyes like headlights of a truck, and his penis lashing around him, snapping at the floor, like a bullwhip.

"So," he thought quietly, "he has found you, eh? My brother has had you, and now he is trying to become part of you. Come. Get on the bed. I must have you now. Do not worry. I will not harm you, but

I must show you who is lord and master in your life..."

"Get rid of those horrible snakes and rats, Janu...they frighten me...."

He laughed at me, but those vile creatures were gone instantly, and all of my destroyed property—books and furniture and other belongings—were restored instantly to their former selves, intact.

Janu moved toward me and held something between his long fingers.

"Put this on," he said. "Since you wear the ring of the Sun from my brother, so you must wear the ring of Night from Janu." He slipped the circle of glimmering ebony around the second finger of my left hand. "After tomorrow night, one of these must come off."

I backed away from him and he watched me, amused.

"Janu, I do not hate you. I fear you, for you want everything from me. I cannot become part of you. Let me have something of my own."

He shook his head, grinning, and his penis shot out and wrapped around my stomach and jerked me up against my dark master.

"No, you must be totally of me. Nothing apart."

His organ had been stroking my thighs soothingly but now it shot like a serpent up my hole so quickly that I screamed.

He began taking me, so deeply and completely that I went into a near trance. His great hips rose and lunged, thrust and dug away into me. But as the hours passed, he did not stop once nor say anything except:

"Can your golden Jozna make you feel as I can?"

"No," I gasped, "he is more...gentle, Janu, he is—"

"You like it gentle...or like *that?*" And he pushed

55

himself viciously into me. Although I screamed, he had succeeded in turning me into a human motor that wanted to go faster.

"Oh, God, Janu, don't stop now. Keep doing it…do it harder.…"

But as I shrieked those words, he was gone, disappearing diabolically.

Later that morning, I found his message on my bathroom mirror. The words were scrawled in greenish-tinted sperm, and they directed me to come to this hotel room "to await the one who is victorious."

Jozna was waiting for me—glowing like a metal sculpture under the dim sun. We said nothing, and he loved me all day. Tenderly, thoughtfully, he plumbed my depths until I was in a stupor and I felt both of us falling, falling into water and finally resting within a crystal bubble at the bottom of the ocean. He entered me and stayed there constantly. He whispered, "When you and I are together at last, we will live here, in my home."

He took me back to the shore, for it was growing late. Embracing me, he gave me the same directions as Janu: "There is going to be a battle within a few hours. You must wait in Room 10,001 at the hotel. It is a chamber that my brother and I have chosen as the place of betrothal. After tonight—"

"One of you…" I continued.

"Will come for you…for better or for worse."

And so I sit here at my table, tearing some of the hard, unsalted bread apart with my fingers. I think of Janu, so dark, brutal, but in some terrible way, fascinating. And I think of Jozna, like an angel, yet powerful, like a child, yet like a wise old man. Being loved by Janu was like being in the midst of a hurricane; with Jozna, I felt bathed by butterflies, cool water, warm sunlight...a splash of gold on my soul. The candlelight flickers, and the colored shadows seems to flicker upon one particular passage on the page of poetry:

> *"Halts by me that footfall—*
> *Is my gloom, after all,*
> *Shade of His hand, outstretched caressingly?*
> *Ah, fondest, blindest, weakest,*
> *I am He Whom thou seekest!..."*

Something is moving about in this isolated hotel; I can hear nothing but I can sense it, the presence of another one. There! There it is, the soft closing of the elevator door and....

Footsteps...moving toward my room. I glide away from my chair and back up against the wall, trembling...

Someone now stands in front of my door; I can hear the heavy panting of hard breathing; the door opens...

And I can see who stands outside now, hesitating. Now he moves swiftly toward me, his arms outstretched and...

"You!" I whisper...joyously....

57

STRANGE YOUNG MAN

When the Age of Aquarius dawned in the spring of
1969, I embraced it feverishly by becoming the town's
first hippie.

While crew cuts were the order of the day, my gold
locks soon swept my shoulders. Instead of the local
uniform of jeans and white T-shirt, I preened in bell-
bottoms and sandals from Woolworth's. Along with
my Indian jewelry, I created such a stir in Carson
City, North Carolina (population 301) that country-
folk drove miles on the weekends in hopes of glimps-
ing this long-haired weirdo.

Rednecks and truck drivers were unusually enthusiastic about my appearance. From windows of their
trucks they leaned out, spit streams of tobacco juice
in my direction, and hollered, "Goddamned fruitcake! Get outta this town before we string you up!"

What? Leave Carson City where the deadbeats

clustered in front of Johnny Bobb's Esso station each morning to swat flies and sweat from their potbellies and bald heads? Where I would be forever known not only as the Town Hippie but the Town Queer? (Question: Does sucking off one fat slob make you a town queer? Answer: If you're the only queer in town, it does.)

There had to be a better place to live than Carson City. So, as the Trailways bus swept me away to California that May morning of 1970, my handsome, black-haired father receded into the distance. He had made me pin my return ticket and four fifty-dollar bills to the inside of my shirt.

Before I left, he gave me two pieces of advice: First, "You'll find happiness in life only when you discover it within yourself." Second, he gave me the warning that parents have given to headstrong kids since time began: "Be careful!"

Dorothy Gale found her Emerald City in the Land of Oz by following the Yellow Brick Road. I felt I had found such a road to take me to my own Emerald City when I stepped off the bus three days later. I was in the Haight-Ashbury section of San Francisco, and hippies were everywhere! In ponchos, flowing scarves, and masses of hair, two of them handed me a sunflower and made the peace sign with two fingers. A half-naked hippie boy skated by, blowing bubbles from a plastic dime-store bottle.

On the curb before the bus station sat a strange young man who strummed a guitar. He was strange, because even before I saw him, he was watching me with dark, glinting eyes, and smiling broadly. Turning his face toward the sun, he sang in a thin voice an old ballad made popular by Joan Baez that year: "Strange young man, Come into my garden/Strange young man, Passerby..."

Jumping to his feet, he put an arm around my shoulder. "Hey, honey! Gonna let a strange man come into your garden? He might just bring you a little bit of heaven and a whole lot of hell."

I pulled away from him. What was he trying to tell me? His dark eyes frightened me, and I moved past him, for he was casting a shadow over my first few moments in gaga land. My wariness attracted him, though, and he moved along with me, talking and teasing. Against my better judgment, I found him attractive, in an ugly way. He certainly wasn't like the farmboys in Carson City. Standing at exactly my height of five-foot-three, he had brown eyes that glittered like burning matches in a face the color of Ivory Soap. Dry, long hair and beard suggested more a Jesus Freak than a flower child.

"Getting much cock, honey?" he suddenly asked.

"Sure! Tons of it."

I lied, for I was still a virgin, and his words shocked me. You asked a question like that in Carson City and you got your head blown off.

Putting an arm around my shoulder, he pulled me against him. Although he smelled of sweat, he felt lean, warm, and strong. "You're scared and lonely, aren't you? You miss your Daddy. I can be your Daddy. Come on and join my commune in L.A. See that old school bus yonder? I'm leaving in just a few minutes. Other hippie kids like you are already aboard. And—you can have all the cock you want at my commune. I've got some big studs there."

His perceptions were startling, for I did miss my beautiful father, and I was beginning to think more and more about cock. Suddenly he began kissing me. As he did so, he pulled a dark, sturdy penis out of his suede leather pants and began masturbating rapidly. A man had never kissed me before, let alone beat off on a side street with people and cars passing by around the corner. I felt dizzy, and the sudden wetness on my toes felt beautiful. The stranger fell to his knees and slurped up the sperm from my feet.

"Will you come with me, honey, and be happy forever?"

"Are—are you going to hurt me?"

He stood and kissed me again for a long time, his tongue darting deep into my mouth like a swollen penis. "Do I look like I'd hurt you—you sweet little angel from Mars?"

I could call him Daddy, he continued, for I was the small, boyish type who would always need a father throughout his life. His name for me would be Angel, for men such as he, he explained, would always need a golden-haired beauty to give meaning to their existence, to show them the light.

"Come with me, you angel from Dixie," he repeated.

"Be careful," my real father seemed to whisper... but could someone in a cowdab like Carson City know about life and love? I took my new Daddy's outstretched hand and went with him. Later—much later—I realized the meek won't inherit the earth. The stupid will, for our tribe is legion.

If I were on a Yellow Brick Road, then it was one Dorothy could never have imagined. The old school bus rolled to a stop two days later before a group of wooden buildings. Somewhere, over a steep hill nearby, snaked the Los Angeles Freeway, but we were hidden away from the world in a literal ghost town, once used by television studios for their Westerns, but now abandoned.

In the empty dirt street, Daddy was shouting, "Come out, come out!"

Tumbling out of the bus, I followed four other

flower children into the blazing sun. From the rickety structures appeared a dozen members of Daddy's "family." From the way they greeted him, you would have thought he was Santa Claus or Jesus Christ.

He was something of both, for I had concluded by then that this small, intense man was extraordinary. He could be a devil or an angel—incredibly sensual, vicious or tender. Along the highway, for example, he had picked up over a dozen hitchhiking flower children. After fucking them all—male and female—he had kicked them off the bus, minus their clothes and belongings. The only ones he let remain were Timmy of Kansas City, who had run away from home, Keith, a tall, sullen youth from Mississippi, and two sisters, Molly and Judy. All of them stayed stoned, thanks to Daddy's abundant supply of drugs. When I refused to get high, he was amused, but didn't press me.

Now he introduced us to his older family members by calling them his "Oldies" and us his "Newies." There were eight girls and four boys. The girls were all naked. The boys wore jeans or shorts. All had long hair. To welcome us, they formed a line and hugged us, crying out, "Peace, brothers and sisters! Love and harmony forever!"

During this time, my attention was drawn to a handsome giant who seemed disgusted by the way his cohorts fawned and gushed over their leader. Except for dirty blond hair, swept back into a ponytail, he bore an astonishing resemblance to my own father: even to the thick moustache. His powerful six-foot-five torso was propped against the hood of a dune buggy. A cowboy hat was pulled down over his brow. A skimpy leather vest did nothing to hide enormous pectorals, which billowed over big arms folded across his chest.

Just as I was about to introduce myself, Daddy

topped me and held up a hand for silence. "I want you all to meet this beautiful little gay guy, Angel."

The men shifted their feet uneasily. Although the ones on the bus had balled with Daddy, they had made it clear that gay sex wasn't their bag at all. The muscular Samson in the vest also seemed unusually nervous. With his face turning a bright red, he studied the tips of his boots, as if aware of something about to happen, something involving him. And he was right.

Daddy grinned, "Angel, this fine-looking man is Mr. Billy Bull. We call him that for obvious reasons. Billy, strip off them clothes and give our new family member a big mouthful of something real good. I done promised him a bull dick, and you got it."

"Fuck, no!" barked the charming Mr. Bull. "Look, dammit, you swore that fag I fucked for you last week would be my last fag! You know I dig the chicks!"

Daddy pushed his face closer to the blazing features of the scowling Hercules. "I'm giving you an order, Billy Bull. Strip, so the sun's burning your white butt and the breeze is kissing your big dick." Then he lowered his voice to a menacing whisper. "The cops would love to know where you're hiding. How many warrants they got on you now?"

For a long moment, their eyes remained locked. Then, with a muttered "Christ almighty damn!" Billy Bull thrilled us all by ripping off his cowboy hat, vest, and boots. Finally, after a long moment, he then peeled off his paper-thin jeans. A collective gasp greeted his stunning nudity—and by what jiggled between his huge thighs. I'd never seen anything like it.

Like a star stripper in an all-male revue, the commune stud leaned back against the car hood. His hands were clasped behind his head, and his muscles were wet and like a champion bodybuilder.

As if he had discovered a new toy, Daddy grasped

the base of Billy Bull's genitals and flapped them at me like douche bag. "Come on, Angel, come and get you a mouthful of the best meat in California!"

"Get on it and get it over with!" Billy Bull snarled. At that moment, I knew I had reached a radical turning point in my life. Four days before, I had knelt before my minister to take communion in the First Baptist Church of Carson City. Now I knelt in the dirt of a Hollywood ghost town, before a magnificent naked man, with my hand around his floppy phallus, while fifteen hippies chanted, "Suck him dry! Suck him dry! Suck him dry!"

Grasping his cock was like holding the arm of a healthy infant—one with a fist covered by a thick glove of flesh. Impatient to begin the ritual, Billy Bull ripped back his thick foreskin and crammed the head into my mouth. His stalk bulged and doubled in size as he brutally tried to rape my mouth. Slamming his hips forward, the thick column shot into my throat. I gagged violently and shoved his hips backward, until only the tip was left inside me. Willingly, I worked on that, which seemed to be okay with him. When I glanced up, his eyes were closed, his full lips parted, while his big balls banged against my chin and throat. His thrusting increased.

Just when I was getting the hang of blowing a young bull like Billy, however, Daddy shoved me aside roughly, dropped to his knees, and crammed the growing erection into his own mouth.

Snorting and gagging, the older man grasped Billy's buttocks from behind to bring the muscle stud's hips against his mouth. Finally, Daddy's flaring nostrils were hidden in Billy's thick pubic hair. All of us saw him gulping, choking, his face turning purple and his eyes bulging. The recipient of his lust was flipping out. Billy Bull writhed against the car hood his hands raising at first to push the sucker away, but then to let his fingers pull at his own nipples and rub his rippled stomach. When he finally ejaculated, Daddy gagged so hard, he coughed the hard-on right out of his mouth. He lay there in the dirt, gasping for air while Billy Bull slung the wetness from his main claim to fame, spit, and thrusting his clothes and boots under his arm, walked away naked. *If he hates gay men,* I thought, *then he must really hate Daddy.* As I was to discover, my adopted parent broke all the rules when it came to human behavior.

As the days passed, I saw that everyone treated Daddy like God—or the Devil—two figures who usually inspire awe and fear in the meek. He became exactly what you wanted him to be. To those who yearned for a firm, parental hand, he could be tough, snarling, and masterful. For example, vicious beatings were given to the women who felt they needed proof of male dominance. Since nearly all my cohorts had run away from home, he became their father—an unusual one, indeed, who dispensed sex and drugs, or withheld them as punishment.

"You're special," he explained to me my first night there. "You're my little yaller-haired angel-pie, and nobody's gonna touch you except me. Only—not now. The right time will come. Just be patient, honey, and it'll be well worth it."

He proved his adoration by rewarding me with my own private room at the end of the dusty corridor from his. Other rooms along the hallway of the broken-down hotel were inhabited by his most ardent "Oldies," one of the most devoted of which was a hard-faced girl named Minnie. She loathed me on sight, as I did her, and she was startled to see I could top her insults with no difficulty. When you have been the Town Queer, you learn to defend yourself.

Strangely enough, Billy Bull was also considered off-limits to any horny admirer, male or female. Daddy chose when and where his prize stallion could fuck or get sucked, and by whom. Consequently, Billy Bull lived apart from the others, in a wooden shack where the ammunition was stored. Yes, ammunition. For a family which professed to meditate on peace and love, there sure was a lot of talk about hate and war and blood around there.

It was our third night there. Around a communal table, we gathered for supper and ate bologna sandwiches and drank warm Kool-Aid. Billy Bull sat alone in a corner. Several times our eyes met, but he always looked away quickly.

Like a preacher, Daddy sermonized to us about how Judgment Day was fast approaching. It would be a war to end all wars, he declared, and we were the target of "pigs...honkies ..and niggers." Why? Because we were so fucking beautiful and sweet and attuned to nature, he claimed. As I glanced around the spellbound group, I would have laughed at such crap, if I hadn't realized how intensely they all believed in him.

Then, he went to each of us "Newies." Stooping down before each one, he asked the same questions over and over: "Are you willing to kill for your family when Judgment Day comes? Can you kill your soul, your family, and any pig or honky, so I can lead you out of the wilderness?"

As he spoke, he placed a tablet of LSD on each tongue. Soon all of my new family acted like crazy people attending a revival meeting as they groveled at his feet.

"Oh, God, yes, yes!" they cried.

When he came to me, all eyes watched intently

67

Billy Bull leaned forward, for even in the three days I had been there, it was clear I was no follower. My real father had always encouraged me to be myself and to be independent.

Staring into my eyes, Daddy repeated his chant and held forth a small cube of "dynamite." I ignored it. Taking a deep breath, I delivered what sounded like a speech—that's just what it was. I wanted them to know exactly where I stood.

"I've got a father down South who I love more than anybody on earth—including God," I announced. "I have an uncle who's a sheriff in Georgia. You couldn't find a sweeter man. No, I wouldn't kill them or anybody else. And no, I don't do drugs."

The silence was so intense, breathing was audible around me.

Minnie muttered, "Fucking little goody two-shoes."

From his corner, Billy Bull winked, as if approving of my stand.

Suddenly Daddy leaped to his feet while yanking out a hunting knife from its sheath.

"Don't you know I'm the Devil, and I'm doing the Devil's work?"

His followers erupted into shouts of "Amen! Hallelujah!" Yet, in one of his startling mood changes, he began to laugh and silenced everyone. "Hey, it's no sweat. I can live with that. It's cool. I love a challenge." He turned, his eyes glanced, and smiled menacingly at me. "In a month, I'll have you so turned around you could go right home and kill that sweet ole pappy of yours."

"Don't hold your breath on that one, Daddy Dearest." I smiled, but all eyes studied me coldly. Once more, I was the outsider, and from a lifetime of experience in being one, I resigned myself to it. I left the group with a chill hovering over me. Something about that atmosphere suggested that Daddy had already asked certain of his followers to do what he had just now suggested to me—and that they had already obeyed.

Quickly, I planned my escape. I still had my return bus ticket and my money. In the meantime, I would have to play the game prisoners have played for centuries: to be quiet, to watch, to listen—and then to get the hell out of there when the right moment came.

Daddy delighted in exhibiting his lust for Billy Bull. Hardly a day passed that our leader would not go up to that blond hunk, preferably in the dining hall, where we would all be an audience for him. Without any warning, he would suddenly stoop down in front of the stunning young man, unbuckle, unzip, and quickly capture the monumental penis in his mouth.

You had to laugh at Billy Bull's mixture of emotions. While his mouth would still be stuffed with food, he would curse and try to push that ravenous mouth away. By then, though, Daddy would have already embedded the tip of the big penis in his throat. Giving in, then, Billy Bull would fall back on the table, scattering food and plates onto the ground, while others would strip off his clothes. Soon, stark naked, he would snarl and mutter curses which always ended in gasps of ecstasy.

Seeing Daddy in such a position reminded me of the time I saw a python at the zoo being fed a rabbit. In both cases, rubbery lips trapped the object greedily. Daddy's upper lip pressed deep into the blond pubic hair while his bottom lip squeezed the base of the bulging shaft, milking it in steady motions, until it exploded, its syrup dribbling out the sides of Daddy's mouth. And when he finally slid the drained organ from his lips, he gasped for breath while the rest of us stared in wonder at the bloated penis which shook as Billy Bull sat up to rub the tender tip. More often than not, though, Daddy would want a second orgasm, and once more he would startle Billy by again throwing his mouth over the swollen phallus, causing Billy to whoop as Daddy's strong hands pinned the muscular hips firmly against the table, and started all over again.

One day I overheard Minnie laugh about her experiences in different prisons. Other "Oldies" joined in with their memoirs of jailhouse life, and I was shocked to realize they were all ex-convicts. What had I gotten myself into?

The "Oldies" studied us "Newies" as if we were fresh meat on the hoof—especially me—since Daddy made it clear that I was his "property." This may have soothed his ego, but it did absolutely nothing for my libido. I wanted sex! But he forbade either me or Billy Bull to ball with anyone—least of all each other. We belonged to him.

"You beautiful little angel," he often said, "when our night comes, and it's a-coming, you're gonna feel like you've died and gone to hell."

"Couldn't I go to heaven? " I'd reply. "I hear it's cooler up there."

"Hell's our favorite place, and we just love it real darned hot!"

Although he laughed, he was too intense about "hell...The devil...Satan" for me to believe he was joking. That's when I put my plan for escape into high gear.

Forget the dune buggies and the bus, I decided. Anyway, Daddy kept the keys locked up. I would have to make the expressway by foot. Daddy often warned us about trying such a plan. The hill behind the buildings was steep. Past that, you had to walk three miles over rattlesnake-infested terrain.

My fellow "Newies" were astonished by my plan. Why, they would ask, leave such a great place? You had no worries, you did a few minor chores, and for that, you were given food, shelter, drugs, and sex. Timmy and Keith loved fucking the girls and getting blowjobs from Daddy. Molly and Judy loved being part of a family of hippies and getting screwed by the men. Everyone was convinced this was the end of the Yellow Brick Road, the Emerald City at last.

They were so scornful of my escape idea that I was startled when Timmy did just that. Following a wild night of sex and drugs and booze—from which Billy Bull and I were excluded—Timmy was nowhere to be seen. He ran away, Daddy told us with sorrow in his eyes. He couldn't imagine why—after all, didn't Timmy had everything he wanted here? I couldn't figure it out, either. Not at first.

Three nights later, another big orgy was held. Locked in my room, I was so horny that I jacked off three times. I thought I'd go crazy from the loudspeaker, which blasted out Daddy's favorite recording, The Beatles' new hit, *The White Album* over and over. How could they love an album which had so much screaming in it, I wondered. When I fell asleep, I could still hear the screams.

This time, Keith had vanished. When I asked the girls, Molly and Judy, if they had seen him, they seemed nervous. Both had taken so many drugs the night before that the only thing they *did* remember was seeing Keith being blown by Daddy while one of the straight dudes fucked him.

71

I thought of those screams. They hadn't come from the record, they were real.

I didn't sleep that night. Daddy was holding another party in his room. Several times I heard stealthy footsteps come up to my locked door. Someone breathed heavily outside, but no one tried to enter. *The White Album* was played at car-blasting level, but even so, I could hear screams once more.

The next day, the two sisters were gone. When I asked about them, the other members smirked and drawled, "Maybe you kids just don't know how to live in a commune."

I was the only "Newie" left.

During the next few days, I glimpsed Billy Bull now and then. He was staying to himself a lot in his little wooden shack. Something told me I could trust him, and I was hurrying to find him when I passed Daddy sitting on the stoop of the porch, playing his guitar. At his feet, in the dirt, were six of his most ardent followers, who watched his every move with adoration.

When he saw me, he plucked some chords and sang: "Strange young man, come into my garden…"

I cut in. "What happened to Molly and Judy?"

"Maybe they couldn't handle Judgment Day—which is coming soon."

"What in the world are you talking about?"

"Judgment Day! Judgment Day!" he screamed, leaping to his feet. "It's a-coming for you and for me!"

The others cried their "amens" and "hallelujahs."

I left them, but as I turned the corner of the building, a powerful arm grabbed me and a hand clamped over my mouth. Struggling, I was carried into one of the small wooden buildings. It was Billy Bull, and I was in his home.

"Shut up!' he hissed. "They hear everything. You've got to get out of here before dawn, or they'll kill you—like they did your buddies!"

"Oh, my God! What are you saying?"

These people, weren't hippies I realized suddenly. They were a band of murderers who liked to kill. Blood turned them on. They played around with Satanism. It gave them a kick to perform human sacrifice. Billy Bull confirmed my fears by telling me that ten or more young hippies lay chopped up and buried around the commune, and that I was to be their prize victim, for I was blond, and they had never had a blond before.

"Be careful," my father had warned me. And now look where I had ended up! I covered my face and began to weep. If only I could get back home to my real Daddy! There was a moment of awkward silence from Billy Bull, and then, to my amazement, I felt strong arms pull me against his bare chest.

"I'm leaving here tonight," he whispered. "I'm tired of running from the cops on those drug warrants. Or never knowing when I'll have my throat cut. Wanna come along?"

I hugged him tightly and nodded. Before I knew what was happening, he had picked me up and carried me to his bunk. Quickly, he stripped off his clothes, and I did mine. As he began kissing me, he muttered about how I was the first male he had ever desired, and how much he had really wanted to get it on with me—in private.

In his arms, I felt warm and safe. His huge pectorals felt so wonderful, and I instantly bent down to suck on his nipples. Quickly, I covered the tip of his penis with my mouth and began to suck on it. He grasped my fists in his as we worked them up and down on his thickening organ. When he ejaculated,

73

he did so quietly. I was hardly expecting the abundance of sperm which filled my mouth.

Then he whispered, "Now it's my turn."

With that, he buried his face between my legs, wrapped his massive arms around my butt, and pulled me into his throat. It was not the most skillful sex I've ever had, but the realization that Billy Bull was going down on me set off one of the most powerful orgasms I have ever had. Afterward, he was deeply silent.

Not wanting to leave his protective presence, I began sucking him again for a long time while my fists churned his erection for its cream. He rewarded my efforts with another orgasm, after which he spoke almost immediately. "You have to leave," he warned, "or Daddy'll become suspicious. We'll leave at midnight, cross the hill, and make it out onto the expressway." He kissed me again. "Whatever you do, don't go into Daddy's bedroom. If you do, you'll never come out of it alive."

It was late when I entered the old hotel. No one was around. As I turned into the corridor that led to my room, I froze. Standing before my room was Daddy. Watching me, his eyes were black holes from the dim overhead light. He looked like the Prince of Darkness.

"Tonight's the night, honey," he smiled. "Our big night together. Are you happy?"

"I can't believe it! It's about time!" I beamed. His hand grabbed my arm as he pulled me toward his bedroom at the end of the corridor.

I hung back, though. "Daddy, wait a minute! If we're finally going to do it, can't I just change my clothes, wash up a little? I'm so sweaty and dirty. I don't feel like your angel right now..." I smiled, flirtatiously innocent.

His dark eyes studied me, glinting with that unearthly glimmer. "Five minutes then. But hurry, hurry! Judgment Day is coming!" No sooner had I entered my room than I leaped through my bathroom window to the dusty ground outside.

Billy Bull bolted from his bed when I flew into his room.

"Billy, he's come for me! We've got to go now!" I screamed.

Saying nothing, my protector thrust a deadly-looking .22-caliber pistol into my hand, threw on his own holster, a belt of ammunition and, grabbing my hand, pulled me out into the darkness. Somewhere close by, we heard Daddy laughing.

"Angel! Where are you? Judgment Day's here!"

From afar, the hill looked like a breeze to climb. As we desperately struggled upward, however I knew I could never make it out to the expressway.

"Come on!" Billy Bull hissed. "If they find us, they'll butcher us!"

A bullet exploded on the dirt just a few inches away. Dawn was erasing our protection. Below, Daddy grinned up at us as he and his flock clapped and laughed.

I fired my pistol and was gratified to see Minnie grab her arm and scream. Billy aimed, fired, and nicked Daddy in the ear. This sent them into a frenzy, and they vanished for a moment, only to reappear in two dune buggies, in which began their furious ascent. With their long hair blowing around their faces, with their guns and swords raised in the air, they looked like demons from hell with their mad master at the wheel.

Billy pulled me to the top of the hill. We were both exhausted. For a moment, we couldn't believe our eyes, though. Along the narrow road below us, which led into the commune, glided a small cavalcade of law-enforcement cars. Troopers, sheriffs, police vehicles. Silently, instantly, we tumbled and hit the ground. Behind us, our pursuers raced closer, unaware of what was coming between us.

In the next room, my father turned on the television in our den. It was Sunday. We were preparing our ritual of pigging out while watching the first big football game of the season. Steaks and baked potatoes were almost ready. A peach cobbler cooled on the windowsill. Beyond that, a line of clean clothes snapped in the October wind.

Billy Bull had sent me a postcard the day before—from Boulder, Colorado. He was hiding there, in fear of his life. Daddy and his followers had been released from jail after they were arrested that day three months before. The armada of officers who swept down that morning had actually come to arrest the hippie group on suspicions of operating a stolen-car and credit-card ring. Because the wrong date had been affixed to the search warrant, however, the violent mob was released. None of the officers had believed Billy or me when we told them they had a madman and his disciples who had killed many times in their possession.

I crept up behind my handsome father, who stood before the TV, and gooched him. He grunted, grabbed me, and held me tight against him as he continued watching the game.

Big, muscular, with black curls and eyes the color of lime candy, he kissed my cheek. How wonderful to be with him once more—smelling his clean flesh, the whiff of Giorgio Armani cologne, and feeling the strength of his powerful muscles. Like Billy Bull, he dwarfed me.

"Hey, what the fuck?" he muttered. On the screen,

an "NBC News Bulletin" broke into the football game. A reporter breathlessly reported that seven hippies were arrested that morning in the horrifying ritual murder of a young screen starlet and her four friends in Los Angeles. The slaughter had shocked the nation, with its hints of satanic rites.

A line of handcuffed young hippies were shown as they were led into the jailhouse. Bedlam broke out when the leader of the bizarre little band appeared at the end of the manacled group. He stared into the camera lens, his flat, dark eyes betraying nothing. I could almost hear him humming, "Strange young man..."

"Damn fool kids," my real Daddy said, looking down at me. "How could they get mixed up with a freak like that?"

FORBIDDEN FRUIT

"Have you seen *it*?" Randy squealed. "The patient in 401?"

Before answering, I sipped my coffee, blew cigarette smoke into the air, and resisted a powerful impulse to slap the lascivious smirk off the face of my fellow nurse's aide.

"No, Randy," I drawled. "Should I?"

His reaction was predictable, since I had seen it many times during that summer of 1962. With a roll of his eyes, he licked his lips and squeezed his crotch. Any male patient at Ocean Isle Sanitarium, who still had teeth, hair, and wasn't in a wheelchair, sent Randy into spasms of hysteria.

"Put your coffee down and come see for yourself. You'll simply flip out!"

Since I had to make my rounds of the wards, anyway, I followed Randy's big-hipped figure down the hall.

Room 401 was on the violent—or high-securi-
ty—wing. The dozen men there were considered a
danger to either themselves or to others. Some would
be there only temporarily, since their conditions were
curable. The rest had already plunged into the abyss
of insanity. They would never see the outside world
again. Would the newcomer in 401 be one of those
lost souls?

For once, Randy was right. When I peered into
Room 401, I very nearly did flip, faint, and ejaculate.
Occasionally, Ocean Isle received a handsome hunk
who kept the women and gays in a dither. None I had
seen so far, though, could hold a candle to this stunning Adonis.

He was young, probably in his early twenties, and
like the other men on this wing, he lay spread-eagled
on his back. Thick straps secured his wrists and
ankles. Sedation had knocked him out, so that he was
oblivious to the twin pairs of eyes devouring him.

The patient was also stark naked, except for a
small towel folded across his lap. Muted light from
the barred window bathed his stunning torso with
enough illumination to make it glisten beneath its
sheen of sweat. As for his dark hair, it was swept
back from a face both rugged and sensitive, yet haggard, too. Some traumatic ordeal had left its mark in
the fine lines around his eyes and mouth. His lips
were ragged where he had chewed them.

The handsome face was merely an appetizer
before the main feast. His powerful body—nearly too
big for the bed—was bronzed except for the startling
strip of white around the hips. From his broad chest
billowed enormous pectorals, each crowned with a
thick nipple. His stomach sank in dramatically to
form a hollow, ridged with muscles that were defined
sharply. Finally, his strong thighs were parted entic-

ingly. Seeing my rapt expression, Randy pranced up to the unconscious patient and did a typical Randy thing. He whipped away the towel and scooped up the impressive genitalia in his hands. The thick penis hung heavily over his fingers like a condom bulging with warm water. In his other palm rested testicles that resembled plump plums wrapped in pink silk.

Grasping the luscious organ with his fist, Randy flapped it playfully at me, and then he held it taut, while his other hand rolled down the long foreskin brutally.

"He's so uncut!" Randy drooled. "See how long I can stretch it out? Just like pizza dough. Been playing with it all afternoon."

He thrust his fingers into the snout of the fleshy overhang, fanning it out to an incredible length so that it resembled a white bowl.

"Cut it out, Randy!" I hissed. "How can you take advantage of the poor guy? Hasn't he got enough troubles without you abusing him?"

"Oh, shut up, Miss Goody-Two-Shoes! You know you want to gobble on this big meat stick just like the rest of us. "

"I'll do my balling with men outside of the hospital. Now you cut it out, or I'm reporting you!"

Randy heard nothing, for he was too busy squeezing the man's penis slit wide so that a big bubble of lubricant oozed out. Suddenly the patient stirred, and Randy sprang back.

"Scotty, Scotty," the man muttered in his sleep. "Didn't mean to do it! Forgive me, little brother!"

There was so much distress in his words that I yanked Randy out into the hallway.

On the way back to the nurse's station, he gloated. "Ha! Miss Piss-Elegant got turned on back there, but she won't admit it."

"Shut up, Randy. You make me sick."

And he did, for I was repulsed by his brutal attitude toward the male patients. There were several workers here who thought nothing of raping a man who had been knocked out by medication or shock treatments. Some of the patients were certainly tempting enough, but there were certain things I would not do. I wanted a clean conscience when I went to bed at night.

"I'm putting you on special duty with a new patient," my boss, Dr. Foster, informed me that morning. "You did a terrific job with Bob Johnson last month. He's back on his feet, hasn't touched any drugs, and he's getting married next month. Now I'm giving you a real challenge."

"So who is the lucky man?"

"He came in overnight. He's Paul Darling in Room 401."

"Huh! That's Paul Darling? I didn't even recognize him."

"No reason why you should. He's had a severe emotional breakdown."

For the past two weeks, the local media had been full of stories about Paul Darling—star athlete and scholar at Duke University. He had accidentally shot and killed his brother in a freak hunting accident.

"Paul's become extremely suicidal," the silver-haired psychiatrist told me. "He's vowed to kill himself, and that's why we're keeping him in restraints. Some of these patients can kill themselves with the damnedest things. A toothbrush, a pair of shoelaces, a light bulb."

I was to take care of Paul's body, he explained. I would wash it, massage it, shave it, feed it, give it enemas, if necessary, and see to all his needs. I was also to encourage him to pour out his troubles.

"Thanks, Doc, for giving me Paul Darling," I said meaningfully—for Dr. Foster knew I was gay.

"Wait, now," he snorted good-naturedly. "You know we call a patient like that 'forbidden fruit.' He might look very, very tempting, but don't try tasting it. It could be dangerous."

"But forbidden fruit is always the most delicious!"

"Now, Jason…"

When I entered 401 with my tray of medications and instruments, Paul Darling's eyes were open. I was struck by how confused and filled with pain they were.

"Nurse, nurse," he whimpered, tugging at his restraints. "Please give me some water and the urinal. I've got to piss fucking bad!"

He was not exaggerating, for his swollen penis had risen up and pushed aside the towel. It was a startling sight to see something that big and blue pulsing against his flat stomach. A gush of urine spurted from his slit.

"Nurse, I can't keep it in any longer! Please hurry with that urinal!"

I grabbed the metal vessel from the bathroom and propped it up beneath his genitals. Taking his hard penis, I guided the tip into the mouth of the container.

"I'm Jason Fury," I smiled, "and I've been assigned to be your private nurse as long as you're here. Anything you want, just ask me. I'm taking care of you."

He began jerking his straps and tried to sit up. "Then get me out of these horrible straps, Jason! They're driving me crazy. Why are they doing this to me?"

"We want to protect you against yourself, Paul. Don't you remember putting the noose around your

83

neck in the barn last week and trying to kill yourself?"

A grin twitched his lips. "I was just kidding. Would you kill me if I asked you, too?"

His face crumbled, and suddenly he shook with sobs. "I should be killed, Jason! I killed my brother Scotty. He thought I was God, and I shot half his head off."

With startling swiftness, his weeping stopped, and he asked me for some ice water. I held it to his mouth, and he gulped it down.

He made no protest when I told him I had to take his temperature rectally. The doctors wouldn't dare let him have an oral thermometer because he might crush the glass and swallow it. As my finger sought his rectum, my face lowered close to his lap. His genitals were exposed again, and I could now sniff—just inches away—the wonderful spermy aroma of healthy young male. Finding his hole, I slid the thermometer up into him. While holding it, I had to lift his testicles. Paul lay there quietly with his eyes closed. He didn't indicate that he saw anything unusual in the way his privates were being handled so regularly by his new nurse.

After that, I shaved him—and bathed him literally from head to toe, especially around the genital area. After brushing back his hair and putting some Mennen Skin Bracer on his face, I stood up and smiled at him.

"Well, how do you feel? You look a lot better."

"Yeah, yeah, I do," he nodded, while studying me. "You're nice, Jason. I think you want to be my friend. I'd like that. You're not like that fat little creep who keeps sneaking in here and playing with my dick."

"Oh, God, don't tell me. I told Randy to cut it out. What's he doing, Paul?"

"He keeps playing with my foreskin. Stretches it,

yanks on it, and then he tries sticking his finger down my dickhole. He even tried pushing a bottle up my butt. If I wasn't tied down, I'd break his fucking neck."

"Randy won't be back, Paul. I can promise you that. Now you just relax while I get your supper tray."

I found Dr. Foster and told him why Randy would have to go. It wasn't just Paul he was harassing. It was any male patient who couldn't fight back. Randy was fired later that night, but I knew he wasn't the only one I would have to worry about. Ocean Isle was a huge complex, and there were a lot of the "old bulls," the scruffier older workers who were just as bad as Randy.

I knew temptation would win out when we first turned Paul over on his stomach. His incredible rump was going to be an irresistible target for those old bulls. The first time the three other workers and I saw Paul's ass, there was a moment of complete silence. It stunned us all.

His buttocks jutted out abruptly from the base of his back like twin bowling balls the color of white satin. High, curvaceous, completely without blemish or hair, it could give even a straight man a hard-on. And with the room being so hot, Paul begged us not to cover his derrière with even a towel. He complained it itched and chapped him.

So I was the lucky one who could slather lotion all over his torso, letting my hands linger as they massaged the cream into those gleaming swellings of white—and deep into his cleft. I made sure that my most trusted buddies took turns looking in on Paul when I wasn't there. I didn't want any of those old bulls nosing around my patient.

85

However, word spread rapidly through the sanitarium about the gorgeous young hunk. Suddenly young nurses found all kinds of reasons for having to visit the violent ward and to peer into Room 401. It quickly became legend that in mass alone, Paul Darling surpassed any other male at Ocean Isle. As for that dazzling rump, it, too, was something that couldn't be described. Finally Dr. Foster put a stop to this constant traffic, but the word was already out. Paul Darling wasn't just a contender for the title of Mr. Universe, the boy was *hung!*

All agreed it was heartbreaking to see this male beauty tied down and helpless, but his mental state was still in chaos. And when the dreaded shock treatments began, he grew even more confused and depressed. He would scream and do his best to tear off the restraints.

"I want to die, you fuckers. Kill me! Tear off my cock! Blow my brains out!" he shouted.

Weeks passed, and I watched Paul begin to emerge from the shock sessions. I was with him every day, not even taking the weekends off. It was when patients were in this state that the old bulls always attacked—and, sure enough, a half-dozen ambled by at different times, hoping to catch Paul alone so they could rape him. Whenever I wasn't there, I made sure that people I trusted were.

His spirits improved steadily, and I knew he was on the way to recovery when I entered his room one morning. As usual, his penis had bloated up to an awesome size with its content of urine.

"It's time for a good, long tinkle." He grinned.

"So I can see," I laughed. "What would you do if I didn't give you the urinal?"

He knew I was only joking, and his eyes danced. "I'd just have to do…this!"

He shot a stream of urine into the air, and I quickly grabbed the urinal and thrust it in place. Sitting beside him, I rested my arm on his powerful chest while I held his spurting penis. It felt like a full-grown erection...a fleshy tree trunk.

I emptied the metal container and brought it back because he always had a *lot* of piss. While he continued emptying his bladder, I let my free hand glide over his chest and tug at his nipple.

"Your tits are so big, Paul!" I teased. "Your nipples are the size of the tip of my little finger."

He winked. "Maybe it's because I'm horny as hell, and I ain't had no relief in weeks."

I swallowed hard for I could sense an intense sexual energy flowing from him. The last drops of urine trickled into the can, but I didn't release his penis. I slid the foreskin back and forth, slowly, over the head.

"Jason," he whispered, "you promised to help me out and make me feel comfortable. Please beat me off! I want to come so bad, sometimes I think I'm going to faint. Just give it a few jerks, and I'll do the rest."

If possible, his erection was growing steadily larger as my fist began to move up and down its bulging length. The head was enormous now, and I watched his slit widen until lubricant was drooling out. Soon my hand was covered with this sticky wetness.

His body rippled as his breathing grew faster. I was fascinated by the interlocking patterns of his stomach muscles. Paul opened his mouth, letting out a sharp gasp as his hard-on began to pulsate frantically in my hand. In astonishment, I watched streams of sperm spraying into the urinal. It wasn't like coming, it was like pissing out white cream. I could feel his phallus squirting, squirting out his incredible abundance of semen.

"Good God, Paul! Where did it all come from? You must have shot out at least a half cup of cum."

He laughed and winked again. "Mother Nature blessed me, I guess. I've always shot really big. And you know what, I can do it like that a couple of times a day. Give me an hour, and I'll pump it out again, just like the first time."

I had just cleaned up his semen and folded a towel across his lap, when the door opened and Dr. Foster entered with three other doctors.

"Well, well, well," he boomed. "We've got some good news for you, Paul! We're taking you out of those restraints and moving you to the open wing."

Paul whooped and laughed as we undid the bonds. When he tried standing, however, he swayed, and I grabbed him around the waist. I saw the admiring glances of the men as they took in the superb physique of the patient who showed little ill effects.

His private suite was posh with thick carpeting and lace curtains, but he had absolutely no privacy. None of the patients could have locks on their doors. Although I was still assigned to him, we never knew when the door would fly open and some R.N. or doctor would enter. Still, he was delighted to be able to move around with minimal supervision.

That night, he dressed up in a suit and tie, as did I, and we entered the dining room. It was filled with staff and patients, and as the hostess led us to our table, there was much whispering and staring.

I knew what they were thinking: so here is the gorgeous, young Adonis everyone has been talking about—the one with a six-foot-four torso packed with incredible muscles. The one with a cock and an ass that have to be seen to be believed.

The next morning, Paul created another sensation. I was waiting for him in the lobby. We were to go to the sanitarium's private beach for some swimming. I looked up from my magazine at the sudden buzzing of voices. Paul came toward me, and my eyes probably grew as big as the dozens of others around us. He was virtually naked except for a tiny black bikini brief. With each step, his muscles danced, his huge pectorals shimmered, and the stunning bulge in his crotch shimmied. When we left the building for the nearby cove, I nudged my elbow into his ribs.

"Every man and woman back there was ready to rape you because it looks like you've got a big, fat hard-on."

He laughed and ran a hand over his crotch. "I should have ripped off my briefs and really gotten a hard-on for them. Just imagine what they would have done if I had shot for them."

To get to the private beach, we had to pass through a small but fascinating garden of exotic fauna and small trees. Dark, lush, and spattered with brilliant flowers, it was a special place where the staff encouraged patients to work.

Over the decades, hundreds of patients had planted unusual and foreign-looking plants.

"Look at this, Jason," Paul said, touching my shoulder. "Isn't this strange looking?"

He indicated a small bush that was set apart from the others. Beautiful white flowers seemed to watch us like small faces. Nestled among the petals was a prickly looking ball, like a small apple. Paul started to pluck it, but I pulled him back because I recognized it for what it was.

"Paul, leave it alone! Don't touch that! That's nightshade, a poisonous kind of fruit."

At college, I remembered writing a term paper on poisonous plants in America. Among the most virulent was nightshade—or jimsonweed as it was called,

89

too. There was a description of it that remained in my mind: "The victim suffers the most intense agonies and dies in maniacal delirium."

"It's so small and pretty to be so deadly," Paul murmured. "Thanks for warning me. Come on, and let's hit the water."

The cove was small and very private, hidden away by rocks and dunes, while providing the visitor with a breathtaking vista of the ocean. Many an affair had begun and ended on this stretch of white sand. Now Paul and I were finally alone—two men who had come together strangely in a barred room. Something powerful had flowed between us from that very first moment, and now we were stretching out on the blanket, beneath a pale sun and a few dark clouds that were forming on the horizon.

Paul suddenly pulled me tight against him. With a groan, his mouth covered mine. Warm, moist, and tender, his kiss made me dizzy as did the beautiful aromas of his moist skin, hair, and clean breath. I slid my hands down his hard back to the top of his briefs, which I pushed down. He tore them off and quickly got me out of mine. Rolling over on his back, he pulled me on top of him. My lips moved hungrily down that incredible terrain of lustrous skin, pausing to suck on his nipples, then to the finely chiseled muscles of his stomach, and finally onto the center of his being.

After he achieved orgasm, he buried his face in my lap and sucked me off. Then I went down on him again. If coming made him happy, then he was probably the happiest man on earth that unforgettable afternoon. His sperm supply was astonishing.

But all good things come to an end. Both Paul and I

had only a week left before we both returned to college. He would be a senior that fall at Duke, while I would be a sophomore at Auburn University in Alabama.

On that final morning, we had breakfast together, and then walked out to the private beach. Both our families would be arriving anytime to take us home. We kissed for a long time, and then I dropped to my knees, unzipped him and blew him right there—for the final time.

I savored everything about our last sexual tryst—the warm taste of his penis, its thick length, the way his balls bounced from my energetic fellatio, and having him grunt and squirt out his volley of seed.

In his arms again, I looked up at him. "Paul, promise me you won't try anything when you leave here, like…"

"…killing myself?" He smiled strangely. "When I killed my brother, I killed myself, so I won't have to do it again."

A chill prickled my skin that had nothing to do with the crisp wind. "Paul, don't say that! You've got so much going for you."

His eyes darkened, and he kissed me again before we headed back to the main building. Before joining his family in the lobby, he stared into my eyes for a long time, and then he smiled—one that dazzled in its certain happiness.

"Thank you, Jason, for showing me the way."

It was Christmas break, and on my trip back home to Carson City, North Carolina, I decided to take up Dr. Foster's invitation to drop by the sanitarium for a visit.

I was delighted to be returning to this beautiful,

91

quiet place because it brought my memories of Paul back vividly. He had written me several times, and we were getting together after Christmas.

In his office, Dr. Foster greeted me warmly and fixed me a cocktail from his private bar. Although we made polite conversation for a minute or two, I knew something hung heavily over him. His eyes were blurred from lack of sleep, and his hands trembled slightly.

"Is something wrong, Dr. Foster?"

"Well, we're all still pretty shaken up about Paul Darling. How that boy fooled us all!"

My heart jumped. A terrible coldness surged within me, spreading rapidly through my chest and into my mind. I put my glass down slowly and leaned forward. "Paul Darling? What do you mean, Dr. Foster? We're getting together after Christmas..."

"Oh, my God! I thought you'd heard!"

He slumped back in his chair and ran a hand over his face. "I'm sorry. I should have called you. He killed himself. Two days ago—and the way he died was so horrible!"

"Paul...killed himself? I—I can't believe it. We were getting together in a few weeks." Everything around me had dimmed. Through the window, I could see part of the garden. Beyond that, hidden away, was the white beach. "How did he do it?" I asked finally.

"Poisoned himself. Damnedest thing. He took nightshade—the kind that grows in the ground—and he swallowed some of its fruit. Nobody knows where he could have gotten it. It doesn't grow just anywhere."

"Forbidden fruit," I whispered.

"Of course it's forbidden fruit. It kills."

And then I knew what Paul had meant that day

92

before we left: *"Thank you for showing me the way."*
When I had pointed out the nightshade plant in the
garden that day, I had shown him how to end his own
life.

"The victim suffers the most intense agonies and
dies in maniacal delirium," I said slowly.

The doctor studied me curiously. "That's exactly
the way he died. It was horrible. But how did you
know?"

I shook my head, unable to say anything. I didn't
want him to know he was looking at the man who
had helped murder his own lover.

KISS ME, KILL ME

Thirteen convicts sat before me that October morning two years ago. Black, white, wary, attentive, they were my first students in the only creative writing course to be taught in a North Carolina state prison.

There was Lennie, who looked like a Baptist minister but had been one of the biggest drug kings in all the South. There was dark-skinned Maurice. He might have been a choirboy, except he was actually twenty-seven years old and had killed three of his four children.

But the inmate who caught my eye and held my interest from the start sat well back in the corner, away from everyone, like a king on his dais. The Silver Fox: that was the name the media had given Jack Corday. He was serving twenty years for the rape and torture of a young Florida housewife. "I'm innocent," he proclaimed to everyone, and indeed his lawyers had found a legal loophole that would allow him a new trial next month.

But that wasn't all. On the same day as the rape, a rookie trooper had been brutally murdered a short distance away. An eyewitness claimed it was the Silver Fox who had emptied his gun into the young body of Trooper Tommy Lambeth. As the result of a tangle of legal technicalities, however, that case had still not come to trial. The judge said there was not enough evidence; the state needed a more reliable witness. Yet nearly everything pointed to the guilt of the handsome, dashing Silver Fox, who claimed that in this case, too, he was innocent.

Moving between the school desks, I handed out Xeroxed copies of my assignments. I stopped in front of the notorious criminal. Newspaper pictures had done him a disservice. If fate had spun his life story differently, he might have been a TV idol, an older, handsomer version of Rambo.

I studied him briefly: at forty-four, white hair cropped close in a punk crew cut…a magnificent, deep chest…eyes glinting light blue from within deep slits, surrounded by startling black lashes…skin as fair and lustrous as a Swede's. This was the criminal described by the tabloids as a psychopath who "grinned when he raped and laughed when he killed"—words protested by his hundreds of groupies. "He's too beautiful to kill," they chorused, as if beauty were a gauge of one's soul.

The Silver Fox looked up at me and winked. His finger tapped a book on his desk. It was my novel, which, surprisingly, had become a best seller—and a bible to thousands of convicts. They all identified with my antihero, Paul, who is released from prison, grows disillusioned with society, and deliberately commits a crime so he can return to his concrete home.

96

"You've got good taste," I drawled. He and the others laughed.

The men were delighted when I had coffee and cake brought in at the end of class that first day. While the others crowded around me, asking about my book, the Silver Fox stood aside, slurping coffee and wolf-ing down cake.

As the crowd withdrew, he came over. At five-feet-five, I had to bend my head back to look up at his six-feet-four. His shirt was halfway unbuttoned. A stiff nipple, mounted on an enormous pectoral, protruded.

"Hi," he said quietly. "I'm Jack Corday. Wanted to talk to you alone. Your book was great. I want to play Paul in the movie, if they ever make it. Smoke? '

"Sure."

He pulled out a pack of Camels. But instead of giving me one, he put two between his lips and lit them both. When I put my cigarette to my mouth, I tasted a trace of his saliva. It made me think of what his dick must be like. Watching me steadily, he grinned suddenly, showing perfect white teeth, as if reading my thoughts.

The body heat the newspapers had commented on was intense. He isn't like a silver fox, I thought. He's more like a silver stallion, a silver bull, a powerful animal whose size alone would knock aside any obstacles.

He put his fists in his pants pockets and propped a foot beside me on the wall. His crotch was only a few inches away. Inside the pockets, his hands moved as they massaged his impressive bulge.

"Somebody said you based your book on a lover you once had," he said softly. "A convict. Like me. Write a book about me. Because I'm taking you to bed if it's the last thing I do."

97

My eyes widened slightly and followed the cigarette smoke upward. "Well, Jack, I don't know if I can wait twenty years for you to get out."

"Twenty years, shit. I'll be out in a month, after my new trial. If they don't acquit me, then I'll—"

Our conversation ended when the prison warden joined us. In his mid forties, Jimmy Morgan was a good-looking bear of a man. The death of his wife the year before had crumpled him, but he always brightened up around me. The Silver Fox glared and stalked off.

"Did I break up something?" Jimmy grinned.

I raised my eyebrows. "No. Except the Silver Fox says he'll be a free man in a month."

"So what else is new?" the warden snorted as he walked me to my car.

"You see my greatness," Corday wrote the following week. "You see it, but it's been a struggle trying to keep my greatness since people have always seen me as just a big, fucking animal—to suck off or get fucked by. You're interested in my dick, right? Most people are. I want you to see it. At the tip of the stalk is a big, shiny meatball, uncut. The slit pooches out like nigger lips. When that drool starts pouring out, you know somebody's gonna get splashed good. Think about me and my big body tonight. I've got a big hard-on right now as I write this. One day it'll be sliding in one end of your body."

There was nothing subtle about Jack Corday. He didn't play games, except those he would win.

My pupils bent over their notebooks as they wrote their essay exam: "Who Is Your Favorite Author?" Everybody was writing except Jack. He kept glancing at me over the top of an upraised book. His face was flushed, and when I walked up behind him, I saw why. He had his hard-on out and was playing with it. The tip was indeed enormous, and he squeezed it so the slit gaped wide. He'd scribbled on a piece of paper: "Spit in it!" I looked around. No one was watching. I spat directly into the slit, which Jack then squeezed tight. Skillfully, he slipped on a rubber, rolling it down just over the head. Giving his stiff prick a few strokes, he pumped its burden into the fragile container.

At once Jack rolled off the rubber and knotted the tip like a balloon. How could one man produce so much semen! He gave it to me with a wink.

The following month, during the second trial, the judge refused to change Jack's sentencing. Worse still, the State Troopers Federation announced it was working day and night to bring him to trial for the murder of the young officer.

The next time we got together for our two-cigarette ritual, Jack refused to discuss his legal problems. Instead, he wanted me to describe my farmhouse. So I did. The house was only three miles away. There was a fireplace, my cat, a color TV but no phone, a stained-glass window in my bedroom.

"Yeah," he blinked slowly, "I can just make it out at night from my window. Purple, pink, and blue. I try to imagine you in bed, naked.

"You should join me."

His face hardened. "Don't torture me."

I ground out my cigarette in my coffee cup. "They call you the Silver Fox. Then act like one. What good is it to me, or you, if you're behind bars and I'm..."

He grabbed my arm. "Can I really trust you?" he whispered. "Sometimes you look at me like you hate me, other times like—"

"I love you? What do you think, Jack? Keep watching my window. Think of me there, naked, with another guy...."

"You're a fuckin' asshole."

When *Cell Men,* our first collection of poetry, came out Jack Corday received extravagant praise for his contribution. Reviewers singled out a poem, "To J. F.," as unusually brilliant. One stanza began:

> *Stay away, flashing gold,*
> *blue and honey*
> *Stirring up the old, dark times...*

I was in my kitchen, preparing lunch, when a big, cold hand clamped over my mouth. "Hi, hon. Just thought I'd drop in for a little visit. Got any coffee?" He released me, then turned me around.

"Oh, my God, Jack! What're you doing here? They'll find you. You're crazy!"

The prison sirens had wailed all morning long. On television, a bulletin notified the community that Jack Corday had escaped from the prison just after dawn. Bribing another inmate to take his place in kitchen duty, the Silver Fox had somehow hidden in the back of a delivery truck. He was believed to be heading toward New York City.

But now he stood before me, less than three miles from his former concrete home. His face glowed with excitement, joy, and triumph.

"Jack, the warden and the troopers were here just an hour ago. They'll be back."

"I've been watching the place from your barn. By the time they get back here, I'll be heading to Alabama. You're driving me. It's only eight hours by car. We'll leave at dawn, and it's all interstate. I've

100

got good buddies there. You can stay or you can come on back."

Putting his gun on the counter, he walked to the fireplace. There he stripped. Jack proved to be one stunning sight. Muscles danced beneath his white skin. Between his legs hung the equipment he'd boasted of—justifiably.

"Strip, hon, strip! Let's get down and boogie!" He stuck his rear closer to the fire, spread his buttocks, wriggled, groaned: "Uh-huh! Feels fuckin' good. Thought I'd freeze my ass out there under that hay."

I was naked now and he whistled. "Holy shit, you're a knockout. Like I thought you'd be, you ...haired, blue-eyed little bitch." He hoisted himself up on the kitchen counter and held out his arms for me. "Come over here, hon. Wanna slide my dick up that butt of yours. I shoulda gone on to Alabama, but God, I've been dreaming about this, and your bedroom with the stained-glass window. You scared, or what?"

"Jack, what do you think you're doing? You pop in here while they're scouring the countryside for you...." He heard nothing I said. All his attention was on his penis.

"Look at it," he whispered. "Ain't it a beauty?" He had ripped down the thick foreskin and now ran a palm over the glowing blue head. "Get on over here. Let's give this little fella a workout."

He picked me up easily in his powerful arms, spread my legs around his waist and lowered me over his upright organ. As the tip pushed into my rectum, I cried out and grabbed him around the neck. He loved that, hugging me close while settling me down on his lap. At last I felt his testicles bulging beneath my buttocks.

"Just hold tight." He fucked steadily, deeply, stop-

101

ping for nothing as his hands held my waist, guiding me expertly. His physical power turned me on so much that I ejaculated all over his rippled stomach.

"Oh, you're sweet, sweet," he murmured and kissed me even more fervently as his hip movements grew faster. "I want you to see how much cream I've been saving up for this fuck." He raised me off his bloated organ. The sperm shot high into the air. He didn't even gasp; it was as if he were spitting, nothing more. Using my dishcloth, he wiped his cock clean and put me on my feet.

"While I take a shit, fix me something to eat, and then a hideaway, in case anybody comes."

Checking the window, he lit a cigarette, then walked toward the bathroom. I was spellbound—by his high buttocks undulating sharply from side to side, by the way his huge shoulders tapered to the narrow waist. He paused in the door and glanced back over his shoulder.

"Not bad, eh, for a forty-four-year-old murderer?" He shook his shapely butt and then sat it down on the commode.

I had barely showed Jack the sub-basement, which the landlord had planned as a bomb shelter, when suddenly he hissed, "Shit! Somebody's coming up the driveway." From the cellar window, we saw several cars crunching over the snow and ice. Troopers.

"Get on inside!" I ordered. He started to, then grabbed me. "Look, everything depends on you. If you protect me, I'll owe you a big one. If you let me down—God help you."

"Trust me, Jack. Now move! They're knocking at the door!"

Warden Jimmy Morgan and four husky troopers

crowded into my kitchen. Eagerly, they accepted the hot coffee and buttered biscuits I offered.

Jimmy said, "you've heard the news that he's probably heading north? You see anything unusual around here, Jason?"

Sipping my coffee, I shrugged. "Who knows where the Silver Fox is?"

For a moment longer, Jimmy studied my face. Then he nodded toward the others. "Okay, boys, let's get going."

Jack laughed and kissed me as we both got into the shower. "I owe you a big one, honeybunch." But suddenly his arms tightened around me painfully. "I think you're double-crossing me, you prickteaser," he hissed. "You and that warden are up to something. I seen the way you looked at him."

His arms were like iron. He could easily have crushed me if he wanted to, and that gave him a lot of pleasure. "You're paranoid!" I managed to gasp. "All you prisoners are. Jack, let go. You can trust me. You know you can, Jack!"

Staring down at me, his blue eyes glinting both cold and warm, he muttered, "Maybe you're right, only—sometimes you look at me like you want to kill me, and then like you want me to fuck you. I don't know which."

I pressed my mouth against his right nipple, which swelled instantly into a fleshy gumdrop. He gasped and mashed my lips harder on his bulging, shimmering pectoral.

In bed, he bent over me, studying my face. "You're a mysterious little fucker. I don't know nothing about you. You got family?"

"They're all dead. I'm all alone, except for a beautiful big animal like you." I traced my lips over his

103

chest again, then down to his stomach, which sank in sharply as my tongue licked the sharply defined ridges. Then I put my hands around his phallus. It was stiff and warm. The tip looked mean and angry with the lips of the slit parted to ooze out thick honey.

I sucked on it strenuously, concentrating on the head and digging my tongue deep into the opening. Suddenly Jack filled my mouth with sharp jets of sperm.

He grunted. "Didn't mean to cum that fast. There's more backed up in there." He pulled me up and held me tightly in his arms. Reflections from the flames in the fireplace glinted on the gun, now lying on my nightstand.

"You mentioned that book you wanted to write about me," he said. "What'cha wanna know?" Jack reached for the gun. "Wanna hear about the time I gun-fucked a guy?"

Jack slid his mouth down my chest until it rested on my cock. Lightly, even gently, he patted my asshole with the gun barrel. Then he began sucking me, while his finger toyed with the trigger. Trembling from fear and that strange kind of excitement which comes from danger, I shot quickly. He put the gun back on the table and stuck his own pistol of muscle and blood up my ass.

"I'm a dangerous animal, honeybunch. You're balling with a time bomb. Okay, what you wanna ask me? Anything."

"That young trooper—did you really kill him? Everybody wonders, but nobody knows."

He began to laugh. "Shit, yeah, I killed the little sonofabitch. There I was, trying to get the fuck away from that screaming cunt, and then this young kid stops me and asks me ever so politely, 'Sir, I need to see your license.' You shoulda seen him when I shot him. He was on the ground, still alive, begging me, 'Please don't kill me, please don't kill me. I got a wife and a li'l baby."

"And—you laughed when you killed him?"

"Damn right. That scared-shitless look on his face—and when I finished, I pulled his britches down and did to him what I coulda done to you with my gun."

I didn't want him to see my expression. "Turn over."

"Ha, you're a slut. Ouch, don't bite my ass so hard. You trying to hurt me or something?"

I put down my coffee cup. The sun was barely turning the gray sky pink and yellow through the kitchen window.

"Jack, you'd better check my car and see if it starts. It got down to five degrees last night. I'll bring the blankets."

"It'd better start, or your ass is up shit creek." Nervousness was making him mean. I went with him to the front porch. After checking the landscape carefully, he ran to the big barn where I kept my car.

I watched him enter the building. Suddenly there was a shout and a gunshot. A small army of troopers surged from within and behind the barn.

I slumped against the wall. It was done. It had worked after all. Jimmy Morgan ran up and hugged me to him. "Holy shit, it worked. You okay?"

"Yeah, yeah."

Like magic, nine or ten cop cars raced in from the main road. From the barn, a group of officers dragged their manacled prisoner to a van. He looked over at me and the warden. I turned away.

"Did he find out that your brother was the trooper he killed?" Jimmy asked.

"If he had, I wouldn't be here now."

We had planned it carefully. I was convinced that Jack Corday had murdered my younger brother, but how could anyone get him to admit it? The creative writing course was my idea, a way for us to meet. No one knew anything about my personal life, since I always used my novelist's pseudonym. The signal for the warden was also my idea: *Who knows where the Silver Fox is?*

His arm around me, Jimmy Morgan led me down the drive. The prison van passed us. The eyes of the murderer met mine. He stared at me for a moment, as if seeing something deep in me that even I did not know was there. A smile played around his lips, which he puckered into a silent kiss. Then he was gone.

"My baby brother," I whispered as the cold wind blew harder, "murdered by the man I slept with last night...I did the right thing, didn't I? He told me he did it. I'll testify to that."

Before helping me into his car, Jimmy looked at me sharply. "Did you love Jack Corday?"

I said nothing as the car sped toward town. And I wept as I thought of my brother—and the Silver Fox.

ERIC'S BODY

Through the day I watched them—the men, trickling into this old dorm with their suitcases and new looks. Even with their wives, I could still pick out what remained of boys I'd once seen swagger into this very building from classes twenty-five years before.

Where did they vanish to—all those youths who became husbands and then fathers? All those former classmates who are now fat, old, skinny, bald, and the few who have held their own against time? It was appalling to see the number who had lost the battle of the paunch.

Eric had taunted me all those years ago about returning to this particular reunion. "You'll be back," he observed that day. "Twenty-five years from now, you'll be right here in this room, because you'll be looking for me."

"You'll be so fat and bald and toothless, Eric,

107

they'll have to wheel you in on a hospital bed," I retorted.

Lighting a cigarette, he snorted and watched me intently, as if he were trying to discover something within me which had always eluded him.

I went to the window and stared down twelve stories. It was a strange afternoon, mystical not only in its appearance, but also in its ambience. Final exams were over. Everyone had left the dorm except us.

Outside, the sky brooded with thunderclouds. Ahead of me, the thick wood was turning pale as the wind of the approaching storm turned the leaves over.

Around me, I surveyed the death of a room. Possessions were packed, beds stripped, walls nude, closets empty, beer cans piled high in the trash can. The room still smelled like the ghost of hundreds of nights when strawberry incense and scented candles burned in the dark, as freezing winds and sleet howled outside.

During those nights, Eric and I would lie together, warm beneath an old quilt, whispering, licking, and kissing each other—fingers exploring the other's body like exotic territory never before savored.

As we prepared to leave that day, he held out a hand for me to come to him. When I did, he pulled me against him easily. Copper bracelets gleamed like huge wedding bands above the corded biceps of this formidable young man. I licked the chest which had served as a soothing pillow during all those nights and which was now naked beneath its leather vest. As he leaned down to kiss me, I ran my fingers through those dark, moist curls.

His tongue had long explored most of my secrets, as mine had discovered his. For several minutes, we concentrated on this fast-ebbing ritual, which soon would be ended.

108

"Whatever happens," he whispered, "let's be here—right back in this room—in twenty-five years. No matter how much we've changed."

Outside, rain slashed the windows. We hugged tighter. He had never begrudged me the use of his body whenever I wanted it. All those nights I would creep over to his bed, lift up the covers, and slide next to his nude torso.

Like a powerful animal, he would always wrap his big arms around me and pull me against him.

"Don't worry, Eric," I told him. "I'll be here. Even if I look like hell. And I'll get this room if I have to pay a thousand for it. I'll be here—"

"—and so will I," he answered. "At midnight sharp, I'll be tapping on this door."

He turned quickly, picked up his cardboard suitcase, and left. At the window, I looked down and saw him enter his old Ford. As it sped away, he glanced upward. Our eyes met for the last time.

Twenty-five years later, I was standing in that very same room at that very same window. I stared down into that newly cemented parking lot filled with late-model cars. None of them had brought me the man who had haunted me all those years. That was not surprising. For the past twenty years, he had lain beneath the Georgia soil. I was there alone, seeking out his ghost. That beautiful body of his had long since turned to dust.

From the day we left school, I dreamed of seeing Eric again—just once more. Although I was an atheist, many a night I would kneel down and pray: "Just one more time, let me see Eric slipping quietly into our room at night...locking the door behind him, standing there for a moment: watching me watching him from our bed...the candles and the incense burning,

109

through the night, mixed with cigarette smoke...cold sips of beer which we kept chilled on our window ledge...his leather jacket, boots, jeans hitting the floor...then his naked torso slipping between the sheets next to me...and muscular arms wrapping around me with a grunt of satisfaction...."

Eric's body was like a glorious machine—warm, sleek, hard, packed with muscles. Every movement was beautiful. Most stunning of all, though, was when he would lie on his back, his thighs slightly raised and parted, his hands locked behind his head while my fists were locked around his thick, muscular cock.

For long minutes, he would lie there still, trembling slightly, his body moving slightly due to my strenuous exercise of it. Then he would begin to writhe a little, to moan, to whimper, moving his hands through my hair, thrilling to the fact that I was grooving so intensely on his abundant machismo. He would be sweating profusely by this time, his breathing heavier and more rapid.

"Want me to come?" he would ask. "Huh? Want to suck it longer? Go ahead, I'll try to hold it back awhile longer, but ohhh, it's hurtin' some! Come now, let me blow it out now! I'll have more for you. No? Look, dammit, I'm gonna pop it out anyway. Oh God, it's comin'. Can you feel it risin'? God...! Whew! Swallow it, take it all, you li'l fucker. You wanted it so bad!"

As he cooled down some, he would watch me play with his floppy cock...squeezing the slit and watching the remaining globs of semen ooze out...digging my tongue deep into his large urethra, making him squirm, wince, but also causing his big "wee-wee" to begin to thicken once again. This time my sucking would be even more feverish as I savored the cum remnants on the tip and the stalk. Eric would begin to groan, toss, and grip the sheets with his hands as I drove him once more to the point of orgasm.

And then there would be sleep—but not ordinary sleep. A steady thud-thud beneath my ear, which was right next to the nipple that was still wet from my spit and pink from my sucking. All this would lull me to sleep. While we remained in that narrow bed with the white spread, beneath the window with no shade so that we received the full rays of the moon, we were one...a merging of two opposites.

Sometimes I would sit up and study Eric as he slept...the moonrays picking out his full, parted lips...the hard swell of his biceps, the gleaming curve of his pectorals, the nipples protruding like gumdrops...the flat stomach rising and falling...and the long, sticky, but now soft phallus lying on his thigh, the tip shrouded once more by its thick fleshsock. And, from its snout, a pearl of translucent honey would glimmer.

Sinking back beneath the quilts, I would snuggle up to him, delighting in his warmth, exulting in the breath on my face from his lips...fully aware that there were many who would pay a small fortune to be where I was every night...next to Eric's body.

It was a freezing morning in February. An old wood stove provided the only heat in the art class of Dr. Cartier. Seven art students sat around, sipping coffee, some smoking cigarettes, when the door opened and our model appeared.

Dr. Cartier had propositioned me several times, but I turned him down. He took his rejection good-naturedly and even told me that I would probably get quite a charge out of some of his nude male models. Especially one named Eric who had a spectacular physique which no one on campus had touched. He was an enigma, a real loner who stayed pretty much to himself, but who worked out daily with weights and in the gym.

This particular art professor was notorious for his blatant flirting with good-looking males. I was small for my age, five-foot-three, with curly golden-blond hair, large blue eyes, and a compactly built physique. Men had always been attracted to me, and that can make you bold and confident. And when I saw Eric that cold afternoon, I vowed to myself: "Sooner or later, I am going to have you."

Eric was a brooding beauty who stunned me with the casual way he stripped naked for the small art class. Kicking off his boots and frayed denim jacket, he smoked his cigarette while peeling off the jeans, socks, T-shirt. Like a skilled stripper, he knocked out cigarette ash before completing the last act of his performance: pushing down his white BVDs and throwing them indifferently onto his pile of clothes in the chair.

With the cigarette dangling from his full lips, he ran his hands over his chest and genitals before sitting down on the stool. His cock and balls were right there in front of me. Parting his thighs, he leaned back slightly, his hands behind his torso, gripping the stool, and stared at some point above my head.

I had seen nude men before, but it was usually in places you expect to find some bare asses, like the showers or in the privacy of a room. Seeing a beautiful naked male in this type of setting was an exciting turn-on. All of us were clothed—but Eric wore nothing. His shoulders, arms, and legs were powerful. His chest was broad, with enormous pectorals. On each, a thick pink nipple jutted out. The fact that his body was cleanly shaved emphasized his sensual quality. No hair darkened his pubic area, which made the

112

thick cock hanging down heavily between his thighs even more succulent. "If I could just push that fore- skin of his back and see the tip..." I thought.

Eric's stomach muscles rippled continually as he breathed. He seemed to be in a world of his own, his eyes never meeting ours, but there was something thrilling in the way he was offering his body so gener- ously for us to sketch in all its gleaming curves, indentations, and bulges.

During the next two hours, he changed positions several times at the command of Dr. Cartier. At one point, he braced his knee on the stool and leaned for- ward with his back to us so that his high buttocks were emphasized. As he positioned himself, his cheeks parted so that all of us glimpsed his hairless crack—and his pink hole.

"God," I said to myself, "if I could only have him for a few hours, having him to pose in any position I wanted him in!"

After class that day, he was in no hurry to put his clothes back on. Instead, he sat there, still naked, and accepted the brandy Dr. Cartier poured for him. I joined them and was startled by Eric's body heat. He exuded an intense animal-like energy. He was polite to both of us, but seemed to keep himself aloof. I glanced down at his genitals. They were just a few inches from my fingers.

Suddenly he stood up. His warm privates brushed my hand, but again he seemed indifferent to the con- tact.

I lived for those art classes when Eric modeled. I would see him on campus, but he was never with any- body. He was always smoking, and his mind seemed a thousand miles away.

We had the same English class, and he sat in the back of the room. I could imagine him studying me

113

intently. If he was, he didn't want it to go further than that.

One day, though, everything changed in our relationship radically. I had just gone outside into the hallway, and there he was. Thrilled to see his powerful figure, I started to speak, but then he interrupted me, saying, "Uh, can I talk to you a minute? It's pretty important."

He told me he was flunking English, and it was no secret that I was the top student in the class. My themes were always lauded by the professor. Could I help him write his midterm theme? It would be crucial in helping him get a passing grade.

"I can pay you whatever you need," he added desperately.

I had fantasized constantly about a moment such as this, but still managed to say calmly, "I'll be happy to help you, Eric." I smiled. "You don't have to pay me a penny—but I would like to ask something from you."

Relieved and happy, he laughed. "Sure! Anything."

"Model for me. Alone. For three Saturday afternoons. That's all you have to do. I'll have us some wine and beer. I'd like to draw you in all kinds of positions. You're pretty broad-minded, though—it shouldn't bother you."

Dragging on his cigarette for a moment, he looked off into the distance. "Okay," he said, smiling. "It's a deal. When do you want me over?"

When he came to my room the next afternoon, at first he acted no differently then when he had entered the studio. He took the glass of wine and complimented me on the way I had fixed up my room with movie posters.

Lighting up a cigarette, he took off his jacket. "You want me to strip all the way, right?"

"If you don't mind."

"Naw. Not a bit."

His nonchalance immediately charged the atmosphere with a raw sensuality. He was so casual and relaxed about baring it all that I didn't try to hide my keen interest in watching him strip.

And then he was naked, just a few feet away from me. I had him stretch out on the thick rug on the floor. Smoking his cigarette, sipping more wine, he lay like that for a long time while I went through the pretext of sketching the gleaming lines of his torso.

Then, from my drawer, I pulled out a small posing pouch I had made from a swath of silk and rubber bands. When I asked him to put it on, he laughed.

"You think I can fit all of my cock in this thing? Okay, I'll try."

Both of us laughed as he tried futilely to bring the material up over his cock. The silk barely covered the tip.

"I'm sure that pouch was made big enough, Eric. Uh, would you mind if I tried to fit it on you?"

He shrugged good-naturedly. "Go ahead. But like you can see it just barely covers one of my balls."

I was trembling as he sat down on the edge of my desk, and I stooped down between his thighs. I put my hand around his dick—and felt the hot organ throb slightly at my touch. Then I went through the motions of trying to guide it into the outrageously tiny pouch. In doing so, I pulled back that soft wattle of foreskin so that the sensitive glans rubbed against the material. His cockslit was enormous, and I let a finger rub the pink lips. His stomach was beginning to rise and fall more rapidly.

115

"Whew!" he laughed. "All that touching is getting me just a little bit hard."

"Eric...can I bring it down for you?"

Saying nothing, he sighed, nodded his head and closed his eyes, and leaned back—while I wrapped my hands around the thick column that tapered to a narrow neck, then expanded into a huge tip.

I covered the head with my mouth. He whistled, breathed deep, and tensed himself as the rest of his cock vanished between my lips. It was almost too big to suck effectively, but it was beautifully malleable—warm, rubbery, and tasty.

From the way his body began to twitch, I sensed he was preparing for orgasm. When he did ejaculate, he just sighed and let it squirt out. Even as it was still pulsating, I began sucking him again. He didn't move. His organ had become soft and floppy in my mouth, but as I continued to suck him, it began to expand and harden again. After a brief time, he again emptied his semen into my mouth.

"Eric, would you lie on your stomach—so I can lick your ass?"

Slowly, but smiling silently, he obeyed as if he were taking directions in art class. His derriere was magnificent—white, lustrous—and when I parted his cheeks and my tongue found his hole, he began to really move around that bed.

It was obvious that he had never been rimmed before, and he flipped out over it. We lost track of time. Before we realized it, it was past midnight. We had said little since we were both caught up in the powerful flow of sensuality between us.

As he held me close against him, kissing me, he finally whispered, "Christ, I didn't think all this would happen. I knew you admired my body—I could see that in class. You must have really wanted it bad, though."

"Eric, let's live together. I can help you out in so many ways—just as you can help me."

When he said yes, I kissed him on his full lips and then began to suck his nipples once again—and then every other part of his stunning body.

Before, I'd been the target of constant verbal and physical abuse from the fraternity boys. They hated me because I was so upfront about my homosexuality—and this was almost unheard of twenty-five years ago, when most gay men were terrified about being found out.

Eric became my protector, and his powerful physique alone quelled most bullies from trying to start anything. Over the months, I discovered that Eric came from a poverty-stricken home where his parents struggled to keep their small farm going.

He would mutter now and then, "I'm just a penniless redneck who's got only one thing to be proud of: his fucking body. That's it. Just a lotta muscles, a big dick, and not much else."

When Eric got into those kind of moods, nothing I could say would bring him out of them. I grew to love Eric, and he learned to love me, too. To me, he became more than just a breathtaking body. I knew he would do almost anything for me in his quiet way. And I helped him pass our courses, which built up his always-weak self-image.

That negative trait would sometimes make him mean and bitter. "You don't like me a fuckin' bit," he'd snarl after drinking too much wine. "All you see in me is a fuckin' stud—a bunch of muscles and a big dick."

"Oh, cut it out, Eric," I'd sigh. "You know that's not true. You've got something rare: great physical

117

beauty. Few men have what you've got, Eric. Don't be ashamed of it. Use it. Don't hate me for wanting to enjoy that."

Toward the end of school, he began talking constantly about us meeting again in twenty-five years. "That's when we'll get together again," he'd say.

"Eric, I'm seeing you *before* twenty-five years."

He'd shake his head and say that both of us would journey along different paths in life. But no matter what happened, he emphasized, it was crucial that we come together again in twenty-five years.

Each night we saw a glittering orb of golden light from our bed. It shimmered from a mountaintop. We never knew its source, but to me it became a symbol of permanence.

It was our last night together. Both of us would begin our "journey" apart from each other the following day. Eric had to return to his family's farm for a while to help them through a bad time. I would be moving to New York to enter Pratt Institute. We bought beer, wine, candles. He locked the door. I watched him strip off his clothes. Sweat glinted on the curves of his chest and shoulder muscles.

It was wonderful having him—and his stunning body—lying there beside me, completely vulnerable to anything I wanted to do with it. For the last time, my tongue traced over his nipples and pectorals. Then I took all of his cock into my mouth until my lips were pressed against the smooth pubic area. Eric began to writhe, moaning as he tossed his head and grabbed the headboard with both fists.

After coming abundantly, he got above me, pulled my legs around his strong back, and gently pushed himself up into me. "Our last fuck," he said smiling sadly.

"Eric, I'm not going to New York. I'm going everywhere you go."

He shook his head. "We can't take what we have in here anywhere else. It wouldn't work."

I knew he was right and, as we merged together, we both noticed that strange light shimmering through the night.

I recognized almost no one at the alumni reunion cocktail party that night. Many eyes studied me. There were a lot of head shakes, and someone gasped, "It can't be him. He's too young. It must be his son."

In the corner stood a striking man with silver hair and blue eyes. Our eyes met. He held up a glass at me and grinned. It was Rex, one of Eric's few friends, and one who had known us both well.

"Rex! I can't believe it! You look wonderful."

He blushed, a beautiful trait that made him look boyish and sexy. "You're the one who looks incredible!" he said, grinning. "I've seen you in those jeans ads."

We laughed. I had become a well-known model who earned some fame as the good-looking man who dances up a storm in my jeans while everyone around me faints.

He told me of owning a car dealership in Louisiana, and of getting his second divorce. His eyes had been studying me, and then he said quietly, "You know about Eric's death. Can you believe it? A beautiful man like that killed by an overturned tractor?"

I suddenly had a vision of that once-glorious body moldering in the soil of a Southern grave. I put a hand to my eyes and shook my head. "Please, Rex, don't..."

"I'm really sorry. Didn't mean to bother you, but

that guy really did love you. I mean, he *really* loved you. Can we get together later and talk some?"

"Maybe, Rex. I'm expecting someone around midnight. If he doesn't show up, maybe I'll drop by."

As he watched me leave, I wondered what he would have said if I had told him my date was with a ghost?

One minute to midnight. I had taken a long, hot bath and put on a new blue silk robe, and now I took my glass of champagne over to the window. Only a single candle flickered in the room. Several people were talking and laughing loudly in the parking lot below.

The campus chimes began to toll. The cold October wind moaned around the building. And through the darkness shone that brilliant orb of light. So it was still there after more than two decades.

Someone tapped at my door.

My drink nearly fell to the floor. "Of course," I thought, "it's Rex." But still I trembled violently as I crossed the room and opened the door. The hallway was dark. Standing before me was a big man with broad shoulders. His face was obscured by the shadows and a wide-brimmed cowboy hat. There was something familiar about the frayed denim jacket, the faded jeans, and the thick curls brimming around the shoulders.

"Jason?" the stranger whispered. "Is it you?"

I backed away, shaking my head. *"Eric!* Oh my God! It can't be! I thought you were dead...."

As he moved forward, he tore off the hat, and I recognized that same square face, the mustache above pink lips, but the eyes—instead of brown, these are blue.

"Eric *is* dead. He was my father. I'm his son Kyle."

I could only shake my head, weeping harshly and

muttering, "I can't believe this is happening…it's too unreal…"

Sounding uncannily like his father, he began to talk as his big hands gripped my shoulders. His father had often told him how important this night was. He knew that it was profoundly important that Eric and I meet once again.

"Tonight, if you'll let me, Jason, I'm taking Daddy's place," he said quietly. "He always told me that if anything should ever happen to him, for me to come in his place. I even wore his clothes for the occasion." He stripped off his father's old jacket, the boots, and the rest of his attire.

In the muted illumination of the candle, I saw revealed the magnificent torso of the son whose father had been my boyfriend.

"Eric didn't really die," I thought. "He's come back through his son." Only one man in the world had a body like that—and there it was before me again.

Kyle picked me up easily in those brawny arms and carried me to bed.

My face rests now in the hollow of his shoulder. He still holds me tight, but he has dozed off now. After his strenuous lovemaking, I can understand why.

Through the darkness outside, that diamond point of light continues to burn with renewed brilliance. I think of Eric and know that, like that night, he'll never really vanish.

His son stirs. I kiss those full lips, and he smiles. Pulling me closer to him, he murmurs sleepily, "Daddy was right. You and I were destined to meet."

And I snuggle up to the man who inherited Eric's body.

121

THE RETURN OF BUBBA LEE

Bubba Lee was coming home.

The good people of Carson City, North Carolina, talked about nothing else all last August. "Bubba Lee's getting out of the penitentiary!" they said. There was eagerness in some and fear in others at the thought of again encountering this young man who had murdered his own father.

In a big city, the crime of patricide—taking the life of one's own father—would hardly warrant the blink of an eye. In a small Bible Belt town like Carson City, such a crime is unthinkable, right up there with incest. God would never forgive such blasphemy. Still, in this case, some argued that He just might.

Everyone followed the sensational trial in which both my father and I were key witnesses because the Lees lived right behind us. The prosecution painted a picture of Bubba Lee as a powerful eighteen-year-old who had murdered his father because the man had refused to pay Bubba's college tuition. Crafty, psychotic, spoiled to the point of amorality, Bubba Lee was a killer who should fry in the electric chair. They hinted, too, that he was capable of committing other atrocities, such as the unsolved strangulation of old Miss Clara Barker.

Bubba Lee's attorneys countered with a shocking defense: Mr. Lee had been a sadistic madman who had used his wife as a punching bag and had beaten and sexually abused his daughter and son since childhood.

No one in the courtroom that day would ever forget the weeping, handsome youth confessing on the witness stand: "That night, I saw Daddy beating Mama until her face was so bloody you couldn't recognize her. And then I knew I had to do what I did—to save us all."

Old Judge Lawson was notorious for his harsh sentences, and he sent Bubba Lee to the state prison for fifteen years. This raised such a public outcry and inspired so many outraged editorials that the judge was forced into early retirement and the young man's sentence was eventually reduced to six years for good behavior.

It was no accident that I flew home to Carson City from New York to visit my father at that time. I wanted to greet my former lover with open arms because there would be many who wouldn't.

I had just turned eighteen on the day, six years earlier, when my father and I stepped over the low hedge which separated our backyard from that of our new neighbors, the Lee family. I had baked a chocolate cake and Daddy had brought along two jars of his famous Southern chili.

The minute we entered the hallway of the colonial mansion, we sensed something was wrong. Tension was almost palpable. Mrs. Lee was a small, timid woman who was so jittery she couldn't finish her sentences. Her daughter Lisa was pale, quiet and nervous. Mr. Lee was a giant of a man, paunchy, balding, with a loud laugh and a nose red with veins from too much boozing. In the background stood Bubba Lee, darkly handsome, my own age. His haunted eyes missed nothing.

Mr. Lee ushered my father to a huge bar while ordering his son to take me outside and show me their new cars. He had brought three that morning: one for him, one for his wife and a shining Ford for his son. A retired military big shot, the old man seemed to be loaded.

The silent Bubba had been mowing the lawn before we came and wore only black bathing trunks. He motioned me to follow him into the kitchen, where he got us a couple of Cokes, then led me out to the back of the house. He sipped his drink while leaning back against the hood of his car and studying me. At five-feet-three, I had a mop of gold curls and was thin as a rail. He was well over six-feet tall and I was dazzled by all his exposed, beautiful flesh. Brown hair was combed back from his square face. Sweat trickled down his broad chest already heavy with big pectorals. It was difficult to think of him as only eighteen. A twenty-four-year-old man was more like it, especially when he spoke in that low, deep drawl.

"Is that your real hair color, or did you bleach it?" he smiled. "I've never seen blond hair that light. Any girls around here worth fucking?"

He ran a hand over his crotch as if he were used to fucking. Little did he know he was talking to the town's Number-One Weirdo. Since my father had always taught me to be independent and to ignore peer pressure and public opinion, my reputation had grown as someone "fuckin' unreal, man."

"Gee, I wouldn't know anything about that, Bubba. I've never dated before and, God willing, I never will."

His dark eyes squinted in amused disbelief. "You shitting me? You're eighteen and never gotten any pussy before?"

"So what's the big deal? Dating's never interested me, and if you're not interested in girls, why fake it?"

He shook his head and laughed. Then he· slid his hands along his thighs to his basket.

"You ever sucked a hard dick before? Hey, I didn't mean to embarrass you, Blondie, but whenever you wanna try, I'll give you mine to practice on. Ain't had any complaints so far."

I was shocked, thrilled and excited, to be offered something so wonderful so casually. And when he put an arm around my shoulder and escorted me back into the house, I thought I'd piss and cream in my jeans for sure.

From the beginning, Bubba didn't have a chance in school. Mysterious demons rode him, and no one could help. Each morning, he picked me up in his new car for the drive to school. I never knew what mood he would be in; from a sullen, pale-faced robot, he could change suddenly to a singing, finger-banging-on-dashboard doll.

Among our classmates, he created immediate hostility with his expensive clothes and jewelry. Carson City is a poor area of the state. Few have cars, and new clothes are only dreamed about. Teachers and students alike were either frustrated with him or

126

loathed him. Bubba sailed through it all, seeming neither to notice nor to care.

Daddy and I both speculated as to what went on
in the Lee residence at night. We often heard
screams and shouting, doors slamming, a car screeching off into the night. Mrs. Lee was often in the hospital. Her husband explained that she was accident
prone. Mr. Lee became the town joke, staggering
down Main Street with his pants unzipped and wet
with piss. Once, when I was getting into Bubba's car
for school, the elder Lee stumbled toward us with his
robe flapping around his nude hairy body.

Holding out his limp gray penis, he humped his
hips. "Want something good, queer boy?" Bubba
screeched off while his father shook with drunken
laughter.

Football season rolled around. My handsome
father, who was the high-school football coach, was
busy at school every night. When I invited Bubba
over for supper, he surprised me by accepting. We
enjoyed the pork chops and candied yams and other
vegetables I prepared. Later, in my bedroom, he
stretched out on the bed, kicked off his shoes, and
watched me bring over some of my design sketches.
At that time, I was determined to be a Hollywood
fashion designer. As I drew closer, he caught my
hand and pulled me down beside him on the bed.

"You know something, Blondie, you hurt my feelings. You never took up my offer of going down on
me. What's the matter? You getting it someplace
else?"

I shook from nervousness and desire. "Bubba, I
didn't know if you were serious and—"

He had already unbuckled and unzipped himself
and pushed his tweed slacks onto the floor. Raising
his hips, he stripped off his white BVDs and pressed

127

my hand against his warm genitals. I pulled on his penis as though it were a toy and rubbed the trimmed tip, which was shaped like a small apple. Sex honey glistened in the large urethra, which I rubbed, causing him to gasp.

I lowered my head and took his still-soft organ into my mouth. I was amazed at how good it tasted and how alive it felt. After a few powerful sucks, I could feel it respond by expanding a little and becoming bigger.

Pushing me aside gently, Bubba stripped off his sweater and shirt and sprawled out completely naked, encouraging me to enjoy his body. His penis was completely erect now. I wrapped my fist around its center while my other hand kneaded his plump testicles. I could taste the lubricant oozing out more profusely now, and when he ejaculated, I was amazed at the abundance of sperm which squirted out of his cock as if out of a water pistol.

Turning over, he ordered me to lick his asshole, which was buried deep in the valley of his firm white buttocks. Bubba squirmed and gasped as my tongue fucked him, and when he turned over, his phallus was bigger and bluer than before. Quickly, I helped release its liquid contents for the second time and Bubba gathered me up in his arms and kissed me for a long time.

The windows were streaming with icy rain and the room was dark except for the light from a single candle. I lay in Bubba Lee's arms, stroking his nipples and biceps and muscles while he smoked his Camel and studied the wet windowpanes.

"I've got to kill me a rat at home," he muttered suddenly.

"A rat? I didn't think you had any, Bubba."

"It's a big, fat rat that needs killing."

"How will you kill it?"

He slid a big, strong hand easily around my throat, tightened it until I protested, and then replaced his fingers with his mouth.

A week later, the body of former schoolteacher Clara Barker was found strangled at her isolated farmhouse. The crime was never to be solved.

Two weeks later, Bubba took a gun and shot six bullets into his daddy. When the police arrived, they found the body still on the commode, where Mr. Lee had been answering nature's call when his son decided to murder him in cold blood.

"Boo! What're you doing out here, Jason Fury?"

I was reclining on a lounge chair in my backyard, completely engrossed in *The Password to Larkspur Lane,* my favorite Nancy Drew mystery, and jumped at the sound of the familiar voice. When I looked up, I could only stare for several moments at that handsome face, set against the backdrop of the deep blue of a September afternoon sky.

"Bubba Lee! You weren't supposed to be home until tomorrow!"

I jumped up and threw my arms around his neck and he hugged me close, a rather pleasant experience since he wore only tight white tennis shorts and white socks and tennis shoes.

He had become even more powerful looking, rippling with formidable muscles. If possible, his pectorals were even bigger. Dark hair glistened with mousse, and brown eyes danced as he looked me over with devious pleasure. You would have thought he had just returned from a health spa instead of prison.

Still holding me tight, he kissed my cheek.

"Wow, I hope everyone will be as friendly as you

129

are, Jason. Mama told me you'd flown in from New York. I was flattered because I thought it might be because of me."

"I wouldn't have missed seeing you for anything, Bubba Lee."

"Come on," he commanded, taking my hand and guiding me to his garage. "Let's go for a little spin and get out of this cowdab. We got some catching up to do."

Sitting behind the wheel of his mother's white Cadillac convertible, Bubba steered us down the Main Street of the town he had come to hate. The few shoppers and drivers all stopped to watch the startling sight of the town's two most notorious men sitting side-by-side: one, a convicted murderer whose case had created national headlines, and the other an acknowledged homosexual who was an internationally acclaimed writer. You couldn't get more decadent than this!

At the outskirts of town, Bubba accelerated and we zipped through the lush countryside, and we talked. His sister had left home, moved to Chicago, and married a newspaper reporter. She never came to visit; she refused to set foot in the Lee mansion ever again. My letters and gifts through the years had cheered him up through many a dark hour. Was I aware that I had a fan club in prison? All the cons read my stories.

"When I told them that you were my neighbor, they all laughed and called me a liar."

"You should have told them you were my first man, too, Bubba."

He smiled. "Yeah. I remember that day very well." Taking my hand, he pressed it between his legs. "I hope we can pick up where we left off."

"That would suit me fine."

I was surprised when he stopped at a luxury motel in Sanford, about ten miles from Carson City. He was living there until he and his mother moved to their new condominium in Raleigh in two weeks.

"I just don't like staying in that house," he admitted. "It don't seem to bother Mama none."

"She's been a recluse, Bubba. No one ever sees her."

"Yeah, I know. You mind if I clean up some?"

"Go ahead—just let me watch you undress. Carson City doesn't have many good-looking men and when I find one like you, I want to see everything."

Teasingly, he pushed down his white shorts and kicked them, along with his shoes and socks, into a corner. Only a jockstrap covered his privates now, and he laughed and wriggled his hips so his pouch shook from its impressive contents.

When he came out of the bathroom, only a white towel covered his nudity. Sitting close beside me on the bed, his brown skin gleamed +6 from a thin sheen of coconut oil. I pushed his towel away as he put his arms around me and we fell back onto the bed.

Bubba whispered, "When I read your stories in prison, it seemed like you were always describing me with my big muscles and big dick."

"So I was," I admitted. He was bronzed all over, except for a startling white strip around his hips. Prison life had taught him how to shave his body so that even his pubic area was shorn smooth of any hair. It made the banana-shaped penis look even more formidable as it sprouted out from his pelvis—all pink and smooth and wet-tipped.

Bubba kissed me deeply, stuffing his tongue into my mouth as I pretended it was his penis I was sucking. From his lips, my mouth moved down to savor

131

his nipples, then over the rippled stomach, and finally onto his erection, which he thrust deep into my mouth.

Grunting and crying out, he fucked my mouth thoroughly before squirting out his semen in thick white spurts. As he sat up, still breathing heavily, he watched the last trickle of semen slide down his swollen organ.

"You must have been saving up for months," I smiled.

"A week. I wanted to impress you. Did I?"

My answer was to go down on him again and, after he came a second time, he turned over and I buried my face deep inside his magnificent rump. While I tongued his pink anus, I wondered how many other men had been there and how many orgasms he had rewarded them with for their diligent efforts to bring him relief.

Although Bubba Lee and his mother were busy preparing for their move, he and I got together each night. I saw the few local residents who dropped by to wish him well and express their regrets over his incarceration. But I was also aware, when we were out in public, that many of the citizens of Carson City would always consider Bubba Lee as a cold-blooded murderer.

One night we walked the few blocks from our street to Bobby's Grocery Mart to buy the makings for ice cream. As usual, about a dozen men sat around the color TV, watching Andy Griffith in "Mayberry, R.F.D." Big, stout Bobby Smith stood behind the counter and barely acknowledged our greetings. From the corner of my eyes, I saw the men nudging each other and glancing our way furtively.

When we carried our groceries to the counter,

132

Bubba attempted to be friendly by holding out his hand to the unsmiling, tobacco-chomping Bobby.

"You probably don't remember me, Bobby, but I'm Bubba Lee."

Bobby shot a stream of tobacco juice into the trash can and ignored the outstretched hand.

"Yep, I know who you are. And I know'd your daddy, too. Too bad he ain't with us no more."

He smirked and glanced at his chuckling cronies to see how well he had performed. Bubba's face was pale. I grabbed his arm and steered us both to the door, leaving our purchases sitting on the counter.

"We don't need these greasy groceries from this greasy slob. We'll go elsewhere."

My voice carried loud and clear throughout the store. Later, I heard that Bobby hadn't liked it one damn bit that a queer like Jason Fury had called him a "greasy slob."

Bubba finally saw his mother safely ensconced in their big condominium in Raleigh. The night before he was to join her, he wanted to sleep one last time in his old bedroom, "to exorcise the past." When he asked me to join him, I agreed reluctantly. To me, there was something dark and mysterious about that house where a man's blood had been spilled.

Bubba fixed us steaks and vegetables. We topped it off with a bottle of chilled champagne. There was no wind to speak of, and I wondered why the old house creaked so much.

Bubba had prepared us a bed on the floor of his room. A candle flickered nearby, and I was frankly glad to slip naked under the blankets beside Bubba and to have his comforting presence so warm and close. Sensing my fear, Bubba held me tightly.

"Get closer to me and you'll feel better."

133

A draft made the candle flicker, and in the dancing shadows I could almost see the big, naked body of the dead Mr. Lee standing there, grinning at us. Bubba's arms tightened around me and his big, hard penis pushed against my stomach. I scooted down beneath the quilt, took it in my hands, and proceeded to suck hard on it. Bubba grunted in appreciation. More and more, it seemed, Bubba couldn't get enough of good head.

Soon Bubba pulled his cock out of my mouth and fucked me so energetically that I forgot my fears and the cold. His strong arms squeezed the breath out of me while he pumped loads of his semen inside me. Afterward we took a break. Bubba lit up a cigarette and stared dreamily at the window, just as he had done that night in my room six years before. I lay with his powerful arm around me and traced with my finger the outline of his pecs, the still-erect nipples and full sensual lips.

"Does it feel strange, Bubba, to sleep here in your old room for the last time?"

Instead of answering my question, he seemed to answer an unspoken one of his own.

"I'm glad I killed that old rat," he whispered into my ear. "I paid the price, but that rat ain't around to bother anybody anymore."

"What will you do if another rat comes into your life?"

The candle's flame dimmed and shimmered for a moment, as if someone had moved closer to hear his reply.

Crushing his cigarette, he sat up and looked down at me.

"You don't know me. Nobody does. I'd just put my fingers around the rat's throat, like this, and—"

His big, formidable hands easily gasped my neck

134

and tightened. But, as I tensed, he replaced this potential weapon with kisses and we made love until dawn.

The next morning, Bubba left for Raleigh. The way he said good-bye, at the front door of that big, old house, convinced me that I would never see him again. I watched his car disappear around the street corner and dispiritedly climbed the stairs to my room in my father's house. I took my suitcase out of the closet and opened it up on the bed and started packing. Tears splashed down on my clothes as I placed them in the bag. I was crying, but I wasn't sure why.

MR. WHITE LIGHTNING

As Governor George Wallace droned on about how wonderful it was that Montgomery finally had its own drug-treatment center, I studied the other men sitting behind him on the podium. On that chilly October morning ten years ago, fate had brought together three of the sexiest men in Alabama for this dedication ceremony. If a Colt Studio photographer had been there at that time, he would have flipped over these luscious "Daddy" types. I, as the star reporter for the *Montgomery Tribune,* knew each of these he-men, who were regularly involved in news-worthy events which I covered for the paper.

To the left of the stage was suave, sensual Senator Jess Jernigan, who was struggling to keep his eyes open. A notorious womanizer, I suspected him of other proclivities as well. Whenever I visited his office for a story, he flirted outrageously with me.

People always told me I attracted attention because of my unusual coloring. My close-cropped curls were so blond they were almost white. My large blue eyes and boyish stature conveyed the deceptive image of a high-school kid who was really a twenty-four-year-old pro. Considered the most smartly dressed politician at the state capital, Senator Jernigan once confided to me that he got blinding headaches unless he ejaculated twice a day, preferably with the assistance of another person.

"Oh, you poor little boy," I told him. "Did you ever try aspirin?"

"Aspirin's faster, but sex is better," he drawled.

The senator now saw me sitting in the front row in all my splendor and nodded to me.

He was sexy, all right, but two seats down from him sat Detective Johnny-Mack McCabe of the Montgomery Drug Unit. Cute, tough looking, with a pitted complexion and bull-like in physique, he resembled a burly ex-marine—which he was. Once, when riding around with him at night for a feature I was doing on prostitution, he casually unzipped himself, pulled out a dark length of fleshy hose, and whammed it hard on the steering wheel.

"I'm a guy who likes it rough," he sneered.

Our subsequent dates confirmed his boast. Now he gave me a quick wink from behind his Hollywood shades and crossed his legs. To me, it was obvious what was going through his mind: He didn't want the hundred or more spectators to see the bulge growing in his britches. I gave him a knowing grin, which he tried to ignore.

As impressive as these hunks were, though, they were overshadowed by the man sitting between them. He was the main reason there were so many women present. Seen by thousands each week on television, he was Montgomery's own evangelist, Reverend Andrew Lightner—"Mr. White Lightning," as his adoring flock dubbed him. By just touching people, he claimed to cure them of paralysis, tumors, heart problems, blindness, and even cancer. They didn't have to spend years in therapy or in hospitals. He could effect healing in just seconds—thus his sobriquet, "Mr. White Lightning." His syndicated TV show, "Love the Lord," better known as "The LTL Show," was popular at that time throughout the Deep South, yet, many of us were repulsed by the way he seemed to play on the gullibility of his audience. On his knees, he wept and keened as he beseeched viewers to send in their dimes and dollars for his worldwide LTL Ministry. Tearing off his sport coat and tie, with his shirt unbuttoned halfway down his broad chest, he would sing gospel hymns and then rip into the "great evils of the world": communists, drug pushers, and homosexuals. The camera would pan over his frenzied congregation with their hands stretched upward as they shouted "Amen!" to his condemnations.

Such diatribes turned my stomach and I wondered cynically how much of him was sham and how much was sincere. For all his begging, the man lived well: his huge mansion had been bought outright—with cash—as had his Mercedes and private jet. I had met a number of ministers in Alabama who screamed about the evils of "sex perverts" from their pulpits, yet in private were wilder in bed than any of the homosexuals they crucified each Sunday—and I wondered whether "Mr. White Lightning" had a darker side.

Reverend Lightner was extremely active in those city agencies that dealt with alcohol, drug, and mental problems. I covered them for the newspaper, and it had been inevitable that we would meet. That happened last year at the opening of his Lordland theme park. Determined to snub him, I was instantly overpowered by his charm, wit, and sensuality. Since then our paths had crossed half a dozen times, and each time I wondered which was the real Andrew Lightner: this charismatic male or the shouting red-faced hysteric on the stage who expounded intolerance for men of my sexual persuasion?

On that October morning, I studied him sharply, trying to pierce his facade. An expensive suit of dark tweed emphasized his powerful physique. A former star athlete, boxer, and air force captain, he towered over most men with his six-foot-four height. Black hair was slicked back into a gleaming helmet around his large head. Eyes of a brilliant blue sparkled in a face tanned and creased attractively around the mouth. Lips, already pink and full, were even more inviting beneath the dashing mustache. A former country-western singer, he made me think of what Elvis Presley would have been, had he matured into middle age and worked out with weights. He held his program at crotch level, his muscular thighs spread enticingly. I was startled when he, too, gave me a playful wink and smile. I returned the smile, and once again hated myself for my weakness.

A high school band played "God Bless America" and Governor Wallace finally cut the red ribbon to the new treatment center. As a hunky state trooper pushed the governor away in his wheelchair, Senator Jernigan sauntered over to me.

"You want a scoop for tomorrow's *Tribune?*" he leered. "Senator Jernigan has a pounding headache, because he hasn't come once today."

"Can we get a picture of you beating off for page one?"

"Sure—if you give me a helping hand."

"That's too old-fashioned for the *Tribune*. How about a mouth?"

"Where can I find a mouth?"

"You're looking at one. And I've got an ass, too."

The senator whooped with laughter. He loved talking dirty. Before leaving, he made me promise to have a *long* lunch with him in his office the following week.

Detective Johnny-Mack stood alone and yanked his head for me to join him. He reeked of Jade East, a cologne every man in Montgomery seemed to be wearing that year. His dark eyes glinted sexily when I looked up at him.

"Stop flirting with all the guys," he snarled in his charming way. "Let's get together tonight. About ten."

"What did you have in mind, Johnny-Mack?"

"You know fuckin' well what I got in mind. I got two days' supply backed up in my nuts. They need cleaning out. You like draining me, and don't say you don't."

"I'm just an innocent little country boy."

"Yeah," he laughed, "and I'm Mae West. See ya around ten, Goldilocks."

"I'll be waiting."

It was obviously my day, for no sooner had Johnny-Mack left me than Reverend Lightner broke away from his gaggle of admirers and came toward me with his arms spread.

"Jason Fury! Just the fella I want to see!"

Like most evangelists, he was a very physical man When he talked to another male, he seemed unable to restrain himself from touching, hugging, squeezing shoulders, shaking hands, patting cheeks. I was grateful for this trait, because he now took my hand

141

between his two big ones, held it tight while locking an arm around my shoulders, and pulled me close against him as he led me off to a secluded spot. As I leaned against the wall of the building, I looked up into those startling eyes. His hands gripped my shoulders, and for a moment, I thought his moist lips were about to press against mine.

Instead, he spoke. "I've got a big favor to ask you, Jason, m'friend. People read every blessed word you write. We need you desperately, or we're goin' under. As God is m'witness, we won't be able to survive."

"We? Who do you mean?"

"Let me refresh your memory, he began, in that seductive voice of his. "For five years, the civic clubs of the city have been tryin' to open up a nonprofit camp for orphans and abused children, about a hundred miles from Montgomery. It's nearly complete, but we need more money to pay for staff and another building. Now, I'm goin' to the campsite tomorrow," he said urgently, as his fists kneaded my arms. "Other civic leaders will be there and about a hundred National Guardsmen. We're all goin' to work like demons, and make that camp look good, to kick off our campaign for additional funds. I'd like you to come along. As my guest. It'll make a great story, I swear. Would you do it—for me? Please?"

Good God, but this man was something else! Tears brimmed his beautiful eyes. Both my hands were in his now, and his lips were so close I could feel his hot breath on mine. For a moment, I almost believed my decision would save or destroy the world.

"Well...uh.... Sure, Reverend—"

"God bless you. That's wonderful! That's great!" His knuckles tapped my chin, almost playfully. "And call me Andy."

142

He hugged me close against his hard, warm body, our crotches pressed tight. He was not fully erect, but he was not flaccid, either. To strangers, we probably resembled a father and son deep in conversation, as he walked me to my car. I put my arm around his waist, and when we came to my Volkswagen, I let my hand linger on his hip, and then slide over his high buttocks. That didn't seem to faze him. In fact, his face was radiant when he told me he would come by for me at nine the next day. I thought briefly of something I'd read once about how closely related the sexual and spiritual impulses are and, for the first time, I understood the connection.

In spite of myself, I was in a daze. It had been a long time since a man had swept me up emotionally the way this gorgeous hunk had done.

When I turned in my story of the dedication to the crusty old editor, Hargrove, he gave me a suspicious look.

"Whatsa matter with you, Bubble Brain? You on drugs or something?"

"I've found religion." I raised my hands in a hallelujah gesture and sailed out of the office.

When I heard a knock on my door that night, I allowed myself a momentary fantasy that my gentleman caller would be "Mr. White Lightning," now fully erect. I opened the door.

"Oh, it's you."

Detective McCabe lumbered by me.

"Hey, thanks for the overwhelming welcome. Feel my nuts, while I open up a Bud. Oh, yeah, that's it. Don't they feel like they're about ready to pop? Strip me, you little prickteaser, and let's get this fucking sex show on the fucking bed!"

Nobody could stay in a trance with Johnny-Mack

McCabe around. I stripped off his clothes, pushed him back on the bed, and grasped his floppy cock in my fist. When I took it in my mouth, he grunted, guzzled his can of beer, and watched me work it up. When it was soft, I could take it all; but the thicker and harder it got, the less I could take. It was simply too thick. So I concentrated on the oval tip—sucking and pulling on it with my lips and digging my tongue deep into his slit—until I had the red-faced detective squirming.

Johnny-Mack always proved to be a wonderful animal in heat, who didn't give a fuck how brutally you treated his pride and joy—just so you eventually got around to milking the sperm out of his purple stalk.

"I'm gonna pop," he muttered.

Just in time, I took his hardness from my mouth to watch it squirt out that startling first gush, which always shot straight up two feet into the air. Subsequent spurts were nearly as impressive, and soon his broad chest was coated with his own cum. Unfazed by this energetic orgasm, Johnny-Mack merely clicked open another can of beer.

"Ummmm-*mmmm!* Not bad, huh? Wanna try for seconds? I gotta be hitting the road pretty soon."

He pulled me up into his arms and began kissing me. You wouldn't think he would know anything about lovemaking, except to get sucked off. But Johnny-Mack always amazed you with his physical skills—he could kiss you in a way that made warm chills fly up and down your body. Distracting chills that made you hardly feel the firm tip of his penis being positioned against your rectum, until, with a hump of his hips, he shot it up inside you. By then it didn't matter. With each slow, penetrating lunge, you could tell that here was a man who lived through his

144

cock. His face was scrunched up in ecstasy as he shot out the pressure in his nuts, then lay back shuddering and jerking with after-tremors. It never occurred to him that you might want to come, too.

As he dressed, I asked him about Reverend Lightner. Johnny-Mack shrugged. All he knew was that the evangelist drove the women crazy, but not one word of scandal had ever surfaced on this man. His entourage would make sure of that, even if there were something to hide. He had been married to his mousy little wife, Edith, for fifteen years. They had two teenage boys (both ugly as sin), and the preacher seemed to be a decent guy, when he wasn't screaming about hellfire and damnation.

Johnny-Mack kissed me again before he left.

"You got the hots for 'White Lightning'? Well, if you find out he sucks cock, send him over to me. I always wondered how it'd feel to be sucked off by a preacher."

Today, ten years later, I've forgotten nothing about that weekend at the camp for abused children. I can still see vividly that handsome man behind the wheel of his white Mercedes, clad only in a pair of brief chino shorts and a Ralph Lauren polo shirt. His brawny physique was clearly outlined beneath the thin materials. And those tits—his nipples pushed out against his jersey like fingertips.

The hundred-mile trip passed quickly. He had read all of my stories and columns, and said several times that I was one of the most powerful people in Montgomery, that I could make or break a person. Flattered, in spite of myself, I replied that I didn't do either unless a person deserved it. After we arrived at camp, he insisted on carrying my bag and kept an arm around me as he helped me over the potholes

145

and tree stumps. He seemed to move through life in a state of semierection.

We were staying in the main building, I soon learned, along with several other men from Montgomery's civic clubs. I was amazed, though, when Andy told me we were occupying the corner unit. We—he and I. His bedroom was on one side, mine on the other, with only a communal bathroom separating us.

"You'll probably want to ask me a lot of questions about the camp and I thought we could get together later tonight," he smiled. He pulled me against him and squeezed me tight. "Bless you, Jason, bless you."

There were dozens of husky National Guardsmen present, trying to clear up the bramble and weeds. Andy assigned two of them to show me around the camp while he went off to supervise work on the final cabin. Ordinarily, I would have lusted after either of my guides, but I hardly noticed them—I had been blinded by "White Lightning."

Since it had become hot, nearly all the men stripped off their shirts. My beefy companions were soon barechested, and jokingly asked me to photograph them for my story. I obliged, without my customary enthusiasm. I had brought plenty of film, but by far the most dramatic shots I got were of Andy, naked except for his shorts, hammering away at the cabin. Sweat made his muscles gleam, and the white sweatband around his forehead made him look like a weight lifter. One of the guardsmen nicknamed him "Mr. Muscles," and he accepted his new title with a smile.

I noticed how everyone—men and women alike—sooner or later studied his pectorals and nipples. They were so noticeable, and now and then Andy would absentmindedly pluck at the swollen pink tips, which made them even more stiff. The gesture seemed subconscious; I doubt that he realized how frequently he repeated it.

At dusk, everyone washed up and gathered around charcoal grills, where thick steaks cooked. Tin tubs of iced beer and soda pop were everywhere. I noticed how Andy drank only Coke, while the guardsmen (and I) got mellow on chilled suds.

By nine, I had showered again, put on a blue shaving robe, and was curled up on the floor in front of my fireplace with pad and pencil. Andy had said he would come by after he cleaned up, and I could hear him moving around the bathroom. Then he knocked on my door. When he entered, he made a dazzling sight. Only a brief bathing suit of white terry cloth protected his modesty. His white skin rippled and gleamed beneath a light coating of oil, which smelt faintly of coconut.

"Mind if I join you down there? You look mighty comfortable and relaxed." Smiling, he stretched out on his stomach and settled close to me on the cushions. His shoulders had turned pink from the sun.

"You're gonna burn," I said, running a hand lightly over his hot flesh.

"Whew! A little bit sensitive."

"You need something on it, Andy. I have some lotion—"

"Would you mind very much rubbin' some on? I'd appreciate it a whole lot."

I couldn't believe it. The seduction scenario was happening too easily. You see someone beautiful, you fantasize about him, and that's usually as far as it goes. You know there will be no chance in hell of getting near him. But now, literally beneath my fingertips, I had possibly the most attractive man in Montgomery, who would be naked but for that snug bathing suit which hugged his buttocks like silk.

147

He closed his eyes as my fingers began swirling the Noxzema into his lustrous skin. There were no blemishes anywhere, and soon I had come to the top of his bathing suit. I began rubbing some of the cream beneath the waistband, but just as I did, he sat up and turned over on his back.

What was going on here?

"That felt really nice, Jason," he smiled. "Now, if you could rub some of that stuff on my front—I'd be truly obliged."

In my mind, I had been peeling his bathing suit down to his ankles, parting his buttocks and burying my face into the warm cleft. In a single movement, he had destroyed that fantasy, and it took me a moment to get myself back together.

I rubbed large dollops of cream over his nipples and pulled on them gently, until I felt them becoming stiff. I dropped more gobs of the cream onto his stomach, but as my fingers inched past his navel and to the top of his bathing suit, he once again shifted position.

"M'friend, that felt wonderful." He laughed and stood up, then strode to the bathroom door. Yawning, he stretched until his fingers touched the ceiling. "After that, I swear I could sleep for a month of Sundays. Thanks, good buddy. You will be in my prayers, tonight."

I was stunned. Nothing was going to happen after all. And I had been so sure. Could he possibly have not known how completely he had won me over? When a man feels your fingers creeping beneath his waistband, he has to have enough brains to know you aren't trying to find your car keys down there.

I poured myself a big glass of Scotch and was determined to get drunk. In bed, I wept tears of self-pity and wanted to scream. I contemplated how wonderful it would be to burst into his bedroom, rape him at knife point, and then cut his throat. The two-bit, redneck evangelist! Then I considered praying for him to return. In fact, I did—briefly—then returned to my Scotch.

Less than an hour had passed, and I was still nowhere to getting drunk, when there was a soft knock on the door.

"Jason?" It sounded like his voice. "Can I come in?"

Instantly, I forgot how much I wanted to break his neck, and raced to open the door. Except for the flames in the hearth, the room was dark now. Despite my vows of revenge, my heart beat faster when I saw him again—this time clad only in a brief towel. Without a word, he stepped inside and closed the door behind him.

If possible, he looked even sexier than before. A lock of black hair had fallen over his forehead. His magnificent body rippled with each movement, and he seemed distressed.

Sitting on the edge of my bed, close to me, he took my hand and began to stroke it. "I know how you must hate me, Jason," he murmured. "You have a right to. I led you on—because I wanted it to happen as bad as you did. My flesh is as weak as any man's. I've always fought it—all my life. If anybody knew the desires I have..."

I took his hand. "No one will. You can trust me. I swear."

"I'm hurtin' so bad..."

I watched the front of his towel rise, tremble, and slip away as an enormous erection freed itself from the terry cloth and throbbed, clear and shiny and wet

"Take the sin out of my flesh, Jason. Cleanse me."

149

Ignoring the metaphysical implications of his plea, I knelt and took his erection in my mouth. The reverend gasped sharply and pushed his fingers rigidly through my curls. Unable to take more than half of Johnny-Mack's erection, I was somehow able to engulf all of Andy's, although he was as thick as the detective's and even longer.

I had always thought that a talent for "deep-throating" was just a boast of some men. A large penis was more often a complication than a pleasure. That night, though, I performed my first and last "deep-throat" ritual when I worked Andy's organ down to the pubic bone. He was so sensual, so hot, so electrifying in his desperate, naked splendor that I would have swallowed his fist to the elbow, had he asked me to.

"Deeper, deeper," he kept chanting. "Just another inch and you'll get to the depths of my sin—ummm, you got it all! Oh, Lord, take it...take my sin."

Just as he spoke, I felt his penis pulsating, squirting out its "sinful" seed deep in my throat, and then in turn, my mouth, which was soon overflowing with his long pent-up "white lightning." The damnedest things come into your mind at times like that: I recalled, with a smile, how often I'd referred to good sex as a "religious experience."

"Bless you, Jason," he whispered, putting his arms around me and kissing me wildly. "Now, my nipples. Cleanse them, cleanse them, too." I obeyed, marveling over their thickness, amazed at his recuperative powers. He was hard again. Raising my hips slightly, he skillfully pushed himself up into me. I clung to him tightly, and he kissed me as he slid the whole length of his staff up into me.

He was so exhilarated by this experience that tears sparkled on his cheeks. Through the darkness, I could see his white buttocks bobbing up and down as he fucked me to another soul-shattering orgasm.

"Greatest night of my life!" he muttered. "Lord God, the greatest night ever in my life!"

The moment he pulled out, I rolled him over, and when I spread his buttocks and began to rim him, he shivered.

"Yes, my whole body—cleanse my whole body— pound the sin out of my flesh."

His asshole was amazingly limber, almost loose. I slid in effortlessly, and fucked him doggy style, then missionary. By the time he turned over, he was hard once more. This time he writhed even more as I simultaneously sucked and fucked him, until at last I unleashed a little white lightning of my own. But that was not enough for him.

"Pound the devil out of me," he begged, taking my fist and guiding it to his ass. It was surprisingly easy to push half my arm up into him as he raised his heels to heaven.

When I awoke, light was breaking over the trees outside. The fire in the hearth was dead. The reverend, apparently exorcised at last, held me in his arms and smoothed my hair back while kissing my face.

"Wake up, m'friend. Time we got dressed. It's Sunday, so we got to put on a Sunday face for everybody."

"I don't like being a hypocrite, Andy."

"Think of it as being all things to all people," he said, a bit smugly.

"Just as you were what I wanted you to be, so I'd write the story you want?"

"I'm only human…"

"Do you really mean all those things you say about gay people in your sermons? Surely, you can't be serious—not after last night."

151

He shrugged indifferently. "That's what my audiences want me to say. They pay me to do a job. Without them, there'd be no 'Mr. White Lightning.'"

I wrote the story he wanted. In some quarters, it was a great success. I made sure there were several photographs to accompany it, showing the gorgeous, young evangelist in all his sweaty splendor, hammer in hand, outlined heroically against the sky. This added greatly to his image, while it took away from mine. Readers wept over my portraits of orphans having no camp to go to, and thousands of dollars swelled the coffers; my colleagues were appalled I could write such a gushing piece of fluff.

In time, on "Love the Lord" stationery, he wrote me a formal thank-you note and ended it with "God Bless." That was that. We never again bedded down together. On the phone he was friendly but remote; in person, charming but polite. He had gotten what he wanted from me and there was nothing more. I waited, though, never writing the exposé I wanted to, hoping (I suppose) that "White Lightning" would strike twice.

Today he is famous as a charismatic evangelist beyond the Deep South. All those nickels and dimes he cajoled from viewers over years have turned him into a millionaire, but he still hasn't gotten so rich that he won't get down on his knees to weep and beg for more—while steadily adding to his earthly mansions, luxury cars, jets, and entourage.

Was I really his first?

He swore I was—yet a lover as masterful as he could not have acquired his expertise through fantasy alone. If nothing else, how could he know the technique of fisting without having experienced it? Still, there were moments when he was so wide-eyed with expectancy, so thrilled with something I did, that he did act like a virgin. And all that talk of cleansing—was it self-delusion—or strictly for my benefit?

Today he rarely lets a weekly sermon pass without ripping into the gay life-style. AIDS is God's plague on homosexuals, he assures his television audience regularly. When confronted by a group of gay protesters and accused of spreading homophobia, he claims he has never put down homosexuals. He is merely repeating what God tells him. And I can hear him saying as clearly as though it were yesterday, "That's what my audience wants me to say."

More than most, Reverend Lightner's life is like an onion. He shows you the layer you want to see. He revealed one of them to me that memorable night ten years ago. I'm sure a different layer is presented to his family, to his followers, and to anyone who can help him. I was but one of many.

One day there will be no layers left, and his core will be revealed. I would not like to be around when that happens.

POOCHIE WOOCHIE

His real name was Steven, though some called him Steve.

To his many friends, though, he was Poochie. No one knows why, but everyone agreed that the nickname suited him. When I came along, I added Woochie to Poochie. Poochie Woochie.

No one else dared call him that; only I was allowed the use of that moniker. It was a sign of our special friendship, a friendship which mystified everyone on campus. After all, he was Poochie—King of the Macho Jocks; I was Jason—Queen of the Flaming Weirdoes.

Everyone *adored* Poochie. He was a sweet guy with a crooked grin and eyes which always laughed or glistened with warmth. His finely muscled body towered at six-feet-two over my puny five-feet-three frame. To me, he was like a big, beautiful giant.

In my yearbook of fifteen years ago, he stares out unsmiling and bored like the rest of us. Those squares of black and white evoke nothing of the real person frozen within. But if the yearbook conveys nothing about him, I have something which does. From a drawer where I store memorabilia from the past, I pull out a jockstrap—his. The passage of nearly two decades has turned it dingy, yet piss and sweat stains are still visible. My fingers explore the elastic pouch which once contained the most treasured part of Poochie's body and slide along those rear straps which had clung to his buttocks through many a game...

So many drooled over him, but few touched. I was his most fervid drooler—and he knew it.

"Need some help?"

I looked up from the *huge* trunk I had been trying for the last fifteen minutes to push down the hallway toward my room. I wasn't the biggest guy in the world, and a childhood accident had left me with a permanent limp which didn't help things much, either. Looking down at me was a tall guy with a good-natured smile on his face. He had apparently just stepped out of the shower; water glistened on his slender, muscular torso, and a white towel was tied around his waist.

"Wow, I'd love some help! I'll be here until fucking doomsday trying to move this fucking trunk to my fucking room."

"Maybe it needs a little fucking." The stranger grinned. He made some humping gestures with his hips. "Here, let me take it. What room are you in?"

I told him and watched, fascinated, as he easily swooped the trunk up onto one shoulder as if it were a bag of cotton and padded down the hall, whistling

merrily, What a broad back he had, and what a narrow waist! Suddenly his towel came off and fluttered
to the floor. He whooped, and a couple of guys coming toward him applauded.

"Cover up that big cock of yours, stud!" one called
out. "You trying to get us all excited?"

My hero laughed, not in the least embarrassed. I
picked up his towel and followed him, mesmerized by
the round, lustrous buttocks which made my mouth
water. He set the trunk down easily in my room and
turned to retrieve his towel from my trembling hand
I was just able to catch a glimpse of his impressive
cock—uncut, floppy, thick, and dark. Like it had seen
some use in its time.

"Hope my towel dropping off didn't embarrass
you too much." He smiled. "We're pretty informal up
here on fourteen. I'm Poochie."

I told him my name was Jason and as I shook his
hand, his eyes were scanning my new blond hairdo,
the touch of mascara, the red sweater and black
slacks. This was an era when *every* guy sported crew
cuts, jeans, and T-shirts. Not me!

I was so small for my age that I looked barely old
enough to be in junior high school, let alone college.
A mop of glistening gold curls and huge blue eyes
made me look even younger.

When our eyes met, I sensed that he understood
exactly who and what I was. And he liked me just the
same! Laughing softly, he squeezed my shoulder.
"Glad I could help you out. I'm just down the hall. If
you need anything, holler."

As he left the room, I took his advice and
hollered, "Poochie!"

He stuck his head in the door. "Yeah? What'cha
need?"

"You, that's who!" I went up to him. "You're nice.

157

Thanks for everything. You're the first person I've met here. Maybe it's a good sign."

He blushed, but seemed pleased. "Maybe I'm just a mean old sumbitch." But I discovered he was one of the most popular boys on campus. He liked to laugh and have a good time and date the campus beauties.

While he fitted exactly the image of Mr. All-American Boy, circa 1967, I would have won the title of Mr. Anti-American Boy hands down. Most of the students had never seen anything like me. The sissies in their hometowns usually stayed out of sight, creeping around as if apologizing for having been born.

I was flamboyant and colorful and said exactly what I thought. It was assumed rightly that boys—not girls—were my cup of tea. I didn't wear a sign proclaiming *I'm Gay,* nor did I go around screaming out that fact. The way I acted and looked and thought said it all. Which was just the way I wanted it.

Therefore, I was labeled one of them thar *thangs* (read: faggot, sissy, homo, queer, pervert, cocksucker, deviant, nellie queen, she-he, girl-boy, prissy drawers, etc.). Most men on campus were terrified of being seen talking to me—unless it was in a crowd. Being alone with me would destroy their reputations—so they thought.

On the other hand, I became an instant hit with the weirdo set: those shaggy-haired boys and girls in sandals and wrinkled clothes who thought they were tomorrow's Jack Kerouac (their god), or Bob Dylan or Jackson Pollock.

They welcomed anybody different. When I came along, they knew you couldn't come any more different unless you were from Mars. What other male student actually wore a trace of blue mascara, a touch of powder, and sometimes, on the weekend, a dab of lipstick and Intimate perfume? I wasn't in the least surprised at the catcalls, insults or threats. I was used to being ostracized and would have been shocked if I hadn't been treated that way. At least I knew I was being true to myself. On my deathbed, I would have that consolation.

Even my fellow weirdoes, though, were stunned when I began a brazen affair with Johnny Ramirez, the campus legend. This loner lived in a small trailer off campus. He wrote gloomy, incomprehensible poetry, strummed the guitar, and sang like Bob Dylan at campus coffeehouses.

He was also one fucking knockout. Black hair hung to his shoulders. He had been a boxer, marine, bouncer, divorced twice, and now he was the campus hippie.

Our clique was the only one he would get near, and I knew he had been watching me closely. When I camped it up in our group, he always laughed the loudest. One night I was coming out of the library when he stepped from behind some bushes.

He smiled and said, "Can I fuck you? I don't mean that as a joke. I'm truly serious. Just looking at your ass gives me a hard-on."

I was thrilled, delighted. I smiled and replied, "Your place or mine?"

Johnny Ramirez was not gay or even bisexual. At that time, though, he wanted to try anything that might shock the philistines among us. When he slid beneath the sheets next to me in his trailer, he was stunning—with a chest Steve Reeves would have killed for. I liked balling with him because he let you do anything you wanted to. As he lay stretched out on his back, I sucked on his nipples and rubbed around his pectorals. They fascinated me. How could a man have tits as big as a woman's?

When I put my lips around the tip of his cut, bullet-shaped penis, he whistled softly. His hips moved slightly upward, pushing his phallus deeper into my mouth, as if he thought it was a cunt. That's what excited me about Johnny. He treated me exactly as if I were a woman: he drove his penis feverishly into my mouth and up my rectum as if they were vaginas.

Hippie or not, Johnny Ramirez was incredibly vain! He loved watching the candlelight flicker on his superb physique, highlighting the muscles and the skin which he rubbed daily with Vaseline and baby oil. I liked to tease him about seeing an imaginary pimple on his butt. He would nearly flip out. He didn't think my jokes were funny. But then, that was Johnny's biggest problem: he had no sense of humor, particularly about himself.

Neither of us wanted to be together constantly. We were both too independent for that. Still, we made a point of being seen in public enough to cause heads to swivel and tongues to dart.

I had promised Poochie Woochie I would write a poem for him which he needed for English composition. He had promised to "try" to repay me in some way.

He was one of the big shots of the turf, so I had seen him only in blurs since football season was fast approaching. When he came strolling into my room one night, dressed only in his white BVDs, I whooped and clapped.

"Hiya, handsome! Park your ass. I've written you a wonderful poem!"

Laughing, he sat down on the edge of the desk beside me and tousled my curls. "Hey, Goldilocks. Ouch! You trying to get fresh?" I had pinched his hard thigh, just inches from his crotch.

"Be glad I didn't pinch you where you live." He

covered his lap in mock terror and leaned back
against the wall. As a joke, I began reading my dirty
rhyme about him:

> They say Poochie Woochie
> Has got a big coochie
> And he plays with it day and night
> But when his hands get tired
> And he needs some help,
> You can show him how to do it right!

He listened to it good-naturedly, sighing deeply, trying, to look disgusted and pissed off, but then he
began laughing. "You're nuts! Absolutely nuts!" Of
course, he loved the real poem I had written, which
was the kind his teacher thrilled to: about winter and
death and nature awakening to spring.

"That's real nice of you," he said. "You know
something? You're a famous person on campus.
Everybody's talking about you—"

"—and Johnny Ramirez? Isn't he gorgeous,
Poochie? He's the sexiest guy I've ever met—next to
you. When I go to his trailer and he's lying there
naked, waiting for me, it's—its just like Christmas!"

Poochie listened to this babble with his eyes
squinted. Cocking his head, he finally shook it, as if
he couldn't believe what he was hearing.

"I—I—you simply amaze me, Jason! I swear to
God I've never heard talk like that before from
another guy. But I'll say this, honey. I admire the hell
out of you, for being yourself."

Standing in front of him, I leaned forward and put
my hands on his spread thighs. "Poochie Woochie,
you said you would repay me for the poem, didn't
you?" I ran my hands up his arms. "You said you'd
be nice to me, didn't you?"

161

He swallowed hard and nodded. "Yep, I said it, but I ain't gonna do with you what Johnny Ramirez does. Still, he didn't get up, He just sat there, smiling, waiting for my next move.

"I don't want you to. You might end up in hellfire. The devil's already got a place reserved for me and Johnny. Just give me a teensy-weensy, tiny little kiss. Now don't back off. You said you should repay me and—"

He started shaking with laughter. "Shee-it, if you ain't the craziest little guy I've ever met." Then he asked quietly, "Is that door locked?" I ran and bolted it. Then I skipped back. He was standing up now. Clasping his hands together in a mock praying position, he rolled his eyes upward. "Oh, Lordy, don't let this turn me into a fruit."

I burst out laughing and hugged him. He snickered and acted silly and then he pooched his lips out like Cheetah the Chimp. I slapped him lightly on the face.

"Stop it, you clown! Be serious now, Poochie. Pretend this is the greatest moment of your life."

Still laughing, he put his arms around me and drew me closer. I felt his smooth skin, the strength of his arms and shoulders, and drawing his face down to me—I kissed him. It was like making love to a tree. He just stood there, doing nothing, but as my hands continued to stroke his chest, nipples and hair, I felt his tongue move cautiously between my lips. His clasp became stronger, then his tongue more probing, his lips firmer and warmer.

He sat down on the desk again, pulling me into his lap where he cradled me like a child, kissing me even more ardently. Moaning, he licked my face, then stuffed his tongue deep into my mouth. When my hand began moving beneath the waistband above his crotch, the spell was broken.

162

Poochie drew back, flushed, breathing hard and looked at me in astonishment as if seeing me for the first time. "Holy shit!" he whispered. "I—I forgot you was a boy, Jason, and—holy shit!"

"Are we still friends, Poochie Woochie?"

As he headed for the door, he looked at me over his shoulder. "Well," he smiled, "if I can give you a kiss like that, honeybunch, it sure don't mean I hate you."

"Show me your ass, Poochie."

He pushed his shorts down and wriggled his buttocks. "That turn you on?"

"*That's* what I'm kissing the next time I see you!"

Johnny left, with his usual secretiveness. He had left a note taped to his trailer door which I found when I went to visit him the next day. He had gone to New York. He was going to be a big singing success, like Bob Dylan, who I always said sounded like a sick cow. He was sorry he didn't say good-bye. Time was running out and...

Shattered by the loss of this wonderful lover, I returned to the dormitory. Passing Poochie's room, I saw him sitting in his BVDs at the desk. I've always been a good actor. Now I forced tears to instantly well up in my eyes, and ran wailing into the room.

"Poochie! I've got a problem! A big problem!"

Alarmed, he jumped up and locked the door. At his desk, he patted his knee for me to sit on. He put his arms around me and hugged me to him.

"What's your problem, blondie?" he whispered tenderly. I told him about Johnny Ramirez, the shit, and how I wanted to kill myself. Poochie rubbed his face against mine, "Don't do that. You'll find another guy. Maybe—"

Then he began kissing me, and this time he was

163

even more passionate than the time before, He guided my hand down to his lap. His erection bulged
against the thin briefs. Poochie sat up a little and
then pushed them on down.

"Wanna play with me a little bit?" he whispered.
"We'll have to hurry. My roomie's coming back anytime. Want me to cum for you? I'll do it if you want
me to."

His penis was fully erect—dark, wet, with the purple tip fully free of its covering. My finger rubbed the
lips of his urethra, which dripped profusely with lube
oil, Poochie put his fists over mine as we began to
steadily stroke him.

With his body gleaming with sweat, his stomach
suddenly began to move in and out rapidly. He closed
his eyes, breathing heavily and suddenly his phallus
began to pulsate in our hands. His ejaculation squirted
out upon his books and against the sides of the desk.

He ignored the wet mess and pulled my mouth
against his, kissing me again. "You love me?" he
smiled.

"You know I do. I wish we could—"

At that moment, his roomie began knocking on
the door. Poochie and I worked fast to mop up the
proof of our relationship.

The game between our school and Wake Forest that
rainy, freezing day had been unusually brutal.
Tempers flared, players slid, the ball was fumbled. I
knew nothing about football. I just wanted to sit and
study player number 23. My Poochie Woochie.

Suddenly he was hurled beneath a pile of fighting,
kicking players. After they got up, he didn't.
Everyone stood up, alarmed, and when an ambulance rushed him to the hospital, I was terrified. He
was suffering from torn chest muscles.

I wanted to see him alone in his hospital room. While waiting for my chance the next day, I heard conversations in the lobby among his friends. His heart had been bruised badly. He might have to drop out of sports.

Half-expecting a white-faced wreck, I was delighted to find my friend sitting up in bed, as chipper and impish-looking as ever. "Hiya, handsome!" I called out.

"Hey, blondie! It's about time you came by!" He gladly took the stack of comic books and the bag of Snickers candy bars which were his passion.

Sitting on the edge of the bed, I took his big hand and squeezed it. "You okay, Poochie? Your chest, was it—?"

"Aw, wasn't nothing serious. Nothing at all." But, as he glanced at the ice-covered window, I saw a glint of fear in his eye.

"Poochie, please tell me. You know I love you."

He closed his eyes tight and when he opened them, I could see he was scared. "I'm just a little worried, Jason. Coach Dickson says it ain't nothing. But I've been having these real bad pains in my chest. *Real sharp.* Like a knife's stabbing me. They gave me these pills and—"

"Poochie Woochie, if you get back out there on that field—"

"I've gotta. I'm on a sports scholarship. I'm poor, Jason."

I leaned down and gave him a quick kiss. Laughing, he pushed me away. "Hey, cut it out! Somebody might see us."

"Let 'em. I love you, and I don't give a fuck."

I went straight to his doctor's office on the third floor. When I asked him for the truth about Poochie's condition, he hemmed and hawed and

165

said things weren't that bad. Then he added something chilling: to the coach, the game was everything. All injuries could be repaired. Poochie was too valuable a player to just lie in bed because of a minor injury.

There was little time for us to see each other. One night, though, shortly after the last game, I entered the elevator to find Poochie standing there. White-faced and sweating, he leaned against the wall, breathing loudly.

"Poochie! Are you okay? What's wrong?"

He had a hand on his chest and rubbed it cautiously. "It's okay now. Just a pain—a real sharp pain."

I put my arm around his waist and walked him to his door. "Are you still going to the doctor like you're supposed to?"

He had gone just that afternoon. The doctor had given him a firm command: no more football. When Poochie told me this, suddenly he began to weep. I hurried him into his room and put my arms around him as he continued to cry. He rubbed his eyes like a little boy and told me what a tragedy it was. Sports was his life. Everything he had done had been aimed toward becoming a great athlete. For an hour or more, I continued to hug him, consoling him as he wept. Finally he looked at me and tapped a fist against my chin.

"Thanks, Jason. You're a wonderful guy. I owe you one."

A week later, I stuck my head in his door. "Hey, you lazy-assed schmuck! Let's haul ass and go for a walk or something!"

He had been lying in bed with a biology book propped up on his chest. He threw it across the room, whooped, and jumped up.

166

"Let's go, blondie!" He pulled on walking shorts, tennis shoes and a windbreaker. Walking closely together, we went out of the back of the building and toward the thick woods at the bottom of the hill.

It was spring break. Everybody had split for the coast or the mountains. Only a few remained. I was joyous when Poochie said he would be staying to catch up on his studies.

Dusk was turning the sky a powdery pink and blue. As we kept walking, I stopped to catch my breath. "Poochie, let's rest. My bum leg is killing me."

"Climb up on my back. I guess I'll just have to carry you."

Stooping down, I climbed on, and he carried me easily to the small pond which was a favorite for young lovers. My hands ran beneath the windbreaker to feel his naked chest. I plucked at his stiff nipples.

"Hey, cut it out, you little fag! Want me to drop you in the water?" By the time we sat on a bench that fronted the pond. The moon had come out. Fireflies flickered around us. We were completely alone. I thrilled to being here at last with this beautiful young man.

He had taken off his jacket and sat bare-chested. I couldn't take my eyes off him. With an arm resting behind my head, he seemed perfectly at ease. Looking down at me, he smiled. "You like what you see?"

"Poochie, you know how I feel about you."

He pulled me against him and began kissing me. His other hand pushed his shorts down and he kicked them aside. My hand squeezed his genitals, which were swelling up rapidly.

"You want it, don't you? It's yours, Jason." I sank down to my knees, between his hairy thighs, and

167

grasped his penis. Pulling down the fleshy covering, I covered the wet tip with my mouth.

Poochie gasped and threw his head back as I inched more of him into me. His body throbbed with an extraordinary sexual energy which caused the sweat to spring out, his testicles to churn, his penis to become harder, sleeker and bigger.

By the time he ejaculated, it lasted for several seconds. With each surge, Poochie cried softly, rolling his head and his eyes. It was his first blowjob, he told me later, and he had never felt anything so wonderful in his life.

Later, in his room, he bent over me, kissing me intensely and inching the point of his organ up into me. He penetrated so deeply and thoroughly, it was as if he had become part of me. He pumped his hips, pausing now and then so he wouldn't lose his load. Finally he could hold back no longer.

"I'm coming!" he muttered. He fell beside me as his body jerked with each squirt of his seed into me. During that night, a permanent bond was created between us.

I can smell and see and taste Poochie Woochie as clearly now as if he and I had parted only fifteen seconds ago—and not fifteen years.

It was a Friday morning, and I got up early, threw on my robe, and headed for the showers. A week had passed since Poochie and I had spent our night together, and I was still floating around. Johnny Ramirez had been a great stud. Poochie Woochie was a wonderful lover. There is a paramount difference between the two.

And who should be coming out of the showers but my very own Poochie Woochie! He was alone and he looked magnificent with his white towel around his hips, his body so lean and strong. His smile for me was dazzling. And best of all, the doctor had just informed him that his heart was in stable condition again. He *might* be able to play ball next year!

Nobody was around. He pulled me into the empty shower stall and gave me a quick, passionate kiss. I grasped his thick penis beneath the towel and pushed my finger deep into his foreskin.

"We've *got* to get together tonight!" he whispered. "I'm leaving in two days. Working in Colorado for three months. How about the woods?"

"I'll be there at seven."

He smiled. His eyes rolled back. Then he fell heavily to the floor. As he writhed, gasping for breath, his face was turning a hideous pink and then blue. "My heart—it's killing me!"

Other boys were entering the bathroom now. I shouted for them to call a doctor. In the ambulance. I held his hand tightly. "Poochie—Poochie, hold on to me! You'll make it! We're almost there now, baby!"

While the paramedics worked feverishly to save him, I was horrified to see how his face had changed. Fifteen minutes before, he had been laughing. Now his skin had become blue. His features had contorted into the face of an old man.

"Poochie?"

His eyelids parted to a slit. Something flashed in them as they looked at me. Then he closed them—and sighed. The young nurse who had been working so hard to keep him breathing suddenly began to sob.

"Is he—?" I whispered. She nodded her head.

The heat in the church that Sunday was so intense that one lady fainted. Poochie's jock buddies, girl-friends, teachers—all were there, all wept. Students

169

who didn't know him personally had come to pay their respects. Poochie was admired by everyone.

I waited until everyone had passed by his coffin. Finally I was staring down at him as he lay there—tall, broad-shouldered and unnatural looking in his blue suit. The sleeves were too short, the collar too big. He did not often wear such attire.

His face, once glowing with merriment and high spirits, was now like pink parchment. There was a terrible finality in the firm set of his tightly closed eyes and mouth.

Touching his big hands, I whispered, "Good-bye, Poochie Woochie." Maybe I imagined it, but I thought his mouth twitched in a brief smile at the sound of the name which no one but I had ever called him.

Tonight I press the jockstrap to my face and think: *Oh, Poochie Woochie! Why did you have to leave us so soon?*

(Author's note: This story is dedicated to the memory of P. W.—*"One day we'll be together again."*)

THE LEADER OF THE PACK

I knew I was on my way out of the teaching profession when I was assigned to Classroom 401—also known as "Punk Hell," around St. James School.

This special-education project had the most notorious reputation of any in the Alabama school system. As one of those federally funded pilot projects for "youthful offenders," it was a howl. All the guys in that particular class were in their late teens, but had been around the block more than any average John Q. Citizen. Some were even unmarried fathers.

The only reason they would be in the class was by court order. Either take remedial education and get that diploma—or it was back into prison. Four teachers before me had given up that year. One had a breakdown, one became a drunk, and another was literally run out of the class by these rambunctious hoodlums.

I kept hearing rumors of a certain Cal Trezetti, the supposed leader of this pack of roughnecks. Cal's education so far had been in drug dealing, sexual assault, and robbery. He was either a devil or a god, depending on who you talked to. One of my fallen predecessors told me he was a "big sonofabitch, but bright. He controls that classroom. Get him on your side if you can. There's another devil—a black kid, Jo Jo. He wants to be leader, too, so it's like a war in there."

And so what had I done to deserve such punishment? At the age of twenty-two, I was just starting my teaching career. Within a month, I had been propositioned twice by Principal Donahue, my boss. He was the most repulsive man I had ever come across. Donahue crashed the scales at two hundred eighty pounds, though he was only five feet eight; his breath smelled like onions, beer and Juicy Fruit gum, so lethal it would knock out Hulk Hogan. And did he have to drown himself in Jade East cologne? To top it off, he was a known sadist who delighted in slapping students around. I hated him. He knew it, which made him pursue me even more passionately.

He knew my weaknesses, too. I had no experience working with problem kids. At five-feet-five, most of my students were bigger than I was. And I attracted a lot of attention because of my looks. I have hair so blond it's almost white, big blue eyes, a well-proportioned, slim torso, and a spectacular ass which tends to twitch when I walk. Men—and boys—were always grabbing at me.

That first morning found me so nervous that the two Valiums I had taken did nothing to calm me down. Fifteen pairs of hostile eyes watched me silently as I strode to my desk—and found an enormous pile of human excrement in my chair.

172

"Did anything human do this?" I drawled. "Or did some tiny little bird fly over and decide to have a little shit?" The boys burst into laughter, and two of the tamer rogues volunteered to get rid of the mess.

Some of the others protested that I was violating their civil rights when I demanded they get rid of the live blacksnake—and huge rat—which were squirming around in my desk drawers. They said they were students, not janitors.

"Get them out," I snapped, "or nobody's getting out of this room!" As I moved around the room, I saw my students stirring. They were exchanging looks and snickering. Well, they've finally got my number, I thought. They were already labeling me "faggot." Sure enough, none other than the notorious Jo Jo—a big, hulking kid on the front row—slid down in his desk, spread his legs, and began massaging his genitals. Mock gasps of sexual pain could soon be heard as he squirmed and humped his hips. Some of his nearby buddies began imitating him.

"You have a headache or something, Jo Jo? Maybe you'd better run up to Principal Donahue's office and ask him for a helping hand. What you need is relief, but I don't think aspirin's going to help." The pupils roared when I glanced at his crotch while saying that. Some of the tension eased, and I saw looks of suspicion replaced by stares of interest.

I was wearing a pair of *very* snug linen pants that morning. They fit like a second skin; I wore no underwear. As I walked down the first row, I saw several young toughs ogle my butt and squeeze their equipment unconsciously. Suddenly I stopped short. I had wondered where he was, but now saw that he had pushed his desk away from the others, into a corner. He might have been a warrior and a thug—but Lord, he was gorgeous!

173

With his fair skin, and hair like me, Cal Trezetti could have passed for a Swede. His chin rested on a magnificent chest—for he was fast asleep. Dirty, yellow hair was slicked back, pushed away from a face that was square and strong, with a scar on one cheek. His biker's cap, complete with a skull and crossbones medallion, was also pushed back, giving him a sweet, angelic quality. Gold lashes rested on his cheeks. His chest was bare except for a skimpy vest, which hung open. Powerful arms, with an American eagle tattooed on both bulging biceps, were folded across huge pecs which billowed out. Each was crowned by a thick nipple, fully erect. Encased in soft, pale denim were muscular thighs, and something thick, big and swollen strained against the stained crotch. His lips, pink and sensual, were parted slightly.

I could have watched him forever, but the sleeping beauty awoke when Jo Jo and company began whooping it up. "Hey, Mr. Trezetti, hey, you, white boy, wake up so teacher can unzip you.... Mr. Cal Trezetti, you are being paged to beat your meat for the teach..."

Cal balled up his fists and was ready to lunge forward, but I pushed him back and whirled around. "Shut the hell up, Jo Jo, or get out of this room."

He made kissing sounds. "Gotta help white boy, huh, teach? Want that big dick, huh, teach?"

"One more crack, bozo, and you're heading back to the school with the bars."

Jo Jo jumped out of his chair and headed for me, but something huge, in the form of Cal Trezetti, came between us. "Back, Jo Jo," he said softly. "Or you're flying out that window."

"Do as he says, Jo Jo, or I'm writing you up and out you go."

Muttering and glaring, Jo Jo slumped back in his

174

chair. Cal, passing me, looked down into my eyes. A strange light glinted in his own ocean-colored eyes, an expression of amusement, curiosity...and something else I couldn't define.

Cal was the last to leave at the end of that exhausting day. Perhaps he stayed behind to protect me. I went back to his desk, where he was combing his hair, chewing his gum, and getting his books together. I told him how much I appreciated what he had done that day. He had been watching me steadily for hours.

Wiping his comb on his thigh, he put it away and tapped his biker's cap into place on his head.

He blinked and shrugged. "Wasn't nothing," he said quietly. He moved closer, and suddenly I could smell his sweat, and the Vaseline hair tonic he used, the wet leather vest. "There's something I'd like to know, teach."

"I'll try to help you if I can."

He moved still closer, until my back touched the wall. He put a big hand on the wall above my head, so I could see drops of sweat glistening in his hairy armpits. He spit his gum out and bent his face closer to mine, while his other big hand turned my face closer to his. Instinctively, I closed my eyes, hardly daring to believe this was happening. The leader of the pack, and me...but nothing happened. I opened my eyes, and he was staring at me cooly.

"Just as I thought," he snorted. "We got a fuckin' faggot teach."

Enraged, I hit his chest with my fists—which was like a gumdrop bouncing against Mount Rushmore. "You sonofabitch. The only thing you're capable of kissing is what you see in the mirror in the morning—asshole!"

With the back of his hand, he slapped me against

175

the wall. Tearing off his cap, he slammed himself close against me. "I'll show you what a fuckin' kisser I am!" I was suddenly engulfed in hard, hot muscles as his arms went around me and his mouth ground against mine. He was brutal, determined to hurt, and I kicked and tried to get away. But suddenly I felt a difference in his attack. His wet, deep kiss became more tender; his big arms drew me closer to him. I ran my hands over his wet pecs and pulled at his swollen nipples. His crotch felt like a mound of warm rubber against my stomach. But then, just as abruptly, he began to pull away. He looked down at me with astonishment in his eyes. "Shit," he stammered, "I didn't think I'd..." And then suddenly he pushed me away, grabbed his cap, and slammed out of the classroom.

I drove home in a daze, and thought: *being kissed by a punk bruiser like Cal Trezetti is something every teacher should experience.* For weeks after that, though, I wanted to kill him. He ignored me; he pouted, sulked, and acted like a slob. And every afternoon, I'd run to the window and watch him climb on his big black motorcycle and roar off like a scowling young god.

But he was watching me—when he thought I wasn't aware. I'd see him peering at me from beneath those gold lashes in the hallway, while his buddies surrounded him. One night I worked late, and when I drove out of the parking lot I heard the roar of a motorcycle pulling off in the opposite direction. He had been waiting for me—but why? And when the class got out of hand, and I could do nothing with them, just one snarl from Cal would quiet them: "Shut the fuck up, will you guys?"

I heard that his father wouldn't let him come home, and beat him when he did. He slept around wherever he could. He owed his magnificent physique to working on a construction crew sometimes, after school and on the weekends. Already he was a man, and he was trying desperately to get a diploma.

Principal Donahue was giving me hell for not keeping discipline in my class. He took to dropping in unexpectedly, surveying those roughnecks for whom the school was receiving a small fortune in federal aid. I'd see Jo Jo sneaking out of his office now and then, and knew he was blabbing lies about me. One morning Principal Donahue entered the room quietly. He was staring at Cal in the back of the room. Cal was asleep, looking glorious, with his hands behind his head and his chest exposed. Grinning, Donahue tiptoed swiftly up to him. I hurried up behind him, for I knew what was going to happen. Before I could stop him, he grabbed a handful of gold hair and snapped Cal's face back. His other hand raised to give him a powerful slap, but I pushed him aside.

"Don't you slap any of my students in here unless they deserve it," I hissed. "And he doesn't deserve it." Cal looked dazed by what was happening. If looks could kill, I would have been dead from the look my boss gave me.

"You know who's boss in this school system?" he hollered.

"The school board is, and they'd love to know you're still beating up on kids."

"I want to see you in my office immediately," he bellowed.

In his office, he screamed and carried on until I finally got up and left. My days were clearly numbered, but suddenly I didn't give a fuck. Back in my classroom, the students—with the exception of Jo

177

Jo—looked at me with new respect. Cal watched me for the rest of the day, from beneath those gold lashes, and when class was over, he came up to me and sat on the edge of my desk.

"You didn't have to do what you did, teach."

"I was glad to, stud—isn't that short for 'student'? Let's get something cold to drink. Just something to drink—and nothing else, okay?"

"Let's go." he said quietly, looking down at me, and putting a hand under my arm to help me up. He led the way out to his motorcycle, and ordered me to climb on behind him. "I might fall off, Cal,"

"Just hold onto me, teach, and nothing's gonna happen."

And so I wrapped my arms around that powerful young body, and we went roaring out into the country. I didn't care if I was fired tomorrow because I was holding on to the punk I loved.

Sally's was a dark little truck stop out in the middle of nowhere. She knew Cal, though, and when he held up two fingers, she gave him two cold cans of Black Label. The place was empty, and Cal led me to a secluded corner booth. It was so tiny that I had to squeeze my knees between his thighs as he sat across from me. I could feel the heat from his crotch.

He stripped off his vest. Sweat trickled down his muscular arms, and light danced on his pecs. His nipples always seemed to be hard.

"How'm I doing with the other guys, Cal? Do they like me okay?"

His blue eyes twinkled as he sipped his beer. "Yeah, they like you, but maybe not in a way you'd appreciate. They want to get into your britches. When you shake that ass of yours around the classroom, you give those guys big hard-ons."

178

I sipped the cold beer. "And do I give you one, Cal?"

He put his hands under the table for a moment. "Reach down and see for yourself, teach."

My hand eagerly slid along a warm, hard thigh, and then up to something hot, wet, and long. "You see, Jason?" he whispered. "That's what happened the first day I saw you."

The tip of his organ dripped with honey, and I pushed my thumb along his cockslit. Cal gasped, put his fists around mine, and stroked it some. He raised his hips and peeled his jeans down to his ankles.

The barmaid was laughing at "I Love Lucy" in the front—and my student sat virtually naked across from me! His sac was swollen with cream, and I kneaded it roughly, feeling the balls slip up and down between my fingers. Cal pursed his lips and closed his eyes. "I'm gonna blow," he whispered—and instantly my hands were dripping with wet, warm sperm, which overflowed onto the floor.

"Oh, Jason," Cal moaned, "get down there and lick it off. Eat me. You'll love it—all the girls love sucking me off. I've got a lot more cum back up in there." I was trembling now; I was losing control of myself. I could be ruined professionally if anyone saw me—a teacher jerking off a student in a barroom!

"Cal, you're crazy. We could both get thrown out of school."

"Come on, teach," he whimpered, "have some fun with ol' Cal's dick. See, it's getting hard again."

I got to my feet and started to leave. "Cal, if things were different..."

"What's a matter, teach?" he asked bitterly. "Ain't I good enough for you? Is that it? I'm just a punk stud, right?"

179

I bent down and kissed him on those moist pink lips.

"That's what I think of you," I whispered, and hurried out, leaving him with a startled look on his tough young face.

A motorcycle roared up my driveway around midnight, followed by a firm knock.

Cal leaned in my doorway. He was shirtless, wet with sweat, and looked more luscious than ever. I had just come out of the bathtub with only a towel around me. He pulled the towel away and yanked me against him.

"Can I live with you for a while? My Daddy won't let me come home, and I ain't got anyplace to stay, and..."

I knew the dangerous game I was playing, but said, "My home is yours."

He carried me into the bedroom and began stripping off his clothes. Completely naked now, he looked even more beautiful. No one could ever mistake him for a boy. He pulled me onto the bed and let me enjoy him in any way I wanted. I began by sucking his big nipples until, squirming and panting, he pushed my head down his hard stomach, onto the object that throbbed against it. He held his dick in both hands and guided the tip into my mouth. It was still gummy from being jerked off that afternoon. I had been on it for only a few minutes when I nearly choked on an abundance of fresh sperm.

And that was only the beginning. He was eager to show me his sexual prowess, and I was astonished at his seemingly inexhaustible prick. At dawn, he finally fell asleep in my arms. I watched his glistening organ stirring on his right thigh: I saw the sac turn slightly as it replenished itself with fresh semen. He had the

180

body of a young giant and the face of a lost little boy.
And I was going to help him find his way.

Tension mounted steadily all that week. Principal
Donahue kept my class under constant watch. Spies
gleefully reported to him anything I did wrong. Jo Jo
became more bold in his attempt to take over as
ruler of the classroom, but the other students simply
didn't worship him the way they did Cal. The sullen,
brutal Jo Jo lacked two indispensable qualities:
charisma and physical beauty.

One Friday afternoon, after working late, I hurried to leave. I would be fixing Cal and me a big
Italian supper, and then we planned to watch some
porno videocassettes. I gathered my papers and
walked out into the dark hallway. Only a single light
glowed ahead of me. Suddenly I realized I wasn't
alone. Three bulky shapes stepped from behind the
lockers, and surrounded me.

"Hey, teach," Jo Jo grinned. "Where's your big-
dicked lover boy? Huh? We know he's fucking you;
everybody does. We thought you might like to see
how us black boys can fuck, too!" They dragged me,
yelling and kicking, into the parking lot, and began to
tear off my clothes. But suddenly they stopped. One
of them snarled, "Shit a mile!" I looked up, and there
were Cal and four of his big, husky buddies. He
picked me up from the ground and thrust me behind
him. "Get on home, baby. We'll take care of this." As
I got into my car, I caught a glimpse of chains and
knives swinging through the air, and heard curses,
screams, and gasps.

I waited for hours. At around three in the morning,
my guardian angels came in—bloodied and bruised,
but greatly excited. While I served them lasagna and

181

beer, they kept telling me I'd never be bothered by Jo Jo again.

"You didn't kill him?"

They roared with laughter, and said that no, the prick wasn't dead, but he should have been. At eight, Cal's buddies left, and he told me to get ready to go to school. It was time we faced the music.

My classroom was almost hysterical with excitement, for word had gotten around that Jo Jo and Cal had finally had their war—and now my blond bruiser was even more the leader of the pack. Before I had even sat down, though, the principal's secretary sent word that both Cal Trezetti and I were wanted immediately in Donahue's office.

Cal went in first, while I waited outside. I heard the fat buffoon's voice screaming about Jo Jo and his buddies being treated in the emergency room for fractured ribs, sprained wrists, and miscellaneous bruises.

My lover emerged while the principal was still screaming, and grinned and winked at me. "It's your turn," he said. A crowd was gathering in the hallway when I entered—and, before Donahue could say anything, I told the fat slob where to stuff it. "Working here has been like amateur night in Dixie."

"I'll see you never work anywhere again…"

"Try it, and I'll take your ass to court."

I went outside, and saw Cal waiting for me beside his big chopper. Oblivious to the hundreds of staring eyes at the windows of the school, he pulled me close to him and kissed me. "Come on, teach. Let's get moving." I climbed on behind him as he started up the motor.

"What's going to happen to us, Cal?"

"I'll think of something. Come on, let's go back to bed!"

As we roared off into the sunlight, I hung on to his powerful, strong body for dear life. It never occurred to me to question him. You don't do that to the leader of the pack.

A Merry Little Christmas

It was the morning of Christmas Eve when Michael O'Shannon flew into a fine Irish rage, accusing me of hiding his liquor bottle. I retorted (truthfully) that he'd guzzled up the entire contents the night before.

Pulling on his jacket and tweed cap, he stomped to the door and roared loud enough to awaken St. Patrick, "Go fuck yourself then, and the devil can fuck you, too! You won't be seein' the likes of Michael O'Shannon ever again!"

Michael's brogue thickens considerably when he's emotional—and when he's been swilling too much bourbon,

"Great!" I shot back. "Drink yourself to death! Barf out your brains! Blow your money in!"

The door slammed behind him and I ran to the window to watch my dark, gorgeous Irishman swagger down the block to Clancy's Bar and Grill,

Michael's home away from home these days. There, he would find plenty of cronies to lift a glass with him right through the evening.

God, how I wanted to break that stubborn neck of his! Yet, I had to smile at his arrogant strut—the way his shoulders were thrown back, the proud tilt of his head, the black curls at the nape of his neck dancing in the December wind. Michael O'Shannon can always put on a grand front to hide the demons raging within him.

He's such a big guy, this handsome heartbreaker from Dublin. Still, he can act like a little boy, too. Just when I'd be convinced I could no longer endure his brooding, sulking, and temper tantrums, he would do a complete turnabout and become a dream lover, turning on that charm with which the saints have blessed him so abundantly.

He would buy me something sweet and boyish— some candy bars, scented soap, cologne— but best of all, he would suddenly pick me up and carry me to bed. When he was like that—naked, vulnerable, aroused and tender—I never wanted to leave our bedroom with the gold-shaded lamp glowing on the nightstand and a red candle flickering before our framed portrait on the dresser as if it were a religious icon.

At that moment, the bedroom was a mess. It smelled of stale cigarettes and liquor, testaments to Michael's brooding. Usually so neat, he had left his socks and skivvies on the floor. I picked them up and pressed them to my nostrils and it was like having him there in the room with me: a whiff of Menen's Skin Bracer and a trace of Irish Spring soap. His BVDs were still warm from nestling his genitals.

In the window sat a small Christmas tree. Only a few gifts lay beneath it, the cause of Michael's torment. Last year, he had made good money and had delighted in piling up mounds of presents for me. This year had been rough. He hadn't worked steadily in six months. My meager earnings from writing and a part-time secretarial job barely got us through each week.

On the dresser sat a framed portrait of my handsome Heathcliff and this transplanted Southerner, showing me leaning back against him with my arms around his neck, his rugged face nuzzling mine. I am blond, blue-eyed and my small frame gives me the look of a sixteen-year-old.

Michael's emerald-colored eyes glinted at me through black lashes, a stunning sight in that rugged face. A tough smile showed dazzling teeth. A shadow darkened his stubborn jaw, the traces of his ever-present beard. He, too, was fair-skinned, and from a sleeveless turquoise T-shirt powerful arms shot out to wrap securely around me.

Beautiful Mike. Bad, mad Mike. He would come back. He had to. All year long we had planned for this day. Tomorrow was Christmas, our favorite day of the year. Yet I remembered him whispering to me once in bed, "God help anybody who loves an Irishman."

Through the window, I saw the first flakes of snow. The weather report had been right: it would be a white Christmas. I turned away from the window and picked up the picture, looking closely for some assurance in those dazzling green eyes. Instead I felt a pang of alarm. Maybe this time he wouldn't return.

"What's your name?" I asked the half-naked man.

Minutes before, he had casually carried off my apartment door as if it were cardboard and was now installing a new one. He and several other workers

187

were making repairs on the old building in which I lived. I had watched this particular hunk for days, and now here he was, alone and looking more luscious than ever. This candidate for a centerfold was stripped to the waist and his jeans clung wetly to the lower half of his muscular body. A green rag was tied around unruly black curls, keeping the sweat out of the startling eyes that resembled chips of jade. He was big, over six-feet-four and beneath his smooth white skin rippling muscles denoted awesome power and brute strength.

He leaned against the wall, wiped his face with a towel, and glanced down at me as if I were an alien from a hostile planet. His bunched biceps resembled a softball. I had just had my hair done into a golden mop of curls. I looked girlish and small, smelled of Royal Bain de Champagne cologne and had a dash of mascara around my big blue eyes. I didn't look at all like your average all-American boy.

"Michael O'Shannon's the name," he answered with a thick Irish brogue.

And cockteasing's the game, I thought. Aloud, I said, "Is it now? Don't tell me—you're from Ireland."

A smile actually softened the tight line of his lips. "Well, I'm not from Puerto Rico—that's for sure."

Still, he watched me as though I were a king cobra, poised to strike. I had always heard how homophobic Irishmen were. In New York, there were constant rumors of fag bashings by these men, attributed to their religion, which preached to them that homosexuals were evil and encouraged them to hate the perversion, even as they touted love of one's fellow man.

What a pity, I thought, giving Michael O'Shannon's stunning physique one final glance before returning to my typewriter. I couldn't concentrate though—not with this magnificent giant working just a few feet away. Suddenly he let out a loud yell. His hammer went flying across the room, inches past my head, and clattered to the floor. Startled, I looked up to see him bent over almost double and holding his right wrist in his left hand and making strangling noises in his throat while his feet did a mad two-step on my linoleum. It didn't take long to deduce that he had hit his finger with the hammer.

"Michael, get on over here, and I'll fix it."

I led him to the kitchen sink and held his big, warm hand under the cold water. Then I massaged cooling cream into it, gently. I sensed he was the type of man who was used to being mothered, so I wrapped two big Band-Aids around his finger.

My reward was to see his face soften and hear him thank me in that low, musical baritone. He was standing so close to me then that I could smell his clean sweat and feel his warm breath on my face.

"You live around here, Michael?"

He sniffed. "You kidding? Begod, I wouldn't live in this faggot hangout." At that time, I lived on Christopher Street, in the heart of Greenwich Village. I pretended to be angry. *"Well!* I just *happen* to *be* one of those *faggots!"*

I was gratified to see him blush and roll those glorious green eyes around. He muttered an apology.

"It's okay, Michael." I smiled. "I've heard things about you Irishmen, too. Like how many of you it takes to screw in a light bulb, and how there aren't many of you who would turn down a cold beer. Are you one of them?"

His face lit up. "You wouldn't have to twist my arm,"

I glanced at his formidable arms, "Believe me, Michael, I wouldn't try to twist your arm. You could break me in two using just one of them!"

189

"Who?" he grinned. "Me?" Then he went into an Incredible Hulk pose, gritting his teeth and growling and causing all his biceps to bulge and shiver. When he left me an hour later, his barrier had dropped some. He still watched me warily, but I had made him howl as I recounted some of my experience in interviewing celebrities for gay magazines.

I was thrilled when Michael began dropping by each afternoon with a shopping bag of beer. Never did he wear a shirt. It got to the point when he saw me as a person and not some wild-eyed, drooling degenerate, which is what he had been taught to expect.

He liked to kid me. "Hit me in the stomach," he'd say. "As hard as you can." I would and it was like hitting a block of wood. Michael didn't even blink. That tickled him. He began to let me feel his hard biceps while he teased me for being small and delicate looking.

"I could pick you up like a wee baby," he taunted me one day and promptly grabbed me and held me above his head while he twirled me around on both hands as though I were a helicopter blade. I became so dizzy that when he put me down I had to hold on to him, thrilling to the feel of his strong shoulders and arms. I knew our relationship had progressed when he pulled me against him and we walked into the kitchen. "Me thirsty!" he barked. "Me want beer! Take me to your fridge!"

He sat across from me, his hands behind his head, leaning back in his chair. Sweat gleamed on his solid shoulders and chest. It was his final day on the job. His buddies had already left, and I insisted that he come by for a farewell drink, something stronger than beer.

190

I prepared him a powerful gin and tonic—the only drink worth drinking if you're from the hot, sultry South. It must have loosened his tongue, for he described how a woman down the hall had propositioned him. She said she charged only fifty bucks for a fuck. He told her he could fuck a pig for free.

As I laughed, I watched that strong hand of his slide down to his crotch. "You know of any women around here who might want to get fucked?"

"No, but I know a lot of guys who would."

He grinned and shook his head. "You're too much." After a pause, Michael moistened his lips. "How's about you, Goldilocks?"

"Ha! And get my neck broken, Michael O'Shannon? No, thanks. I've seen too many men like you. You tease, but God help the gay guy who falls for your line."

As I got up to get more ice, he grabbed my hand and pulled me into his lap. Although I protested weakly, he held me tighter. His strength was overwhelming!

"You're scared of me now, aren't you?" he muttered. His brogue had become strongly pronounced. Taking my right hand, he pressed it against the swelling of his right pec. The nipple felt like a bullet of warm flesh. "I've been thinkin' of you, and you're a nice little laddie and I wouldn't hurt ya for anything in the world." I trembled with delight, nervousness, and fear. A friend of mine had been sent to the hospital from his encounter with a handsome cockteaser from Belfast. But Michael's arousal was so genuine, the expression in his jade eyes so longing and hot that I blanked out my misgivings."

Michael, I'm trusting you now...."

By the time Michael left me that night, he seemed to be in a trance. His face was flushed, his eyes glazed slightly, and he had trouble speaking. Still, he smiled as he hugged me to him and looked down at me. Then, laughing softly, he kissed me for a long time.

A month later, we decided to live together.

The twelfth-floor apartment we found on the Upper East Side of Manhattan faced the East River. Best of all, it had one fireplace in the living room and one in the bedroom. We got it cheaply because it was in such poor condition. Michael knew he could fix it up and, within a month, he had done just that. He even turned a huge walk-in closet into an office where I could work undisturbed on my novel.

"No more part-time jobs," he told me on our first night in our new home. "Your book is the most important thing in the world. Don't worry about anything now. I'll take care of you. I'll never let anything happen to you."

We both hated dirt and disorder. Luckily, I enjoyed keeping house, even washing dishes. It was our bedroom that I worked hardest to make the most comfortable, for it was here our most memorable moments were spent. Our window looked out upon the river. In the window, I put a small copper bowl of red geraniums, and over this I hung a curtain of light-blue lace. Beside our bed was a nightstand crowded with our favorite books and a gold-shaded lamp. The big bed dominated the room, covered with a white spread and a patchwork quilt of crimson, blue, and yellow squares folded neatly at the foot.

I loved to watch Michael sleep. Raised up on my elbow, I would study him: His muscular arms wrapped around the pillow with his face turned to me; pink lips parted slightly as he breathed quietly; long lashes resting on cheeks like feathers the color of coal; and, when he turned over the symmetry of his powerful back, starting from broad, white shoulders and tapering to a narrow waist.

Sometimes, unable to resist this magnificent hunk sleeping next to me, I would slip the covers down his back, past the naked hips to his knees, exposing the naked buttocks, luminous and pale in the moonlight.

Sometimes he would awaken and catch me studying him and, smiling sleepily, he would reach out and pull me up against his massive chest, wrapping his arms around me like a powerful lion gathering in a restless cub.

The next morning, he would admonish me.

"You love me too much," he would warn. "The good Lord knows I've got my vices. Don't idolize me. You'll just get your little self hurt."

He was right. You didn't love a man as complex as Michael O'Shannon without paying a price. Both of us were basically loners and independent types. I had been attracted to difficult men before, and though I had become experienced in dealing with their quirks and eccentricities, Michael was something else again. He would brood sometimes for days over the death of his parents, who had been blown up by a terrorist bomb in Belfast two years earlier.

And he was still ambivalent about our relationship. You couldn't just suddenly forget a lifetime of teachings that homosexuality was an abomination in a country where males were shunned and beaten at the slightest sign of effeminacy.

Luckily, these dark spells were rare; as suddenly as they came over him, they would leave. I knew he was his old self again when he sank down beside me on the bed, his muscular arm wrapping around me and pulling me up against him with his hard penis pressed between us.

193

Eager to atone for his surliness, he would urge me to do anything I pleased, even guiding my face down his warm torso until my mouth had engulfed his erection—fragrant, warm, pulsing with energy and pungent with his macho aroma. I would sometimes fellate him until dawn, and he would have several orgasms. And when I'd finally nestle in his arms, exhausted by our lovemaking, he would stroke my hair and shoulders gently, as if he held a young boy in his arms rather than a twenty-four-year-old man.

Sometimes we would walk along the East River, watching snow-covered barges gliding by, their brilliant spotlights shining through the falling snow as they dodged huge chunks of ice bobbing in the gray water. Then we would return to our apartment in the sky. Michael would fix us a couple of hot toddies, and we would curl up on cushions before the fire and watch old movies on our VCR. Neither of us had any interest in going out and socializing much. We found in each other everything we needed to feel complete. Loneliness was a strong bond that bound us together.

Clancy's Bar and Grill was just a block away from our apartment. It was the hangout of the area's musicians and Irish expatriates. Friday night was amateur night. Anyone who had the guts to get up and perform was spotlighted. First prize was unlimited drinks for the winner and his date. Michael became a regular winner, singing folk songs and accompanying himself on the guitar. His voice was a beautiful baritone, and his repertoire of Irish and American ballads was outstanding. By midnight, he would be feeling no pain, and I was forced to enlist some of his cronies to get him home, strip him and put him under a cold shower. One night, after we laid him out on the bed, naked and asleep, one of the men from the bar murmured, "God, but he is one hell of a fine-looking man!"

When the small construction firm for which Michael worked folded, Michael was stunned. He had fore-seen a glowing future as the firm's best carpenter. He couldn't apply for any type of governmental help because he was an illegal alien. Having come to America two years before on a visitor's visa. Michael had never applied for citizenship, for he had a horror of being sent back to the poverty from which he had escaped. He soon discovered that no reputable con-struction firm in New York would hire him without the green card attesting to his citizenship. The few that offered him work did so at a salary so low and for work so backbreaking that it was an insult. I could make much more as a temporary word proces-sor on Wall Street.

We had saved up some money, but that vanishes fast in the most expensive city in the United States Although Michael enjoyed his liquor, he always watched himself carefully except for those once-a-week binges at Clancy's. Now he began drinking more as his efforts to find work proved futile.

One morning I got dressed and went up to him at the window as he stared out at the icy weather out-side. "Look, sweets," I smiled, "I'm taking a one-week word-processing assignment on Wall Street. I don't mind. The money's good and—"

"Dammit, I mind!" he bellowed. "I don't want somebody taking care of me."

"We're in this together," I reminded him. "You've been good to me, Michael. It's my turn to be good to you." When I left him, I thought I had never seen a face so bleak as his.

195

With the help of a crafty lawyer friend of mine I made him apply for citizenship, which was a start in the right direction. In the meantime, he wanted to work. Each day he would go out in search of a job, but when I returned home each night, I'd find him nodding drunkenly before the fire with his new companion—his bottle—sitting next to him on the floor.

It was nearly midnight, nearly Christmas, and he hadn't yet returned. In the window, the pink-and-gold lights glowed brightly on our small tree. Michael had once said that such a sight on a snowy night is one of the most beautiful in the world. And the snow was falling heavier....

Having stashed away some money for just this occasion, I had gone out earlier and splurged on the making of an elaborate Christmas Eve dinner. The turkey was basting in the oven, along with an aromatic chestnut dressing. On the counter sat a platter of appetizers—the kind Michael loves—a bottle of champagne stood chilled and ready. I had showered and put on the blue silk robe Michael loves me to wear and sprayed myself with Royal Bain de Champagne, a scent he swears gives him a hard-on.

What if he doesn't come back? I brushed aside the thought and put a Judy Garland Christmas album on the turntable.

The front door opened quietly and Michael entered with his back to me, the way he usually did when he felt sheepish over a blowup. I was struck dumb with joy at the sight of that broad back, the black curls, the comforting size of him. He turned at last and grinned. His arms were filled with gaily wrapped packages.

"Mike!" I gasped, finding my voice. "Where in the

196

name of God have you been? What'd you do—rob Macy's?"

Laughing, he dropped his bounty into a chair and embraced me so hard I could barely breathe. He didn't smell of liquor for a change; instead, I sniffed the cold wind, the snow, the leather of his jacket and *him.*

"I start work next week at Clancy's Bar," he whispered. "I tend bar through the week and sing on the weekends. I should take in at least four hundred dollars a week."

"I knew you'd find something!" I took his hand and led him over to the counter where I poured us champagne. From the record player, Judy Garland was urging Michael and me to "Have yourself a merry little Christmas..."

We clinked our goblets together and drank the bubbly liquid. Suddenly Michael's laughter boomed out again, surrounding me like a warm blanket, bouncing off the walls and saturating the very air. With one massive arm, he swept me up, crushed me against his chest, and began to dance slowly around the room.

"...let your hearts be gay," Judy sang.

And I thought, *Don't worry, Judy. We will. We will!*

COCK OF THE WALK

Friends always ask me about the coffee mug.

It sits alone—prominently—in a place of honor on a shelf in my den. It looks like an ordinary cup, except it's bigger than most. And across its black surface is painted in gaudy red the words "Dixie's Fairhaired Boy."

Above it is a large color photograph taken ten years ago. I am in that picture, along with a magnificent young man. While he is laughing uproariously, with an arm around my shoulder, I am scrunching up my face, because he's pouring a can of beer over my head. We're both in bathing suits—me in green. and he in crimson—at the edge of a blue swimming pool.

"What's the story with the mug, and who's that gorgeous hunk with the mustache?" a visitor will ask.

"Carson. He gave me that coffee mug."

199

"Carson? Was he the Vietnam vet? The state trooper? The cop...the...?"

"Carson was the reporter."

"What reporter? This is new to me. Wow, he's incredible looking. Looks just like Don Johnson in 'Miami Vice.'"

In a way, the guy in the photograph does resemble that handsome television hunk. Carson, however, was over six feet tall, with a heavier, more muscular build...with eyes the color of lime candy...skin bronzed with a trace of rose in the cheeks...a mustache above lips full and pink...glossy dark hair which he slicked back from a square, stubborn face. Carson is one of those memories I like to keep to myself. I don't share him with others. I savor him on nights when it's cold and rainy, and I can pretend he's here with me again, as it was back in the days when we were younger and both of us thought he was the cock of the walk.

During my first day at the *Montgomery Tribune,* where I had begun work as a feature writer, I kept hearing the name of Carson Drew: "Let's put Carson Drew on that story... Leave a note for Carson to call the governor's office... Get Carson for me."

And when the swinging doors at the end of the newsroom suddenly swung open later that afternoon, I saw him. A suit of pale yellow linen covered the broad shoulders and the rest of his powerful young torso. A panama hat of the same color with a pink band was set jauntily above dancing jade eyes. I noticed how all the female staffers suddenly perked up. Some refreshed their makeup. Excitement pervaded the dark, cluttered old newsroom at his mere presence.

A black cigarillo was clenched between white

teeth. Snapping his fingers, he was whistling "Yankee Doodle Dandy." After throwing his notebooks on his desk, he introduced himself, shook my hand with gusto, and clutched my shoulder enthusiastically.

"Hi, theah!" he boomed. "Ah'm Carson Drew and ah'm mighty glad to know ya, li'l buddy. And mah God, ya *ah* little!"

Like many others, he seemed startled by my appearance. At five-feet-three, I looked more like a schoolkid than a man of twenty-one. My light blond curls and huge blue eyes added to my deceptive illusion of innocence.

I was stunned by this male beauty. The reporters I had known usually thought little of their personal appearance or bodies. Most were paunchy. Now, this dazzling peacock was stripping off his hat, tie, and coat, rolling up his sleeves, and unbuttoning his shirt to the navel. I glimpsed impressive pecs, dusted lightly with hair, a flat stomach enclosed by muscled ridges. He was like something out of a movie. So alive! Electricity seemed to pour out of him.

One of the secretaries had taken his coffee mug and brought it back filled with the steaming beverage. He tossed her a "thanks, dahlin'," and threw me a wink as she left, pink and radiant. "Dixie's Fairhaired Boy" were the words written on the cup in scarlet. He matched those words perfectly.

At once, his fingers flew over the keyboard, as he pounded out his stories. Now and then, he would lean back and close his eyes to think. His crotch was pointed directly at me. The tight fabric stretched over the thick thighs indicated outlines of an impressive organ. And I suspected he was not wearing underwear. He scratched this protuberance occasionally. Then he'd run a hand over his chest, plucking at his nipples and hair and patting his flat stomach. A moment later, he would return to his typing, seemingly unaware of the glances of lust being cast his way by the women reporters—and the blond, blue-eyed slut sitting across from him.

Later that afternoon, my temperature rose higher when he went to the city desk to confer with an editor. Leaning down, his ass stuck up in the air. It was a spectacular derriere that should have been showcased on a Colt all-male calendar. The thin fabric hugged his round buttocks and had been sucked into his crack. This Southern cannonball did *not* wear underwear!

"Dixie's Fair-haired Boy" was clearly interfering with my attempts to write a Fourth of July parade story. In response to my piteous pleas for help, he came to my rescue gallantly. Kneeling down beside me, he put a hand on my neck with his face only an inch or two from mine to study my story. I forgot my problems completely. I was dizzy from feeling his warm breath on my cheek, the moist lips near my ear, the scent of his body—a mixture of clean sweat, tobacco, and a cologne tinted lightly with citrus and musk. His sea-colored eyes sparkled when they looked into mine.

"Now, heah," he smiled sweetly. "Jest move this li'l paragraph down a mite, dahlin', and it might read a tad bettah."

I was so thrilled! He called me—darling! Later, I discovered Carson called everyone (even crooks and enemies) "honey"…"dahlin'"…"babe"…"sugah"…

After work, he insisted I join him and the "gang" down at Quinn's Bar, a dark little watering hole beneath the streets of Montgomery. It was so packed, I was squeezed between him and Nicky, a *Tribune* photographer I had met earlier that day. They were easily the two handsomest men in that room.

My hand brushed Carson's thigh several times, but he had forgotten me. He was much too busy flirting with the girls who were raping him and Nicky with their eyes.

Nicky ignored them. He was too busy flirting with me. He was wearing a pink golf shirt which enhanced his swarthy features, and his wicked eyes flashed "bedroom, bedroom" at me. I decided in the heat of the moment to forget Carson for a while. When my hand brushed Nick's thigh accidentally, his hand quickly covered mine and guided it beneath the table to his crotch. I began to massage it vigorously until I felt the mound begin to expand.

"That big enough for ya?" he whispered. "Wanna have some fun with it? It's a big dick. Ah jerked off after seein' you this mornin'. That li'l boy's butt of yours, twitchin' around, whew, Ah—"

His words of love were suddenly drowned out by the blaring of Marvin Gaye's classic, "I Heard It through the Grapevine." A miniskirted woman grabbed Carson's hands and dragged him to the dance floor where other couples were twisting. Soon, everybody was watching Dixie's Fair-haired Stud put on a sizzling routine that Chippendale's would have loved. Shaking his ass to the rhythm, he humped his hips, stripped off his shirt and whirled it above his head, while hollering and screeching like a cat in heat. The crowd loved it. They whistled and shouted, "Do it, Carson! Shake that thing!" I wanted to see more, but Nicky was dragging me out of that mob. He couldn't stand it anymore.

"I've gotta come, Jason, or I'll have a stroke."

"Don't do that!" I giggled. "*I'll* stroke it!"

In the months thereafter, Nicky proved to be a perfect sex partner. We made no ties on each other. He just wanted to ball—it was his main interest in life. That first night, at my place, he stripped us both in record time, picked me up, and promptly positioned my ass on my kitchen counter. I soon learned he didn't like doing it in bed—either a floor or a counter was fine, though.

Sweat glistened on his husky body as he pushed the plum-shaped tip of his penis up into me. Sighing with relief, he edged the remainder of the narrow stalk into my rectum. Then he proceeded to confirm his reputation as a superstud. He fucked relentlessly, skillfully, silently, to milk out the large deposit of sperm which was causing him so much sexual pain.

Nicky bent over me, kissed me passionately, moaning, almost sobbing, as he moved his hips faster and faster. With his eyes shut now, he drilled me steadily until he stopped, tensed, and shuddered as he achieved orgasm.

"Godalmighty, but that felt good!" He smiled. "You wanna suck me now? Let's git on the floor."

We lay down on my thick rug. Nicky spread his hairy thighs and held his penis up for me to enjoy. Although it was still sticky with newly spilt semen, I felt it begin to thicken after a few minutes of my blowing him. Soon, he had a full-sized erection. Now, Nicky wasn't one of those sensitive souls who whines, "Hey, be careful" or "Stop biting me." His organ was like smooth leather, and I could do whatever I wanted with it. Both of us were eager to see this ejaculation, and he helped me beat out endless strands of white syrup.

Afterward, as we paused for some cold beer, he pointed to something through my window. My apartment was one of a dozen clustered around a huge swimming pool. You could walk a few feet from my door and jump in. Nicky now indicated the unit directly across from me.

"Did you know—that's where your handsome hunk, Mr. Carson Drew, lives."

I was delighted by this incredible stroke of fate. "Oh, God, I hope he goes skinny-dipping. Did you see him shake that ass of his tonight? I've got to have him, Nicky."

"You're barkin' up the wrong tree, toots," warned Nicky. "He's super straight. Shit, honey, he's gettin' married in three months."

My heart sank. I sat down at the table gloomily. It couldn't be true. He was too young, handsome, and sexy to tie a noose around his neck. Maybe I could get him to change his mind....

Oh, those were the glory days at the *Tribune*. We worked hard and played hard. Each day I fell more in love with Carson. He was fond of me, too, and treated me like a younger brother in need of his protection and guidance.

Many a night, after a few beers at Quinn's Bar, we'd all speed over to Carson's or my place. Dixie's Fair-haired Boy always changed into his uniform: a pair of red boxer swim trunks. (He liked jumping into the water now and then, which, he said, knocked some of the booze out of him.) The trunks set off his deep tan, his white grin, and rippling musculature, much of which came from having played football at the University of Alabama where he had been a star jock.

He adored teasing and picking on me. Many nights I'd go to my door and find him in his trunks, adorable and wet from the pool. When I would tell him I didn't want to swim, he'd pick me up and jump into the water with me, regardless of what I was

205

wearing. The angrier I got, the more tickled he got.

"You act like a li'l ole kitten," he'd grin and gooch me.

And you couldn't stay mad at him—not with his red-hot charm and good looks. Oh, how I wanted to go to bed with him. One night he pounded on my door, and when I opened it, he was (as usual) wet from the pool. Water glistened on his big bearlike torso. He was also a little drunk. When I told him I was not going into the pool with him, he grabbed me, and we wrestled all around the living room. I was in heaven putting my hands all over him. Finally he hugged me against him tight. His face was only a few inches from mine.

"Mean li'l ole thing." He smiled tenderly, staring at me with those lustrous green eyes. "You're my li'l buddy, and I love ya like a brothuh."

I rubbed his bulging pectorals as he continued smiling. "You're the greatest guy in the world, Carson." He pressed my face against his chest and patted it with his hand, as if in perfect agreement. What he said next, though, sent a chill through me.

"Ah'm glad ya ain't no fruity fag. A guy told me today he thought ya wuh, and Ah 'bout broke his neck. You kin be damned sissified when ya want to be, but Ah kin spot a fruitcake a mile off."

I had been pulling his nipples, which had become white and thick. "What would you do if I were a homo—a fruity fag?"

He doubled up his big fist and waved it in front of me. "Why, Ah'd break that sweet li'l ole neck of yours, and throw you to the 'gators."

Wanting to lighten things up, I pretended to suddenly pant in lust. "Gasp, gasp—Carson, quick—let me have that big dick of yours—you know how us queers are!"

I rubbed his chest, stomach, and crotch. He howled

with laughter and, to my delight, pushed his trunks
down and flipped his phallus at me.

"Woo-weee!" he laughed. "Come and git it, you
li'l burr-headed cocksuckuh!"

Carson was *big*. While his cock was probably no
more than six, seven inches soft, it was so big around,
it was like a flesh-colored bottle in his hands. He
flopped it on the table and moved it around while
making feigned sounds of a man having orgasm. All
that movement was causing the tip to slide out from
its large covering of soft flesh. I started to touch it
but Carson stuffed it back into his trunks.

"Let's don't get *real* fruity," he grinned—but then
he hugged me to him again and nuzzled his face
against mine. "See? Ah kin cut up and kid with ya.
'cause Ah know you ain't a homo."

I took his face with my hands while he made comical expressions and sounds. "Carson, I can promise
you if I was a homo, I'd be as proud of that fact as
you are in being a big-dicked stud."

He snickered, belched, and gooched me. And then
I put on a Ruth Brown album, and she began wailing
about "Wild, Wild Young Men." Carson grabbed me
and started dancing like he did that night at Quinn's
Bar. As he swung me around, making those screeching cat sounds, I thought, *You are a wild, wild young
man.* And God, did I love him!

After that night, Carson adored talking "dirty talk"
or "fag talk." Like an impish little boy, he'd sneak up
to me at work and whisper, "Hey, fruity-pie, you gittin' any cock lately?"

Rubbing my jaw, I'd come back with, "Wow, after
eating that big stiff one of yours last night, Carson, I
didn't want no more."

My buddy laughed until he was gasping. He'd slap

207

his desk and stagger around it. Best of all, when no one was looking, he'd lean back in his seat and rub the outlines of his cock.

"Whew, Ah'm hurtin' mighty bad. How's about a quickie?"

Licking my lips, I'd gasp, "Christ, yes, let me have it! I'm just a slut!" Carson would howl so hard he'd have to leave the room.

Or I'd leave him dirty notes, addressed to: "Mr. Cock of the Walk" or "My Beloved Ten-Incher" or "Dixie's Fair-haired Hard-On." He loved them all.

When I told him he had a fabulous-looking butt, he made a point of always pausing in front of my desk and twitching it. When I pinched it one day, he grinned, but pulled away.

"Hey, let's don't get too fruity, Goldilocks."

That was his favorite name for me. Goldilocks. Besides "sugah," "honey," and "babe." When I told him Nicky was coming down from Atlanta (where he'd gone to work on the newspaper there), Carson pouted.

"Nicky, Nicky, Nicky!" he grumbled. "All you talk about anymore is Nicky. What's that guy have that Ah don't have?" At that moment, he was leaning back in his desk chair. With his legs spread and his crotch clearly visible, I glanced at it pointedly.

"Carson, I can promise you that few men have what you've got." He blushed a beautiful pink and tried to look disgusted, but succeeded only in looking pleasant.

"Your mind's always in the guttah," he muttered.

With Nicky around, my mind stayed in the gutter. He wanted me to be a slut, and if enjoying sex means being a slut, then I was the number-one slut in Montgomery.

"What d'ya wanna do first?" Nicky asked me that

night. "Wanna suck me off? Want me to fuck you?"

I pulled him down to the kitchen rug, pushed aside his thighs, and went down on him right there. I had behaved myself since his last visit a month before, and I was starving for blunt, plain sex. His penis quickly swelled up in my mouth, as I took it all the way to the pubic hair. My tongue dug into his slit (which always set him afire) and as the tip hardened, he began to pulsate and then ejaculate. He whistled silently and arched his hips to make sure the head stayed in my mouth until he finished.

Suddenly I felt a draft of wind on my face. The kitchen door had opened. Nicky was trying to push me away when I looked up and saw Carson staring down at me. His face was white, his eyes shocked. "Fuck, no! Shit, no! Ya really *ah* a fag!" Knotting up his fist, he rammed it through a pane of glass in my door. Then he jumped back into the water and swam away from me.

For the next few days at work, Carson ignored me. If we passed each other in the hall, he'd look straight ahead or down at the floor. I no longer existed. I felt sorry for his disillusionment, but I wasn't going to let him make me feel guilty.

When he saw me going about my job, laughing and talking to the other staffers with no signs of an impending breakdown, he decided to change his tactics. Waiting for me one morning, he held his coffee mug to his lips and watched me settle down at my desk.

"Well, well, well," he smirked. "Ya gettin' enough cock from your Eye-talian stud? Or ah ya goin' to the bus station and the fruit bars for mo' meat?"

I smiled sweetly as if he had complimented me. "You should have stuck around, Carson. Nicky fucked me after you left. He said I'm great at both ends. Wanna give it a try?"

He made an inarticulate sound of horror and fled to the coffee room. After that, he began to taunt me constantly. It was like the days when he and I would "joke" about fags and such—only now his teasing was edged with malice.

"There's a big black buck out theah unloadin' a truck," he grinned one afternoon. "Should Ah see if he wants you to suck that big ole black dick of his?"

"Sure," I sneered. "Bet I'd have more fun with him than I would with you—he's got so much more to offer."

"Ya make me *sick!* Ye'd love thet, wouldn't ya?"

"I'm not apologizing for the way I am, Carson. If I saw you fucking a girl, I wouldn't go off the deep end like you've done."

He seemed startled by my comparison and became quiet.

It was late that night when I left the *Tribune.* I had thought about Carson all day, and now he stepped out of a doorway and joined me.

"Hi," I smiled. "Aren't you afraid I might attack you or something?"

"Shut up," he grumbled. "Ya know it's gettin' rough around heah at night. And since ya don't know nothin' 'bout takin' care of yourself, Ah guess Ah'll have to do it."

I stopped and grabbed his arm. "Carson, please be my friend again."

We were at my car now, and suddenly he grabbed my shoulders. "Jason, Ah've figured it out. Let me git ya some dates lined up—real girls. That'd change ya whole outlook. Git some pussy—"

"Carson, I don't want a fucking girlfriend. I love a

210

man. You. I love everything about you—your muscles, charm, your ass—"

He ran a hand over his face and hair. "Sweet Jesus, you're—you're crazy as a bedbug. G'wan. G'wan home, now. Ya hear?"

After that, though, he became quieter. He was still struggling with having to readjust to a side of me he couldn't understand. Faggots were the lowest of the low; yet people liked me, respected me—even he had been close to me. That didn't jibe with what he had been taught to believe.

At that point, neither of us had time to battle over my sexuality. Within weeks, Carson would be marrying his childhood sweetheart. Worse for me, though, was the death of Nicky.

I was the first one on the scene of that horrible car smashup just outside my apartment. Nicky had just left me to return to Atlanta when the drunken driver of the tractor trailer smashed his small sports car into junk. Imagine (if you can) seeing a man who has just made love to you—handsome, warm, talented—now a mass of flesh, blood, and bones. I remember little of what happened next. Somehow Carson found me and pulled me away as the ambulance people went to work. He took me to his place, fixed me stiff drinks, and held me in his arms.

Pressed close to him, I heard him say, "Ah know how much ya loved him. Ah'm really sorry, honey."

"I loved him, Carson," I said groggily, "but I love you, too."

"Shhh, don't say that, baby. Be quiet now. Ah'm takin' care of ya now." As my head lay against his bare, warm shoulder, he stroked my hair, and then I felt warm lips touch it gently. "Git yourself to sleep."

Carson couldn't spend his days taking care of me.

211

His wedding was fast approaching, and I knew I was losing him. He and his new bride were leaving immediately after the wedding for Florida, where he had taken a job as editor of a small newspaper in a posh resort area.

He was changing before my eyes. Gone were much of the high spirits and animal beauty I had loved so. Now, he was becoming more mature, more serious—but nothing could hide the fact that he was still one of the most dazzling males in the heart of the Confederacy.

And then came the day when I watched through the window, as Carson and his buddies moved his belongings out of his little bachelor pad. Deeply depressed, I spent the day like someone in mourning. By midnight I had taken a hot bath and was preparing for bed.

Someone knocked on my door. When I opened it, I could say nothing for a moment.

"If'n ya'd rather Ah didn't come in," he said quietly.

"Carson! You didn't forget me!" Like the old days, he wore just his red swim trunks. Cold water glistened on his luscious tan. His nipples were white and erect. "Come in, of course."

Impulsively, I threw my arms around his neck. Laughing, he half-carried me back into the living room. He had brought along a bottle of champagne, and we opened it.

"Here's to your future, Carson," I smiled. "You don't know how much I'll miss you."

He put his glass down and held out an arm toward me, beckoning me to come over to him. When I did, he hugged me tight and began talking: in twenty-four hours he would be a married man. He was going to respect his vows, settle down, and raise a family. He wanted children. Before all this happened, though, he wondered if we could—well, have a few hours together.

I took his big hands and pulled him into the bed-room. "Come on, gorgeous," I smiled. "Let's go to bed."

He was nervous at first. We were doing something he had always been taught was so evil as to be unthinkable. I vowed to him that it would be our secret. No one would ever know. And just to think of me as a girl, and things would be wonderful.

Carson proved to be an even better lover than I had fantasized. When I snuggled up to him, his golden body rippled as it went into motion. His mustache tickled as he kissed me, awkwardly at first, then with more mastery. Moving down from his mouth, I feasted greedily on his nipples (which were thick and smooth), his chest, and his stomach (which sunk in deeply when I kissed it). And then I began to push his penis into my mouth. He held down his foreskin as I licked at the slit, and then enveloped the head, which was lustrous and soft. Quickly, though, his entire organ began to stiffen, as I sucked it, licked it, and squeezed it.

While all this was going on, Carson was writhing and twitching and panting. His body gleamed with sweat, and when I saw his stomach rapidly sinking in and out, I knew he was close to orgasm.

"It's gonna bust open!" he muttered, to confirm my thoughts. As I took his penis out of my mouth, it pulsated suddenly. Sperm blew through the opening in thick streams. I watched it glisten on his stomach and chest. "Ah guess ah've been savin' it up for tonight," he admitted sheepishly. I immediately kissed him, for it was like having the old Carson back with me.

"Carson, you know you've got an ass that drives

213

people crazy. May I—?" Even before I could finish the sentence, he was turning over on his stomach and presenting me with a lustrous white treasure more perfect than most men behold in a lifetime.

I parted the round buttocks. My face sank slowly into the cleft which was unbelievably warm, moist, and fragrant. Quickly, my tongue danced into his rectum and pushed in between the tight lips. Carson began to squirm, really squirm.

No one had ever done that to him (nor was anyone likely to do it in the future—certainly not his Southern wife). For nearly an hour, he had a rimming that I've never forgotten—and when he turned over, his erection was a sight to behold. A pinkish blue, it was thumping steadily against his stomach. A small puddle of transparent honey had oozed out of the slit nearly into his navel. Once again I began to suck on him, but could only get the upper portion into my mouth—it was too thick around. And when he tried to fuck me, he could only get half of it in. But what he did slip in felt wonderful.

And it went on like that until dawn, when he finally pulled on his red trunks and we walked to my door.

"You'll be at mah weddin' today?"

I shook my head. "Don't torture me, Carson. You know you'll be the only man I'll ever love."

He hugged me tight and kissed me again. "Thanks, Goldilocks," he whispered. "Ah'll always remembuh that—and Ah'll remembuh this night." I watched him dive into the pool and swim in long, strong strokes over to his empty apartment.

And that was the last I ever saw of him.

I found his mug on my desk the next day. Taped to it was a brief note: "Remember me when you drink from my mug."

A friend sent me a clipping from a Florida news-paper recently. It showed a balding man with a defi-nite paunch and his wife and four daughters. The headline read: "Newspaper publisher Carson Drew and family celebrate tenth wedding anniversary."

On special occasions, I take out that precious mug, and tonight I've filled it with something stronger than coffee, for today is the anniversary of the first time I ever saw him on the Fourth of July, ten years ago.

Holding it up to the picture of him and me, I toast aloud: "To Dixie's Fair-haired Boy, for what might have been—the cock of the walk who will never grow old!"

WILD, WILD YOUNG MEN

The first time the Thompson kids met me, I was wearing full makeup, and my Mama had just chased me into the Atlantic Ocean.

That dramatic encounter set the tone for our relationship during that summer of 1958. Things were also happening to us—and I seemed to be the lightning rod which drew down upon us all the good and the bad times.

A sea breeze stirred the curtains beside me that August morning. Sitting at my Mama's dressing table, I was oblivious to the sunbathers and swimmers outside our rented cottage. We were spending a month at beautiful Wrightsville Beach, North Carolina.

This was our first morning there—but was I interested in working on a tan? Huh uh! I was more fascinated in watching my face change beneath the makeup I was trying on. Mama and Daddy had gone out for a walk. Good riddance. We had bickered all the way from Charleston that morning over the fact that I was a "queer" and not a "real boy"—an argument I had heard all my life.

Mascara and eyebrow pencil made my eyes more lustrous and blue. Revlon's Pink Sin lipstick transformed my mouth into luscious petals of rose. My white skin needed no pancake or powder. A spray of Chanel No. 5 transported me even further (in my mind) onto the set of a big Hollywood spectacle.

I stood up and fluffed my gold curls I really did look like my goddess—Marilyn Monroe. Several of my jock buddies in high school had told me that, after pinching my rear end which (they leered) also had a startling resemblance to that of the sex goddess.

White short shorts and a blue jersey set off my five-foot-tall torso and I preened in all my eighteen-year-old-glory. *Just wait till I enter college in four weeks! I'll really have the boys lapping at my heels.* I was reaching for the earrings when I froze. Watching me with horror from the doorway were my parents. *Oh, God,* I thought, *here we go again.*

"Mama," I drawled, "you're nearly out of lipstick."

With a shriek, she lunged for me I jumped through the window and landed on the soft sand. She raced out of the house after me with a broom raised in the air.

"We're sending you to the marines!" she screamed.

We raced past startled families and sun worshipers, until I plunged into the water. Mama watched me from the shore, shaking the broom like the crazy woman she was.

"Just you wait, Jason Fury. I'll get you!"

"Come on in and get your jockstrap wet!" I trilled.

Finally she stomped away. I emerged wet and bedraggled. Nearly a dozen people gaped at me as if I were the *Creature from the Ocean Floor*. A young woman and two good-looking men came up to me, smiling.

"Wow!" the girl laughed. "Here's a towel." She and her companions watched, fascinated, as I began wiping off the ruined makeup. "Your Mama's sure on the warpath."

"Oh, that old bitch is always on the warpath. You should have seen her that night she caught me trying on her blue organdy and ermine stole."

I did an imitation of her, and the three doubled up laughing. Long ago I had discovered never to take myself that seriously—especially if you're as obviously effeminate as I am.

The girl introduced herself as Tina Thompson. The boys were her brothers—gorgeous, broad-shouldered Keith and cute, husky Scotty. Both would be returning to Duke University that fall, where they played football. Tina said she had dropped out of college to be "a writer—like Ayn Rand."

I was struck by how gorgeous they all were. Tina was plump, with long, dark hair and beautiful skin and makeup. With his black crew cut and light-blue eyes, Keith was a breathtaking version of what Montgomery Clift would have been if he were six-foot-three. Scotty made me think of Tom Sawyer or Huck Finn with his round, freckled face and goofy sweet grin. Only a foot taller than I was, he (like his bigger brother) had a powerful physique. His sandy hair was shorn into a crew cut—the only hairstyle for American boys at that time.

Johnny Mercer's Pier, *the* hangout for the beach crowd, was just a short distance away. We could hear the jukebox booming out the big summer dance hit,

219

Ruth Brown's version of "Wild, Wild Young Men." I suddenly began to scream along with her and did some wild dance steps. The Thompsons laughed, and Tina grabbed my hand and started running.

"I'll bet you're a great dancer, Jason Fury! Come on and let's show them how to really dance!" Her brothers ran with us, and as we laughed and whooped and whirled around, Ruth Brown wailed how wild young men just liked to whoop and holler and yell "Oooo-weeee!"

And all of us screamed: "Ooooo-weeeee!"

First we gobbled down hot dogs with sauerkraut and guzzled icy Cokes (the kind you *drink*) while watching the small dance pavilion jammed with tanned guys and girls. Boys didn't wear bikini briefs back then. All were attired in ugly boxer trunks, or worse still, Bermuda shorts. Still, some of the trunks hung low enough on slim hips to indicate what might lie beneath.

Tina punched "Wild, Wild Young Men" on the jukebox, pulled me out to the dance floor, and soon nearly everyone was watching us put on a show. Like most heavy people I've known, she was a great dancer. From the corner of my eye, I saw her hunky brothers, along with their gang of bronzed beach buddies, studying me—nodding in approval, whooping and stomping on the floor.

Etta James came on the jukebox with the finger-snapping "Good Rockin' Daddy." The Thompson boys got on the floor with their partners. Poor Keith! So big, so gorgeous—yet he had not one ounce of rhythm. Still, that made him even more attractive as he just laughed and shuffled his feet around. Scotty, though, was a sexy dancer—bumping and grinding his hips with a lazy grin on his mouth and a hot look in his eyes.

Tina and I took a Coke break, and while we leaned against the wall, watching the waves below, I blurted out, "Your brothers are so cute!"

She smiled knowingly and raised her eyebrows. "Oh? Which one is cuter? Want me to tell you about them?"

Keith was the real lady-killer. Girls chased him constantly, I learned sometimes he became vain and arrogant because of the powerful spell his muscles and football uniform worked on people. Basically, he was sweet but could be a smart-ass.

Scotty worshiped Keith. He tried to do everything his older brother did, but to no avail. While Keith was a natural scholar, Scotty was a terrible student. Neither was he physically graceful, but the girls still liked him although he didn't seem to care.

"He's so shy!" Tina sighed. "He won't ask any girls for dates. Something's bothering him. He won't tell us. He's gotten real quiet. It worries me a lot. You think maybe he could be—?"

"I'd love to find out."

She laughed and punched me on the arm.

The Thompson kids and I became inseparable. Since no one's ever accused me of being boring, I kept them captivated for hours as I did my imitations of Patti Page, Etta James, and Ruth Brown. I had them laughing hysterically at some of the stories I spun about the fights between me and Mama. Other times, while I went on about how gorgeous James Dean and Montgomery Clift were, Tina giggled and the boys listened wide-eyed.

I could be so nauseatingly piss-elegant during that time, too, that Keith and Scotty would have to bring me down to earth. They would play tricks on me.

221

Keith came up to me one day, his eyes dancing, and told me to sit on his shoulders. He wanted to show me a trick.

"What kind of trick, Keith Thompson?" I demanded.

Tina called out, "Don't you hurt Jason, you big lug."

But Scotty and Keith persuaded me to get on Keith's broad shoulders. When I did, he raced out to the water with me screaming, and dunked me. While they howled, I pretended to be enraged, but then I ended up laughing, too.

One afternoon, Tina came up to me. With her was her "boyfriend," a handsome businessman in his early forties who owned one of the hotels.

"Honey," she said, "I've got a date with Sal here tonight. Keith's got a date, too. But Scotty doesn't have anybody to be with tonight. Would you mind going to the movies with him? He thinks you're fabulous, and he's so lonely and—"

"Will he give me a kiss on our first date?" I drawled.

Tina and Sal burst out laughing. "He might give you more than a kiss," Tina giggled. Then, growing more serious, she added, "Something's bugging that little guy. He won't talk to us, Jason. You work on him."

"Oh, you!"

Scotty looked so cute that night when I met him at Johnny Mercer's Pier. His white T-shirt emphasized his dark tan and muscles. The jeans, too, outlined his trim torso. Grinning shyly, his smoky blue eyes lit up when I came over to the hot dog stand to join him. I had put on a pink T-shirt and chino shorts. Mama said they made me look like a two-bit slut. I told her I was the biggest slut on the beach, so why not dress

222

the part? She chased me out of the house with her broom.

"Gee," Scotty blushed, "you look real nice. Hungry? How 'bout a hot dog or two and a Coke? I'm treating."

"Sounds great." We lived on hot dogs and Cokes that summer, sometimes having them for breakfast, lunch, and supper. But you know what? We never got tired of them.

Afterward, we took in the summer's big movie, Elizabeth Taylor in *Cat on a Hot Tin Roof*. And then we were alone as we walked along the deserted beach. Scotty took my fingers into his hand now and then as we brushed against each other. He felt so warm and comforting and he kept glancing at me, even when we weren't talking. We found a grassy knoll that overlooked the glimmering Atlantic. Before sitting down, he stripped off his T-shirt and spread it on the ground.

He sat close to me, and I could feel the warmth of his naked skin. After talking about college and movies for a while, I put my hand on his arm. "Scotty, you're so cute. I'll bet you've got thousands of girlfriends."

"Naw," he sighed sadly. "I don't have any." After I prodded him gently for a few minutes, he finally confessed the Dark Tragedy that had befallen him two summers before at the family's lakehouse.

At that time, Scotty had had the hots for this particular girl. She had tits out to there, he explained. The problem was that she started dating Keith. One night, the girl came looking for Keith who had gone out for a while. Scotty and she were alone.

"One thing led to another—I stripped off my shorts—and when she saw what I had, she died laughing. Then she told me that next to Keith I looked—like a midget."

He confessed that he thought about what she had said all the time and vowed never again to have sex with a girl. I urged Scotty to forget what the bitch said, but he shook his head.

"She was right," he groaned. "Keith's got a cock like a cucumber—and mine—mine's tiny."

"I'll bet you've got a real nice one, Scotty. I can tell."

"You—you can? How?"

"The way you walk. In your shorts, something nice is sure jiggling around in there. Tell you what. I've seen lots of naked guys. Let me see yours. I'll give you my honest opinion."

"Well, I dunno. Promise you won't laugh at me?"

After promising him, I was thrilled to see him unzip himself, raise his hips to pull his jeans off, and then fold them neatly. Next, he peeled off his white BVDs. Immediately, I could smell a warm, spermy aroma.

"It's so dark out here, Scotty, I can't really see," I said. "I'll have to feel you up some." He had a beautiful set of genitals—a thick, average-sized penis with a tip that was firm and trimmed. I squeezed his testicles, which were warm and plump. "Scotty! You're really big!"

"Aw, come off that. You're just being nice."

"No, I'm not! And—oh, my God, it's getting bigger."

"Hey, I—I really am! Wow! It's not bad, is it?"

My fingers kept caressing his penis, rubbing it, pulling at it until it had expanded and grown impressively. I bent down and took the cocktip into my mouth. Scotty whistled as I began to suck on it. My tongue parted the large urethra easily and dug down inside it until he was squirming. When I finally enveloped the organ down to the pubic hair, he was breathing harshly and trembling.

224

"Hey, Jason, this is my first blowjob," he managed to whisper. "And shit, it sure does feel like Christmas!" He paused nervously. "Hey—could you take more? All the way into your mouth, huh?"

As I did so, I felt his cock pulsate. Instantly my mouth was filled with large gusts of sperm. After he finished, he sat up, still nervous.

"That's another thing," he said. "I come so fast. I know some guys who can hold it in for hours. But me—well, my first orgasm just pops right out."

"Those guys who can hold it in for hours are just bullshitting, Scotty. Lots of guys shoot right away. Besides, it's the second time that counts, and I'll bet you can get it up again real soon, can't you?"

Eagerly, he told me to help him, and I ordered him over on his stomach. His butt was like the rest of him: smooth, lightly dusted with hair and freckles, and as round as two melons strung together. Pushing them apart, I buried my face deep into his crack. Scotty began to squirm in joy. That had never been done to him, either.

As I tongued his asshole, I felt his genitals beneath my chin swelling up again. Pulling his penis back between his thighs, I sucked him thoroughly. Very quickly, he gifted my efforts with another ejaculation.

Afterward, Scotty took me into his arms and kissed me for a long time. "This is the greatest night of my life, Jason," he whispered. "You made me feel like a real man for the first time. Hey, can I try something else—like trying to fuck you?"

"God, Scotty, you are such a stud! That bitch didn't know what she was turning down!"

Naturally, I was being a little too enthusiastic, but not much. Scotty was a passionate little guy, and I knew how much my words meant to him. He threw himself into this new sexual practice with tremendous

225

gusto and rewarded me with his third load in less than an hour. Before we parted that night, he kissed me again.

Tears were in his eyes when he whispered, "Damn, Jason, this is a night I'll never forget. You're a dream."

After that night, there was a definite change in Scotty. Before, he had been quiet and awkward around the girls. Now he would go up to them at the dance pavilion and lead them out to the floor with confidence. Soon, he was seeing a different girl every night. Still, he found time for me. We got together at least once a day for hot, passionate sex in his car. He seemed to know where all the good parking spots were out in the Carolina countryside.

It was as if he had finally discovered how much fun his cock could bring him, and he was trying to make up for all the lost time. Both Tina and Keith teased me constantly about that night of my date with Scotty.

"Whatever did you do?" Tina laughed. "Ovenight, he suddenly came out of his shell."

Poker-faced, I replied, "What a dirty mind you have, Tina. "We just *talked.*"

"Liar! Don't tell your Aunt Tina, then. But whatever happened—thanks."

Keith, too, was dying to know about my date. He and I were lying together on a blanket one morning. Scotty frolicked in the water with his new girlfriend, Kathy, and Tina was horsing around in the waves with her new boyfriend, Sal. Keith rolled over on his stomach and propped his chin in his hand, staring up at me from beneath those thick jet-black lashes. His eyes, as blue as the sky, danced with high spirits. Taking my hand into his big paw, he began to squeeze it. He adored teasing me.

226

"Tell me, Jason Fury, what did you and my kid brother do that night when you two dated? He's a changed kid. Did you...uh...do a little hanky-panky?"

"That's for me to know, hotshot, and you to find out." He squeezed my hand tighter until I cried out. "You're always picking on me, Keith! Stop it!"

He just laughed. "I'd like to find out, Goldilocks. Maybe we could take a walk one night—"

"And have you rape me, Keith Thompson? No, thanks!"

Keith whooped and turned over on his back, laughing crazily. "You're too fucking much, squirt." He jumped to his feet and held out his hand. "Come on. I want you to show me how to do some of those sexy dance steps you do at the pier. Let's go to the house and have some Cokes."

The Thompsons had the biggest house on the beach. I had been to several parties there and loved his parents. They didn't seem to do anything all day but sit in front of their huge TV console and watch comedies. After I greeted them, Keith said I was going to show him how to dance.

"Ha!" laughed Mrs. Thompson, a slender, young-looking woman. "If you can do that, Jason, you've accomplished a miracle."

Keith grinned at the good-natured ribbing and we went on up to the big game room at the top of the house. It had a huge jukebox with all the latest hits and a fridge filled with Cokes. As we sipped our icy drinks, Keith punched several songs. Then he came to me and put his arms around me.

"Okay, Goldilocks, how do you do it—that sexy kind of stuff you do with your shoulders and ass?"

"Pretend I'm a girl, Keith—"

"That won't be hard to do," he grinned.

227

I punched him lightly on his chiseled stomach, and he feigned great pain. I hardly knew what I was doing, for here I was, in the muscular arms of the Adonis of Wrightsville Beach. His black trunks hung low on his narrow hips. His sea-colored eyes stared intensely into mine, and his pink lips were parted. As he pulled me closer to him, I noted again how all his muscles rippled with the slightest gesture.

"Let's start with a nice, slow song, Keith."

"Which one you wanna hear?"

"'You've Got the Magic Touch?'"

"You really think so? All the girls tell me that."

"Play the song, stupid."

He put his arms around me again, as the Platters began crooning the love song.

"If you're gonna be a girl," he said shortly, "then act like one. Put your head on my shoulder." His strong, warm shoulder felt wonderful against my face as we moved in a small circle. As he dipped me to the floor, my thigh naturally pressed against his crotch. As he continued holding me in that position, he chuckled. "Did Scotty tell you I've got a cock like a cucumber? Come on. Admit it. He tells everybody that. What do you think? You can feel it, can't you?" He brought me back to my feet. "Well?"

"I couldn't tell, Keith. I felt something—it could be the size of a peanut."

He grabbed my hand and stuffed it down the front of his trunks. My hand felt a penis that was warm, moist, and—long.

"That's just soft. When it gets hard, it—"

"It what, Keith?"

"It gets as big as a fucking watermelon!"

I burst out laughing, and then so did he. Before I left, I promised to meet him that night at seven sharp near the lifeguard's station.

At seven-thirty in the evening, he jumped screaming over the sand dune, grabbed me, and whirled me around.

"Sorry, I'm late!" he panted. "Had to get dressed."

"Keith, I could kill you! You scared me shitless! And you getting dressed? You're wearing the same black trunks you wear everyday."

"Yeah," he teased, "I *did* forget to put on my shirt. But you see, Jason, when I wear these ole trunks, I can slip 'em off and on in no time. That comes in handy on a date."

"You oversexed maniac!" I laughed.

He acted crazy, first running around me and then throwing me over his shoulders and running toward the water. I screamed and he, laughing all the way, carried me back to the dunes. Taking my hand, he led me to a grassy knoll that looked much like the one Scotty and I had used for our night of passion.

Before we sat down, Keith told me to wait. I was startled to see him strip off his trunks and put them down beneath us. He was completely naked. Although it was dark and no one was around, I was thrilled with the brazen display of exhibitionism.

"You're cold," he said. "Come on down. I'll warm you up."

He pulled me against him, his powerful arms hugging me close to him. It was electrifying—to find this naked, beautiful young man pressing himself sensually against me. With Scotty, there had been so much shyness and fear on his part before he finally "did" it; with Keith, it was exactly the opposite. He was brazenly open about what he wanted.

"Will you be as nice to me as you were with Scotty?" he whispered. "He told me how wonderful you were—how great it felt. Please do it to me, too, Jason! I get so sexed up sometimes I really hurt!"

229

JASON FURY

As his lips pressed against mine, his tongue quickly began exploring my mouth, and his body jerked
and trembled in excitement. He gasped in delight
when my mouth started its journey over his magnificent nudity—sucking at his nipples, licking the ridges
of his chiseled stomach, and then finally settling upon
that wet, dark length of muscle that did, indeed, feel
like a warm cucumber of flesh.

I pulled down the tight foreskin so that the wet tip
popped out, as if from an elastic sock. Keith cried out
when my tongue pushed deep into his slit, but I left
that quickly to slide as much of the stiff member into
my mouth as I could get. My fists wrapped around
the base of his erection while I sucked on the tip.
Steadily, my hands milked the lower portion, as if it
were a leathery cow teat, until finally his organ
throbbed. Out squirted a large gob of semen, then
another and another, until I could not swallow fast
enough to take it all.

Afterward, he pulled me up against his wet body
and began to kiss me wildly. "Was I okay?" he whispered. "Did you like my dick? Am I as good as
Scotty?"

"You were incredible, Keith." I reached down to
pat his cock reassuringly, only to discover he was
already hard again. "Keith!"

"I've got to fuck you, Jason. Scotty said there's no
feeling like it—and you've got an incredible ass. I
won't hurt you. I know I'm real big and thick, but I'll
be careful."

"Well, give me a second to catch my breath."

I was terrified he might tear me. I'd heard horror
stories of gay guys having to be sewn back up and
explaining to the doctor what had happened. Still, I
lay back and spread my legs. Amazingly, as big as
Keith was, he was tender and skilled. No wonder the

girls were crazy about him. He paused for a moment so he wouldn't shoot. When he did, he let me feel of the thick base of his phallus and I was astonished that all *that* was lodged up inside my cute little blond ass.

When he finished, I had him turn over. Those Thompson boys had such glorious rear ends. Keith was so bronzed that by comparison his buttocks were a lustrous white. When I parted his buns, he moaned; when I dug my tongue into his butthole, he whimpered and writhed. I wanted to see him shoot, so he turned over obligingly and let me beat out his sperm. He covered my hands with a big gush, and when I lay back in his arms, I asked him how he liked it all.

"The sucking part was wonderful," he drawled. "Getting my butt eaten out was something terrific, too. As far as fucking goes, though, I think I like cunt best."

"Oh, you!" I laughed. "What do *you* know?"

He had been teasing me, and now he had me get up on his shoulders. With both of us still naked, he ran hooting and hollering crazily out into the ocean.

It was nine in the morning. We had just finished our breakfast. You guessed it: hot dogs and Cokes. Out onto the dance pavilion we went. It was too early for most dancers, but already we could see a few young bodies moving along the beach toward the pier. Soon things would be rocking.

Within an hour, I would be heading back to Charleston. Tina, Keith, and Scotty watched me silently as I moved to the jukebox. They were sad, and nothing we said could lift our feeling of gloom. Although we swore to always stay in touch with each other, each of us knew this would be just another closed chapter in our lives after we separated.

"Dammit!" I yelled. "I wanna have some fuckin'

231

fun! Let's get down and boogie!" I punched "Wild, Wild Young Men." We all moved in close for the last time that summer—and then we whooped and hollered and acted crazy. First Tina twirled me around, then Keith, and then Scotty. Then all of us hugged.

An hour later, I looked out the back window of my parents' car as we passed the pier on our journey home. I could make out the forms of my good buddies—still dancing, with new partners, as Ruth Brown urged them all to "whoop and holler—and yell ooo-weeee!"

WHITE GODS

When people ask me to describe Pearl Harbor before the war, I tell them it was both heaven and hell.

It was heaven for me because I was madly in love with Rudy, definitely one of the most gorgeous native boys ever to strut his stuff along the white sands of Waikiki Beach.

I was his passion, too, and when I study the pictures I took of him in his green loincloth, against the cobalt blue of the Pacific Ocean, I think again that they don't make 'em like Rudy anymore. Like the other men I knew back then, he had that boyish look of wide-eyed innocence which World War II seemed to obliterate forever.

It was hell, those last months of 1941. We knew something was going to happen to us there. Honolulu was a feverish nest of intrigue and spies that made Casablanca look like Podunk. Since I lived there with my father, Rear Admiral Edward J. Fury, of the U.S. Navy, I heard all the latest rumors.

Dad was half-crazed with frustration over this situation. Nothing he told his superiors in Washington made them share his fears that Pearl Harbor was going to be attacked by the Japanese.

Added to his torment was another shocker. In September 1941 he just happened to be visiting our Washington home when I arrived from South Carolina. The letter from Citadel Military Academy—which all the Fury men had attended for generations—had preceded me. In cold, clinical words, it informed my father that I was a "degenerate." I can recall how ugly that word sounded as he spat it out in his study. Chewing gum and smoking a Camel, I pretended to be cool as I watched him at his desk, running a hand through his thick hair. The letter informed him that I simply couldn't keep my busy little hands off the husky torsos of the cadets. Worse, many of them had been more than willing to assist me in my oral research into what makes a military man shoot.

Remember that this was an era when the word "homosexual" was rarely even whispered—let alone discussed—unless you were in a mental hospital. Although my father sighed, muttered, and closed his eyes as he continued to read, I thought he looked too handsome and young to be a man of forty-one. Slender and broad-shouldered, his age was belied by full lips and an unlined face. However, his serene, blue eyes burned with fiery emotion.

"I...I simply can't believe this!" he sputtered for the billionth time. "A Fury...a queer? It's impossible! What do you have to say, son?"

At that time in my life, I wanted more than anything to look like Betty Grable and act like Bette Davis. My hair was a froth of gold curls around my

234

tiny head. I was exactly the same height as my favorite screen goddesses—just over five-feet tall. My skin was flawless porcelain, my eyes a striking blue.

The red sweater and black slacks I wore that morning emphasized my well-proportioned boyish figure. It always drew admiring winks and whistles from the dozens of military men cruising the area around the White House.

"Don't call me a queer," I drawled. "I'm a homosexual. It's right there in the dictionary. You sound like one of 'them thar' redneck yahoos from down yonder in Dixie."

Actually, I was teasing him, for I'd been raised in North Carolina. Did I imagine it or did his eyes suddenly dance with amusement? He jumped from his chair and began to pace the floor, glaring at me the whole time since I was acting as if I were waiting for a bus.

"If anyone knew about this, it'd ruin me!" he snarled.

Infuriated by his contempt, I blew smoke in his direction and snapped, "If any of my navy boyfriends knew you were my father, it'd ruin *me!*"

He wheeled around and slapped me hard in the face. I enjoyed volatile scenes I could turn into big productions. I crashed into the liquor cart, overturning it, and fell to the floor. Groaning in mock pain, I was overjoyed to see a trickle of blood running from my nose. My groans grew louder.

And what did my father do? He just stood there, his hands clasped behind his back, staring down at me, a grin growing on his lips.

"My, my," he taunted. "Bette Davis couldn't have done it better!"

When he began to laugh, I blew up. I thought I looked pretty damned dramatic!

"You bastard!" I shouted. "You don't even know me! All you do is ship me off to one school after another. No wonder I'm a fuckin' faggot! *You've* never given me any affection, so I'll find it elsewhere!"

His expression changed from one of amusement to one of pain. Helping me to my feet, he announced I would be returning with him to Hawaii, where he had been stationed for the past year. I was thrilled. "At least there I can keep an eye on you," he said sternly.

"Great, Dad! All those gorgeous young officers and marines and native men and—"

He gripped my shoulders and hissed between clenched teeth, "You *will* behave yourself! You will do nothing to disgrace me or the U.S. Navy! Don't you understand that men have been hanged for doing the things you do!"

I pushed him away and lit up another cigarette. "At least when I'm hanged I can go to heaven happy!"

His mouth fell open. He blinked his eyes in disbelief. Then he sat down on the edge of his desk, shaking his head. Suddenly he began to tremble with laughter. "I can't believe we're having this conversation! No one would believe it! Go on, get packed!"

When I left the room, I could still hear his laughter, a rare, touching sound from a man who acted older than his years.

I couldn't believe it. The day before I was snowbound in Washington. Now I was in balmy Hawaii. Throwing a short robe over my naked body, I went out to the balcony of my second-story bedroom.

Dad had rented us a big residence on the side of a small mountain in Aloha Heights, just outside of Honolulu. A dirt road wound down past a small church to the highway below. Directly below me was Pearl Harbor. The seven warships were lined up like futuristic skyscrapers. Smaller barges and ships swarmed around them like insects. Thousands of men lived on those ships.

It wasn't even eight o'clock, yet the harbor teemed with life. I still hear that noise—the constant hammering, riveting, drilling, engines roaring, whistles blowing, men calling to each other. Beyond the harbor shimmered the Pacific Ocean like a giant cape of silver sequins.

Below me, a jeep with two handsome navy officers pulled up in front of the house. The sight of them sent blood rushing to my cock. I heard Dad call out that he would be out in a minute. I leaned over the balcony and greeted the men. Startled at first at seeing a young blond guy waving at them, they winked and smiled. I knew my robe showed them everything I had, but I didn't care. I was proud of my body. Suddenly a big hand gripped my shoulder and pulled me back into the room.

"So you can't stop flirting, can you?" growled my father. "Going out there and showing them everything God gave you and—"

"If they haven't seen it by this time, Dad, then you'd better send *them* to the funny farm."

I heard a snort of laughter and then noticed the stranger leaning against the door. He was a heavily tanned powerful young man. In baggy trousers and shirt, and black-rimmed glasses, his big arms were folded across his chest as he watched me with keen interest.

As if he were on the brink of a breakdown, Dad ran his hand through his hair and blinked rapidly. "Rudy, this is my son, Jason. Yes, *the* Jason, so you'll have your hands full." Throwing on his jacket, Dad

237

hurried to the door. "Rudy'll explain to you what I expect from you. And you *will* obey! Is that clearly understood?"

Turning my back to Rudy, I bowed from my hips so he could get a good view of my naked rear end. "Yes, massa. Anything you say, massa. Wan' me to pick dah cotton—or is it coconuts over here?" This time Rudy laughed aloud and Father, rolling his eyes and shaking his head, stalked out of the room.

When I turned to Rudy, he had taken off his glasses and was stripping off his shirt. Dad had told me the night before he was assigning a bodyguard to me because of a recent outbreak of violence against American civilians, especially against the families of high-ranking military men. And Rudy was sure big enough to be a bodyguard.

"Are you preparing to attack me, Rudy?" I teased.

He smiled. "I thought I'd look more professional on our first meeting if I wore my glasses and shirt. But I don't feel comfortable in them."

"Do you wrestle or box, Rudy? You've got a lot of muscles."

He did jobs for my father and other military officials, he told me, in addition to being a private security guard.

"You will be safe with me," he said in beautifully accented English. "I know all the martial arts, and I can take on a dozen men. I'm to go everywhere with you. I will sleep in the next room."

As he talked, Rudy impressed me even more. Pacing with a kingly air, he reminded me of a magnificent lion: sleek, muscular, proud, and graceful. His eyes were slanted and of a clear brown color. His lips were full and his skin was a burnished gold, enhanced with ivory tones. Black hair hung halfway to his shoulders. He had the build of a professional football player. His round pectorals were made even more voluptuous by thick nipples.

He came over to where I sat, knelt, and took my hand in his. It was so warm and smooth that an electric jolt shot through me.

"Think of me as your friend, Jason, not your keeper. Your father will be away a lot. I will try to take his place in some ways. I want you to enjoy your stay here."

It's impossible to convey how sensual, handsome, and dazzling he was at that first meeting. I was so overcome that I kissed him on the cheek. Rudy reddened slightly.

"That means we're friends, then?" he grinned.

"Sure does!" I laughed. "Let's go for a swim."

"Great idea. I'll go change."

When he returned, I was so dumbstruck, I would have whistled if I hadn't been speechless. Rudy was naked, except for a very brief thong of white cotton. I had a nearly unobstructed view of his smooth hips and his high, rounded buttocks. The light fabric enhanced his lustrous darkness and glorious form of his young body.

"Oh, my God," I said, "you look like Tarzan of the Jungle!"

Smiling, he went into some muscle-man poses for me. Then, holding out his hand, he took mine. "Let's go!"

In his battered jeep, Rudy drove us to a lagoon several miles away. It could have been the soundstage of an MGM movie about romance in the South Seas. I stood paralyzed for a moment, stunned by the beauty of this isolated tropical dreamscape. It was small, completely shrouded by thick palm trees and masses of white and yellow orchids, with a centerpiece of pure white sand speckled with seashells. Even the glittering green-purple water and sky full of pink-tinted clouds looked unreal, the creation of a master set designer.

"It's incredible, Rudy," I whispered.

"This is my secret place," he said quietly. "Only a few people have been here with me."

He walked to the edge of the water, but warned me about the sharks—and the stingrays *and* the devilfish. Naturally, I refused to go in. He laughed and, holding out his hand, told me to climb on his back.

"I won't let anything hurt you," he said, with a reassuring smile. He swam around the lagoon with me clinging to him. When we emerged, I lay down on the blanket and watched him, standing above me, drying off. His beautiful body rippled as he lay down beside me. The gauzy thong, still wet, molded itself even tighter around his hips and bulging crotch.

"It's chilly, Rudy."

"Move closer to me. I'm always warm."

I remembered my father's order that I obey my new chaperon. Drops of water glistened on his lustrous skin.

"You remind me so much of Valentino," I told him.

"That's why my mother called me Rudy." He raised himself on his elbow and looked at me even more intently.

"Your father told me about your homosexuality. He doesn't expect you to live like an old maid, so I promised to try to find some nice, decent men for you."

Startled by this revelation, I bolted up. "Am I, uh, hearing you correctly? Good God! I can't believe

240

what you just said! *My* father said *that?* And it doesn't bother you?"

Rudy didn't seem to be at all embarrassed. He just shrugged those massive shoulders. "Naw. I shouldn't have much trouble finding you men. There aren't that many young men who look like you in this region: slim, fair-skinned, with golden curls."

I snuggled closer to him. "Rudy, why not *you?* You're mature and strong…and beautiful."

He seemed to blush beneath his dark skin and looked away. "Not me. Stick to your sailor boys."

"Rudy, think about it. You wouldn't have to worry about getting me pregnant. Just stick it in, stir it around, and shoot."

His brown eyes watched as my fingers caressed one of his nipples, which hardened instantly into a thick nugget of pink. "What…what would you like to do with my body?"

My body. Those two words had the effect of an aphrodisiac. He *was* aware of the beauty of his splendid torso—and of its power over me. Instead of answering, I pressed my lips around his nipple and tongued it. His gasp was quiet, really just a short sharp intake of air. As my mouth moved downward to the succulent terrain of his rippled stomach, his body twitched slightly and his breathing grew harsher. His fingers helped mine in untying his thong so that it fell away from his hips, bringing to light his hidden treasure.

It was indeed a glorious treasure for anyone to behold, as if the light cloth were wrapped around it until the right worshiper came forward to pay it homage. Large testicles, the color of rosé wine, served as a velvet bed for the uncut penis to lie upon. His foreskin was unusually long, hanging nearly two inches over the bulbous tip. Gently, I pushed the

241

fleshy sock back to disclose a plum-shaped head: shiny, pink, and soft.

"Ah" he whimpered, "when the air hits my tip, that's when I feel really exposed."

In the wide slit was a larger bubble of sparkling natural lubricant. I dug my tongue deep into it, pushing it far down into the wide urethra. Rudy shuddered before I finally enveloped the organ with my mouth, then raised his hips slightly to push more of himself into my mouth. That wasn't hard to do. His penis, while firm, was still very malleable. It thickened only a little more before it suddenly began to pulsate as it squirted out large gushes of semen. It was a quick orgasm. When I raised my head, Rudy smiled.

"The first one's always quick. I kind of clean it out. Stay on it and I'll give you another."

In the next hour, I discovered Rudy was that rare phenomenon: a sexual partner who could achieve multiple orgasms with no hint of strain.

He turned over and presented me with his ass which, like the rest of him, was stunning in its smoothness and firmness. Parting his buttocks, I pushed my face deep into the cleft and rimmed him for what seemed like forever. Beneath my chin, his genitals began puffing up once more. Pulling his penis up between his thighs, I blew him in that position. He rewarded my efforts with another heaping mouthful of jizz.

He kissed me for a long time on that deserted stretch of beach. Military planes flew in the distance. Ships sat like metallic clouds on the horizon.

"Thousands of years before," Rudy whispered, "white gods came to this island. They did wonderful things for the people—and then they vanished. More white gods followed in later centuries, but like the others, they left quickly, never to return. Your father makes me think of one," Rudy explained. "He's warm and kind and people love him here. This morning I saw your beautiful bottom, your hair and your skin and I thought, *Jason is one, too.* But," he sighed, "white gods never stay long. You'll leave soon."

"I'll stay forever, Rudy, if I can stay with you," I said urgently.

"No, I'm going to America!" he cried out. "I'll become a movie star or dance in nightclubs."

On my knees, I crawled over sand to him and grasped his naked hips. He stood still, waiting for me to begin my ritual, throwing his head back as I began to suck him off again. As he ejaculated, I swallowed his essence and looked up at him.

If I'm a white god, I thought, *then he's a golden one!*

During my years of growing up, I rarely saw my father. He was always the dashing, handsome navy officer in a photograph on the mantel. When he was home, I knew him only as a stern disciplinarian.

Sometimes I overheard him and my late mother discussing me. It would always go something like this:

"It's pretty obvious, isn't it?... You see how he looks at your navy buddies? I caught him trying on dresses yesterday."

Yet he was never cruel to me. When we left Washington for Hawaii, something had softened between us. He knew what I was. Yet it didn't really bother him. I felt his bluster and displays of indignation were more for show than a heartfelt expression of his true feelings.

In our house in Aloha Heights, he was still a blur—a striking man in white who was literally living on the warships he commanded. Still, he clearly saw that Rudy and I were hitting it off very well. Strangely, this seemed to please him. He acted like a man who had had a heavy burden lifted off his shoulders.

One night, I walked him out onto the large balcony. Rudy insisted on doing the dishes, and as we heard him humming and whistling merrily, Dad looked at me.

"Are you staying out of trouble now?" he said with a smile.

I leaned over and kissed his cheek.

"And what did I do to deserve that?" he laughed.

"You gave me Rudy."

Dad always felt awkward when someone thanked him for anything but, after stuttering for a moment, he put his arm awkwardly around me. There was something serious he needed to talk to the two of us about, he said. Calling Rudy out of the kitchen, Dad informed us that the threat of war was growing worse every day. Although Washington still refused to listen to his fears, Dad had enough information to be certain that Japan was planning an attack on Pearl Harbor. It could be tomorrow or a month from now. He wanted us off the island when that happened. We were to make immediate plans to leave.

Within a week, we were booked to fly out of Hawaii on December 7, 1941. Rudy was overjoyed. At last his dream was coming true! He was going to America. My dad really *was* a white god!

The relationship between Rudy and me had far transcended that of two handsome men who enjoyed great sex together. He was so many things to me: the protective big brother I'd never had, a best friend, a substitute father who had more time to look after me. Only twenty-four, he acted like an older man one moment, an impish kid the next.

As our departure date drew nearer, we visited our

"White Lagoon" almost every day. It was like an enchanted place to us, and each time we would have passionate, uninhibited sex. We drove into Honolulu several times a week. Sometimes, we went at each other in the car, often having to pull over to the side of the road. It was great fun visiting Waikiki Beach and watching the attention both Rudy and I drew from the sex-hungry military men. My heart ached for them. I knew how lonely they were, these young guys far from their small towns and families, who knew that death could come at any moment. Yet Rudy and I never ran around on each other. At night, in his arms, he would softly croon the lullabies his Polynesian mother had sung to him.

Sometimes he'd murmur disturbingly, "Little white god, you'll leave me and never return."

"We'll always be together, Rudy," I assured him quietly and calmly.

He sighed that fate would find some way of separating us.

How well I can evoke that little bedroom of ours—the bed with the white spread, curtains billowing through the night, and Rudy lying there, naked and glorious, beckoning me to join him.

"If you love me, you'll come to me," he would say.

All my bedrooms since then have looked like that one.

Some nights we joined Daddy aboard the ship to watch the Hollywood films flown in, both the latest and the golden oldies, like *Dark Victory, Alexander's Ragtime Band,* and *Grand Hotel.* After the movie, they would play toe-tapping swing music over the loudspeaker. Several of the guys leaped up and began jitterbugging with each other.

One blond hunk grabbed me and whooped, "Come on, Blondie, let's shake a leg!" We brought

245

the house down with our wild dance, and even Daddy and Rudy hollered and stomped their feet with the rest of the crowd.

After Thanksgiving, we watched them string up Christmas lights both in downtown Honolulu and aboard the warships. Rudy found us a fir tree, and we decorated it with popcorn.

After I showed him how to wrap yuletide gifts, he went out one day and brought back a gift which he refused to let me see. I had to wait until the morning of our departure. I bought him a beautiful coral necklace in an old curio shop. He kept trying to sneak looks at it as I wrapped it, and we ended up wrestling all over the living-room floor. At night, I snuggled in his arms and read to him from *Gone with the Wind*. He wept so much at the end, he had to go into the bathroom and compose himself.

Each day, war moved closer. We heard about it on the radio, read about it in the paper, and saw it in the newsreels.

Then the drills began.

On our last night in Hawaii, we cooked a huge feast. Dad joined us. We put on suits and ties, and Rudy made some kind of cocktail he called a "Volcano," which nearly blew our brains out. Afterward, he insisted I leave the dishes to him and spend some time with my father.

"Go to your father," he urged me. "He's alone and he needs you."

Dad did look sad and haggard. During the past few weeks, he had lost weight, and lines had formed around his eyes and mouth. When I joined him on the balcony, he put his arm around me and together we looked down at the seascape below us. All the ships were lit up more brilliantly than any tree in town. Christmas carols from their sound systems echoed around us eerily.

"All those thousands of young men down there," Dad sighed. "They haven't even had a chance to live yet." He turned to me and hugged me to him. "You love Rudy, don't you?" he whispered.

"I love him almost as much as I love you, Dad," I answered truthfully.

He pressed my face against his shoulder and kissed the top of my head. "I'm glad to hear that, because he worships you."

I looked up at him. "Tell me, something, Dad. It really doesn't matter since we're leaving tomorrow. It's just that it might be a long time until I see you again. But...were you and Rudy lovers before I came here?"

He looked away and his smile was sad. "Yes, we were," he said, nodding. "For a year. But when you came along, I *hoped* it would end like this. Understand something, son—he *liked* me, he *loves* you."

I buried my face in my father's chest. "Dad, how I wish we could have been friends before now. All those years..."

As he got behind the wheel of his Jeep, Dad took my face between his hands and kissed me.

"Good-bye. I'll try to stop by for breakfast tomorrow morning. Around eight. But if not..." Suddenly he embraced me tightly. "I'm proud of you, son. You've always been your own man, and sometimes that takes more courage than being on a battlefield."

I wept for a long time in Rudy's strong arms that night—at the thoughts of leaving Hawaii, of Dad not returning from this war. Rudy pushed his soft, warm penis into my hand.

"Put it into your mouth," he coaxed. "It'll make you feel better. Feel how warm and smooth it is? Get down between my thighs. I want you to enjoy your last night here."

He rolled down his foreskin for me so that his tip was waiting for me, taut and hot. I felt his penis thicken a little, then surge, as it continued swelling up between my handling and my sucking. In just a few minutes, Rudy gifted me with his first orgasm of the night. I blew him again until I felt his cock growing stronger. Once more it shook as it shot its load down my throat.

I dozed off in Rudy's arms, only to awaken when I felt my golden god pushing the tip of his cock up against my bottom. He fucked me steadily and passionately, and I was grateful for his dedication to making my last night in Hawaii a memorable one.

The next morning, I saw Rudy hop behind the wheel of his Jeep, wearing only his green thong.

"I'm getting the Sunday papers!" he called.

As he sped off, I yelled, "Hurry back! Dad might be here any minute!"

It was seven-thirty and for once, the constant noise from the harbor below was stilled. It was Sunday. Everyone, including the young navy men, was entitled to their one day of sleeping late. The radio was blaring a new swing tune.

Coffee in hand, I jitterbugged out to the balcony. I stopped abruptly. Suddenly, on the horizon, a plane appeared. I watched as it flew low—so *very* low—over Pearl Harbor. Planes were always flying close to the water, but this one had a strange yellow symbol on the underside of its wing. A metallic object fell from the craft directly above the biggest ship in the fleet, the *Arizona*—the one Dad was on. The ground shook, and I was knocked to the floor. More of these strange planes filled the sky and they were depositing bombs like giant prehistoric birds dropping eggs. Columns of black smoke went up clear to the sky. Bullets were answering the attack now, and I could hear men screaming and cursing.

I ran out to the road. Racing by me was my neighbor, Mrs. Stivers, her robe flying open and her children stumbling behind her. "It's war!" she shrieked. "War! The Japs are here!"

Where was Rudy?

As I ran behind her, I saw Rudy far down the road, crouched over the wheel of his Jeep as he headed toward me. Directly behind him, a Japanese plane was flying so low it nearly sheared the treetops.

"Rudy! Rudy!" I screamed. "Look out! Get off the road!"

All around him, gunfire strafed the ground. Then he fell forward on the wheel as his body was jerked violently by a fusillade of bullets. The Jeep burst into flames. My neighbor and her children were doing a convulsive dance of death as they, too, were rained with bullets. I dived into a ditch just as the plane dropped one more bomb and flew away serenely.

I could put it off no longer.

Nearly fifty years had passed since I left Pearl Harbor. I *had* to return, to exorcise all the bitterness and sadness that had shadowed my life since leaving there at the end of 1941. So, three months ago, I went back.

In the new Arizona Memorial Visitors Center, built in tribute to the largest warship that was destroyed that day, I watched a twenty-minute film depicting the events of the day that would forever "live in infamy." Two thousand, three hundred and thirty-four American servicemen died for their coun-

249

try in the shower of bombs that began World War II for the United States.

A guide pointed out the grave of the sunken battleship *Arizona* to me. In its watery hulk, 1,102 servicemen are still entombed. My father is among them. Rumor had it that he was last seen on deck firing a machine gun at the enemy.

Later, I drove along the nearby Kamehameha Highway to find the community of Aloha Heights, where I had lived those few months. There was nothing left, as if everything else had been blasted away along with Rudy on that fateful morning.

As wind stirred the ferns and tall grasses on the hillside, the memories rushed back. I thought first of the "White Lagoon" flush with orchids. *Was it still there?* Then my cherished image of a handsome man in a white uniform, staring down at the harbor, his arm around me.

"Good-bye," my father had said.

All around me, the wind blew harder, as if ghosts were trying to speak. "White gods never stay long," Rudy had told me.

Slowly, I walked to my car and drove away. Like Rudy's white gods, I would never return.

DANCE WITH THE DEVIL

The door to my dressing room burst open.

Towering there, like a six-foot-five version of Rambo, was Serge. He made a dramatic sight with his big head lowered, those green eyes glaring up at me, and his fists grasping the door frame like Samson preparing to tear down the temple columns.

He was naked, except for a belt of gold around his narrow waist. A swatch of silk fluttered over his impressive genitalia. The covering failed to hide the low-hanging testicles or the circumcised tip of his famous penis. Behind him fluttered another wisp of cloth. It did nothing to cover the cleft of his beautifully mounded buttocks. A gold bracelet, shaped like a serpent, coiled up his powerful arm.

Square, swarthy, and arrogant, his Slavic face was half-concealed by a thick beard and mustache. A cascade of jet curls were bound around his head by a gleaming band of copper.

"Out!" he shouted to David, my dresser, and to Tina, who was helping me with my complicated makeup. *"Out! Out! Out!"* he screamed, and swept a stack of books and photographs of me to the floor. Fearfully, they obeyed, for it was obvious that the fiery Serge—founder and star performer of the famous Stanowslavski Dance Troupe—was experiencing one of his notorious temper tantrums.

"Wow!" I drawled. "You're in a wonderful mood tonight, sweetie-pie." In the mirror, I pretended to ignore him as he crept slowly toward me, half-crouched, like a Roman gladiator ready to destroy an enemy. And I had certainly done much to displease the mighty Serge.

Although I seemed calm, my fingers trembled as they dipped a brush into gold paint and drew a line from my eyes to my temple. Serge was so fucking *big!* His musculature was the envy of bodybuilders everywhere. In fact, he had been featured on the cover of *Muscle Builder* magazine to confirm the theory that male dancers were often in better condition than many physique beauties.

I could feel his body heat as he came nearer. I just continued applying gold paint to my other eye and temple when, suddenly, he knocked the brush from my hand, yanked me from my seat, and whirled me around to face him.

With one savage jerk, he stripped off my robe. Like him, I was naked, too, except for the swaths of transparent material which merely made a mockery of protecting my modesty. Serge had always said that there was no place for modesty in his dance company.

We were the solo performers in the upcoming

252

sequence, *War*. It had already been hailed as the most controversial dance ever performed in America. Serge and I represented two nations.

In the number, we meet, become friends, and then sweethearts. However, we argue and then he kills me. Before dying, I strip away his almost-nonexistent costume, leaving him completely naked. Picking me up and holding me high over his head, my killer then stalks off the stage.

War might just as well describe our own relationship. It, too, was the talk of the dance world. We had loved, fought constantly, and made up passionately. And now I thought he *would* kill me as he shook me furiously, as though I were nothing but a rag doll.

"What was Andy doing here again tonight?" he demanded in his heavily accented voice. "You will *not* make that movie for him. Is that clear? You will stay with me—Serge Stanowslavski! You're on the verge of becoming a great dancer! If you disobey, Serge will tear you into a million leetle pieces like—."

"Serge, will you fuck off!" I shouted above his roar. I knew a crowd stood outside our door, listening to every word, but I wanted them to know where I stood. "We've gone through this a million times! Tonight is my last show! I've told you that and told you that and—"

Suddenly I broke down. For six months I had virtually been in the middle of a "war zone"—pulled violently in opposite directions by both Serge and Andy Pulver, the Hollywood producer.

"Shhhh!" Serge whispered gently. "Clear your mind now, my sweet golden kitten. Look at me! *Look!*"

When I did, his jade eyes glowed. He kissed me on the forehead and nose. Then he began to talk to me

253

the way he always did before we performed an unusually difficult piece.

"Think of nothing, not even the movie," he began. "Imagine you're running from the devil—"

"That shouldn't be hard to do," I smiled.

He raised a hand, as if to strike me. "Shall I kill you now or on-stage? When you dance, think of all the demons in your life trying to catch up with you. Dance fast tonight, my little bear, for the devil can dance even faster!"

"Ten minutes, gentlemen!" a voice called from just beyond the door.

Serge kissed me again, half lifting me up with his big arms, for I stood at only five-foot-three. I might have been a twelve-year-old boy in Serge's arms instead of a twenty-one-year-old man. In the mirror, I glimpsed us. He was dark and saturnine and could have been the devil himself at that moment with his flashing eyes and seductive smile. His thick penis hung visibly beneath the panel of cloth. It looked dark, powerful, and threatening—just like its owner.

I, on the other hand, was white-skinned, with glowing curls of gold and eyes that were big and blue, a perfect contrast. "The new Baryshnikov," they were calling me.

When he put me down, I still clung to his formidable torso. He felt so solid, so warm and strong! "Serge, I can't go out there tonight! I'm scared shitless!"

His sudden slap shocked me. Stooping down to my level, he grasped my face. "Don't ever say that! You will dance tonight as you never have before! Hundreds have been turned away from the box office. The cream of New York's elite is sitting out there tonight. Dance, dance, so even the devil can't catch you tonight!"

Taking my hand, he led me out to my place in the

wings, facing the set of *War*. There was only a huge moon, some gray boulders. Soon two figures would be dancing in a fury across that sparseness.

Serge took his place on the opposite side of the stage, facing me. The woodwinds began their low, mournful sigh. Serge nodded to me. We began to walk toward each other stiffly, with our heads and shoulders thrown back. There were gasps from the audience at the sight of two stunning examples of manhood, almost nude—one of them white and gold, the other dark and glowering. Few in the audience that night would ever forget what they saw. Serge would see to that.

As we began to dance, I threw myself passionately into my role of the "naïve" country boy. And how aptly that particular adjective might describe me—especially when Serge first discovered me that winters morning a year ago.

The male dancers at Madame Le Boc's School of Ballet were wild with excitement. Our guest instructor that week was to be none other than the great Serge Stanowslavski. Rumor had it that he was seeking a performer to groom personally as the star of his exciting new troupe which had shaken up the dance world.

Already, critics hailed him as the third "Serge" which Russia had given to the dance world. The first, of course, had been Serge Diaghilev who, along with his *Ballets Russes* company, had scandalized the civilized world during the early twentieth century. I, personally, had always identified with Diaghilev's young lover, Vaslav Nijinsky, who many believed to have been the greatest dancer who ever lived. Then there was Serge Lifar, whose radical and sensual approach to ballet in the Roaring Twenties created a tremendous uproar.

255

And now there was this latest Serge, who had defected from Russia three years before. I had read the *People* magazine spread: "Russia's Sexy Gift to the Dance World!" He had posed in a brief black bikini with his Russian wolfhounds. He could have played Hercules—which he had done—in the nude, along with a transparent pouch that contained his heavy genitals. He adored to shock, to excite, and to arouse controversy. Nudity was prominent through-out all of the programs of his avant-garde dance troupe, which combined elements of both New Wave and the classical schools. "Dancers can perform much better if they wear nothing," he explained, dis-missing all criticism.

Suddenly, into that drab gray dance hall he appeared, like a magnificent animal bursting with life and sensuality. We were all properly stunned. Most of us twelve students were small, or of medium height.

In pink tights and a sleeveless green T-shirt, he stood before us like a giant stepping from the pages of a Russian folktale. His crotch looked as though he had stuffed a softball into it. When he moved, it jig-gled to an alarming degree. His famous derriere fasci-nated us, too. It was so high and perfectly rounded that it reminded me of what two basketballs would look like if they were joined together.

After introducing himself, and thoroughly mes-merizing us with his charm, he declared, "Let's go to work." And work we did, all of us hungrily desperate to please him.

During a break, I found him alone in the hallway, gulping down water. With a paper cup in my hand, I went up to him. His dark-green ocean-hued eyes studied me boldly and with sharp interest. I smiled up at him.

"You're so big—and so strong, Serge!" I blurted out.

He went into some muscle-man poses, smiling slightly at me as he flexed his enormous muscles while watching me. "I'm glad they impress you."

"Is it true?" I asked mysteriously.

"Possibly," he said softly. "What is it you want to know, leetle Goldilocks?"

"I—I heard you can balance a cup of water on your buttocks. Can you really do that?"

He snorted, his eyes dancing with amusement, and then he turned around. "Try it, Goldilocks." The thin tights hugged his spectacular rear end like oil. He tensed his dimples, and then I ever so carefully set the cup of water on his left cheek. The cup stayed there.

"Well?" he grinned, as I removed it.

"You're a man of many gifts."

"Are you stopping there? Don't you have any imagination? Give me your cup. Let me show you something else the great Serge can do." In astonishment, I watched him lean backwards slightly and place the cup on top of his prominent crotch. The cup remained there. Laughing, he straightened up and told me to go back to class. But I could feel his gaze, following me.

At the end of that day, I was undressing in the locker room with the other boys when Serge entered. He was completely naked—a vision the like of which none of us had ever beheld before.

We were used to seeing trim, nicely proportioned torsos with average genitalia. But Serge! His pecs billowed out like olive-toned balloons. Each was capped by a nipple which was rigid and red. His stomach rippled with a fascinating display of ridges and indentations, flaring out slightly at the hips. He was known to detest body hair and was shaven so closely that even his pubic area glowed lustrous and

257

smooth. And sprouting out from his hips like a tanned banana was his much-talked-about cock. It had been flashed around on stages before thousands of theatergoers—but never enough to permit anyone to become too familiar with it.

He held before him his green T-shirt. As he squeezed it, a puddle of perspiration formed at his feet. *"You have not worked*—until you can do this," he said, in his deep, musical voice.

Most of us, however, were spellbound by his sex organ. The thick stalk of his penis tapered into numerous folds of moist flesh before becoming that round, naked tip. Shorn of its foreskin, the head was broad and slightly oval, like a luscious pink mushroom. Behind it hung two enormous testicles which made me think of two potatoes hanging in a thin sack of reddish silk. Seeing where all our eyes were directed, Serge smiled wickedly.

Grasping his penis with his fist, he suddenly slammed it down so hard on the edge of the dressing table that the tip bounced up like a rubber ball.

"And you aren't a man until you can do *that!*" he mocked.

This man certainly knew how to make an exit. None of us could speak, for we were watching him breathlessly as he strode out of the room. His organ was obviously thicker than it had been when it entered, now swinging heavily from left to right, just as his buttocks did.

I sank down onto the bench and studied the wet spot on the floor, left by his sweat. Here, truly, was the man of my dreams—and I vowed I was going to have him.

It was the last day of class. The other students had already left in dejection. Most had fallen violently in love with Serge. He knew this and drove them—and myself—mad. He taunted us with his stunning physique, even holding us close to him as he guided one of us through a difficult exercise. He could be cruel and tender, sullen or stormy, warm or cold. In other words, he was the type of complex genius who fascinates, if only because one never knew what to expect from him.

I was determined not to leave school that evening without letting Serge know how I felt about him. My friends constantly warned me about always being so candid and frank with others about my feelings—but that was how I was. I knew I would never see him again. I had nothing to lose.

"Well, well well," a deep voice boomed behind me. "My leetle Goldilocks is still here."

Serge had come up silently behind me. I turned slowly, to see him stripping off his old T-shirt. "I am glad you stayed," he added quietly.

"There is something I wanted to discuss with you."

I could barely speak from my nervousness and excitement. "Yes, Serge, there is something I must say, too."

His eyes sparkled, and his smile was warm. He *knew* what it was that I wanted to say. Yet, he played the naïve game. "Oh? Well, let us go into my office, Golden Boy, my blue-eyed kitten, and we can talk."

For a week, he had used all kinds of comical, affectionate names for some of us students. For me, he had many names: 'Goldilocks...Golden Kitten...Leetle Bear...Candy Child...Leetle Sweetie-pie."

My heart beat faster as I watched him lock the door and then remove a huge bottle of vodka from the windowsill where it had been chilling. He filled up two big crystal goblets and handed me one.

"Drink it!" he demanded. "All of it!"

"Serge, I've—I've never drunk vodka before."

"Drink it!" he shouted. "I don't want anemic zombies in my dance troupe! I want artists who have lived, suffered, who've gotten drunk and fucked and puked and done all the things real people—real men—do!"

"*Your troupe?* You mean, I—"

He smiled and watched me swallow a big mouthful of the liquor. I coughed, but then immediately I felt a bolt of flame racing through my veins, hitting my head and making it warm and glowing. I swallowed more as he finished his own drink off and poured himself another.

Through a richly colored haze, I watched him put his drink down and begin peeling off his pink tights. Then, naked, he sat down on the edge of his desk.

"Come closer, my pretty faun," he requested. "Let me see if you're the right person to join my troupe. I said to come closer—like *this!*"

His strong arms grabbed me and pulled me against his chest. His thighs were clamped tightly on either side of me. "Does this bother you?" he whispered. "For a naked man to hold you like this? In my company, you'll be doing this a lot, and even more things."

The alcohol coated my brain to some degree, but I was still lucid when I replied, "It feels wonderful, Serge. Especially when the man doing it is you."

He took my hand and guided it over his pectorals, his nipples, his stomach, and finally down to his thickening penis. "Could you caress me like this—onstage—in front of thousands of people?"

Nodding my head, I pressed my lips against his. With a deep moan, he hugged me tighter against him and laid me down gently on the floor. Quickly, he stripped off my tights. And then, without further ado, he began to make love to me—wildly passionate love. There had been men in my life, but none could have ever come close to the performance of this "Russian bull." Just as he used his body as an instrument for art, so did he now use it as an instrument for sexual expression.

My lips traveled over his luscious terrain of flesh and muscle, licking the surface of his lustrous skin. He squirmed as I sucked hard on his succulent nipples, biting them roughly, twisting them around in my fingers like rubber balls. When I kissed his stomach, it sank in suddenly, like a deep, fleshy bowl. Finally I swallowed the tip of his stiff penis, licking it, savoring it, sucking on the tip, with my tongue digging deep into the wet slit.

For several minutes, as he writhed and groaned I fellated him relentlessly until I felt the stiff organ pulsate. It squirted out an astonishing abundance of sperm, causing his testicles to contract to fig-sized balls. Even before his phallus ceased to throb. I was blowing him once more, this time pressing my mouth all the way down to his smooth pubes.

On that hard, grimy floor, he gave me the most extraordinary fuck of my life. I had never liked to be screwed ever since a black man had fucked me when I was in high school and tore me. When Serge began to slide himself up into me, though, he did it so skillfully that it felt like paradise.

Frantically, he continued kissing me and fucking me. After a brief break, I buried my face between his smooth buttocks. Moist, fragrant, and deep, his cleft was to become my favorite place for hiding my face in the days to come. His rectum throbbed. When my tongue shot up into it. I sucked him off once more as well, marveling at the resiliency of his dark cock—the way I could bend it, double it in two, pull on it, and

261

how it never seemed to bother him. While I played with it, he began to talk to me.

I was to join his troupe. My talent was extraordinary but, equally important, I had blazing beauty—gold, white, and blue—the type the media would go crazy about. I *could* be another Nijinsky.

"And you'll be my Diaghilev," I whispered as he pushed the tip of his penis up into my rectum again.

He grunted before answering, "I'll be anything you want me to be—your bull, your stud, your lover, teacher, father, brother. Just promise to be as great as I think you are."

Within a year, the dance world was saying just that.

My life underwent a radical transformation once Serge took it over. First, he moved me into his brownstone town house in Manhattan. We were to live as a married couple, faithful to each other, "joined together by genius and beauty," he exclaimed, without a shred of modesty.

And when I joined his troupe, I became immersed in a swirling, teeming world of talent, jealousy, sexual obsession, and a passion to please Serge which bordered on madness. Unfortunately, my new "husband" was the focal point of the erotic fantasies of all the gay guys in our group. Only three out of the twelve were either married or had girlfriends.

To his worshipers, he was their father, their brother, their fantasy hunk and, before I had arrived, their lover. Since he absolutely forbade promiscuity in any of us, he dealt with the problem in his own blunt way. Just as most Russian villages of old had boasted of having a single stud who would visit all the lonely women while their husbands were away for months hunting or fighting wars, so did Serge now apply this principle to his dancers. He had blithely designated himself the personal "stud" for the gay men in our company.

I was outraged at his duplicity and let him know so. If I was to be faithful to him, then I expected the same from him. His rugged face looked confused while he heard me out.

"But, Jason, my leetle Candy Boy," he said, in that low voice I loved to hear, "I am doing them a favor. No one has to worry about diseases. I am so safe they could eat off my body and not catch a cold."

Finally he agreed to my stand. And what did he do to prove it? He brought in his handsome cousin, Ivan, a truck driver in Brighton Beach, twice a week. Balding, but husky and charming, Ivan became an instant hit, and the boys finally kept their hands off my Serge.

But both Serge and Ivan had *more* than enough to go around.

With Serge at the helm, my career got off to a blazing start. He insisted that I be his partner in a brief rendition of *Afternoon of a Faun* for a PBS special on dance. Wearing only fancied-up jockstraps, we made an electrifying impression on viewers. Some had seen Serge before, but I was still completely new. Many reviewers lavished me with praise, commenting on my "gold curls and blue eyes and perfectly proportioned body."

Immediately after this, we signed up for an important segment in HBO's television documentary, "Dance World," which emphasized new trends in dance. Once more, we stunned viewers, this time with our audacious take-off of that famous sequence from the film, *Singing in the Rain,* in which Cyd Charisse tries to seduce a wide-eyed Gene Kelly.

In our version, I wore nothing but green tights and

assumed the Charisse role. Serge was attired first in an ugly, wrinkled suit, but I quickly stripped this down to a very abbreviated loincloth. As one magazine wrote later, we "burned up TV tubes across America." It was done with such good humor and taste, however, that no one complained about the gay connotation. Besides, Serge was so fucking butch looking that the possibility of his being homosexual was unthinkable to Middle America.

Offers from Hollywood began to flood in. Serge threw them all into the trash can. "We will not be ruined by drug addicts and their money," Serge explained to me.

I was soaking in the tub one night, exhausted from a day of rehearsals. Our troupe was to open its new show in three months. Much was riding on this production. Serge wanted to cement, once and for all, his place at the top of the dance world. He was determined to dazzle, shock, and create controversy with his new numbers. He even mulled over the idea of having me actually blow him on stage in one sultry skit, but I told him quickly that it was too fucking much—even for New York sophisticates.

"Hollywood just called," Serge said as he came into the bathroom. Wearing only his usual pair of black bikini briefs, he peeled them off and slid into the tub with me. "Andy Pulver, the big-shot movie producer, has the hots for you; he wants to meet you."

Serge sat facing me as I ran the bar of green apple soap over his spellbinding chest. I rubbed his nipples, startled, as always, as to how big and stiff they could grow. "You told him, of course, that I would be thrilled to meet him and become a movie star?"

My master and husband lifted me easily onto his

264

lap. Then he began working the tip of his penis up into my rectum. As I felt it pop in, I cried out and grabbed Serge's neck. He rubbed his face against mine and then kissed me as he continued to slide the rubbery stalk up, up into me, until I felt his testicles pressing against the outside of my buttocks.

"I told Andy Pulver to fuck off," Serge muttered. "You still have lots to learn."

Serge was slow-fucking me, raising my hips until his penis tip nearly popped out, before lowering me again over its blue-toned length.

"I want to be another Garbo, Monroe, Valentino. I want fame and—"

"Destruction," Serge finished darkly. "Trust me, leetle slut. Serge knows what is best for us both."

I sighed, caressed his bulging muscles, kissed him, and then heard him whimper as the bulbous tip of his organ finally erupted—unleashing within me enough Slavic cream to satisfy an entire troupe of dancers.

Serge believed that if people worked hard, then they should play hard, too. Friday night was our night to "howl." Immediately after rehearsals, all of us hopped into taxis and sped toward Leo's, a large bar in Greenwich Village which catered to dancers. Straights and gays both went there, and nothing was considered too shocking.

You might find yourself dancing with a hunky male stripper from the Gaiety Burlesque or an arrogant beauty from "Solid Gold." Serge was always the center of attention. After guzzling down nearly a bottle of 100-proof vodka, you could count on him to do the outrageous. With little prodding, he usually stripped down to his black bikini. And usually that came off a dozen or more times before we left.

One night, he and I both brought the house down

265

by doing a slow, sensuous striptease to Marvin Gaye's classic, "I Heard It Through the Grapevine." Holding our briefs in front of our privates, we gave our asses one last shake before everyone began screaming for more. I noticed one man, in particular, who kept his eyes on me throughout the entire routine. With short-cropped hair, polished white teeth, and blue eyes, he cut quite a figure. As he studied me, he kept pushing his glasses back on his nose.

Dying of thirst, I rushed to the bar. A huge margarita was pushed over to me. "Compliments of your admirer," smiled Tony, the bartender. The stranger came over to me. He was husky and pleasant looking in a middleman way.

"I'm a fan of yours." He smiled warmly. "My name's Andy Pulver. I make movies. In fact, I'd like you to star in one that I'm currently planning. Can we meet for lunch and talk?"

Since I followed the gossip columns regularly, I recognized the name of Andy Pulver immediately, as he was often mentioned in them. I also, of course, remembered Serge's talking about him. Once called the successor to David O. Selznick, his stream of box-office hits was extraordinary. But then something had gone wrong. His last four movies were bombs. I had seen one, *Kiss Me Again,* and could understand nothing about it. "Drugs," people had whispered after the film's failure. Apparently, he hired only people who would snort cocaine with him. From the cameramen to the script girls, his sets were supposed to be a drug pusher's dream.

I thought of that as I ate the meal he had served to us in his dazzling penthouse suite at the Helmsley Palace in midtown Manhattan. Steak, caviar, vegetables, and plenty of champagne. His charm was bold and warm, and the way he kept studying me with those strange blue eyes had me infatuated. He kept going to the bathroom, though, and when he came back, his nose was pinker than before and his eyes more glittering. I forgot that for a moment when he told me that he could pay me $100,000 to star in *The Town That Danced*.

I could hardly believe that incredible figure! I could live on that for the rest of my life! In a daze, I heard him outline the movie's plot: A famous ballet dancer returns to his small hometown to care for his ailing father. Growing bored, he starts a dance school. At first, the townspeople regard this venture like the plague. Soon, however, people begin to join and...

"It doesn't sound very believable," I said frankly.

"Look at *Flashdance*. It was totally unbelievable. It made a fortune, though. Look, Jason, I've got to make this movie a hit! You could make it happen—I saw you in those TV specials. You have great charisma. Say yes, and I'll have half the money put into your account tomorrow and the rest deposited at the completion of the film."

I finally agreed to make the movie, but only after I had finished my three-month run of Serge's all-important production of *Men*.

For those lucky enough to obtain seats to the opening night of *Men*, it was an experience they talk about even today. Everyone, from viewers to critics, was knocked out by the dazzling explosion of energy that filled the auditorium for three hours. Utilizing bold musical selections, from heavy metal to rock to gospel, we put on a show that intoxicated even us.

And the climax to the show always came with the controversial vignette, *War*, which showcased Serge

267

and me as a duet. A few patrons carped about Serge's total nudity, especially when sometimes it looked as if he was sexually aroused, but most were delighted.

Each night from there on, we began to play a game. I would skip ahead of Serge as we walked home along Fifth Avenue, and shout, "If you're the devil, then try to catch me!" Laughing, he would tear after me as we raced up the nearly deserted sidewalk. And when he caught me, he would grab me and throw me up into the air and catch me. "You'll never escape this devil," he would smile, kissing me boldly on the mouth.

"Nor would I want to," I would happily reply, and then I'd put my arm around his waist, and we would return to our snug home. Always hovering over me was that terrible cloud, though—of telling Serge about the movie. And the night I did, his rage was indeed terrifying. He tore up the furniture in our den, ripping apart antique pillows, magazines, and throwing vases through the windows. No one had warned me that Russian geniuses showed their anger in ways that differed from the rest of us.

I would *not* make that movie, he bellowed. Andy Pulver was a worse drug addict now than before. The film would bomb and destroy all the prestige I had so carefully established, and he had honed so carefully.

"You can't leave me," Serge said quietly, pulling me to him and kissing me. "You're my good-luck charm. Since you came to live with me, things have never been better."

"Serge, it's only for four or five months!" I protested. "As soon as I finish the film, I'll return and—"

"No one ever leaves Serge and comes back!" he screamed. "When you go, you're gone for good. Now, forget about the movie. It doesn't exist."

And so on that final night of our record-breaking show, Serge carried me off the stage for what was to be the last time. We put on our black robes and began to make our bows with the rest of the company. Up and down the curtain went; people were screaming and yelling their feelings for us. "Bravo! Bravo!"

Remember this, something told me, *for it may never happen again.*

In my dressing room, I was furious to find Andy Pulver sitting at my dressing table. His face was like wax—white and taut—and he grinned stupidly as he stared at the floor.

"Great!" he babbled. "Simply great!" He was so zonked out on drugs, he didn't even know what he was doing. I tried to ignore him as I finished dressing and began putting my personal things into my duffel. The door opened. Serge stood there, looking incredibly magnificent in his great Russian trench coat with the black fur collar. A wide-brimmed hat was cocked jauntily over his left eye. A black cigarillo was clenched between his perfect white teeth.

His green eyes went from the slack-jawed Andy and then back to me. His voice was low and sad when he said finally, "So long, leetle golden butterfly. Enjoy the big time. The devil's got you at last."

"Serge, wait; don't go like this. I—" I sprang from my seat, but he had already turned and slipped quickly out the stage door.

For a moment, I sat there at my dressing table. Andy was fumbling around in his pockets until he brought forth a small golden box and a matching spoon. The white powder spilled on the tabletop as he tried desperately to pour some onto the spoon. When that failed, he mashed his nostrils down to snort it up. *This is the man who will be handling my future,* I thought sadly.

269

I grabbed my coat from the chair and ran out of the room.

Dense fog coated the alleyway like white velvet, yet I could make out Serge's big figure as he waited at the curb for a taxi.

"Serge! Wait, wait for me!"

As I rushed up to him, he looked down at me. "Well?" he asked quietly. Sometimes action acted more effectively on Serge than words. As if I were back on-stage, I suddenly caressed his face with my hands, exactly as I did in *War*. Then I backed away and began to dance in front of him.

"If you're the devil, then try to catch me!" Running and whirling about, I waited anxiously, my heart beating faster, for his reaction. Had I destroyed everything? Suddenly he stiffened; then he bowed, and he began quickly to chase me down the block, laughing. And then he caught me, embraced me and suddenly lifted me high over his head.

After lowering me, he hugged me tight. "You'll never escape this devil again," he whispered.

"Nor will I want to." I laughed. "Come on, lover, Let's go home!"

THE BULL OF THE BLUE RIDGE MOUNTAINS

His naked body strained, as he pulled me up with him along the steep mountainside. Grunting, crying out with each lunge, he was gradually taking us through the snow, higher, to safety. Around us screamed the wind. Beneath us were our abandoned cars. Around us was death, if we did not reach the top.

I could no longer hold onto him. My hands slipped from his powerful neck and shoulders. I grabbed for his waist—even his genitals—as he held out a hand for me and shouted my name. But already I was falling back into the blizzard.

I awoke violently, as always.

Outside my cottage beats the soothing lapping of the waves. It is fall now. Two hundred miles away, he sleeps somewhere in the Blue Ridge Mountains. Pouring myself a glass of chilled Chablis, I watch the sky turn pink and silver and wonder: Does he ever think of that day and night when he showed me a side of him no one else will ever know? Since he is much like the mountains, he will guard our secret well.

Snow was already falling, as I drove along that mountain road last February. Forecasters were predicting a major blizzard, but I had to get home to my beach cottage on the North Carolina coast. Paul would be waiting, for that night we would celebrate our fourth year of being together. I had been visiting my favorite sister and her husband, who had turned their farm into a famous mountain restaurant, and they had loaded my trunk with vegetables, freshly baked breads, homemade soups, wines, pies, and fried chicken. I had also brought several bottles of liquor, for Paul and I were having several of our favorite friends over to help us celebrate.

The wind was heavier and the snow was becoming thicker. I was relieved to see ahead of me the welcome sight of blue revolving lights on a state trooper's car in the middle of the road. When I stopped, a husky figure hurried up to my window.

"What're you doin' out here, buddy?" he bellowed above the wind. "Ain't you been listenin' to the blizzard warnings? Git on up to the Delmar Motel jest ahead. It's gonna be a bastard! Move!"

I needed no prodding, for the storm was gathering force. But, as I drove on, I could no longer see the road—and didn't even know if I had yet come to the motel or passed it. Before me was a steep incline. As I started up it, my car suddenly slid, and the rear portion was instantly slung over into the ditch. I jumped out, saw it was hopeless, and was beginning to panic, when once again I saw those beautiful revolving lights of a trooper car approaching me. I waved it down and leaped into the front seat. It was the same young officer, and he looked anything but glad to see me.

"What the fuck you doin' out here? Didn't I tell you to go to the Delmar Mo—"

His words stopped short as his vehicle, too, began to spin. Like mine, it careened into the ditch. Cursing and smashing his fist against the wheel, he grabbed his car-radio transmitter—there was nothing but static.

"Come on!" he yelled, jumping out. "We got to git outta here fast, or we'll freeze! There's a cabin up thataway—come on, dammit!"

He leapt across the ditch and began climbing up the steep incline of the mountainside. I tried to follow him, but as he climbed higher, I kept sliding and falling back. Suddenly a big arm wrapped around me and I could hear my rescuer's voice above the wind.

"Hold onto me!"

I grabbed his waist and neck, and he began to pull us both higher. Like an animal determined not to die, he cried out and wept with rage and cussed—but against the screaming wind and the avalanche of snow, he moved steadily for another half-hour, never letting me go. At last, he paused and let out a whoop.

"We made it! It's okay! The cabin's still there!"

Before us was a small two-story log cabin. We hurried up to it, but the door was barred by a padlock. My Lochinvar smashed it away with his gun butt, then with his big body, easily pushed it open. Inside, it was like a freezer, but furnished comfortably.

"Sit down on the sofa and stay outta my way! I'll handle this." The trooper quickly checked the large oil circulator and chortled to find some oil still left in a can. After he got a fire going, he began piling huge logs onto the hearth. Soon a roaring fire was driving

273

away the chill. Then my protector lit a cigarette and glared at me, shivering on the sofa.

"My name's Rick," he snarled. His eyes snapped angrily as he continued, "I oughtta be whuppin' that butt of yours up and down the Blue Ridge. If I hadn't had to stop for you, I could've made it home to my wife and two li'l kids. Now, I don't know if we're gonna make it through the night."

I was too numb from the cold and from trauma to even care what I said. "You've got a wife and kids," I muttered. "And I've got a lover waitin' for me. Our fourth anniversary's tonight. He'll go crazy worryin' about me."

"*He'll* go crazy?" Mr. Tough Guy was making a big display out of showing his disgust. "Oh, Lord, jest what I need. To be trapped up here with a—a homo!"

Anger was replacing my hysteria. "Jest what I need," I mimicked. "To be trapped up here with a supermacho bull."

Rick narrowed his eyes, opened his mouth, and then burst out laughing. This gesture changed him completely. Suddenly he looked gorgeous with his white teeth sparkling beneath his mustache. Brown curls were plastered to his forehead. And although his eyes sparkled with amusement, he tried to look mean.

"You jest keep those hands to yourself," he declared in his deep Southern drawl, "and don't try anything, hear?"

I experienced an electrical bolt of warmth flowing through me as I began to appreciate him as a person.

"Rick," I said lightly, "if you had fifty million bucks taped to your ass, I wouldn't touch it."

He, too, had been studying me sharply, as if suddenly taking in my curly blond hair, blue eyes, and short but trim torso. Suddenly he laughed again, as if I were the funniest thing since Peewee Herman.

"You've taken a big load off my...uh...mind," he replied finally.

I giggled, and he couldn't suppress a grin. But we both turned serious when a blast of wind nearly blew out our window. He muttered something about having to go back and try to reach headquarters. I grabbed his big arm as he began zipping up his leather jacket again.

"Rick, please don't go back out there. If somethin' happened to you—well, I wouldn't know what to do about keepin' this fire goin' or gittin' help or—"

His dark eyes squinted above the smoke of his cigarette. "Seems like you're more concerned about your ass than mine."

"Well, of course—you warned me not to think about your ass, remember?"

He laughed, a beautiful young sound, and left the cabin. I learned a long time ago that if you can make a man laugh, you can make him do anything.

He dumped my two boxes of goodies on the kitchen counter. Red-faced and covered with snow, he whooped and clapped when I began taking out all that great food—and liquor.

Rick began relaxing and soon was in a very lively mood.

Before the roaring fire, he began stripping off his wet clothes as I fixed him a drink.

"You miss me?" he teased.

"Every second," I replied as I filled up an iced-tea glass with gin and added a few drops of tonic water "I started to write you."

He kicked off his boots and pulled off wet socks "Well, I missed you, too," he grinned.

275

I pretended to swoon. "Oh, Rick, are you tryin' to tell me somethin'?" I cooed as I added a shot of tequila to his drink.

"Yeah, like rustle me up some grub and gimme that damned ole drink."

"You sound like a chauvinistic prick—I mean, pig."

"You're lookin' at the guy who invented the word."

"You mean prick or pig?"

"Would you jest shut up please and gimme that drink?" I gave it to him as he grumbled, "I've had a rough day. And you ain't helped things out—" Suddenly, he choked and gasped and turned purple as he swallowed some of the lethal concoction. "Shit fire! What'd you put in this sucker! Nitroglycerin?" But he continued sipping at it as he tore off his T-shirt and then his white BVDs. He glanced at me sideways, his eyes dancing. "I've heard how you gay guys operate. You git a poor stupid bastard like me drunk, and then you take advantage of him."

"That's a damned lie! We just rape the poor stiff."

Rick choked on his drink and howled. Then he began performing muscle-man poses in front of the fire, bunching up his arms and baring his teeth. "You think I'd give a gay guy a hard-on?"

"You'd probably give him a heart attack."

Rick *was* gorgeous. He was like a beautiful, young bull—a powerful Southern male without that phony baggage of blown-up pecs and chiseled stomach—the carefully cultivated artifice that smacks of overblown narcissism. He was built more like a wrestler or boxer. His chest and shoulders were broad, with a light covering of hair over his pectorals. Beneath the flat stomach swung big testicles behind a penis which was thick, sturdy and uncut. Most of all, though, Rick had that irresistible boyish charm which certain Southern men possess—and which can be devastating to more passive gay men like me.

My drink was working wonders on him. He now turned his shapely rear end toward me and patted it. "Would you touch *that* if I had five million bucks taped to it?"

I slapped it, and he whooped.

"You wouldn't have to have a penny stuck up your crack, Rick, for somebody to have his tongue up there," I added.

His clear brown eyes glinted warmly as he plucked at his chest hair. "You sound like a li'l ole whore." He smiled. "I think what I'm gonna do is take a good, hot bath before we eat supper."

"May I scrub your back, Rick? I promise not to touch the goodies. I'll keep my eyes turned toward heaven." I stared at the ceiling while I heard him chuckle. "Promise."

"Okay, I reckon I can risk it. But if your fingers start doin' the walkin' toward my privates, I'll—" He rolled up a big fist.

I ran my hand over his swollen bicep, which seemed to please him.

"And could you fix me 'nother one of these drinks? What do you call it?"

"A Stud Seducer."

He did his damnedest to act disgusted, but succeeded in only looking more luscious.

One of the most beautiful sights I'll carry to my grave is of watching Rick settle his splendid torso into the steaming water. Lying back, he let a faint smile soften his full lips, and he closed his eyes as I soaped up his thick neck. Next came the wide, untanned shoulders. I noticed a scar on the right one, and when I asked

277

him about it, he said he got it while serving a hitch in the marines.

He pointed to a small blue devil above his right nipple. "I got that sucker in the marines, too."

I rubbed the devil and the nipple, and watched it swell. Thus emboldened by his silence, my curious washcloth massaged his biceps and then his stomach.

"Your belly is so hard, Rick."

He looked at me sideways, with a challenging expression. "I thought you'd already figured out I was hard all over."

"I wouldn't know. You've made me too scared to look any lower'n your nose."

"My bark's worse'n my bite."

"I like men whose bite is worse'n their bark."

"You've got a one-track mind," he snorted and closed his eyes.

I made no answer, but let my hand daringly slide to his pubic area—and then into his lap. He said nothing. I trembled as I caressed the soft sac and squeezed the large balls. Slightly rising from the water was his phallus. I ran my hand over it and pulled back the rubbery wattle of foreskin. The tip slid out—glossy and oval. His stomach sank in sharply as I ran a finger along the slit, which had widened. He was rapidly becoming hard. My head was moving closer and closer to this beautiful object when Rick suddenly stood up.

"Party's over. Time to eat!"

Furious at having been teased, I remained on my knees and stared at Rick's semierect penis.

"Yeah, Rick," I spat, "time to eat, huh?"

His hands pulled me up and pressed me against the door. I had to look up into his young, handsome face.

"Now, I done tol' you," he began quietly, "to keep

278

your hands to yourself. I oughtta be beatin' that butt of yours right now—"

His wet body was so close to mine that his thick phallus was pushing against my thigh. I could hardly breathe. I looked away.

"Rick," I whispered, "you're so attractive and so nice—you're makin' it very hard for me not to put my hands all over you."

His fingers touched my chin and forced my face up, so that again I was looking into his eyes. Then he bent his head down and his lips found mine. He kissed me deep and with much curiosity. I felt his organ growing stiffer against my leg. Abruptly, though, he stepped back, breathing harshly, his face flushed.

"Did that help you out?"

He laughed when I rolled my eyes and slumped to the floor, then pulled me up and put an arm around my shoulder.

"Come on now. Let's grab some grub."

Supper was a howling success. Both of us drank too much and gorged too much, but it brought us closer. Beneath that tough-boy exterior, Rick was basically a warm, all-American male—the kind a Lions Club or Jaycees group would love to have—whose presence in a small country church would be welcome and who would naturally be a den father for a Boy Scout troop.

We toasted my sister and her husband for providing us with the magnificent spread we enjoyed before the roaring fireplace: spinach quiche, cream of potato soup, fried chicken, rolls, pickled green tomatoes, and for dessert, sweet potato pie with coffee and brandy.

While the blizzard still continued to scream outside, we were curled up on big cushions before the fire. Rick told me about his wife, Becky, and his two children, Tommy and Scarlett. One day Tommy hoped to be a lawyer and ride the Space Shuttle. Ronald Reagan was his hero.

I told him about my unorthodox life-style—of living half the year in Manhattan and the other half in the South, of trying to survive as a writer. Around nine, though, both of us were yawning. I was horrified when he made it clear I would be sleeping in one bedroom on the second floor and he would be sleeping in the other one down the hall.

"Rick, I'm scared to sleep in there alone!" I wailed.

He sighed heavily with the exhaustion of a man who has had one hell of a day. "Now there ain't nothin' gonna bother you with me around. If you git scared, jest wake ole Rick up. Okay?"

He had found us plenty of comforters and blankets in a closet. I must admit, they felt wonderful when I crawled beneath them. But I kept thinking of that beautiful man down the hall—alone and untasted. Suddenly I awoke. It was just past midnight. Beneath me, on the porch, I heard the unmistakable sounds of someone moving around. I raced to Rick's room. Like a scrumptious teddy bear, he was curled up and snoring. He jumped and growled when I woke him.

"Huh? What? What's matter?"

He listened to my babbling, then slid his brawny body from beneath the covers, threw on an old robe he had found somewhere, picked up his gun, and told me to stay put. I jumped beneath the covers, still warm from his presence, and pulled the comforter up to my ears. When he returned, he laughed softly.

"You look like a scared little cat. Nothin' but a

deer lookin' for some food." He let his robe drop to the floor. "You miss me?"

I nodded.

"Okay," he whispered. "Move on over. I think I want it as bad as you do."

His naked body felt wonderful, as he joined me and pulled me against him. Rick was so warm and strong and comforting. *This*, I thought, *is what he does with his wife each night.*

"I've never done it with a man before," he muttered and then pressed his mouth against mine.

My hands swam over his smooth hardness, trying to record through my fingers everything about him...the way he smelled, the way his nipples swelled up beneath my sucking...the way his stomach caved in sharply when my mouth traveled over it...and then the glossy rod of muscle and blood between my hands. I stooped between his thighs and rested my face there. In the thick shadows, I saw how his hips arched slightly to push more of himself into my mouth. His hands gripped the sheets while my chin rested on the firm pillow of his sac.

When he ejaculated, it was sharp and forceful—much like him. But, as his orgasm tapered away, his strong hands pulled me back up, and he began kissing me again, wildly and intensely—as if he were suddenly discovering a new side of life he had never conceived of before (but was finding most interesting and delightful). *This*, I thought again, *is what his wife can enjoy each night if she wishes to.*

Only moments later, he placed my thighs around his neck and prepared to mount me.

"You okay?" he smiled. "Just hang onto ole Rick, and he'll give you the best fuckin' you ever had."

It did indeed turn out to be the most memorable "fuckin'" I had had up to then. He proved my theory that a married man is a better lover than one who is single. The man with a wife learns sensitivity in bed. He can perfect his shortcomings and improve on his stronger traits. A single man fucks sporadically, usually with a constant changing of partners.

Gently, my new lover pushed himself into me, and paused. He rested it for a few seconds, so I could get used to him, kissing me for a long time before proceeding further with his immemorial "fuckin'." Then he began inching in, until eventually I felt his balls brush my buttocks. That was when Rick began fucking me with short, penetrating lunges, letting the tip pop out occasionally before he pushed it back in forcefully.

"Christ!" he whimpered, "better'n a woman!"

As he prepared to ejaculate, he grabbed me and pulled me into a sitting position in his lap. Within me, I felt his organ pulsate as it emptied itself.

He wrapped his arms around me, shuddered, and I began to pray the blizzard would last forever.

We took a break. I served him a predawn breakfast in bed by candlelight. Lying in his brawny arms, I fed him warmed-over quiche and scrambled eggs, washed down with hot coffee and brandy. And just before the sky began to lighten, my lips took a final trip over his body. They explored all the crevices and bulges and crannies before settling down in his lap. In my mind, I saw him as an embodiment of the mountains—powerful, beautiful, mysterious. One could enjoy them, but one could never plumb their secrets.

Snowplows had already cleared much of the road by the time we descended the hill. Rick easily got not only my car back on the concrete, but his own as well. I was warming up my engine when he came over and rested his elbows within my window.

"More snow comin'. Look."

The sky was clouding up once again with ominous banks of grayness.

"We're back where we started from," I smiled. "You warnin' me and—Rick, I've never met any man like you before. I owe you a big one for savin' me. You've been so wonderful."

He gave me a wink. "You, too. You're somebody I won't ever forget. And you paid me back last night— more'n enough."

But already he was becoming a stranger. Within our cabin, we had created our own fantasy world. Out here, we were two strangers again. The strong wind, tinged with ice and the scent of new snow, was blowing away our illusions. I wanted to suggest we go back to the cabin. I knew I wouldn't. I prayed he would.

I took his right hand. Holding it to my lips, I traced my tongue over the palm and along the fingers. "There," I whispered, "I'm trying' to take you away in my memory. Rick, you're so different out here. Couldn't we...well, get together again? I wouldn't be a problem and..."

He shook his head sadly. "Last night was last night, Jason. When it's over, it's over."

Suddenly he leaned down and kissed me—a long, thorough kiss. We didn't close our eyes, but stared at one another, as if trying to freeze this moment forever. A gust of wind slapped us. He drew back, saying nothing. Then he straightened up and fixed his trooper's hat on his head. By doing that, he put the Rick I had known in the cabin forever into the past.

He got into his car. With blue lights flashing, he sped by me and tapped his horn lightly. I followed at

283

JASON FURY

a slower pace, trying to guide my car along the same tire marks left by Rick in the watery slush. But soon, like him, they vanished, as new snow once again began to cover up reality.

When it's over—it's over.

THE BASTARD OF THE COUNTY

Mama was headed for an early grave. She told everyone this morning, noon, and night, always managing to add that I was the one chasing her into it.

This woman kept herself in a constant frenzy over my failure to develop into a "real boy." I hated sports, getting dirty, or any kind of rough-housing—but I loved men. So when she found those magazine pictures of muscular hunks under my mattress, she dragged me to our family preacher. She took me to him because there were no beds available in the nearby mental hospital "where you belong!"

Remembering all those times that Preacher Anderson had squeezed my bottom, I listened to him drone on about how the Baptist church didn't think too much of "dugenerate" behavior.

"I'm mighty sorry to hear that, Preacher Anderson,"

285

JASON FURY

I drawled, "but frankly I couldn't give a shit about this religious crap."

Mama nearly fainted, and the good minister closed his eyes and prayed feverishly.

"What will the neighbors think?" she screamed afterward. I thought about old Mr. Johnson next door who had once been convicted of sexual misconduct. And then there was li'l ole, sweet Miz Snider further down the street. She played organ at our church and sold her cunt for five dollars a shot to horny high schoolers (all over eighteen, I'm sure). And Mama was afraid of what they would think?

Then came that immortal day when Mama came into the toolshed and found me playing with the oversized tool of Jimmy, our black handyman, who was sprawled buck naked on the floor. Worse, he was in the process of shooting off his first one of the day, which was always a geyser.

"What's the difference between Jimmy's prick and a bar of chocolate? They both taste so good!" I hollered as Mama ran for the leather strap and I grabbed a broom. It was going to be one of *those* fights.

After that beating, I ran away. I had no trouble getting to New Orleans, where my Aunt Rennie lived with her handsome husband, Trass, and her two bouncing boys, Bucky and Bobby Rob Hamilton III. Truckers seemed to enjoy picking up blond, blue-eyed runaways. You might say they took really good care of me along the way.

I had always wanted to visit my aunt and her brood, but next to me, Mama hated her sister Rennie, the most. What happened was that while growing up, Mommie dearest saw herself as the reincarnation of Scarlett O'Hara. After teasing her boyfriends, she

286

loved to dump them. One of the dumpees, Trass Hamilton, asked Scarlett's quiet, gentle sister, Rennie, to marry him. She did, and five years later, Trass had made a fortune with his chain of used-car lots across Mississippi. The couple bought a beautiful plantation outside of New Orleans. This made Mama furious, so she grabbed a handsome rogue for her husband, who later became an alcoholic (married to her, I could see why). After I came along—"I shoulda had an abortion"—she married a greasy-haired wimp who looked like he had been weaned on a dill pickle. He ran our nearby K mart.

My three days at Aunt Rennie's were the happiest of my life up to that time. Bucky was cute, freckle-faced, and my age. Aunt Rennie and Uncle Trass fussed over me as though I had just escaped the Nazis.

It was my older cousin, Bobby Rob III, who messed everything up. I quickly began calling him Bobby the Turd. He was a hulking, sweaty, pimply-faced slob with a fat ass. I thought he resembled a gorilla, and I told him so after he kept needling me about the makeup I wore. For God's sake, it was only a touch of powder, some mascara, and a dab of Cover Girl's Luscious Honeymelon lipstick. The truckers loved it! Bobby the Turd, however, said I looked like a French whore, and I said he smelt like a used Kotex.

"It's fag shit!" he snarled, and I said that if that were the case, why did he always get a hard-on whenever he was around me? He blushed, glared at me, and stomped off to call up my mother, telling her where I was. Mama screamed and yelled until I was put into the station wagon the next morning and driven to the bus station. As the car pulled away from the front porch, I stuck my head out the window and

287

yelled at my scowling, horrible-looking cousin: "I hope you fry in hell, Cousin Bobby! I hope the devil jus' turns you over real slow and burns the shit outta you!"

When I got back to hell house, my new father suddenly joined Mama's constant chorus: "Put a dress on Jason, and he'd be a real purty, little girl."

I spat back, "Put a jockstrap on you and a cigar in your mouth, and you might look like a man."

Furious at being dragged back, I rebelled. I began wearing dresses and heels around the house, and you could hear our fights all the way to the Kmart. Neighbors got used to seeing me running up the street in crinolines and heels, Daddy chasing me with his leather strap, and Mama flying after him, screaming, "Don't mess up that dress, Henry! Just beat him around the head and legs!"

By that time, I was the town's A-Number-One character. Since the white kids would have nothing to do with me because I was a "queer" or "faggot"— they couldn't make up their minds which was worse. What's more, I ran around with a bunch of gorgeous black boys who loved me to act outrageously and camp it up.

They loved even more us piling into a car and driving out into the country where we'd all strip and I'd give them all "lollipop"—licking them from their handsome faces down to their quivering stiff pricks. And after I finished there, they'd all turn over. I'd then start on their backs and end up with my face between those chocolate-colored buns. Lots of times we'd go to a dingy little bar, Ruby's in blacktown, and I'd do a mean striptease to the jukebox accompaniment of Ruth Brown screaming about "Wild, Wild Young Men" and "Daddy, Daddy." Then those black studs would fight over who was

288

going to fuck me first on the bar. Oh, wow, was it crazy!

My adoring parents were going crazy, too. What drove them over the edge was that April morning I came down to the kitchen in my "new" look. Mama screamed and Daddy dropped what was probably his third Bloody Mary. (My mother drove *everybody* to drink sooner or later.) My idol was Boy George, the pop singer. Even my worst critics said I had a great singing voice. So, since I considered this vocalist to be the ultimate, I had created a Boy George look that day. My blond hair was in plaits, my face was white with pancake, and my lips red with scarlet lipstick. My eyes were outstanding in purple and gold mascara. I'd even created a costume identical to the one I saw worn by my musical god in a magazine.

My parents chased me out the door, all the way to the fire station. The area newspapers quickly ran articles about: "Local Teen Discovers Being Boy George No Fun!"

After that day, Mama decided that before she died of a heart attack, she'd make her hated sister, Rennie, go along with her to the great beyond by having me spend the summer with her family in New Orleans. I was thrilled. Most of the people on that Greyhound bus, though, acted like I had AIDS with my Boy George look. Also, I played my idol's theme song, "Do You Really Want to Hurt Me?" over and over again so many times on my portable tape recorder that the bus driver finally screamed, "Would you shut that thing off...ma'am? Or, eh, is it sir? Ha, ha, ha."

"Of course I will, sir—or is it, ma'am?" I replied.

I turned it off, but in revenge I emptied a bottle of Chanel No. 5 all over me. People yanked down their windows and hung their heads out. When the bus finally pulled into the New Orleans bus terminal, the driver staggered off, moaning, "Oh, Christ, give me some aspirin and a stiff drink, and don't let me see another faggot as long as I live."

I yelled after him, "You need a stiff one all right—one up your ass and another down your throat!"

Calmed down, I recognized Aunt Rennie dressed in pink lace. Beside her was Uncle Trass, and next to him was cute, tanned Cousin Bucky. But behind them loomed someone unfamiliar—a knockout in a pink T-shirt, white linen slacks, and bulging muscles. A Rhett Butler mustache made his full lips look even more luscious. Who could he be? I was determined to make an entrance, and so, turning on my tape recorder, I began twisting on the steps of the bus, singing along with Boy George to "Do You Really Want to Hurt Me?" But on the top step, my foot got caught in my full pants leg, and I hit the ground flat on my ass.

As strong hands helped me up, I gasped, "Wow! I knew I'd be a smash hit in New Orleans—but like this?"

My aunt and uncle laughed, and Bucky hugged me. "How ya' doin', stranger!" None of them acted in the least embarrassed by my colorful appearance, which was drawing stares from everybody.

Uncle Trass called out, "Get on over here, Bobby Rob, and greet yo' cousin."

I was astounded! So this living centerfold was my hated cousin! What a difference five years could make. I smiled and went eagerly toward him, but his scowl and his frown made me stop.

"I ain't gonna do it till he scrubs all that damned makeup shit off and stops looking like a damned ole freak."

Instantly, my buried hatred flamed up full force at this hateful man, and I forgot his stunning new appearance. "Don't worry," I told my uncle. "If his opinion meant anything, I'd cut my throat. Since it doesn't, I couldn't give a shit."

And on that friendly note, Bobby Rob Hamilton the Turd jumped into his Jeep and streaked away. We followed in a pink Cadillac with Bucky goosing me and laughing and my aunt and uncle telling me not to worry about Bobby Rob, that he was "just stubborn."

"Like a jackass who hasn't shit in two years," I muttered, and they howled.

Bucky helped me unpack in my beautiful room which overlooked the nearby lake. He was cute and sexy and sweet. I kissed him on the cheek, and he blushed. Rolling his eyes, he laughed, "This is going to be a very interesting summer."

After he left, though, there was a knock on my door, and in strode the human gorilla. Bobby Rob the Turd looked like he was preparing to face a firing squad.

"What do you want?" I snapped.

Blushing, he muttered something about his parents ordering him to show me around the grounds before our barbecue cookout.

"I wouldn't go with you to a gravedigger's convention," I said coolly and looked away. His all-American face hardened. His dark-blue eyes blazed as he moved closer to me. "Maybe I oughtta apologize, Jason, but dammit, you come down here like a wild-eyed…a wild-eyed…"

"Cocksucker? Is that the word you're looking for?" He grabbed my shoulders and shook me. "I heard you'd be trouble, and now I believe it. I've been

291

hearing things about you and those black boys and..."

I pulled away. "You and my mama ought to get together. She's the biggest bitch in her county, and I'll bet you're the biggest bastard in yours." The back of his hand sent me sprawling against the nightstand and onto the floor. The telephone and a pitcher of water fell on my. It didn't hurt, but I pretended it did. My anxious cousin tried helping me to my feet. "Don't touch me!" I spat. "You might get V.D."

That night at the barbecue, I wore a gigantic bandage which nearly hid my face. There was only a small bruise beneath the covering, but I enjoyed watching my big cousin squirm as the others looked horrified. I explained to them that Bobby Rob had "accidentally" struck me while helping me unpack. I made it sound as though he had tried killing me.

Glaring at his son, Uncle Trass muttered, "I want to see you in the library after supper."

"Yes, sir," sighed Cousin Bobby Rob, looking suddenly like a scared little boy. I was delighted.

As the night dragged on, I felt like I would scream if I didn't have some privacy. After everyone went to bed, I showered, got rid of my Boy George look, and put on just a white shirt and shorts. Taking some cans of beer with me, I went out to the lake's edge and leaned back against a huge boulder.

I wasn't alone, though. It was as if he had been waiting for me. Slowly, his figure began emerging from the shadows into the moonlight, moving steadily toward me.

Even through my loathing—and my fear—of him, I had to concede that he would have been a sensation on Fire Island or one of those gay watering holes I had read about. With the moonlight painting his torso silver, he looked unreal—like one of those heroic figures we used to slobber over in comic books.

And my big cousin was naked, except for a pair of skimpy nylon shorts and tennis shoes. A red sweatband kept his black curls from his face. Sweat streamed over his flesh, for he had been running.

"Oh, God!" I groaned to myself. "Bobby Rob, please don't bother me anymore today! Let me have one little moment of peace. You hate me and I hate you and—just go away!"

His deep-set eyes, which were like black slits, never left me as he came closer. I pressed myself against the rock. He loomed huge, menacing, and almighty. I smelt his clean sweat, his moist hair, and thought how abnormally big his nipples were.

"You look mighty nice right now, little cousin," he said softly in that musical, caressing tone some Southern men still have. "I wish you'd always look like that."

"I'll do anything you wish," I snapped sarcastically. "I'll get a crew cut and knock up some girl to prove I'm a man and..."

"Just thought I'd warn you," he broke in, "that nobody comes out here at night, li'l cousin—'cause there's big water moccasins all over the place. They like to curl up in big clumps and wait for somebody to come along that they can sink their fangs into."

Without thinking, I grabbed his big arm instinctively. "Oh, Lord, let's get out of here, then! I'm *horrified* of snakes! Come on, Bobby Rob, let's go!"

He smiled slightly, as if realizing what power he had and what little I possessed in such a situation. I started to withdraw my hand, but he squeezed it comfortingly.

"I'm the only one who could lead you back to the house without stepping on one of them suckers. They can get eight, twelve feet long."

"Stop it, Bobby Rob! You're scaring me! Please, let's go! Why're you so mean to me?"

293

He looked away and a grin twitched at his lips. "My daddy bawled me out tonight because of the way I've been acting. I told him you called me the 'bastard of the county.' He said you might have a point. Maybe I should make you feel more welcome."

Suddenly he leaned forward, bracing his hands on the rock on either side of me. I could feel his warm breath on my face. Behind him, the big, white moon made him look bigger. His hard nipples brushed my chest.

"Have I got something, you might want, li'l cousin Jason?" he whispered. "Anything that might make you feel more welcome?"

I was trembling now from this completely unexpected proposal. He left no doubt what he had in mind. Lust for his body overpowered my loathing for him.

"Push those britches of yours down, Cousin Bobby Rob, and I'll show you what I want."

I saw his shoulders tremble as he pressed his hands harder against the rock—as if steeling himself for what was to come. "You take 'em down, li'l cousin. Anything of mine you want, you got."

My fingers brushed against his hot, smooth flesh as they dug beneath the waistband and pushed the shorts down to the ground. He kicked them away. That left only his jockstrap. Even more intimate was this gesture of pulling away the constricting elastic bands and watching him step out of them. He then pushed off his shoes, so that at last Bobby Rob the Turd stood over me: completely nude, big, sweaty, tough.

He lay on his back on the rock and spread his legs. If Jimmy, our black boy at home, possessed a chocolate bar of a cock, then my magnificent cousin had a

294

vanilla bar. Its oval, cut tip thumped against his navel. I stooped in front of him, put my hands around it, pulled it forth until I had the tip in my mouth. My tongue dug deeply into the big slit. Bobby Rob shuddered.

"Oh!" he whimpered. "Oh, wow, wow, aw, awww!"

I sensed that no one had ever sucked him before. Like most virgins, he was astonished by the sensation of having a wet, velvety mouth suck his phallus. He watched me intently as I moved my lips forward, inching them along that thickening bar until my nose was buried in his black pubic hair.

He might be my tormentor, my demon, but the muscles along his upper thighs and hips felt wonderful beneath my hands. He smelled like Christmas—sweaty, clean, fleshy, spermy. I looked up once as I sucked him strenuously. His head was thrown back, turned upward toward the moon. His stomach had sunk in, and his hips were arched forward. Half his phallus was exposed, and it gleamed with spit. *How lucky I am*, I thought, *To be able to do this to him—this big Southern stud who ordinarily would kill a man who dared put even finger on his thigh*.

He then turned around and offered his ass to me. It was very round, white, and smooth as moist silk. Again, I was certain he was a virgin in getting rimmed. When I spread his buns and sank my face into his cleft, he jerked and gasped, "Oh, shit, fantastic!"

Bobby Rob squatted as I reached between his thighs to milk his sticky penis. "I'm gonna blow real soon!" he whispered into my ear.

I hugged my lips around his swelling organ until he began squirting out sperm at a furious rate. His sac convulsed, and I saw his rectum pulsate rapidly.

Quickly, he pulled on his shorts and announced he would escort me back to my room. Like a true Southern gentleman, he made certain I was safe and sound in my room before leaving me.

But when I entered my room, my younger cousin, Bucky, was lying on my bed, watching Elvira, the vampire hostess of "Creature Features" on television. I was so charged up by my encounter with Bobby Rob that I wasted no time flopping down on the bed beside Bucky. And, unlike his brother, he was no virgin. He sensed I was in a very sexual mood, and he fucked like a married man and sucked like a slut. I kept thinking, though, that it was his brother who was with me in bed, whispering sweet nothings into my ear.

As the days passed, I thought of nothing but that powerful encounter between me and Bobby Rob. Although Bucky was tremendous fun, that's all it was. Fun. With Bobby Rob, it was something powerful and profound. But he said little to me the rest of that week. He was polite, but acted as if I were a boring stranger.

Bobby Rob, it seems, was engaged to a rich little girl named Sheba Sue. They were to be married in a month—and so a big blowout was being held at the nearby country club.

I was sick when Bucky told me this. I told him I would not go, but he and his parents insisted that I attend. Everybody was wanting to meet me and hear me sing, and Bobby Rob would be real hurt, *Ha!* I thought. *He couldn't care less.*

It was a scalding hot night in August when I, in my Boy George costume again, mounted the bandstand there at the club and began singing the current hits: "Karma Chameleon," "The Heart of Rock 'n' Roll,"

296

and "Time After Time." Bucky's young and vivid friends seemed to like and accept me, although the old-timers watched me warily as they tried to shake their asses to the beat. Bobby Rob, I noticed, was surrounded by handsome young bucks. The blonde clinging to his arm looked too much like my mother. I met her later, and she proved herself a bitch by sneering, "Yo' makeup's running, honey. Maybe you shouldn't use those cheap brands."

"Sweetie," I smiled, "if you used lipstick and mascara that cost a million bucks, it wouldn't help your looks."

Bobby Rob and others nearby smothered their grins while Sheba Sue opened her mouth, glared, and flounced off.

By nine, I had had it. I showered, removed all signs of Boy George and, clad in my shorts and white shirt, grabbed a bottle of champagne and went out into the dark. Couples were vanishing into the thick bushes and trees around the club. I was walking down a path toward the water when a fat figure came staggering toward me.

It was Arnold, a wealthy farmer who couldn't take no for an answer. All night, he had pestered me about joining him for "some fun" at his mansion.

"Oh, Lord," he blubbered, "if it ain't my little cutesy-pie!"

Before I could dodge, he threw his fat arms around me and tried dragging me into the brush. Suddenly I saw him being whirled around by a big hand and shoved in the direction of the club.

"Now, get the fuck outta here!" bellowed my big cousin, Bobby Rob Hamilton III. He grabbed my arm and pulled me along with him into some bushes and then closer to the shore. "Come on," he muttered. "Time me and you had a little talk."

297

"Yes, Daddy. Anything you say, Daddy."

He squeezed my arm painfully. "Shut up that sarcastic mouth or I'll throw you out there with all them water moccasins."

"Yes, Dad...I mean, Cousin. Anything you say, Cousin."

He laughed softly.

Frankly, I was scared of him at that moment. He was so big and mean-looking with that scowl and his black curls plastered on his forehead. I watched him strip off his shirt and then his shoes and socks. Finally he started unbuckling his belt.

"What...what are you gonna do, Bobby Rob?"

Stripping off his britches, he glanced at me. "Well, I ain't getting ready to go to church—that's for damned sure."

I tried edging away, but he grabbed me and pulled me against his naked body. There was no way I could escape that formidable fortress of muscle and blood.

"I've been fighting this feeling ever since that first day you came here five years ago...you li'l ole slut," he said tenderly. He ran his mouth over my face and down my neck.

"Well," I managed to say, "you'd better start fighting it a little bit more because I—"

He threw me to the ground. Within seconds, he had managed to rip away most of my flimsy clothes. He was powerful, but he was sweet, too. I was startled by how tender he was when he pushed the tip of his penis into me. He let it stay there for a moment, giving me time to adjust to it—and then he slid it in deeper until it had reached the hilt.

"Am I still the 'bastard of the county?'" he muttered as his white buttocks rose high in the air before plunging deep within me.

I gasped and whispered, "You're something of the county, but I think I'd change that to stud."

The following week, Bobby Rob broke off his engagement to Sheba Sue. This caused a big scandal in New Orleans, one they whisper about even today. Then he took me and Bucky with him on a cross-country trip of America. We even sent Mama a post-card from the Empire State Building. It was signed, "Jason, Bucky, and the Bastard of the County."

HIM

Twenty years had passed.

Two long decades had drifted by since I had last seen him. Within minutes, however, I would once more be setting my eyes on this man who had ruined me for all others. For after having Johnny Ramirez as a lover, every other male was anticlimactic.

I had made my annual call to the alumni office at East Carolina University in North Carolina. Each year I phoned in hopes of finding out something about my former hippie boyfriend. There was never anything. But last week I nearly dropped the phone when the woman replied, "Ramirez? Yes, we have something. In fact he's on the faculty here now Teaches phys ed."

What? I couldn't believe it. The Johnny I knew would never return to that redneck campus where both of us had been so miserable. I thought of all those win-

301

JASON FURY

try nights when I'd snuggle in his big arms and play
with his enormous pectorals and nipples, and we'd talk
about our futures. We had to leave campus and explore
life. After all, he was going to be a famous folksinger
and poet. I was going to be a gay writer—not a mainstream author, which had zero appeal for me, but one
who wrote stories about people he knew.

When it came time for action, though, it was he
who split campus and biked out to California. He had
talked incessantly about joining the communes,
meeting other hippies like himself, discovering what
life was all about. He couldn't flourish as an artist
unless he did it all—which meant everything: sex,
drugs, and protest.

It was as if he had vanished into the Bermuda
Triangle for I never saw him again. I trekked to the
Woodstock Music Festival in 1969 in hopes of finding him there. At one time I was certain I saw him
there, but was never sure. There were 500,000 long-
hairs, and they all blurred into one another. I went
to California, but that's a big state, and there are a
lot of people named Ramirez. He was gone forever.

I now turned my car into Mimosa Drive. His
address was 506. There had to be a mistake, I
thought. Each house along that block was just alike.
White, one-story, with a neat lawn, cars parked in the
drives, Mimosa trees hanging over the street. We had
been so virulent in our scorn for suburbia. It would
be the end for both of us if we ever settled into a
neighborhood like this. An artist would never live in
a cookie-cutter environment.

For myself, I had found a small studio in Manhattan—the kind I had dreamed of, with a big fireplace,
a stunning view of the East River and a small degree
of fame. My gay stories had developed a strong following.

302

Johnny, what happened? Where did all your dreams go? You left saying you would wear flowers in your hair in San Francisco.

I gave myself one last look in my rearview mirror. Oh, God, would he still find me attractive? I was forty-two. He would be forty-five. Two middle-aged men, both of us wiser, changed by life. Time had been kind to me, though. Only five-feet-three, I had kept myself in good condition. People still asked if my blond hair was bleached. Only a few laugh lines radiated from my eyes which were still blue and lustrous. In a way, I had lived my life the way I had because of him. I wanted him to be proud of me, should we ever meet again, not only of my writing career—but my physical self, too.

For a year, we had been the most controversial couple on campus. I had been myself, come hell or high water, and dressed and acted just as I pleased—meaning, I was one of them thar *obvious* homosexuals. Johnny was the campus hippie, and I worshiped him. It wasn't just because of his spectacular physique. Even in the late sixties, you didn't see men who looked like the son of Charles Atlas. His muscles were so big! Coupled with that, though, was the square face from which peered turquoise eyes between jet lashes. He stood at six-foot-four, and his black hair swung like silk around powerful shoulders.

Most importantly, there was his blazing charisma. You *knew* he was somebody special. I got out of my car now and walked up the sidewalk to 506. A small boy was playing with toy cars. When he looked up at me, I froze. There were those same turquoise eyes and jet hair. It must be Johnny's son! I stooped down and smiled at him.

"Hi, there! Anybody home?"

"Uh-huh. Gramps and Grannie."

303

Gramps and Grannie. Perhaps Johnny had his parents living with him. At that moment, a heavy woman came out of the house, smoking a cigarette and frowning.

"Tommy Lee! I've told you not to play out here in this cold! You'll get pneumonia." She yanked him to his feet pushed hair back from her brow and looked at me.

"Can I help you, mister?" She was slightly overweight, a woman in her forties or fifties—it was hard to tell. She wore no make-up but then she didn't need to. She had smooth skin but suspicious eyes.

"Does Johnny Ramirez live here?"

She ground out her cigarette and snorted out a stream of smoke. "John's cleaning up right now. Just got in from the gym. If you're a student, I'd suggest you see him at school."

"I'm an old friend. I've come a long way." She sighed and told me to come into the house. The living room was jammed with huge abstract canvases. The woman went upstairs while little Tommy studied me shyly from behind the door. I heard a rumble of voices and footsteps.

"If he's not a student, then who is he?" a man was asking. I held my breath and tried to control my trembling. The reflection in a mirror reassured me some: I had worn his favorite colors that day: a navy overcoat and scarf.

And suddenly, *he* was there. We said nothing. In his skimpy jogging shorts and cut-off tank top, Johnny was standing before me—older now, but *it was him!*

"Oh, my God!" he whispered. "It can't be."

"Johnny—do you—do you recognize me? It's me. Jason." I was terrified. You know how it is to meet someone from the past, with whom you've had a gay

304

relationship—and you see them years later married, with children, respectable.

Moving toward me, his rugged face suddenly cracked into a grin. "Good God almighty, it *is* you!" he laughed. Picking me up in those powerful arms, he swung me around. Both of us were laughing now, trying to talk, hugging each other. The woman had come into the room, smoking a new cigarette. She put her hand possessively on Johnny's shoulder and looked straight into his eyes.

"Well, you two seem to know each other," she drawled. With his arm around my shoulder he introduced us. This was Stella, his wife. I was Jason Fury, the writer.

Her face hardened. "Oh, yes. John's mentioned you a lot. You write for those—those—"

"Gay magazines? I sure do."

I ignored her, though. I was devouring Johnny up with my eyes. Twenty years...his beautiful black hair that had once blown in the wind was shorn now into a crew cut. Gray touched his temples. He was still a giant, his muscles still bulged as if he were in a Mr. America contest. It was his eyes that had changed. They were still that breathtaking mixture of green and blue but now they looked so—so sad. The sparkle of excitement was gone. He looked tired, bored—defeated.

He guided me out to the porch. "Where you staying, honey?" Honey. That was his favorite term of endearment for me. I was in Room 401 of the Paradise Motel. His wife seeing us whispering, quickly came up to him and put an arm around his waist.

"John, you've got to get that garbage out to the front. Did you fix that water pipe yet? If you're going uptown, be sure and pick up milk for breakfast. You might get the laundry, too, and—"

305

As I drove away, I saw him staring after me just as his wife was staring at him—and nagging, nagging, as if he were an ordinary man. Christ if I had what she had sleeping beside me each night, it would be like Christmas every day of the year.

By the time he got there, everything was ready. I had lit a large scented candle, some strawberry incense—just like we used to in college. There was a big cooler of iced beer. And when he knocked, I had already taken a bath, put on a blue silk robe and the cologne he always liked me to wear: Royal Bain de Champagne.

When I answered the knock to my door, he stood there like Superman, grinning—looking boyish and gorgeous in an old crewneck sweater and jeans.

"Are you that campus freak I've been hearing so much about?" he drawled.

"Sho nuff. And are you that campus hippie?"

His answer was to close the door behind him and pull me to him. "I nearly blacked out when I saw you standing there," he whispered, "looking just like you did when I left you in sixty-eight." His departure was abrupt that long ago morning. When I returned to our house, he had left me just a brief note: *"I've gone to San Francisco to wear some flowers in my hair."*

When he kissed me, I was the one who felt like blacking out. I had forgotten how he tasted—those lips, the scent of his skin and hair. He moaned as his kiss became more intense—as if he were trying to make up in a few seconds what he had missed over the years. He pushed my robe off while kicking off his boots, unzipping his jeans and by the time he carried me to bed, he too, was naked.

"Johnny, you still look so incredible!" I rubbed one of his huge pectorals which he jiggled the way he

306

used to. His skin had lost some of its youthful glow, but his body was still solid and dazzling. No one ever looked as naked as Johnny did when he was naked. He had always kept his body shaven smooth of any hair, even the pubic area. He loved strutting his stuff in all those physique contests.

With the curtains drawn, with the candle flickering, the incense smoldering, it was like we had taken a time machine back into the past—when both of us were young, fearless, and cocksure of our destinies.

Reluctantly, my mouth moved from his to plant itself on his right pectoral—my favorite one because of its oversized nipple. He whistled silently as I began to mouth it and nibble at its succulent thickness, as if I had a miniature penis in my mouth. From his chest, I moved down to his stomach. Those ridges of muscles he had worked on so ferociously were fewer now, less sharply defined, but they still rippled impressively—a far cry from the stomachs of most men his age.

I glanced up. As of old, his big fists gripped the back of the headboard, his eyes were closed, he whimpered softly as I licked his smooth pubis. And then I finally reached his pride. His penis was untrimmed, and it had always reminded me of a flesh-colored cucumber. It seemed to weigh as much, too, and I put my fingers into his foreskin and stretched it out—the way he had always liked it.

"Oh, wow!" he gasped. "Nobody's done that to me since you did it, honeybunch. Man, that's great. Stella hates my foreskin. Wants me to get cut."

"Tell her to go fuck!" I muttered as I yanked it down over the large tip and pushed my tongue deep into his wet urethra. A trickle of sap glistened on the thick stalk. Johnny parted the opening with his fingers to make it even wider for me. His hole was

307

always unusually large, anyway, and now I dipped my thumb tip into it and began massaging the lips, the way I always did.

He was moving now, in sexual pain, urging me to put my mouth on it and so I did, taking it slowly all the way down to the lustrous pubis. Johnny's cock was never the kind that got rockhard. It was always malleable enough so that you could bend it and curve it almost into a knot.

I could tell his ejaculation was not far off now. Nights of sucking him in the past had taught me much about his body language. The head grew more taut, the stalk slightly more rigid, and then I felt it surge as he began squirting out his sperm. He gasped and tossed some more as I kept my mouth on it, startled, as always, at the amount of semen he could produce.

He was still breathing heavily, sweating, and looking glorious when I turned him over. This was always the second part of our sexual routine. He knew what was coming, for he put a pillow under his hips. Johnny had a high, rounded derriere that was made to be rimmed every second of the day. Even now, at forty-five, his rear end had lost little of its beauty. The cleft seemed even deeper as I spread them and found the puckered hole that had given both of us so much joy. I began licking it, then pushing my tongue into it.

Soon Johnny was twitching again, groaning in pleasure. Beneath my chin, I could feel his genitals begin to stir once more. He was so fragrant down there, and sweat trickled down the sides of his buns to join my saliva in his rectum. When he turned over, he was again fully erect. Only a hint of pink head was visible beneath the thick sock of flesh. Both of us had always delighted in the moment when I pulled the foreskin away from the tip. It was as if he were giving me a hidden gift—and this one was a large, oval-shaped ball of meat, the color of glossy grapes.

Once more, I slid it into my mouth, wrapped my fists around the center, and after just a few suction movements, it began to throb as it emptied itself of its fresh semen. In his arms again, he kissed me for a long time and we began to talk.

"Have I changed much?" he asked. "You look so—so incredible! You could still pass for a nineteen-year-old kid. How do you do it? That blond hair, those eyes—wow, I've seen them a million times in my mind."

"Did you ever go to Woodstock, Johnny? I thought I saw you there."

"Woodstock? I dunno." He said that he had indeed gone to California, gotten into the commune scene, moved heavily into drugs. There were months of his life that he couldn't recall. Others had told him they had seen him at Woodstock, too. He tried to write—but now it meant nothing.

"All that stuff I had been writing about—anti-establishment, protest, peace, and love—it was just bullshit. It bored me." He had drifted around the country for a few years, over to Europe for a while. When he returned to North Carolina, he got a construction job on a college campus, met Stella, who was an art major. Her parents had plenty of money, and when she got pregnant, he just decided to get married.

They had a son, Nick, who married. He and his wife were killed in a car wreck a year before. Their little boy, Tommy Lee, was living with Johnny and Stella.

"So you are a grandfather, Johnny?" I said in disbelief. "I can't believe this. We sound like a bunch of old dinosaurs." He laughed and stood up and held out his hand. He wanted us to get fresh air, go see the campus and the house we used to live in.

It was freezing. A thick mist shrouded reality, thus enhancing the dreamlike ambience of this whole experience. Few people were around, and Johnny took my hand, put it into his jacket pocket, and then placed his hand over mine.

Our little wood house had been turned into a bookstore. There was no one there but a bored-looking clerk who left us alone to wander around. There was our bedroom, now lined with rows of paperback books. Johnny pulled me quickly over to one particular shelf. There was my collection of short stories, *Barbed Wire,* which was selling well.

"To think you used to sleep here in this room," he smiled, "and now a part of you is back in here again." There was a large closet in the room. I remembered writing something on one of the walls during my first day there. It was still there.

"Johnny, look! Our inscription." It read: *"Jason Fury lived here with Johnny Ramirez in 1968."* We had both signed our names. His eyes were wet when he hugged me to him—and kissed my cheek.

I recognized almost none of the stores along Main Street. "Do you remember that day, Johnny, when I first saw you on that homecoming float? You were almost naked except for that little G-string and everybody was drooling over your muscles and rear end?"

"Yeah," he laughed, "and my rear end nearly froze off."

"I'm freezing, Johnny. Let's get on back."

He squeezed me to him. "I know why you wanna get back, you slut," he whispered. "Well, I'm ready to go again if you are."

310

My old lover gooched me and suddenly lifted me up into the air above his head as if he held a rag doll—and it was as if both of us were college kids again and would never grow old.

When he came out of the shower, I had my Polaroid camera ready. He eagerly went into all the sizzling positions I asked him to get into. On his knees he spread his buttocks so I could snap his butthole. In another shot, he stretched his foreskin out to an incredible length. There were dozens of other pictures—of Johnny lying stretched out like a centerfold with his erection laying blue and thick against his stomach. If he had lost much over the years, he still had his torso to be proud of.

He looked at his watch. "I gotta be moving on. Nearly midnight. Stella is gonna have one screaming fit."

"Johnny, you can't go! This is a special night. Whose more important anyway? Me—or Stella?" His eyes danced, and suddenly he burst out laughing. Pulling me down onto the bed with him, he hugged me tight.

"You are, you little slut. Okay, I'll spend the night, and dodge pots and pans tomorrow."

Once more he kissed me for a long time, pausing occasionally to draw back and look at me, as if photographing me onto his mind. I had him sit on the edge of the bed so I could get down on my knees between his legs and suck him off. He leaned back slightly as I began inching my lips down around the thick stalk until his testicles touched my chin. Johnny gasped as I began to strenuously suck him, never letting up for a second. I heard him murmur he was "gonna pop" and he did so—squirting, squirting until my mouth couldn't take it all.

311

It was almost dawn. When I came out of the shower I found Johnny still sitting on the edge of the bed, staring at the gray line of dawn, seeping through a crack in the curtains. I got up behind him and wrapped my arms around him and laid my head against his neck.

"Johnny," I whispered, "where are the flowers?"

"Flowers?"

"The flowers you were going to wear in your hair. Why didn't you ever write me, try to find me, too?" He put his hands over his face and for several moments, said nothing. When he removed his fingers, his cheeks were wet.

"This is what I've been afraid of," he said quietly, "of you finding me and seeing I've done none of those spectacular things I said I would."

I squeezed him tighter and kissed his check. "Johnny, you know that would mean nothing to me. I wouldn't care if I found you digging ditches or in prison. You're the only thing I care about."

He began weeping again, this time more harshly and for several minutes we said nothing. "Christ," he sobbed, "I've fucked up my life but good. I sold out, and I hate everything about it."

I got up and sat down in his lap, hugging him tight to me. "Don't talk like that! You're only forty-five for God's sake. Leave it all. Start a new life. Thousands are doing it every day."

He wiped his eyes and smiled ruefully. "For you it's simple. You ain't married, or signed on with a college, or got a grandson."

"Bring your grandson with you to New York. You'll stay with me. Johnny, don't go back to that bitch. She doesn't appreciate you. You know how I'd worship you every second and make you feel like a million."

312

I saw that old sparkle of excitement suddenly flicker in his eyes. "Yeah, maybe, maybe. It's something to think about."

After he dressed, we went to the door. "Give me your phone number and address. I may be giving you a call one day."

"If you don't, Johnny Ramirez, I'll come back here and cause a scandal this town will never forget."

He laughed, kissed me and chucked me under the chin with his fist. Then he said that old phrase we always used when either of us was going to be gone for a while. "Here's looking at you, kid. It was wonderful. And I won't forget you."

I watched him move in that sensual, powerful gait down the lot until he became part of the mist.

As I closed the door of my room, I said aloud, "I'm going to get you back, Johnny Ramirez, if I have to come back here and kidnap you. We were *made* for each other!"

And as I study the Polaroid shot of him above my desk now, he seems to smile slightly, as if in anticipation of my battle—to get *him* back!

THEY WON'T FORGET

"You ain't gonna leave me," Rhett panted between hot kisses that sultry night long ago. "If you do, I'll break that li'l ole neck of yours."

Broken neck or not, I was leaving him. Not that I wanted to, but our days as the cutest hunks on campus ended that afternoon of May 10, 1955, when we received our diplomas from Duke University. Reality had to be faced, careers begun and, most importantly, bills to be paid. Rhett couldn't have me all to himself anymore or fight my battles. He thought this was the way it should be, though, since his six-foot-four torso towered over my trim five-foot-five body. Now my hot-blooded lover, who had scored many a touchdown on the football field, was using his magnificent frame to try and persuade me to change my mind.

To celebrate our graduation, we had rented the Deluxe Honeymoon Suite of the Dew Drop Inn near the campus (complete with black and white television, pink towels and sheets, and king-sized bed). It had long been our plan that after graduation, we would move to Atlanta, where Rhett would join his father's big law firm of Youngblood & Son. I would stay home, keep house for Rhett, and work on my novel. All that changed the week before when I was offered a newspaper job in Boise, Idaho, of all places. Tomorrow I would leave to start my journalism career.

Rhett had rolled over on top of me and was kissing me wildly when I managed to free my mouth and whisper, "Rhett, I've *got* to take that job in Boise! It's my big break. Newspaper jobs are impossible to find!"

"Huh-uh, you ain't gonna leave me," Rhett grunted stubbornly as he suddenly pushed himself up into me—again! Grinding himself deeper into me, he watched my expression while his hips moved as only Rhett Youngblood could move them.

Although a brilliant law student, he loved dressing and talking like a tough cowboy. "There ain't no stud in Idaho who can fuck like me. None of them yokels can give you something—like this!" I cried out as he lunged deeper to allow his ejaculation to erupt within me. How many times had he cum that night? Four—five—?

We took a break and had some icy gin and tonics. I rested my head in his lap. He ran the sticky tip of his penis over my face and throat like a warm hose. Every time I opened my mouth to say anything, Rhett crammed his thick organ into it, like an impish kid. Gradually, however, he saw his ardent lovemaking wasn't changing my mind.

"You don't love me," he pouted, casting down his long lashes and rolling over on his stomach. With his face to the wall, he muttered again. "Naw, you don't love me when I could take good care of you in Atlanta. Something bad's gonna happen to you in Boise. I just know it."

I began kissing his high white buttocks, a rump so dazzling that even his macho teammates referred to it admiringly as "Rhett's greatest ass-et!"—in addition to the one which swung so thick and sturdy in front of him.

"Will you please cut it out, Rhett Youngblood! You can't always protect me. Let me just try it out in Boise and if things don't work out, I'll be home Christmas." He sat up on the edge of the bed and rested his stubborn jaw on his fists. When I tried to kiss him, he jerked away like a sulking little boy. Because of his fabulous good looks—dark curls, hot eyes and a rippling physique which stunned—he was spoiled rotten. His outrageous charm had also helped get him everything he wanted. Now he couldn't understand why anyone would want to leave all that for a stupid job. Suddenly he grabbed me to him and rolled over on top of me.

"You win, you hardheaded li'l sumbitch. If you're leaving tomorrow then let's fuck like crazy tonight."

At dawn, I left him standing in the doorway of the motel room, wearing his cowboy hat, boots, and tight jeans, his powerful chest bare. As my taxi drove out of the courtyard, he touched the brim of his hat and tried to smile—while tears ran down his rugged young face.

Oh Rhett! I moaned. Don't do this to me!

When my bus rolled into Boise on May 14, 1955, I thought it was the most drab and colorless town I'd ever seen. Fifty thousand people resided in this small metropolis where the sidewalks rolled up at six and a

317

church seemed to dot every other corner. Beyond Main Street, neat two-storied houses crowded each other. If you walked past them at night, you could see through windows families gathered around their big console televisions watching "The Milton Berle Show," "Dragnet" or "I Love Lucy."

The sixteen-member staff of *The Plainsman* newspaper were all devout Mormon and Catholic males. When they asked me my religion, I shocked them by stating I had none. I was an atheist.

My editor, Don Owensby, was a grinning, lanky man with thick glasses, thinning red hair and breath that would stop a buffalo in its tracks. When he discovered I wasn't married, he told me half in jest that he would try to change that shameful condition. "We need to get you fixed up with a pretty Boise girl and get you married off. Ha, ha, ha!"

"The only problem with that, Don, is that somebody special's waiting for me back South."

"Is she a blonde or a redhead?"

"This *person's* got black curls," I drawled and was tempted to add "with muscles and ass galore and a cock big enough for two men." Gradually, I was to discover how obsessed everybody seemed in this Mormon-dominated town to get all single people married off and start popping out babies like rabbits.

And so I became a reporter for *The Plainsman* where murders and suicides were buried deep on the inside pages and where the front featured such earth-shaking articles like "Has Anyone Seen My Dog, Topsy? Wails Little Lucy James" or "Ned Jenkins Named American Legionnaire of Year."

I was assigned to cover the civic clubs, of which there seemed to be hundreds. Five days a week, I ate fried chicken, green peas and mashed potatoes as the luncheon speaker would address the all-male members of The Lions, The American Legion, The Jaycees, etc., on "How I Became a Good American" or "Communists Are Still Among Us" (referring to the Communist hysteria of two years before engineered by psychotic Senator Joe McCarthy) and "The Ten Commandments of Happiness" (and you can rest assured that getting married and raising a big family was Commandment Number One).

Most of the men looked hideous in huge floral ties, plaid jackets, and big checked pants. They liked smoking cigars after their meal and picking and sucking at their teeth with toothpicks. Some were cute, though, and the cutest of them all was Brad Summerford. He was a rising bank executive who looked sexy and handsome in his tight pants and white shirts which showed off his muscular figure. His black hair was worn in a flat-top, and his blue eyes were always opened wide, as if he were constantly surprised by life. This, and his boyish grin, made him instantly likable.

I introduced myself to him one day after a luncheon. When he shook my hand, a warm jolt shot through me. His eyes scanned my face and then he flashed me a grin. "Welcome to Boise, pardner. Hope you like living here."

Not much chance of that, I thought as I returned home each night to my small room at the Hotel Astor and thought of a gorgeous Southern buck by the name of Rhett Youngblood.

It was after midnight when I left *The Plainsman* and began my ten-block walk home to the Hotel Astor. Two months had gone by and I knew I'd never fit into this rigid, narrow-minded town where conformity was demanded of everyone. I got so sick of everyone always asking me was I married? Did I have a

319

girlfriend? Oh, you don't, well I know this secretary...
Everyone wanted me to start "dating" or going with
them to church. At the newspaper, those staunch
Mormons and Catholics were always laughing over
jokes about "homos...queers...faggots...fairies."

Don Owensby, the editor, loved going up to different reporters and pinching their asses. Or he might
sneak up behind them and begin massaging their
necks.

"Can you do it a little lower, like beneath my
belt?" they would usually guffaw.

"Whoops!" Don would shriek. "People might talk.
But meet me after work and—" Everyone would dis-
solve into hysterical laughter at the very thought of
Don being considered a "fairy." After all, he was married, with four gangly kids with red hair and freckles.

I smiled when I thought of the hilarious cartoons
Rhett sent to me showing him with monstrous erec-
tions as he fucked everything around him—cars,
trees, butterflies—because I wasn't there with him.
He was actually enjoying his job as a rising young
attorney—but he missed me so much, he wrote, that
sometimes he cried for a long time.

That morning, Don Owensby had stopped by my
desk, grinning broadly. Couldn't he do something
about his yellowing teeth, I thought? Or use a
mouthwash? I held my breath as he began to talk.

"Gee, we're getting a little bit worried about you
not having any dates, pardner. A lot of pretty girls
would shore like to go out with a handsome young
fellow like you."

"I'm afraid my beloved back home wouldn't
approve," I retorted. He stood up and shrugged his
bony shoulders. "Well, you gotta fit in. You don't
want people talking about you—or getting funny
ideas. Ha, ha, ha."

"Don, I've never given a shit what other people think, and I'm not starting now." His face turned a bright red as he abruptly turned and left me.

By now, I knew that the area around the Hotel Astor was the hot spot for cruising homosexuals. Across the hotel was a small park, crisscrossed with paths which wound through thick foliage. There was even a public rest room—making it an ideal place to pick up someone. Young men were always strolling around in tight jeans and jackets, trying to look tough with cigarettes dangling from their lips, and a cool, knowing expression on their faces.

They were playing to the lone men who circled the park in cars. I had managed to control myself so far. Boise frightened me with its strict rigidity of behavior and social codes. More importantly, I had heard a disturbing rumor in the newsroom. A private investigator had been hired by the YMCA to investigate the "strange men" who hung around there—men whom parents claimed shouldn't be around their kids. This situation was hurting the Y in its annual fund drive. The investigator was supposedly preparing a shocking dossier of names of both "victims" and perpetrators which he planned to hand over to probate court for prosecution.

From the corner of my eye, I saw the dark Ford move slowly beside me. Cars were always doing that when I walked home but they passed on by when they saw I wasn't interested. Now I was startled when the car pulled up to the curb and a man's voice called out my name.

"Hey, it's me, Brad Summerford! Hop in and I'll give you a lift."

I was surprised but thrilled at this unexpected encounter. Naturally I was intrigued, too. Why was Brad Summerford driving along "Fairy Lane," as the

321

men at the newspaper jokingly referred to this stretch of street?

The handsome young executive looked dressed for being raped. His white shirt was unbuttoned and pulled away from his big chest. Dark hair dusted his bulging pectorals while his Bermuda shorts looked ready to burst from his muscular thighs and trim hips.

"So where you headed, pardner?" he smiled. "Pardner" was a favorite term of greeting in Boise among men.

"Home at the wonderful Hotel Astor. I've got a room there."

"That's nice. You in a hurry to go home now, or you wanna ride around some? I'm trying to unwind after a really rough day at the office. Fridays are always hell.

"I'm in no hurry to go home, Brad, to that drab little room—especially on a Friday night."

"Ain't that the truth?" he laughed. "You gotta have some fun in this dipshit town."

My pulse beat faster as he turned his car into the dark countryside. Surely he couldn't have the same thing in mind that I wanted. At all the club meetings, he was certainly a mouthwatering sight in his tight britches and all-American good looks. But he was Mr. He Man! Hardly a week passed that our society page didn't run a picture of Brad in tuxedo with a pretty debutante on his arm.

Complaining of the heat, he stripped off his shirt and wiped his wet chest with it. I was fascinated by the play of his big muscles as he did this. Then he pulled out from beneath his seat a half-empty bottle of bourbon. After he drained a few inches, he handed me the bottle. I pressed the rim to my lips, but didn't drink. I just wanted to taste where his mouth had been.

Now, we moved along a narrow country road, deeper into the farmland. Brad lit a cigarette—and then promptly dropped it between his legs.

"Oh, shit, could you get that for me before it burns a hole in something!" It was an obvious ruse, but I was delighted with this excuse to scoot over close to him and slide my hand over his thigh and between his legs. I felt him up freely, squeezing his crotch as he lifted his hips slightly so I could retrieve the cigarette.

I put it between his lips, but kept my hand on his upper thigh. Then I moved it forward to squeeze his warm bulge once more. He stopped the car, turned off the lights and ignition, and threw his cigarette out the window. His big arm pulled me tighter against him.

"Christ," he muttered hoarsely, "I was hoping I'd get you tonight. You've been driving all us guys in cars crazy every night when you walk home from the paper and not giving any of us the time of day."

My hands were kneading his big pectorals and pulling at his nipples. "Maybe I've been waiting for someone like you to come along, Brad. Someone big, muscular, and handsome.

'Thanks," he whispered and covered my mouth with his soft, moist one. I was amazed this was actually happening—me in the arms of the most eligible bachelor in Boise. With ease born of long practice, he stripped off his shorts and sandals so that he was completely naked. Then he helped me out of my clothes in record time and pulled me on top of him as he stretched out on the seat.

No man would ever be a match for Rhett's wild lovemaking and breathtaking beauty. Brad was a good contender, though. His body was hard and warm and strong. I sucked on his thick nipples for a

323

long time before moving on down to his flat stomach. Finally I covered the moist head of his circumcised penis with my mouth.

Brad grunted as I took more of it until it touched my tonsils. I tasted remnants of sperm, and it was obvious I was not the first man he had balled with that night. I didn't care, though, for I was young and horny and used to having my sexual longings gratified by Duke's biggest football player several times a day. My mouth moved up and down and Brad writhed and muttered and gasped that he was ready "to pop off." I felt his erection begin to pulsate rapidly, pumping out all abundance of sperm into my mouth. I had him turn over, and he presented me with a luscious rump, white and firm and round in the moonlight. I buried my face deep into his warm cleft and for several minutes, lost myself in this aromatic valley. When Brad turned over, he was rampant once more. This time, though, he wanted to fuck me. Pushing my thighs back, he pushed the tip of his organ up into me. Slowly, he inched in the rest of it. After a few minutes of energetic drilling, he gasped again and fell beside me. Then he got to his knees and took my hardness into his mouth. I came quickly but he wouldn't take it out. He sucked until I came again.

I drifted into my hotel room on a cloud of euphoria. For the first time since coming to Boise, I felt happy and thought there might be a future for me here. Then I looked out my window and saw the park beneath me. It was almost dawn, but there was still action going on. A tall, lanky male sat on a park bench near the curb. A big, dark car drove up and stopped. The hustler got inside and the automobile, which had just let me off, then headed in the same direction I had just come from. Brad had told me he was oversexed. Now, I believed it. And reckless as well.

We began seeing each other several times a week. Brad made no secret that he was addicted to the tough young punks who hung around the park. He spent a small fortune on them each week for stud services. When he wasn't with me, he would sometimes buy two or three of the young men at night. When Brad drank, he could become incredibly reckless. We always met behind the hotel in its dark parking lot and then head out for a country road. One night I slid into the front seat with him and was shocked to find him completely naked—and a little bit drunk. He laughed at my reaction and said he often drove around the park stark naked to give the boys a look at what they would be getting.

Aside from that, he could be playful, witty, a resilient lover who was obsessed with sex. He introduced me into Boise's homosexual society. At very discreet parties, I met schoolteachers, lawyers, blue-collar workers, even a policeman or two. What amazed me was the number of preachers and priests and politicians who kept popping up. Brad was a great favorite at these gatherings. He would strip naked and make it clear he wanted some sexual relief. Then he would vanish into a bedroom and spend the whole time in there with a string of companions until it was time to go home. I didn't object. He always made sure we got it on until I was satisfied.

Gradually, I realized that I had to stop seeing Brad. He was simply too reckless, and sooner or later he was going to get caught. He even admitted that three of the hustlers were blackmailing him. Somehow they had gotten their hands on photographs showing Brad at a gay orgy, where he was getting fucked. None of this seemed to slow him down. From my window at the hotel one night, I saw three of the young toughs get into his car, and off they went into the countryside.

My editor wanted desperately to get into politics. He brown-nosed a gang of legislators who were Boise's most wealthy and powerful men. Don Owensby would run gushing stories about them and their families on page one of *The Plainsman.*

At that time, there was a flamboyant senator in the Idaho legislature. People wondered if he might be a "fruit" but I knew for sure since he was regularly at the parties I had gone to with Brad. He proved it when he went down on Brad while two dozen or more of us watched.

Senator X was also a millionaire. Don Owensby's crowd hated him and wanted him out of office but there was nothing they could do to dislodge him. Ironically, another person this gang despised was a member of the city council. His son, then attending a military school, was reported to have been the leader of Boise's homosexual crowd.

In October I heard that the private investigator had finished up his work for the YMCA. Several Mormon groups were supposedly urging the man and the Y to turn the findings over to the courts. Something had to be done about the perverts!

To Don Owensby and his cronies, this situation was like a gift from heaven. At last, they had a way which might topple the "screaming faggot at the capital" and the man whose son was also supposed to be a notorious "homo."

Ten teenage boys? And the surface had only been "scratched"? Mothers became hysterical, homosexuals fearful, while Mormons and Catholics gloated. On November 3, the paper fanned the flames of hysteria further with its screaming editorial, *Crush the Monster!* The monster, of course, was all men who liked other men. This species of humans, shrieked the editorial, should all be ferreted out and locked away behind bars.

A week later, one of the three men arrested was sentenced to life imprisonment. Although he had never used force on anyone, he admitted that he had paid young men to have sex with him.

The witch-hunt had begun.

Now arrest followed arrest of men who had been named by hustlers and some of the young boys who hung out at the Y. The male prostitutes tried to act as if they were innocent young farmboys who had been forced into sexual acts. Later they admitted that well, yeah, they did get paid for selling their bodies.

One of the most notorious name-droppers was a tough street slut named Les. He was infamous for approaching men and demanding they have sex with him. When they asked why, he said he needed the money and if they didn't give it to him, he would spread the word around that the victim was a homosexual.

In the newsroom, I heard that the district attorney's office had taken over the prosecution of the homosexuals. His list of suspected men grew daily.

Toward the end of November, the city was rocked when seven more men were arrested. This time, the group included a well-known attorney and Brad Summerford. I had repeatedly tried to warn him of how grave the situation was, and he finally believed me when it was too late. It was heartbreaking to see him in the courtroom with the other men. His young face was pale and gaunt. Shock seemed to have aged

327

him ten years. Someone heard him say to his attorney, "I can't believe this is happening. I hurt nobody. This is supposed to be America, isn't it?"

Hundreds of homosexuals fled Boise during this time, many never returning. One schoolteacher was so horrified over what happened to Brad Summerford that he jumped into his car and headed to California. Two days later, when friends came by to check on him, his untouched breakfast of scrambled eggs, coffee, and toast was still on the table.

At the beginning of the purge, the public was told it was being done to get rid of the "perverts" who preyed on young boys. Quickly, it was clear that the majority of the men being arrested had never touched a minor. Their sexual relationships had been only with consenting adults.

The list of suspects grew into the hundreds. In the media, it was as if this drab little city of the Northwest had magically become the mecca for devouring homosexuals who were flying in from all over the world to enjoy Boise's boys.

After the scandal first broke, Rhett called me up one night. "Hey, honey! What are you doing to Boise? It was dead until you got there, and now I'm reading all these stories about it's become lavender heaven."

"Rhett, I hate this goddamned place! I wish I'd stayed with you and never seen this narrow-minded dungheap."

"Come home," Rhett said simply. "If you made a mistake by going there, then admit it. Nothing to be ashamed of."

"It's my first newspaper job, Rhett! If I leave now, it'll look horrible on my resume. Besides I can't afford to and—"

"Christ almighty damn, but you're one stubborn li'l sumbitch!" he shouted. Rhett always liked to blow off steam by screaming, so I listened to him finally cool down. "Don't say I didn't warn you. When the police come knocking on your door—" His unfinished words chilled me. Like every homosexual in Boise, I expected the police to come pounding on my door at any moment, just as they were doing all over the city.

It wasn't safe now for men to even have lunch together, except at the civic clubs. Landlords were evicting single males; many restaurants and hotels refused to serve them; rednecks cursed and insulted them on the streets. Women were constantly calling the paper to give us names of "suspicious" men, who were often their own husbands or sons or brothers. Unmarried men made big productions out of being seen with "dates." Single women never had it so good. Even the homeliest were besieged with invitations to parties and dinners and movies.

However, the arrests of men who had never touched a minor continued. On December 22 I covered the city council meeting which issued a statement demanding the rounding up of all homosexuals in the city, with each one being convicted and sentenced to prison. One of the council members screaming the loudest for such action was the father of the gay man.

The prosecuting attorney was present. As he put on his coat to leave, I went up to him. "Just what are you trying to do? When you started your cleanup you said you were going after the men who had sex with minors. That's bullshit, and you know it. You're trying to get every man whose had anything to do with another male!"

He was startled by my attack since no one at that time dared question his tactics. "Why does that both-

329

er you?" he snapped. "We're trying to protect the family. Homos are a threat to our family unit."

"You're worse than I thought. *You're* the one who should go to prison."

As I turned to leave, he called out loud enough for others to hear, "Don't trip over your petticoat, precious!" I saw the men exchange knowing grins, and I knew my days in Boise were numbered. I set Christmas as my date of escape.

I didn't know that the following day would end my life in Boise forever.

On December 23, *The Plainsman* carried on its front page the sentencing of five more homosexuals. Punishment ranged from five to ten years in prison. Brad Summerford was locked behind bars for ten.

When I entered the newsroom, Don Owensby was holding court to about twelve reporters and editors who sat around on desktops, sipping coffee, grinning broadly and clapping as Don pranced around with a copy of the paper in his hands.

"Yippee!" he whooped. "We got five more of the fags behind bars. Our district attorney says he's got a list of five hundred more names, and he won't rest until all of them are locked away."

That was more than I could take. Fuck this city and its goons and its witch-hunters. I slammed my chair against my desk and went up to the editor, who was still laughing over his great triumph. *The Plainsman* had gotten the purge going, and look at where it was going. Yippee!

"You turn my stomach!" I spat. "You're ruining lives right and left, and to you it's just fun and games. What's the difference between what you and your goons are doing and what the Nazis did to the Jews in World War II? Have you forgotten that?"

330

The men were stunned by my outburst, and the face of my boss flushed an angry red. "No, I haven't forgotten," he smirked. "Maybe the Nazis had some good ideas about how to get rid of subhumans. They—" His words broke off as he looked at someone behind me.

"And who, sir, might you be? What are you doing here?"

"I've come to take my buddy here back home," a familiar voice drawled. I turned around—and there was Rhett.

He looked like a gorgeous Hollywood cowboy, with his new mustache, his face bronzed, his Western hat tilted rakishly over his brow. His tight jeans and leather jacket swelled with his powerful muscles.

Giving the men a contemptuous glance, he grabbed me to him—and kissed me. Through my dizziness at tasting his luscious lips again, I heard the gasps and the cries of revulsion.

"What the hell are you two men doing?" someone shouted. "What the shit is going on?"

Having created the effect he wanted, Rhett guided me to the door. "Come on, and don't give me no sass. I knew you'd never get out of this shithole until it's too late, so you're coming with me."

"I'm not going to sass you, Rhett," I laughed. I looked at the others who looked shell-shocked. Their faces had drained of blood. They were slowly discovering what they had been working with all these months. I, too was a member of that despicable race of men. I was a—

"Queer?" I smiled. "Homo? Fag? Fruit? Fairy? Yep, boys, I guess I am." I gave them a smart military salute. "Keep up the good work. Adolf Hitler would have been proud of you and the fine citizens of Boise."

Rhett hurried me into his Ford pickup, which was double-parked at the entrance. Then he drove like a maniac out of Boise, never even stopping at the Hotel Astor for my possessions. He raced along all the little back roads, avoiding the main highways, until we were well on our way down South.

Later I discovered that even before we were out of Boise's city limits, police were pounding on my hotel door. My name had "suddenly" appeared on the list of 500 men whose only crime was doing things differently behind a bedroom than some of their hunters.

Their lust for punishment was insatiable. For three years after that, they used every trick in the book to have me returned for "questioning," which would have naturally ended up in a prison term. A sheriff's deputy even came to Atlanta to bring me back. None of them was aware that my lover was one of the South's most up-and-coming young attorneys. He legally thwarted their every attempt at extradition until they finally gave up.

Others weren't so lucky. One schoolteacher was returned to Boise from California by the sheriff for some "routine questioning." The victim was promptly locked away for seven years in the penitentiary. The son of the councilman was thrown out of military school, his future career in the U.S. Armed Services terminated before it began.

Hundreds more had their lives destroyed or ruined forever. The homosexuals with power and money were never even touched. The male prostitutes who did most of the name-dropping never spent a day in jail. None of them protested the daily railroading of gay men into prison by unscrupulous attorneys, law-enforcement officials, opportunists, and religious zealots.

Today they like to pretend a minor incident was blown out of proportion by the media. Worse, many claim it never occurred. The victims will never forget it, and neither should we. When it occurs again, perhaps the hunted will resist this time—and fight back.

(*Author's note:* This story is based on a fact—that of a 1955 homosexual witch-hunt in Boise, Idaho so notorious that its reverberations are still being felt nearly forty years later. While the author is responsible for everything else in this story, he did not invent the historical occurrence of an all-American town trying to purge itself of its homosexual population.)

MIRACLE ON 55TH STREET

The pounding on my door was followed by a shout.

"Open up! It's the police!"

"What do you want? You told me you wouldn't bother me again!"

"You've got five seconds to open up. One! Two! I mean it. Three—"

I flung open the door. The young cop was tall, and his shoulders and chest were broad. The blue uniform of one of New York's finest covered his muscular torso. Moving swiftly toward me, he tore off his cap and dropped his holster into a chair.

"Ain't you glad to see me, you slut!" he sneered.

My back touched the wall, but still he came toward me—until his face was just inches above mine. On either side of me, he pressed his hands on the wall, thus imprisoning me. I felt his warm breath on my face, saw the sweat gleaming on his brow and in his black curls. Spitting out his gum onto the floor, he pushed his hips against me and moved them back and forth sensuously.

"Don't!" I pleaded. "You promised you wouldn't come back. You're so rough and brutal!"

His big hand grasped my face. "Shut up, slut, and give me what I want. Strip!"

I knocked his hand away. "The hell I will, you prick. Now get out!"

"I said *strip!*" he roared and tore off my robe. Looking over my nudity, he squeezed his crotch. "Mmm-mmm! Shit, but you look better each time I see you, Blondie. Let me see that little white butt of yours, boy. Show it or I'm ramming my billyclub up it!"

While his hands caressed my naked rump, his breathing grew harsh. His dark eyes danced with great amusement, while glinting with sexual hunger. A pink tongue slid over full lips, making them glisten beneath his mustache.

"Take off my clothes," he whispered.

Sweat from the scalding August sun had drenched his uniform. After pulling off his shirt, I saw once more how broad his chest was, dusted lightly with dark hair, and how large and round his pectorals were. His nipples glowed pale and thick in erection. His stomach was a fascinating display of sharply defined abdominals.

He kicked off his boots, stepped out of his slacks, and after I peeled down the moist BVDs from his tan line, he grabbed me to him and began to kiss me wildly. I felt myself being picked up easily, as if I were a kid, and carried into my bedroom, where he threw me down on the bed. Before I could escape, he covered my slim, dry body with his big, wet one, and pinioned my hands against the mattress. I felt him move the moist tip of his penis around on my stomach, so that it was crisscrossed with gleaming strands of his abundant lubricant. Suddenly, feeling me cease my struggle, he raised his lips from mine, looked down at me, and grinned.

"How'd I do this time—slut?"

"Not bad—stud!"

Then we burst into laughter as my arms tightened around his warm torso, which felt so hard and power-ful. He rubbed his face against mine, kissed my eyes, nose and my mouth gently.

"Did—did I really scare you this time, Jason?" he asked hopefully.

"I was ready to call in the SWAT team!"

He snickered like a little boy, pleased at his own display of machismo, and began to kiss me anew, this time mashing his genitals hard against my thigh. Once more, we had indulged ourselves in a game he loved to play: Mean Cop. My part in this fantasy was to enact the role of helpless sex object with the utmost conviction.

His fellow police officers at the Nineteenth Precinct in New York City adored rookie officer Jimmy Devereaux for his genuine sweetness and wit. When one teased him about looking like a Boy Scout with his wide-eyed expression of naïveté, he laughed along with them. He left them hysterical with his hilarious takeoff of the caricature of a New York policeman—the sadistic slob who chews up his cigars and fucks anything that moves. His father had been a detective, but was gunned down in a bank robbery. Alone now, with his mother long dead, Jimmy planned to get out of police work, get his degree in physical therapy, and work with handicapped people.

Only twenty-one, he had the muscular torso of an Olympic swimming star and the face of a sensual young cherub. For a brief time he had been married, but that had ended when he finally faced up to the fact that men—not women—turned him on.

Now he was insistently rubbing his stiff penis back and forth across my thigh, as I sucked his tongue. Who would ever think this sweet-looking guy was a rampant stallion in bed? Knowing what he wanted, I scooted down to slide the tip of his hardness into my mouth.

His fists gripped the silk sheets, his body became taut, his muscles bulged—all wet and brown, except for that startling strip of ivory across his hips.

There was no hair on his physique, except for his chest. At my urging, he had recently begun to let me shave him from his waist down to his toes each day. Even his pubic area was shorn clean. I edged more of him into my mouth until my lips touched that baby-lustrous surface. His penis swelled even harder and fuller, as if ready to burst from pressure within. Suddenly it began to pulsate, as it frantically squirted out its liquid contents.

As soon as it stopped, though, I began to suck him off again. Jimmy whistled, for his organ was still sensitive, but he didn't stop me. I felt him calming down some, as I knew he always enjoyed this second workout even more than the first. His eyes were still closed, a smile touching his lips when his penis began responding once more to my energetic lips. I felt his shaft thickening, becoming longer, so I could grasp the lower portion with my fist. And suddenly it began to throb once more as it lobbed out a second load of its spermy burden.

Jimmy's body arched. He gasped, blinked his eyes, and when he came down from his orgasmic high, he kissed me and moved his face down into my lap. My fingers dug into his thick curls as he skillfully brought me relief. We rested only briefly, before we were soon at each other once more. Taking me into his arms again, he began to fuck me in long, deep thrusts. He gloried in the use and the newfound power of his penis, which had been his wife's chief complaint. She had always called him an "oversexed maniac" because he *liked* to fuck! During that time, his rare encounters with men had been furtive and hurried in sleazy bathrooms and arcades. He had never experienced the joy in taking one's time, of having just one partner, of not being ashamed of doing what turned him on—and of realizing that the recipient of his sexual power loved it, too.

Eventually we showered, put on light summer clothing and, as he set the table, I brought out supper, which had been warming in the oven. It was his favorite: a savory meat loaf, mashed potato, and a broccoli casserole, covered with cheese sauce. It was a meal he could easily consume seven days a week and love it.

Our old-fashioned clock chimed six.

"We'd better get a move on, copper," I smiled. "Or I'll be late for the theater."

As we had done every Saturday for three months, we walked together along Broadway through Times Square, enjoying the autumn breeze skimming along the greasy sidewalks, sniffing the scents of pizza, pretzels, and hot dogs with sauerkraut, from the vendors' grills. We had to move slowly, though, because of the crush of people lining up before the box offices of movie houses and theaters.

We turned the corner of 55th Street off Broadway, and stopped to look up at the huge billboard atop the marquee of the Ritz Male Follies Theatre. There I was, twenty times bigger than life, looking down at the passersby, as I blew away the smoke from the tip of a toy pistol. I was garbed in my "cowboy" costume, which didn't consist of much: a white sequined vest, matching short-shorts, white boots, cowboy hat, and nothing more. I was winking—and smiling seductively—as if amused by the words beneath my feet which blinked in yellow lights:

EXCLUSIVE ENGAGEMENT!

JASON, THE GOLDEN BOY

OF MALE BURLESQUE!

AND HIS MUSICAL REVUE!

PLUS NINE HOT BOY DANCERS!

Matt Dempsey, the handsome millionaire owner of the theater, had promised me the star treatment. He had come through, all right, because next to the box office was an impressive display of my reviews from the off-Broadway musicals, cabarets, and posh nightclubs I had performed in. There were some tastefully done photographs of me in my Marilyn Monroe "disguise," and a more provocative one of me preparing to slip off my pants.

Several men, waiting in line, recognized me and asked me for my autograph. After we left them, Jimmy clutched my arm.

"Gee," he whispered gleefully, "I'm living with a real famous person!"

"Gee," I replied, teasingly, "I'm living with a real live police officer!"

Laughing, he put an arm around me and escorted me into the lobby. Later, I peered out of a hole in the curtain to check out the audience. Eddie, the "Surfer Boy" from Australia, was stripping down to his skin, and sitting in the front row in the seat I always reserved for him was the handsomest young cop in New York City.

Looking bronzed, sexy, and gorgeous in his pink

shorts and sleeveless T-shirt, Jimmy would blush and grin through the evening, as the dancers flirted with him—sitting in his lap, running their fingers through his curls, shaking their naked rump and genitals in his face. Everyone had a good laugh over this fleshy display of affection because it was all done in fun. Jimmy and I were a popular couple. We were known to be "tight" and didn't run around on each other.

It was Saturday night. The small, vivid theater with its posh red carpeting and magnificent chandelier was packed. From a dingy porno grindhouse (which had once been one of Broadway's most beautiful theaters), Matt Dempsey had used some of his fortune to restore it to its former grandeur. It was now a gay landmark. From all over the world, men flocked to the Ritz to see the most beautiful men alive strip naked. Unlike its neighboring Gaiety Burlesque and Show Palace theaters, the Ritz Follies was more than just a flesh show of men dropping their clothes to pop tunes. Matt had added live musical entertainment as frosting on the cake. That was how I had zoomed to the top of the male burlesque field.

My fans apparently loved seeing me strip down to my skin, and then reappear an hour later costumed as Marilyn Monroe or performing my imitations of Judy Garland, Barbra Streisand, Aretha Franklin, and even Madonna. A small combo accompanied me along with three gay guys who sang backup. Nature had blessed me with an uncanny gift of mimicry. When I performed Garland's "The Boy Next Door" or Monroe's "Diamonds Are a Girl's Best Friend" or Streisand's "People," some thought I was merely lip-synching to a recording, so exact was my rendition.

"You're next, Jason," whispered Bobby, the little stage manager. "Go tear 'em up, tiger!"

341

For my strip routine, I would begin as a Wall Street executive in my three-piece business suit, starched shirt, tie, hat, glasses—all of which hit the floor within five minutes. I smoothed back my blond curls and tapped my hat into place as Bobby introduced me over the sound system. There was the usual explosion of whistles, applause, and men screaming out my name. I liked dancing to the old rock 'n' roll classics, and that night eschewed the band for a recording by the Creedence Clearwater Revival: "Proud Mary." As it began to throb through the theater, I bounded out on stage, and as I took off my attire, I played to my luscious young lover in the front row—as if we were alone in our bedroom. I loved to watch him blush as he got a hard-on in public.

The night I met Officer Devereaux was the night he saved me from death.

It was around midnight when I left the private dance studio in the Village. For ten hours that day, I had sweated over the routines I would be doing that weekend at the Ritz Follies. Patrons probably thought there wasn't anything to getting up there and shucking your clothes or putting on a wig and gown and looking like Marilyn Monroe and singing some tunes.

Little did they know how fiercely competitive the field was. People always hovered offstage, waiting to replace you. Ricky, a little Southern bitch from Atlanta, was constantly after Matt to let him do his numbers. Fortunately, Matt was on my side. Even in the old days when I'd occasionally danced at his theater just for fun and to make some easy money, he had encouraged me to think of making it my profession.

"To you it's just a game," Matt had criticized me one night over a drink. "Yet you've got what Marilyn Monroe had—a radiant gold quality. When you go out there under those lights, you literally glow with your blond hair, white skin, and those big blue eyes. You don't look like you're over fourteen. Every guy in the theater wants to take you home and fuck you.'

I had scored some success in my singing engagements around Manhattan, in such posh bars and nightclubs as Michael's Pub, Café Carlyle, and Tramps. For fun, one night, I dressed up like Marilyn Monroe and did my impersonations of the superstars—and I was a smash hit. I was onto something big. Matt pleaded with me to return to his theater, where he would make me his "star attraction." I was delighted. Like a modern-day Florenz Ziegfeld, he treated his performers royally. He treated me like a queen, giving me my own dressing room and having chilled champagne waiting for me at the end of each show.

We didn't want to make my routines too piss-elegant. Patrons wanted to be turned on, so I had the handsomest male strippers dance naked in the background to some of my fast songs. The hottest number I did was with Mark, the bulging weight lifter from Paris. We'd have him sitting in the audience, dressed like a regular customer. As I went into my version of the old Etta James rhythm and blues rocker, "Good Rockin' Daddy," I would drag Mark up on the stage. While he pretended to cringe and blush, I would strip *him* naked, and then he would suddenly begin to writhe and rub himself against me while developing his famous hard-on—one I would hang his hat on. The crowds loved it—convinced that this muscle-bound beauty had suddenly turned from bashful businessman into a sex-mad exhibitionist. Once I

343

suggested to Jimmy that he should play the part if Mark ever got sick, but my beloved cop just blushed beet-red and made me promise never to mention the subject again.

Now I wished the powerful Mark were there with me as I hurried up Astor Place to the subway. The street was deserted. I touched the can of Mace in my jacket pocket and the thick iron bar in the other. Around my neck was a police whistle. Because of the AIDS epidemic, homophobia was on the upswing all over the city. Several violent gay bashings had occurred in that very area over the past month. Gangs of punks would drive in from New Jersey, armed with baseball bats and crowbars, to "have some fun with the fags."

A chill ran up my spine when a Chevy Malibu drove by me slowly. Faces of young men peered out, staring at me intently. I looked around for a building to step into. Everything was closed—it was too late. The car made a wild U-turn in the street and screeched to a halt beside me. Even before the doors flew open and three punks wielding baseball bats jumped out, I was blowing my police whistle.

"What do you think you're doin', huh—you fuckin' cocksuckin' fag!" hollered a thin youth with an acne-scarred face. "Want something to suck on, you AIDS-carrying sonofabitch? I'll give you something!"

I had run out into the street, just as a police car turned the corner. A baseball bat grazed my skull. One of the men pulled out a shaving razor, but I had my Mace can out and was spraying it wildly. I even managed to bop two of the creeps hard on their heads with my metal bar. They screamed with pain, but managed to jump back into their cars and race off. A young policeman jumped from the patrol car and ran up to me, while his partner took off after the scum.

344

"You okay, buddy?" he asked. "Christ, you seemed to be doing pretty good defending yourself from that garbage."

He put an arm around my shoulder, and I felt better, even somewhat triumphant, having defeated three cretins in their game of "fag bashing."

"When you're gay in New York City these days, you have to learn how to fight," I said, noting the name on his badge: Devereaux.

The cowards escaped, but Officer Devereaux and his partner drove me back to my apartment and even stayed for coffee.

"You look really familiar," Jimmy said. "I've seen you somewhere before."

"You ever see that big billboard on top of the Ritz Male Follies? That's me up there!" I struck a pose and announced, "Jason! The Golden Boy of Burlesque!" I laughed and relaxed. "Come by some night, and I'll get you in free. You won't be bored."

The young officers both turned pink, but they laughed, too, for you always expected the unexpected in Manhattan. When they left, though, it was Jimmy who gave me a playful wink and a thumbs-up sign of approval. A week later, he called me up.

"I saw your show last night. Wow, my first time in a place like that! You had the place jumping. When you did your Judy Garland tribute, it was like having her right there on-stage."

"Jimmy, drop by for a drink tonight. It's rainy and cold, so I'm not going anywhere."

An hour later, he sat next to me on my couch before the fireplace, where flames snapped away the wintry chill. In his tight, faded jeans and V-neck sweater (which showed much of his bare chest), he made a sizzling picture.

"You were wonderful last night," he repeated.

345

"Would you like me to give you a private performance, Jimmy? Right here, right now?"

"Sure! That'd be wonderful!"

I put the Pointer Sisters' "Slow Hand" on the stereo—and gave the performance of a lifetime. If my fans thought I embodied pure sex in my dance, they should have seen me that night as I danced around the living room. One by one, my white cashmere sweater, black loafers, and wool slacks fell to the floor. Clad only in blue silk bikini briefs, I went up to him—and sat down in his lap. His breathing had grown more rapid. His features reddened, as I put my arms round his neck—and kissed him.

Had I made a mistake? At first he just sat there, perhaps shocked senseless by this unusual proposition. But he didn't protest as my hand slid beneath his sweater to caress his bulging pectoral. His nipple stiffened. That was when he suddenly relaxed, pulled me closer, and jabbed his tongue deep into my mouth. With a moan, he pulled off my briefs and laid me down on the white fur rug before my fireplace. That was when we became lovers.

"It's like a fucking miracle," he said the next morning in bed.

"Well, you fuck like a miracle, Jimmy," I whispered, "so let's do it again!"

Neither of us believed we had seen the last of the gay bashers. Cars filled with hate-spewing hoodlums continued to invade the homosexual areas of the Village. Two lesbians were viciously assaulted with chains and bats and sent to a hospital. A gay man was tied naked to the bumper of a truck and dragged over miles of glass-strewn back streets. More and more concerned, Jimmy took me with him twice a week to a "shooting gallery," where I soon learned how to use a gun.

Before long, I came close to hitting the bull's eye most of the time.

To be on the safe side, I found a different dance studio, a mile away from the old one. Surely the creeps wouldn't bother me there.

Jimmy and I were leaving the studio one night when four figures suddenly rushed around us.

"I told you the faggot was here!" snarled one. "He's the one who Maced me!"

Jimmy shoved me back into the doorway while trying to pull out his revolver. A baseball bat knocked it out of his hand. I lunged for it, but one of the goons grabbed it, aimed it at me, and fired—just as Jimmy jumped him. To my horror, Jimmy was hit. He fell to the ground, blood quickly spreading over him from the hole in his chest.

"Oh, my God!" I cried out. "You sonofabitch, you killed him!"

Suddenly panicked, the lout dropped the weapon and joined the others who ran laughing and whooping to their car. I grabbed the gun and began firing at them. One youth screamed in pain as the others pulled him into the car and sped away. People were rushing to us from everywhere.

"Get an ambulance!" I pleaded. "He's dying!" I looked down at his death-white face. "Jimmy? Jimmy?"

His eyes remained shut as blood gushed from his beautiful young body.

Jimmy Devereaux did not die, though he came close to it. He had nearly bled to death. The bullet had grazed his spinal cord; however, and doctors said he would probably never walk again. Police did catch the bums responsible, but a bleeding-heart judge gave them all probation and a year of "community service." Nothing was done to the creep who pulled the trigger. Because he was only fifteen, he was sent to a juvenile detention home where he enjoyed bragging how he'd taken care of "at least one fag."

One afternoon, I paused in the doorway of Jimmy's room at New York University Medical Center. Lying in bed, he stared out the window, unaware of my presence. *Just a second or two can change our lives forever,* I thought. Because of a budding young criminal, Jimmy's days as an active policeman were over. His dream of being a physical-therapy teacher for the handicapped was destroyed forever. He was now a member of that minority which he had once wanted to help.

His face was pale and haggard, the dark eyes bitter and confused, that magical expression of boyish beauty and innocence lost in quiet rage. I blinked back my tears and put on the "happy face" the doctors told me to always wear with him.

"Hey, gorgeous!" I sang out and put down my magazines and box of bakery goodies he loved. "All the dancers told me to make sure you hurry up and get well, so they can flirt with you in the first row."

All my cohorts at the Ritz Follies had taken turns visiting Jimmy. It was a fascinating sight—to see some of the world's most stunning male strippers sipping coffee in the hallway with some of New York's most macho cops, who were also visiting Jimmy.

"That'll never happen again, Jason," sighed the patient. "If I ever get up again, it'll be on crutches and braces."

"Well, Jimmy Devereaux, at least you'll be up and around."

The doctors were sending him to a rehabilitation center in White Plains, where he would remain for months, and specialists now believed he would be able to use his legs again with the aid of crutches—if only he would work at it.

"My legs aren't completely dead, Jason," he assured me. "You know something? I—I got me a hard-on last night."

I hugged him tight. "Oh, wow—and I'll bet it was a beauty! Did you have one of the pretty nurses help you get it down?"

"I kept wishing you were here. If you want to go out with other guys, I'll understand. I'm no good that way anymore."

I kissed him. "Would you please shut up? I didn't fall in love with a cock, Jimmy—I fell in love with you."

"You—really mean that?" He smiled, and something of the old Jimmy flickered across his face. When I left, he gave me that roguish wink I loved—and his familiar thumbs-up sign of approval.

One night, the bodybuilder, Mark, and I left the stage after bringing down the house with our "Good Rockin' Daddy" routine. He was very naked and very aroused as he embraced me in my Marilyn outfit.

"Mark," I laughed, slapping his naked butt, "don't you *ever* get soft? Every time I see you, you're as hard as a brick."

He kissed me and grinned. "Maybe you keep me hard. Let's get together for a good time after the show tonight."

"Sorry, lover boy, but I'm seeing Jimmy tomorrow."

"Aw, give me a break. He won't be out for years."

"Well, if it means years, I'll *still* be waiting for him."

In his wheelchair, Jimmy whizzed toward me in the corridor of the crowded rehabilitation center. A new short haircut made him look like a little boy lost. His oversized robe and pajamas enhanced that image. We hugged each other tight, and his spirits lifted when he opened up the big box of gifts from the other dancers at the Ritz.

"Wow, I'm glad to see you again, Jimmy! The doctors say you're making progress."

"Yep," he grinned sourly. "From the bed to the wheelchair and one day—crutches! A great future I've got ahead of me." We talked for a while about how the police department would find him a desk job after he returned, and then, suddenly, he leaned forward and grasped my hand. "Do something for me. Don't wait for me. Go out and have some fun. Date all the guys you want. It'll be a fucking long time before I get out."

"The doctors say they're putting you on crutches soon, hotshot," I retorted. "So I'll just keep waiting. There aren't that many guys like you around, Jimmy Devereaux."

"Christ, honey, but you're one stubborn little bastard."

"Bastard? Make that bitch, Jimmy, and you'll have it right." He tried to look exasperated, but finally laughed. When I left, there was hope in his eyes.

No place in Manhattan rocked as hot and loud as the Ritz Male Follies did on Christmas Eve. Dressed in his traditional Santa Claus costume, Matt had an enormous buffet catered in from Sardi's. Champagne flowed like Niagara Falls—after the show. (He wanted his dancers to be able to perform sober.) All of us found fat bonuses tucked into our gifts of expensive sweaters, watches, and bottles of Obsession cologne.

Demand for seats was so great on Christmas Eve that all of them were reserved. At my request, Matt roped off one in the front row and on it he put the sign: "Reserved for Officer Jimmy Devereaux." I knew he wouldn't be there, but it was my gift to him, as I hoped that one night he might be. Doctors had told me that morning on the phone that he was depressed and morose. When I talked to him, he had sounded lost.

"Will you sing something for me tonight?" he'd asked. "Sing 'I'll Be Home for Christmas' and think of me."

All of us had worked like demons for a month on the big musical finale that would close our show that night. Mark, the powerful bodybuilder, nude, as usual, carried me out on the stage atop his brawny shoulders. The audience roared its approval. And for the next hour, I gave an Oscar-winning performance, joking and singing, before I sang the usual yuletide standards. Yet I kept glancing at that empty seat in the front row and thought of Jimmy.

Except for red Santa Claus hats, all the dancers remained naked, and they cavorted around me in most of the numbers. I wondered where Matt was. Usually, the boss loved to get up there and clown around, too. Finally I approached the edge of the stage and held out my hands for silence.

"I promised to dedicate a song tonight to someone who is very special to all of us. He's in the hospital at this moment, but for Police Officer Jimmy Devereaux—who saved my life—this one's for you."

The theater grew quiet instantly. Everyone recognized the name and its meaning to me, for the media had been full of stories about "the paralyzed rookie cop and his gay stripper boyfriend." The lights dimmed, and the dancers moved in closer around me, where they sang with more gusto than harmony:

> *I'll be home for Christmas.*
> *You can count on me...*

There was a slight commotion in the rear of the auditorium. A couple was moving slowly down the aisle. Some of the audience members were gasping and whispering. A ripple of excitement swept the crowd. What was going on? I recognized Matt in his Santa Claus suit. He was helping along a man on crutches. *Surely, it couldn't be...!* Someone grabbed my arm.

"Jason—look, it's Jimmy! He made it!"

Bobby, the little stage manager, took the microphone. "Excuse me, everyone, but we'd like to welcome our very special guest tonight. Police Officer Jimmy Devereaux!"

A collective gasp went up as everyone jumped to his feet. Applause began, grew louder until the little theater trembled from the whistles and cheers and the stomping of feet. The dancers were weeping and hugging me, and then Mark helped me down the steps and into the aisle. Leave it to Matt to provide this dramatic climax to holiday entertainment!

In Jimmy's arms, I kept whispering, "I can't believe it, Jimmy!"

Matt hugged us both. "I had a special limousine bring him in tonight. Merry Christmas, kids!"

Jimmy's body shook with sobs, as I told him, "I saved you a seat tonight."

He wiped away his tears with the back of his hand. "I thought you would. That's why I tried really hard to come down."

Back on-stage, the dancers hoisted me upon their

shoulders and we belted out the words to Jimmy's song request as they'd never been sung before.

And months later, doctors said it was a miracle, the way his spirits, and the improvement in his health, soared after that fateful night in the theater.

On a late morning in May, I saw Jimmy leave my apartment on his crutches as he started his first day of work back with the police department. I remembered what he had told me over coffee an hour earlier.

"A miracle really did occur that Christmas Eve night in that little theater on 55th Street," he'd said. "And his name is Jason Fury."

The Faggot and the Redneck

When I hear people yearn for their good old college days, I want to puke.

I had only been at East Carolina University for a week before most of the 21,000 student population had labeled me "freak." Word spread like wildfire that there was a "flaming faggot"—meaning me—on campus. People clustered in hallways, and hung out windows, to view the hip-shaking, soft-spoken "little blond-haired queer." I reportedly spent my nights on a ball field, taking on hordes of horny boys. It was rumored I had to regularly visit a doctor, to have my asshole sewn up due to my extracurricular activities.

This was during the sixties, when rednecks in button-down shirts, shiny loafers, and short hair ruled the campuses. Gay still meant "happy." Few had ever seen a real-live open homosexual. I didn't try to be a caricature of a campus stud, as the other gays had done. I acted the way I did from the first day I was born, and saw no reason to change. It never bothered me much—except when my mother screamed at me for being "a priss-pot" after I swiped her eyebrow pencil.

At dear ole ECU, fraternity farts would await my arrival in classroom buildings and launch into a rendition of the "Miss America" theme song—with a few differences. "There it isssss," they bellowed. "Mr. Cock-Suckerrrr." They would whoop and flip their wrists and dance around me. They knocked over my lunch trays in the cafeteria, blocked my way in the hallways, pounded on my door when they were drunk, tried pushing me downstairs, threw me out of the showers, and dropped balloons filled with water and piss on my head. If blacks thought they had it rough during the civil rights struggle, I wondered how their experiences compared to those of visible, effeminate homosexuals—both then and now.

When I informed the manager of our dormitory, Ronnie, that I had good reason to fear physical violence, he quickly had me move in with him. Big, blond, husky, he was a good ole boy from Montgomery, Alabama—and, strangely enough, he and I hit it off at once. We were opposite in our personalities, yet similar in our loathing of hypocrisy. (Most of my bullies could be seen attending church faithfully every Sunday.) He immediately appointed himself my bodyguard. And, as Ronnie was on the wrestling and boxing teams, nobody was going to mess with him.

I began meeting some of his buddies. Naturally, they had heard about me, and they studied me the way a bunch of gentle bulldogs might study a pretty little kitten. My effeminacy fascinated them. They had never met anyone like me before. When I told them of some of the things that had happened to me on campus, their handsome young faces scowled and they muttered, "Dumb shits. I'd like to break some necks." But, although I was developing a team of bodyguards, they couldn't be around me all the time. Life continued to be hell outside that room.

One of my worst tormentors was a bronze bruiser named Tommy Joe Dukes. He was a star player on the famed Crimson Tide football team. Black curls framed a square face that was rough, ugly—and yet beautiful. He resembled a convict; a construction worker, and an Adonis, all packed into one magnificent body. He fascinated me, primarily, because he never wore a stitch of clothing around the dormitory. He was a redneck farmboy who was proud of his torso and wanted everyone to see what he had. I'd go to the bathroom and find myself faced with a beautiful round rump, as Tommy Joe bent over a sink to brush his teeth. He hated my guts. Word got to me fast that if that "prissy, cocksucking sumbitch tries touching me, I'll throw that nellie ass of his out the window." He looked like he could do it, too.

While Ronnie was solid and white-skinned, Tommy Joe was bronzed all over, except for the pale strip around his hips. His musculature was sharply defined: big pecs, rippled stomach, powerful shoulders, arms, and thighs. Girls were wild about him. A gaggle of sorority bitches always surrounded him. They'd see me, Tommy Joe would whisper something to them, and they'd all just howl and flip their wrists. Although I hated his guts, I wondered how he'd be in bed. Just passing his nude form in the hallway assured me that, in size if nothing else, this redneck would be a handful. Make that two.

I went to the bathroom to clean up. Mr. Bare Ass himself was also in there, with two of his jock bud-

357

dies. They had been laughing, but became silent when I entered. I was certain I had been the source of their merriment. The only available sink was next to the unclothed wonder. I became intensely aware of not only his hostility, but his abnormal body heat.

"Mind if I use some shaving cream?" he asked, and before I could offer to shave his hairy chest, he grabbed my can of shaving cream—and tossed it into the trash can.

"What's the big idea?"

Looking at his grinning buddies, the football star smirked, "Faggots don't use shaving cream. They use makeup." He flipped his wrists, minced, and patted his hair delicately.

Suddenly fed up with this relentless harassment, I blew up.

"Bullshit! All faggots want is a stiff prick up their asses, like you had yours up in mine last night. Remember, stud? Oops! Did I say something I shouldn't?"

This was a lie, of course but I wanted to hit him where it hurt most—his macho pride—and boy, did I ever! His face looked murderous when he balled up his fists, and started to swing at me—just as my roommate Ronnie, and two of his buddies, appeared in the doorway,

"Hey, there, Tommy Joe," drawled my protector. "You giving boxing lessons, or do you plan on having some fun with my roommate there?"

Tommy Joe's buddies swiftly drifted away—cowards usually do—and my enemy glared at all of us. I had to admit that even in that explosive moment, he was an eyeful: nude, sweaty, muscular, and *very* macho. If only he didn't have that goddamn red neck!

Ronnie put an arm around my shoulder, and his

friends stood protectively close by. "Go back to your li'l ol' room, Tommy Joe. I don't want any trouble, or you're getting that naked ass of yours thrown out of school. You're on probation already. Now, give Jason back his shaving cream."

Muttering and scowling, that handsome troublemaker bent over, and we all had a glimpse of hairless butthole as his cheeks spread. He handed me the can.

Later I discovered that Ronnie and his companions had visited Tommy Joe in his room and laid down the law. No more harassment of me, or he'd be going back to his daddy's one-mule farm in Wilson, North Carolina, to pick cotton. As manager of the dormitory, Ronnie could see that this happened.

There was a marked difference in Tommy Joe's behavior toward me after that. He even nodded at me slightly in the hallway, and his brief glance was filled not only with confusion and hurt...but fascination.

It stormed one night, in late September. I rushed into the lobby of the dorm, and ran for the elevator. And who should come dripping from the storm to join me but my former enemy! We nodded at each other, shifted nervously on our feet, and got into the elevator car. I wanted to scream from nervousness until I heard a low "hi."

I looked up into dark eyes, surrounded by thick lashes, and noticed for the first time a scar above full, moist lips. "Aren't you going to say something?" he grinned.

"Is it safe to?" I said coldly. He ducked his head, rubbed his nose, and began talking. "Look, I've been giving you a hard time. I'm sorry. You hate my guts. You got reason to. I came to apologize. Ronnie says you're okay, even if you are different."

He looked like a little boy, growling the words out,

trying to be tough, but looking only more vulnerable. "Did Ronnie ask you to do this, Tommy Joe?"

He glowered indignantly. "Shit, nobody tells Tommy Joe Dukes what to do! It's me talking." He held out a hand. I put mine in his rough paw and felt an immediate jolt. "Wow, you shocked me!"

The football star grinned, and his eyes danced. I saw then what powerful charm he could turn on when he wanted to. "Yeah, that's what people tell me." We got off on our floor and began to part. "I'll see you around, Tommy?" I watched that gorgeous butt undulate beneath soft, wet denim as he walked down the hall. He turned his head, winked and kept walking.

I told Ronnie about our encounter. "He's just a good ole country boy," my roommate observed. "He wants everybody to think he's a real he-man stud. Doesn't want anybody to think he might be soft—or a sissy."

"Like me? Or is it a faggot?"

Ronnie laughed, and I joined him. With him I could be completely natural—and I knew that my roommate was becoming more interested in me with each passing day. His eyes would light up when I came into the room. He liked to sneak up behind me, put his big arms around me, and wrestle me onto the bed.

Which is what happened one Sunday morning.

I was smearing on face cream when he came out of the showers, naked as a jaybird. Suddenly I felt strong, wet arms embrace me, and felt myself being raised up in the air as he whirled me around the room.

"You redneck jock!" I protested. "Put me down. You're ruining my makeup!"

Laughing, he set me on my feet, but still held me

close to him. I looked up into those clear blue eyes, so innocent and so sweet, and knew what was coming. "I'm really glad you moved in with me, Jason," he said, smiling.

"I think I can feel how glad," I drawled. "Is that a flashlight rubbing against me, or are you just glad to see me?"

He blushed because his erection was pulsing against my stomach. I reached down and squeezed it. He gasped and pulled me down with him on his bed.

"Wow, Jason, you're gonna make me blow!" I slid my mouth down his powerful chest, past his stomach, and onto his white column with the pink tip that beat lightly against his abdomen. I had been wanting to eat him since the day I first saw him, and now I hungrily slid his prick into my mouth. I could feel it swell even larger, and then my mouth was suddenly flooded with sperm.

When I lay in his arms afterward, we kissed until he was hard again. This time, I suggested he slide it up my ass, and he did so. He was clumsy at first—since he'd never fucked a man before—but afterward, he told me it was better than screwing a woman.

As the days passed, and Ronnie and I balled constantly, I know that this was not going to be just a buddy-type sex relationship, where we used each other primarily to get our rocks off. Ronnie genuinely loved me. You have only to look at a person's eyes to realize that. It never bothered him in the least to be seen with me on campus. Most guys could blush and duck away if I tried talking to them outside the dorm. Ronnie had the courage of his convictions, and public opinion meant nothing to him. And, too, nobody could ever conceive of this powerful, butch he-man ever doing anything "queer."

Tommy Joe asked me one day if I could help with

361

an English term paper, since I was reputed to be a "whiz" at writing, I was startled, but interested. He warned me, though, to try not to let anybody see me enter his room: "I don't want them to get the wrong idea."

When I entered his room that night, he wore just a pair of BVDs. He was stretched out on the bed, with his books and papers beside him. I sat at the foot, and it was soon obvious that studying was the *last* thing he had on his mind. I was charmed by his crude and blunt approach. He squeezed his genitals, and said abruptly, "Wanna see something nice? Take a look at this." He pushed his shorts down, and pulled out his uncut slab of meat, and his loose sac of apple-sized balls.

"Suck my dick, Jason. I'm hurtin' read bad." And without further ado, I went down on him—and was surprised at how much fun his cock was. You could bend it, bite it, and twist it, and that made him even wilder. And even after he shot, he told me to lie on my back. He wanted to fuck me. There was no tenderness in the act. All he wanted was to get his rocks off, because the minute he came, he told me to get out: "And don't tell anybody, or I'll kill your ass."

He acted like an animal—but still, even as I lay in Ronnie's arms that night, with his pecker pushed up to the hilt within me, I kept thinking of Tommy Joe's hot, muscled body—the way he whimpered and gasped and threw his whole soul into the sex act. The way you could pull and bite his prick, and the way he could hold his cum until you told him you wanted it. He was a fascinating sensualist.

The next day, he came into the bathroom where I was shaving, and without looking at me, muttered, "Come on by for a quickie. Don't let anybody see you. I'm hurtin' bad." Hating myself, I went—and

362

loved it. In his own way, he grew to like me as we got to know each other better, but I knew, too, he would never accept me for what I was. I'd always be a freak—a convenient suck-and-fuck buddy, and nothing more.

It was a bizarre situation. I was sharing the beds of two of the handsomest men on campus—the kind women would kill for—and both were considered so straight that no one would ever conceive of them as being my lovers. One was so blond, white and blue-eyed that he resembled a Viking, and the other was so swarthy, powerful and high-spirited that he could have been a Gypsy or an Italian.

In bed one night, when Ronnie and I had just had marvelous sex, he startled me by saying, "Don't get mad, but something tells me you're seeing Tommy Joe a lot."

"How...how do you know?"

That night in the bathroom, he had sensed a definite spark between me and the football player. And, one night in my sleep, he had heard me murmur, "Tommy Joe.... Tommy Joe...."

I felt terrible. I told Ronnie I wouldn't see him anymore.

I dreaded telling my wild, bronzed lover this. And I continued putting it off, while Ronnie became quieter—for he know I was under Tommy Joe's sexual spell. One night my roommate held me close, and whispered, "Look, baby, I don't care if you fuck a thousand guys. I'll always be here—and I'll always love you." I wanted to climb into a hole.

It was the night before the first big game of the season—the Crimson Tide would battle Clemson the next day. I met Tommy Joe out in the wooden area behind the dorm, where he had parked his car. From there, he drove out to our usual place, in the middle

363

of an isolated pasture. He was so paranoid about somebody finding out about us that he wanted only "quickies" in his room.

On this particular night, after I had spent nearly an hour with my head between his thighs, eating his prick, balls, and asshole until my jaws were sore, we took a break. Sipping a beer and smoking a cigarette, he was full of excitement as he told me about what fun being a football player could be—out on the field, with thousands of people cheering you on.

"It sounds like that line of poetry," I said. "You know. The one that goes: 'midst the tumult and the shouting and the blue October air.'"

"Hey, that's terrific! Say it again. That's exactly what it is. Write it down, will you?" He repeated the line several times, as if he had discovered something rare and wonderful. Then, before I could say anything about breaking our relationship, he brought the subject up himself.

"By the way, I don't know if you're fucking around with other guys, but if you are, I want you to stop. When I'm going with a girl, I want to be the only one; and, well, you ain't no girl, but still it's the same thing. It's just me, or nobody."

"Oh, come off that, Tommy. You're fucking girls right and left. Why should I be faithful to you?"

He was furious. "It's different. I'm the guy with the meat and the body." He squeezed his genitals and pushed them into my hands. "Looka that cock, and those balls. You won't find any bigger on campus. Anybody would love to be where you are right now, playing with my big dick, eating my cum, and having me fuck you."

"I'll think about it," I said, with much difficulty.

"You let me know tomorrow, okay?" He told me to meet him in the entrance of an empty classroom

364

building next to the stadium. He'd be waiting for me at ten sharp. "And don't let anybody see you, okay?"

Ronnie was unusually passionate that night, as if trying to outdo Tommy Joe in the sex department. I told him of Tommy Joe's ultimatum. Looking down at me, through the darkness, Ronnie asked, "And what will your decision be?"

"I don't know yet."

Ronnie sighed. "I'd like to knock some sense into you—but I'm gonna fuck you instead."

Tommy Joe was waiting for me the next morning. He was crackling with excitement, as thousands of sport fans and students poured into the stadium nearby. We could hear the band playing "When the Saints Go Marching In," the cheerleaders cheering, and the crowds roaring and laughing at something. It was a beautiful autumn day with a chilly nip in the air. Within an hour or two, Tommy Joe would be out there on that field, thrilling his fans, and making tomorrow morning's sports headlines.

"Did anybody see you?" he asked fearfully and pulled me into the drafty old hallway. Looking around nervously, he bent down and kissed me, and pressed my hand against his crotch.

"Look," he whispered, "I...I more than like you, Jason. There are some other guys on campus who want you, like that roommate of yours. I've seen how he looks at you. I don't want to lose you, baby. Understand? You're gonna be mine and nobody else's, right?"

The roar of the crowds nearby sounded louder, as I began backing away. I shook my head. "So long, Tommy Joe. You were great fun, but you've always been ashamed of being seen with me. There are others who aren't. There's one waiting for me right now."

His face was a study of rage, astonishment, and pain. "What the fuck are you doing? You stupid little sonofabitch, you know what you're losing? I'm the man with the meat!"

And so I left him standing there, "midst the tumult and the shouting and the blue October air."

KING OF THE CITY

There are still people on Lower Broadway who remember the days when Mario was head of the Dead Rats—and I was just a small white blur who followed him everywhere.

But when those people speak our names today, they do so with a shake of their heads. How could two half-brothers follow such different paths in life?

The late '70s saw the last gasp of the notorious street gangs of New York—the Muthas, the Bloody Skulls, the Virgin Marys, the Fuckers. By far the most violent gang was the Dead Rats.

They gloried in mayhem, maiming and gang rapes—and in street rumbles that sent many into the hospital and others to Potter's Field to be buried. None of us was surprised when my half-brother Mario assumed leadership of these thugs.

Although I worshiped him, I knew his dark side,

too. By thirteen, he had already fathered a child by a married woman. At sixteen, he acted like a grown man. Years of street fighting had toughened him, but it had not cheapened him. He always had, great inner dignity. With his slicked-back black hair, his square and rugged face scarred above the mouth, he was already a powerful personality on our block near Fourteenth Street and the Hudson River. Whenever I see the *Godfather* movies today, I can see Mario very easily moving around with those swarthy men.

Just as he commanded attention, so did I—in a different way. I was small and white-skinned with glowing blond curls and big blue eyes. At fourteen, I looked like a kid still going to grammar school, since I never grew more than five-foot-three. No one could believe Mario and I were brothers.

In a single bed, we always slept naked together. He would hold me tight against him and tell me the plots of Hollywood gangster movies he had seen. One night he looked up at the cheap print above our bed. It showed the Virgin Mary surrounded by blond-haired angels. My brother kissed me, nuzzling his handsome face against mine, and whispered, "You've got a face just like one of them angels. You've got an angel's face." And to him I would always be Angel Face.

Our mother deserted us; my father died of drink soon thereafter. So we moved in with Carlo, Mario's best friend. Mario was quiet and moody, but Carlo was always fun, impish. We all slept together naked in his bed. I was thrilled that each night I slept between two of the handsomest Italian boys on Lower Broadway.

As Mario began inching his way up in the criminal underground, he did so under a front of working on the docks. Carlo found a safer job in a men's clothing store. After I finished high school, I worked as a secretary for a while, but then won a four-year scholarship to Duke University.

Carlo and Mario were proud—but sad, too, that I would be leaving our little "family." I was elated. For a long time I'd felt I was smothering under their attentions. Although they went out all the time and fucked girls and bragged about it, they sensed I was gay and would have killed any man I dared to be "seen with."

That last summer before I went off to college, there were nights when the three of us would hang out on the rooftop and watch the ships glide by on the huge river. We'd play a game. "When I'm king of this city, I'll buy the biggest place you've ever seen.. When *I'm* king, everybody will know it!..." When, when, when!

It was blazing hot one June night when Carlo came in from work. He dashed into the shower and quickly came out in just a towel. Water still sparkled on his tawny, muscled flesh and in his black curls. Opening a can of beer, he flopped beside me on the bed where I was watching "Saturday Night Live."

"Did you miss me?" he teased.

"I cried into my pillow every second you were gone." He laughed, grabbed me and began to wrestle with me the way he always did. His towel came off, but he didn't put it back on. We were used to seeing each other naked, especially in bed.

"You'll be gone in three months, and I'll be in the Marines," he said sadly, sitting up. "I joined today." Amazed at this news, I hugged him tight.

My hands had been stroking his back, and now they moved down to his hips. They felt so warm and smooth. Carlo began to tremble. He gasped as my hands slid into his lap, began squeezing and stroking

369

the large erection that was already tapping against his flat stomach. His mouth settled on mine. This time I knew he wouldn't be giving me one of those sexless brotherly kisses. Mario wasn't around to spy on me.

Carlo laid me back gently, and then he raised himself over me. I felt his high, moist buttocks and spread them so my finger could trace around his anus. His penis was pushing against my stomach. I grabbed it hard, pushed down the cock covering and ran a finger along the wet urethra, parting the lips and pushing the tip of my thumb into the large opening. Carlo was panting hoarsely now as he raised my legs, put them around his waist, and positioned the tip of his erection against my asshole.

"Am I the first?" he whispered. "Anybody got your cherry yet?"

I shook my head. "You're the first, Carlo."

"Hold tight, then. It might hurt some."

When he popped the tip in, I cried out and clung to him. But eventually, as he inched his way in, slowly, tenderly, I began to relax, to enjoy the exhilarating experience of having this beautiful young man inside my body. His hips moved steadily and rapidly as he continued kissing me, nibbling my ears, licking my face. Our sweat soon soaked the sheets.

"It's coming," he murmured. "Can't hold it back anymore..." His hips slowed their frantic movements, he raised himself slightly, and then he shuddered as he ejaculated.

He had pulled out even before his orgasm was over, so I could see it. I thrust the sticky dick into my mouth and caught the last of his cum. Even then, I continued sucking relentlessly until I felt his dick begin to stir. Carlo was breathing heavily again. And as the head began to swell, I pushed my tongue into the opening. This time he quickly filled my mouth with sperm.

We were kissing each other, laughing softly at having finally made sexual contact, when I felt a draft. We looked up. Mario stood at the foot of the bed.

His face was like a death mask: hard, expressionless. Carlo began to put his feet on the floor, but my brother grabbed him by his hair and slung him against the wall.

"I thought I could trust you with my brother," Mario shouted. "You're worse than any of those old fruits out there on the streets, you fucking faggot!" I was pulling at his arm now, but Mario flung me aside, grabbed Carlo's clothes, and threw them in his face. Then he pushed him out the door.

"If I see you again, I'll kill you!" he yelled as Carlo fumbled with his clothes out in the hallway.

"You sonofabitch!" I screamed. "How could you do that? Carlo's our brother!" Mario slapped me and pushed me back on the bed. He stood over me, staring down at me, biting his lip and shaking his head.

His handsome face looked puzzled and hurt. "Don't you understand anything? You're mine! Nobody's ever gonna have you but me. Can't you understand that?" His words chilled me, but I couldn't let him see that. "Mario, I'm human! You keep me locked up like a prisoner. Carlo was my first man. You know I'm gay. I want sex just like you do when you fuck all your women."

Already he was stripping off his clothes, and all the time his eyes never left my face. Even in that tense moment, I couldn't deny his magnificent beauty. He was heavier, more muscular than Carlo. Hours on the docks had tanned him darkly. His penis hung

371

dark, glossy and untrimmed down his thighs. He put a hand around it, and flapped it at me.

"You want a man? Okay, you got one! Why didn't you tell me? I could've been your stud years ago."

I was stunned. Before I could reply, he had slid beneath the sheets and pulled me to him. His lips were electrifying. I had seen them all my life, had wondered how they would feel touching mine, and now it was happening. His penis had grown thick and was growing bigger. With its wet tip it nudged my stomach like a cucumber fresh from the rain. He guided my mouth down to it. He sat up on the edge of the bed and put me on the floor, between his thighs. I wrapped my fists around the lower portion of the stalk while my mouth enveloped the bullet-shaped cockhead.

On either side of me, his muscular thighs brushed my cheeks. I dug my tongue deep into his cock opening, I stroked it brutally, mashed his testicles until my hands shook—but all this roughness merely excited him. He *liked* it rough!

He grunted in enjoyment while muttering, "Oh, that's nice...that's good...take all you want...nobody else will have it from this day on...it'll always be your dick, Angel Face... Nobody else will ever touch it but you...it's got your name on it... Ohhh, I gotta shoot!... It'll be a big one... You'll Love it... Let me show you..."

He pulled out the swollen organ, all pink and purple. After just a few strong strokes, it squirted an astonishing stream of semen against my chest. Mario grunted, smiling at me, as six or seven more sprays of thick white cum spattered against me.

Mario pulled me up into his lap. He began to rock me as he held me close and whispered, "As long as you're here and you want sex, don't go looking for it.

You come to me and you can have all you want. Anytime. I don't want any other man soiling you."

Fury at what he had done to Carlo still boiled within me. I wanted to humiliate him, make him fail. "I want it now, Mario. Right now. I want you to fuck me good and hard."

He wasn't surprised. He just blinked his eyes and raised my hips slightly. I felt the tip of his penis pop into me. "You got it," he grunted. "Ummmm, you're gonna like my fucking," he smiled sensually.

And for the next three months, not one day passed that I wouldn't ask Mario for sex. Not just once a day, but several times a day. Never once did he protest or try to postpone me. He seemed thrilled to be able to satisfy me. But even when we weren't having sex, I could look up and see those dark eyes watching me...watching me...and he would say, "We'll always be together after you finish college. If you ever try leaving me, I'll kill us both."

The morning I was to leave for Duke, Mario broke down. He wept and pleaded with me to stay. He couldn't get along without me. I kissed him and put my arms around him.

During my four years in college, Mario was a frequent visitor. His fortunes were rising steadily. His friends had helped him by first buying him one restaurant, then another and another. He always looked dazzling and mysterious on his visits, causing the hearts of the girls and my gay friends to beat faster. He sent me beautiful cashmere sweaters, roses, silk pajamas, a VCR, my favorite movies, and money. I kept the gifts but returned the money. I could take care of myself, I told him. He didn't protest, and I think he admired me for it.

On graduation day, he stood out from the thousands with his new black beard, a gray tailored suit, looking like a movie star from a Mafia movie. He gave me an expensive ring and watch. In his big Lincoln Continental, we laughed and talked. In bed, we made up for all the nights we had been apart.

It was then I realized that he had been telling me the truth. No one had touched his genitals except me! The quantity of his sperm was incredible. Of course, we had gotten it on during his visits, but these were only once a month. I had had a number of casual partners in college, but compared with Mario, they were so inexperienced.

During my college years, by reading the New York papers, I had kept up on the various underworld explosions. After one of the top Mafia figures was gunned down, there were rumors a "young don" was being groomed to take over. He was reputed to be movie-star handsome, but he was also eccentric, reclusive. Some thought him crazy. He had a younger brother in a Southern university. This mysterious figure had once led one of the city's most violent youth gangs.

During the trip north from Duke, Mario kept teasing me about a big surprise, yet another graduation present. I began to suspect what it was when the doorman at the most expensive condominium building on the swanky Upper East Side stepped up to the car, saluting smartly. When Mario and I got off the elevator on the 31st floor, we entered a magnificent suite—complete with floor-to-ceiling windows, marble and crystal figurines, a huge fireplace.

"Welcome home." Mario smiled proudly. I looked around me in astonishment. I had seen such aerial homes only in magazine spreads. Expensive oil paintings hung on the walls, huge cushions were scattered around the room, a little Siamese cat with a red silk collar came up and brushed against Mario's legs.

374

"Mario! I can't believe it! Good God, it must have cost millions." He opened a bottle of chilled champagne and handed me a brimming goblet. Pulling me close to him, he guided me out onto the balcony. Before us stretched the glittering landscape of Manhattan. To our left flowed the East River.

"We always wondered who would be king of the city," he said quietly. "I'm getting there. One day everybody out there will know me, and you'll have everything you want."

The wind was freezing. He picked me up and carried me into "our" bedroom. I knew then that he had no intention of letting me have my own space. At last he had me, and he was never going to let me go. I forgot my misgivings quickly, though. Mario was rampant, delighted at having me again at his side. His sexual resilience that night was extraordinary. His penis stayed hard, even after his second, third, and fourth copious ejaculations. Mario was indeed on his way to becoming king of the city—and then some.

One November day, as I waited for a traffic light to change, I was overwhelmed by the feeling that I had to get away. I wanted my own life and my own career. I knew, too, that Mario would never allow it. As he'd often said, he would not only kill me for trying to leave him—he would then kill himself. "We live in one another," he would mutter. "Can't you understand that? We live in one another!"

A young policeman had been studying me as I balanced on the curb. Uneasily, I watched him walk toward me, whirling his nightstick and whistling a tune. He stood beside me now, staring at me intently.

"Could you by any chance be Angel Face?"

I was astonished. Only Mario and Carlo had ever called me that.

375

"Carlo!"

Laughing, he grabbed me and whirled me around.

He was amazed when I showed him my new home. Luckily my half-brother was out of town. Sipping the drink I had made for him, he stared for a long time at the huge painting of Mario and me above the fireplace.

"So he's still got you," Carlo said. "It's not normal, Angel Face. You've got to get away from him."

"I am—eventually. But tell me about what you've been doing."

The years had matured him into a fine-looking young man. He had grown a thick mustache, but his eyes still danced occasionally with the high spirits and mischief I had always loved. He had married a German girl, they soon split, he had screwed around California for a while, then decided to become a cop.

Putting down his drink, he came over to me, pulled me against him and began kissing me. We found ourselves in the bedroom, stripped and in bed. He resumed just where he had left off five years before. He had become more experienced during the time. So had I. While Mario was thicker, Carlo was longer—and the easy sliding of his penis into me seemed to last forever.

He had thought about me all the time, he whispered as his hips moved faster. Even when fucking his wife, he would pretend it was me. He had been afraid to make contact with me because of Mario. He knew that to Mario murder was the same as throwing a newspaper into a garbage can. I told Carlo to cum in my mouth. He withdrew and thrust his bulging penis between my lips. As soon as he did, he began to ejaculate in powerful spurts. And we fucked like that all through the night.

376

Before he left, I told him I wanted Mario and him to become friends again. Carlo was wary, but I was insistent. When I told Mario of seeing Carlo again, he was surprisingly enthusiastic about the reunion. He felt bad about what had happened five years before and wanted to make amends.

We were uneasy at first, but after a few drinks, all three of us began laughing and remembering the good times.

When we went out onto the balcony, Carlo swept his hand across the cityscape. "Well, you made it, Mario. Of us three, you really did become king of the city."

"Not yet," my brother said quietly, "but I'll be getting there, very soon. And soon everyone will know me."

As I walked Carlo to the subway, he suddenly grabbed my arm and shook me. "You've got to get out of there!" he hissed. "Mario's crazy! The way he keeps watching you. And the FBI is watching your place. I hear things at the police department. They know Mario's preparing to take over as headman."

I, too, knew I couldn't wait any longer. I would have to move fast. Although I loved Mario, he was driving me to a nervous breakdown with his abnormal possessiveness. I arranged to move in with Carlo that weekend while Mario was in Miami for a "convention."

Carlo opened the door to his small studio in the Village. I was shaking from fear after running away from Mario, but in Carlo's arms I began to feel safe.

He wore nothing but a pair of sheer bikini briefs the color of a spring sky. His warm, hard body, his firm muscles and his passionate mouth soon made me tingle. I pushed down his briefs, and he stepped out of them.

377

"Come on, I'll make you feel better." Rolling his eyes comically and letting his tongue loll around, he flipped his cock at me. "You little slut. You need some of Carlo's big hot dog to cheer you up."

In bed, as he kissed me, he kept repeating, "Don't worry, baby. I'll protect you. Mario will never find you here. A lotta cops live around here. It's the safest place in Manhattan."

He pushed himself up into me. "There," he grunted. "You feel better? Ummm, there's some more. That feel good?" His hips began moving in a steady rhythm as he studied my face, kissed me, dug deeper.

Looking over his shoulder and watching the white buttocks bob up and down, I saw the door open slowly. There stood Mario, a huge revolver in his hand. It was pointed at us.

"Carlo! Look out!" I shouted. He pulled out and rolled over on his back. Holding his hands out, he told Mario to cool it.

"Mario, don't hurt your brother! Now, I'm leaving here and—" It was just like that day five years before, when Mario had found us together.

"I should have killed you back then. Turning my brother into an animal like you!" I sprang out of bed and started toward him as she moved closer to Carlo. Before I could reach him, he pushed the gun toward Carlo and began firing. Horrified, I watched dark holes bloom all over Carlo's body. I tried to knock the gun from Mario's hand, but he flung me against the wall.

As I struggled to get up, Mario let the gun drop to the floor. He left the room, saying over his shoulder, "You know where to find me." I ran over to Carlo. A woman down the hall was screaming. I heard men shouting, the wail of a police siren...footsteps running down the sidewalk...people rushing into Carlo's apartment.

I grabbed Carlo and held him against me. Incredibly, he was still alive. In his eyes, though, I saw his life receding...slipping away....

"Angel Face," he whispered. When the paramedics pulled me away, there was so much blood on me, they thought I'd been shot, too. Two young officers comforted me as we watched the Carlo's body being zipped up into a rubber bag.

I killed him, I thought. *If only I had stayed with Mario....*

Mario now lives at Riker's Island. He will be there for life. He murdered a cop, and in the halls of justice, there is no crime worse than that. He will be eligible for parole in fifteen years.

When I was with him yesterday, he was as well groomed as usual, even in prison, but his skin was washed out. Yet his eyes sparkled with an abnormal light when he saw me again.

"Why did you have to kill him, Mario?" I asked him again. "He loved you. He was our brother." I looked around the dingy visiting area with the bulletproof partition that separated us. "You were going to be king of the city—and you got this."

Lighting up a cigarette, he snorted. "Yeah, I am the king. I'm the big shot of this city of meatballs, airheads, and assholes."

He said this with such a light, mocking air, I had to laugh. A smile softened his full lips. His charm was not yet extinguished.

"Will you wait for me, Angel Face? When I get out—will you be there?"

"Wait for you? Good Lord, Mario, you won't be free until after the year 2000!"

He laughed softly. "There's no law against dreaming."

379

"Oh, Mario! Don't you ever give up?"

His eyes were dark and he licked his lips as he answered, *"No!"*

I can still see his eyes, watching me...watching me...as they always will...even as I write this. He sent me a letter yesterday. It contained only five words: *We live in one another.*

THE LAST OF THE SEVEN BEAUTIES

I read the neatly typed invitation once more, although
I know the words by heart:

You are hereby commanded to attend the gala
reunion of the last of the Seven Beauties of
Wrightsville Beach—Kris the Body, Chick the Stud,
you, the Boy Beautiful, and yours truly, Tyler the Kid.
Bring your own wheelchair, hearing aid and other
necessities of old age, if need be, for this blast from
the past, commencing October 23, at the Ramada Inn
(which I now manage).
                    P.S. Hey, Jason! Remember "Adorable."

How could I ever forget that golden oldie by The
Drifters? No matter where we all went that crazy year
of 1967, someone would inevitably punch up
"Adorable" on the jukebox and my fellow "Beauties"

could proceed to squabble over who would dance with me. And when my chosen partner swung me out on the floor, the others could act like fools, scampering around us, pretending to fight over my choice, and then bellowing out the words to "my" song: "You're adorable...when you're here in my arms...."

We were so close that Tyler, in fact, never really recovered after our separation. For twenty years he had been trying—unsuccessfully—to get us all back together again. He even sent out an annual newsletter providing us remaining survivors with updates on who was doing what.

Along with the invitation, he had enclosed an old snapshot which he captioned: *The Seven Beauties in Action.* I had to laugh at our tag with which someone had christened us one night when we had crashed a party at one of the beach houses. As we crowded into the living room, the host drawled: "Well, I'll be damned. If it ain't the Seven Beauties."

We may have joked about our new name but we never disputed it. Each of us was indeed a unique specimen.

In the snapshot, the blue Atlantic glistens in the background as we clowned around on the beach.

I stand in the very center of the group, wrapped in a pink bedspread, only partially shielding me from the cold. They dubbed me the Boy Beautiful because at that time I had a mane of golden hair, huge eyes of periwinkle blue, and a trim, lithe body which barely reached the shoulders of the others.

Pretending to strangle me was my steady boyfriend, Beautiful Mike Gerraty. We called him Beautiful Mike because he was a dazzling hunk, with jet hair, green eyes, and a boxer's build. His high spirits made him a favorite of everyone. He's "officially" been dead for eighteen years, though, having vanished into the limbo of Vietnam.

Chick the Stud is mimicking a menacing ape, an animal with which many thought he shared much in common—in habits, not appearance. Fleshy and sensual, with sleek, good looks, he fascinated us all because of his unabashed fascination with his cock. He was our personal jerk-off champion and loved doing it for others. In the seventies, he even appeared in some terrible porno flicks cranked out in Florida, and then stayed on down there to manage a string of strip joints.

Flexing his incredible torso in a typical bodybuilder stance is six-feet-five Kris the Body. His eye-popping physique would stop traffic when he appeared in one of his skimpy pairs of briefs. He went on to become a successful and popular pro football player. He's married now, with two kids, and runs a chain of health spas, and from time to time competes in physique contests and still manages to snatch a win now and then.

Kneeling down, and trying almost desperately to look comical, is Tyler the Kid. We called him that because his face was so childlike despite his being handsome and husky. Even the mustache he eventually grew made him look more vulnerable than adult.

Ashley is in a praying position. Ironically, or maybe not, he's dead now, too. When the folksinging craze died, so did his modest career on the East Coast. In Los Angeles he had no luck, either, and ended up panhandling. His emaciated body was found a year ago in an alleyway, his hands clutched around his battered old guitar and an empty bottle of Thunderbird wine.

And there is swarthy Mario, the Italian stallion, another who we'll never see again although not because of death. A wealthy widow snatched him up after his wild days as an artists' model. Today he's a grandfather in Maryland, complete with gray hair and paunch. His wife is reputed to be terrified of his ever encountering any of the rest of us "Beauties" because of our "scandalous" reputations.

I put the picture and invitation aside, checking myself out in the mirror before leaving the room Tyler had assigned me. My shoulder-length locks have long been shorn into a mass of gold curls. A dab of mascara makes my eyes look even more blue and lustrous.

I *have* to look good since becoming a celebrated drag queen of Broadway. My boyish torso is clad in a cashmere sweater of dusty blue and matching tweed slacks. My rump still draws wolf whistles from construction crews when I swish by them at lunchtime. "Hey, blondie, wanna play with my hammer and nuts? I'll give you a coupla screws, too, ha, ha, ha!"

Okay, Boy Beautiful, this is it. Your blast from the past. I gulped down a shot of vodka for courage, popped in a Tic Tac, sprayed myself once more with some Royal Bain de Champagne and headed for the bar to meet what's left of the Seven Beauties—all of whom had been my sex partners and lovers before I promised myself to Beautiful Mike Gerraty.

"California Dreamin'" was finished up on the jukebox. Yep, that meant the boys were definitely around somewhere. That too had been one of "our" songs. It was so dim in the bar I could barely see, but then behind me, someone gasped: "Ho-leeee, *shit*! It's Jason! Hit 'Adorable'!"

The Drifters began crooning, "You're adorable... as sweet as can be..." And joining them were three men who came dancing and twisting out of the shad-

384

ows with their arms outstretched. "You're excitable...when kissed once or twice...."

"Oh, my God!" I laughed. "Don't tell me! The last of the Seven Beauties!" Others in the bar watched in amusement as my old flames and I danced an connected, becoming a human knot.

"So you're strutting your stuff on Broadway! Still giving all the guys hard-ons, eh?" The beefy man hugging me looked vaguely like Chick the Stud; the sleek young animal I once know had lost much of his hair but those dark eyes of his still glowed like candles in a bedroom. He had become even more like a big, well-fed bear, but one who sported a diamond on his pinkie, a gold chain that glittered against his hairy chest with an expensive silk shirt and designer suit covering his heavy body.

A second man pulled me tight against him and we rocked back and forth. "Wow, wow!" he kept murmuring. "Jason, I can't believe you're here. It's just like the good old days already!" *This was Tyler?* Still slender, handsome in a boyish way, there was nevertheless a weary stoop to his shoulders. His face was still that of a confused, lost kid. His dark brows and mustache were striking set against the gray of his still-thick hair.

A big hand turned me around as a pair of powerful arms embraced me, and I looked up, up into the all-American face of Kris the Body. He had always been a knockout of a hulk but now, in his mid-forties, he was even more massive. His shoulders and arms strained the material of his wool jacket. He still sported his black crewcut and those baby-blue eyes lit up to see me.

"Incredible!" he grinned. "You don't look a day older than twenty. I've read all your stories and heard about your show-biz career. You're famous."

385

"And, believe it or not, I watched you play in all your football games whenever they were televised. I actually became a sports fan. You look fantastic."

"Come on, all you old Beauties!" Tyler announced. "My apartment's in the back of the building, Let's get this blast from the past started."

Nearly midnight, and I was yawning. The long drive down from New York had left me exhausted. Then, too, we had spent hours watching old home movies of the gang, gone through scrapbooks, laughing and reminiscing about the good old days.

When I announced I was turning in, the others jumped to their feet, each offering to walk me back to my room. It was Chick, though, who grabbed my arm and pulled me to the door.

"*I'll* see Jason to his room," he proclaimed. I had to smother a grin at his brazen arrogance. He had not changed a bit in this regard in twenty-one years, and when we stepped into my room, he immediately went into action. Locking the door, he kicked off his shoes, stripped off his coat and shirt in less than a minute, and then grabbed me and pulled me toward him.

Holding me close, he looked down at me with those hot eyes of his and muttered, "Christ, thought we'd never get out of there. I've had a hard-on all night; feel it, baby. Do you think it's gotten bigger over the years?"

I rubbed the long bulge in his pants and then unbuckled them. "Chick, time may move on, but not *you*. You're a human walking cock!"

He snickered and stripped off his bikini briefs. "Yeah, I guess I'll always be a sex maniac. Give your old daddy a big, fat, wet kiss." One thing I always liked about Chick was that he didn't play games. He got down to basics fast, and before I knew it, he had me stripped naked and flat on my back on the bed.

"Well, what do you think, huh? Not bad, eh?" He asked, dangling his cock in front of me. "I can still fuck twelve times a day and beat off a dozen more and be rarin' to go." He resembled a scrumptious teddy-bear. Like a pinkish grape popsicle, his hard-on was standing straight up, quivering with anticipation. I had rarely seen it otherwise.

Glancing at his watch, he quickly got up and dressed. "Gotta run, Blondie. Gotta date with these two swingers I met in the bar tonight. Man and woman. Hey, wanna join us and make it a foursome? The guy looks like he might be hung. Ummm, can hardly wait to get my mouth on his big knob and suck out his spunk while fucking the cunt."

We kissed and just as he left me, I called out, "Chick, man, I'm proud of the way you've kept it up all these years!" He squeezed his crotch, laughed, and hurried off, as he always had in his never-ending search for more partners to service his hyperactive cock.

In the background, The Beatles chanted, "Nowhere Man," and Tyler and I lay on the soft cushions in front of the roaring fire, sipping gin and tonics. We recalled when the Seven Beauties first began. I had been a reporter for the nearby *Wilmington Star News* when I had interviewed Tyler for an article. He was then head of the Drama Department at Wilmington College. We had clicked immediately and even slept together several times. He would rave about this handsome, sexy football player, Michael Gerraty, who was straight but knew the score with gay people. When I finally met Mike, we, too had clicked and then gone to bed together. Then he had introduced Tyler and myself to this incredible young body-builder, Kris, who in turn, knew this sex maniac, Chick, who in turn knew Mario. About the same time we met Ashley at some party and not long after, all decided to move in together at the rambling, old Barbee Apartments. And thus was born the Seven Beauties. Except for Tyler, all the others were basically superstraight—yet, each had fought to ball with me before I finally settled down with Beautiful Mike.

"Sometimes I hated you," Tyler smiled sheepishly, "because all the guys flocked around you. I know you didn't force them to. And then I really hated you for leaving us. *That's* when our group broke up."

He was right. I was offered a big job with the Associated Press in Charlotte, and it had been the chance of a lifetime. It killed me at the time to leave my buddies, but I was also ambitious, and the offer gave me a chance to move up in the journalism world. But Tyler was right. As soon as I left the gang, everyone else began drifting apart and moving away. And then two of them had died.

"You know Mike was the only guy I ever loved," Tyler whispered in confession. "I *know* he loved you and that you loved him, but I didn't care. He's still listed as missing in action, and I keep hoping he'll come back, Jason. I bought him a tombstone even though there's nothing in it. One day, maybe that door will open and…"

"Listen." The Drifters were singing their old ballad, "Your Promise to Be Mine." Mike and I always thought it was the most powerful blues number ever recorded; in fact, each time he would make love to me, he put that song on the record player.

"Mike and I loved that song," I said.

"I know. That's why I put it on. I was hoping (*we* could, perhaps—"

Tyler leaned over and kissed me. It was a soft, boyish kiss, warm and sweet. I saw the longing in his eyes, and I pulled his face closer. He grabbed me tightly against him and we began making love.

Tyler sucked in his breath as I trailed my mouth down his still-lean and tanned body aching for his hardness. I had forgotten how long his penis was. His unusually large mass of foreskin covered the head like a wrinkled sock. I paused to play with it, pushing my fingers deep into it and then fanning it out before rolling it down over the tip.

As I licked the acorn-shaped head, his hand stroked my curls and massaged my scalp. His erection was easy to take because it was so pliant and malleable.

When he came, he grunted softly but made no effort to pull away. I remembered how he adored being sucked and after I worked on him for a few minutes more, he shot again.

Tyler took me in his arms again, kissing me while positioning his hips above mine and then I felt the rubbery tip of his phallus pressed against my rectum. Then, ever so carefully, he pushed himself in. After fucking me hard for a while, he paused to catch his breath. "Ohhh, it feels *so* incredible! No wonder Mike never looked at another man or woman with you around. Your ass drove all of us crazy," he shouted, shooting gobs of cum into my guts.

While I dressed, Tyler told me he wanted us to visit Mike's grave the next morning before we began heading home. "I'm not sure I can handle it, Tyler. When I think of Mike, especially being here, I get all choked up."

Tyler's face glowed as he smiled and answered,

"Just keep thinking he's still alive, Jason, and that one day he'll come home again." I didn't say anything as I left, not wanting to utter words that would destroy his fantasy—the only one which kept him alive.

Back at my motel room, I found a note attached to my door. *Where you been, Boy Beautiful? Drop by and let's shoot the shit. Your ninety-eight pound weakling buddy, Kris the Body.*

When he opened his door, sweat was streaming down his face. His workout suit was soaked. "Whew, hi, come in. Just finished my workout," he beamed.

I feigned amazement. "You mean *you* work out with weights? Why, I *never* would have guessed it!" His motel room resembled his apartment next to mine twenty-one years ago. Weights and barbells were everywhere. Bottles of vitamins and juices littered the dresser.

"Yeah," he grinned, "I guess I'll always be a body-building freak. Get yourself a beer out of the cooler while I shower. I bought 'em just for you—in case you popped by," he said grinning sheepishly.

"Will you show me some of your prize-winning poses?"

He looked over his shoulder and winked. "Maybe I'll even show you some that were too hot for the judges!"

I pretended to fan myself. "Quick, take your shower—and then show me!"

When he emerged from the bathroom, all wet and shiny and breathtaking, I gave him a long wolf whistle. Only the skimpy towel around his waist kept him from being stark naked. If possible, Kris had become even more awesome looking over the decades.

390

Always so vain about his pectorals, they were enormous now and jutted out like twin hubcaps.

Each was capped by a thick pink nipple. His huge chest tapered to a waist that was criminally small, his abs a series of rows of sharply cut muscles. His shoulders, arms and thighs were massive. Beneath his dark crew cut, Kris's cute face crinkled up into a Boy Scout grin.

"So you think the old codger can stay out of the nursing home for a few more years, eh?"

"Kris, if I had you in my burlesque revue at the Ritz Male Follies, you'd knock 'em right out of their fucking seats."

"Really, now?" he joked, smiling sexily. "Eh, and, what would you and *I* be doing in your act?"

He had been watching MTV before I had arrived. Now, I turned it up when I saw one of my favorite videos, "On My Own," with Patti Labelle and Michael McDonald, appear on the screen.

I put my hand on Kris's shoulder and he took my other one. "Pretend we're doing a slow dance to this song in front of hundreds of horny men. I like having a big, muscle stud to dance with—one who's completely bare-assed or nearly that way."

"I'm a married man, remember?" he teased. Nevertheless he pulled me tight against his warm, powerful body, his right nipple nudging my cheek like a gumdrop. He gasped when I covered it with my mouth and began sucking on it. My hands slid down his back to his waist. When I unfastened his towel, Kris guided my hand down to his pubic area.

"Feel," he whispered. "Isn't it smooth and satiny? I keep my whole body shaved. Feel my ass. Put your hand in my crack. See? Not a hair anywhere." My hands caressed his incredibly tight rump before vanishing into the cleft. Sure enough, it was like warming my hands in a tight, moist glove.

Kris lowered his face to kiss me. I nearly fainted. I had forgotten what a great kisser he was. Easily, as if I were one of his young sons, this stunning giant picked me up in those strong arms and carried me to bed with his moist erection already pressed hard against my buttocks.

I had been Kris's first and—unless I was wrong—only man. He was superstraight and, because so many girls were always chasing him, it had taken me a long time to get him into bed. But once it happened, he had eagerly given me his body whenever I wanted it.

Kris knew how turned on I had always been by his fabulous physique, so he just lay there, trembling in expectation and excitement as my tongue tasted his splendid nudity...his spectacular pecs, billowing out so high from his chest...the luscious nipples which made me think of berries waiting to be savored slowly. And when I kissed his flat stomach, it caved in in response, to a startling depth.

He was gasping now and flushed. "Jason, I'm going crazy! Do me!" I pulled his shiny hard-on back up between his thighs and sucked him off within seconds.

All through that night, I saw that every time Kris was ready to ejaculate, his enormous tits would billow and shimmer and his stomach would ripple like an accordion. His kisses made me positively lightheaded, and when he fucked me I even thought I might faint.

The three of us stood silently at the foot of the small tombstone.

It was a gray morning and the wind was wet and

chilled. Chick had refused to come, explaining that visiting graves, *even* that of an old friend, just "wasn't his bag."

Kris stood between Tyler and me, his big arms hugging our shoulders. He sensed how much we needed his support for this moment. Since Mike's body was never recovered, the coffin was empty, and there was no date of death on the stone.

I knelt down and placed a cluster of red roses on the grave. He loved scarlet flowers. Underneath them I put an old 45 record, "Your Promise to Be Mine" by The Drifters, "our song."

In my mind I could see him again, drinking a beer and grabbing me to him as we would dance around our apartment. "That's *our* song," he would whisper, holding me tight against him. "We'll play it until we're old."

It was becoming too much for me. Kris instinctively put his arms around me and hugged me. Tyler turned and clutched both of us. For long minutes we stood there. We wept not just for Mike but for a time in our lives that was gone forever.

I closed the lid of my car trunk and turned to look at the others.

"Well, guys, this is it. It's been great fun. Tyler, thanks for everything."

"You'll come back real soon, won't you?" he pleaded. "It gets so lonely here. With you here, it's almost like 1967 all over again." I looked into those sad, lost eyes and knew that until the end of his days, Tyler would never really move out of that magical year.

Snapping his gum, Chick hugged me and leered. "Come on down to Florida; work one of my strip palaces and I'll make you a star." We all laughed, but

I watched his attention shift as an attractive woman moved her suitcases from her car. Chick's eyes glinted and he rubbed his crotch unconsciously. The past meant nothing to him. Nostalgia was for people in nursing homes. His cock was his life, and as long as it responded to stimuli, nothing else mattered.

Kris held me tight, and I wanted to melt into his magnificent body. He smiled. "If I can leave the wife and kids for a while, maybe I can come and see you in New York." My heart sank. Already he was changing, returning to his role of husband and father. I couldn't ever expect Kris to drop all of that just to resume an old relationship.

As I drove away, I looked into my rearview mirror and watched my old buddies recede against the gray landscape. There they were, the last of the Seven Beauties. Perhaps I would see them again one day. Somehow I doubted it, though.

Author's Note

During the past two decades, readers from around
the world—especially from Japan and Russia, for
some reason—have often written me and asked
about both my stories and my personal life. I tell
them this: my real name is Jery Tillotson. I was raised
in the deep South. All my stories are based on fact.
My life has been most bizarre and I now live as a
recluse in Manhattan.